"We'll have to be ... was saying. "I wou... bounty money to the ... our hideout." He pa... himself to do what mus... sir. You have the honor ... most sought-after Indian in the entire Southwest."

At any other time, Delgadito would have been flattered, but at that moment, all he wanted to do was what he should have done weeks earlier. Bunching his shoulder muscles, he banished his doubt, drew back his arm, and lunged at Taggart.

QUICK KILLER

Clay hesitated. It had been easy to pronounce judgment on the trappers when he hadn't set eyes on them. But now there they were: living, breathing human beings. Then he thought of his promise to the Apaches. He waved the rifle once.

The poachers never had a prayer. The four Apaches swooped into the gully like ferocious birds of prey, pouncing on the startled trappers before they could bring a rifle or pistol into play.

And just like that it was over. The three trappers lay in spreading pools of blood.

Clay walked to the bottom. He stood over one of the men and saw the trapper's eyes widen. "Your eyes! They're blue!" the man said, then erupted in a coughing fit. "You're the one we heard about, aren't you? You're the White Apache!"

Other *White Apache* Doubles:
HANGMAN'S KNOT/WARPATH

Jake McMasters

WHITE APACHE

WARRIOR BORN
QUICK KILLER

LEISURE BOOKS　　**L**　　**NEW YORK CITY**

To Judy, Joshua, and Shane

A LEISURE BOOK®

April 1997

Published by

Dorchester Publishing Co., Inc.
276 Fifth Avenue
New York, NY 10001

WARRIOR BORN

Chapter One

Billy Santee liked to kill and most folks knew it. Not the newcomers to Tucson, of course, who could never have guessed from his smooth, babylike features and twinkling green eyes that he had a cruel streak a mile wide. But most of the regular residents were all too aware of his habit of resorting to his six-shooters at the least little provocation. So they gave him a wide berth when he made his nightly rounds of various saloons and dance halls.

This night was no exception. Thumbs hooked in his polished gunbelts, Santee sauntered along the dusty street, his wide-brimmed black hat pushed jauntily back on his head. He scoured the street as might a bird of prey, secretly amused whenever anyone did a double take on seeing him and then scampered out of his way.

Santee got a thrill out of their fear. To his way of

thinking the good people of Tucson were little better than sheep, and he was the lean, hungry wolf who moved among them as he pleased and did whatever he wanted whenever he wanted. He liked the feeling of power it gave him.

As Santee strolled into the Lucky Dollar, shoving the bat-wing doors wide in a grand entrance, he saw all eyes swing toward him, and he smirked with glee. Spurs jingling, he ambled to the bar, his smirk widening as several men scurried to make themselves scarce.

"Howdy, Santee," the barkeep greeted him. "What's your poison? Coffin varnish, as usual?"

"Nothin' else is fit for a man to drink," Santee declared, resting his left forearm on the counter but keeping his right arm at his side so his hand was close to his holster.

The bartender started to reach for a bottle on a shelf behind him when a loud snicker and a sarcastic comment from the end of the bar froze him in place.

"A man! Is that what you call yourself? Tarnation, you're not old enough to put on your britches without help."

A deathly hush fell abruptly over the smoky room as all eyes turned toward the speaker, a swarthy man in grimy clothes, who lifted a glass to his damp mouth and took a greedy swallow.

"That will be enough out of you, Simmons," the bartender said, casting a nervous glance at the young gunman for emphasis. "You've had too damn much to drink for your own good."

Simmons chuckled, then wiped his mouth with his sleeve. "I'll be the judge of when I've had too many, thank you. And I stand by what I said." Simmons jerked a thumb at Santee. "This strutting rooster don't scare me none, not like he does all of you."

Clearing his throat, the bartender said gruffly, "I'm warning you. If you can't keep a civil tongue, I'll toss you out on your ear."

"Civil tongue?" Simmons exploded in hearty laughter. "Are you loco, Will? Most of those here wouldn't know how to talk decent if their lives depended on it."

"Sometimes they do," Will said, adding another meaningful glance at the gunman.

Santee had not spoken or twitched a muscle. Outwardly he seemed composed and unruffled, but inwardly he seethed at the public insult. Adopting his trademark smirk, he sidled down the bar until he stood six feet from Simmons. "I have to admire a man who speaks his peace no matter what, old-timer," he said pleasantly, "but it sure does puzzle me some that you're courtin' your Maker this way."

Four men at a card table to the rear of the drunk promptly rose and moved over against the wall.

"Hold on, Santee," Will said. "I don't want no trouble in my place."

"Too late to be frettin' about that," Santee replied, without taking his gaze off Simmons.

"Why waste lead on old Art?" Will persisted. "Everyone knows how he is. There isn't a soul in town who takes his word seriously."

"I must be the exception, then."

The bartender tried another angle. "The marshal won't take kindly to gunplay. It won't make no difference to him who you work for."

"Reckon so, do you?" Santee said, showing his even white teeth. "Why then, you'd best have someone run along and go fetch him."

"You think I won't?" Will said boldly. He hopefully scanned his customers. "Which one of you will it be? You'll probably find the marshal over at Ma Evert's eatery having a late supper."

No one volunteered.

"What's gotten into all of you?" Will demanded, exasperated, although he knew full well why none stepped forward. There wasn't a man there willing to tempt fate by angering the gunman.

All this time, Simmons had been sipping at his drink. In the awkward silence that greeted the bartender's question, he set it down hard, sloshing what little whiskey remained, and squared his drooping shoulders. Bloodshot eyes narrowing, he strode around the bar, swaying as he walked. "I can handle my own affairs," he announced. "The rest of you cold-footed bastards don't owe me a thing."

"Don't pay him no mind," Will told the listeners. "It's the liquor talking. Which one of you will go?"

Faces lined with varying degrees of shame either looked away or down at the floor.

"Hell!" Will said. "I'll go myself, then." Removing his apron and tossing it on the bar, he hastened out.

Simmons, meanwhile, had halted in front of Santee and stood glowering at the younger man. "Liquor or not, it's high time someone put you in your place, you no-account gun shark."

"And you figure you're the one to do it?" Santee asked in amusement.

"If I was twenty years younger I would," the drunk blustered. "But as it is, a tongue-lashing will have to do."

"My pa used to give me tongue-lashings," Santee recollected grimly.

"They never sank in, did they?"

"They sank in, all right, but not like he thought they would." Santee frowned at the memory. "It got so he gave me one every time I turned around. One day I just had enough, so I grabbed me a hickory stick and beat him within an inch of his death." He reached out and seized hold of the drunk's shirt. "Just like I'm fixing to do to you if you don't apologize."

"And just like you did to Rufus Blake," Simmons said defiantly, making no attempt to pull free.

"Who?"

"Don't you remember? Last month you pistol-whipped him so bad you cracked his skull."

The memory sent a tingle of satisfaction down Santee's spine. Yes, he did remember beating a harebrained old codger who had blundered into his horse, spooking the animal and nearly causing him to be bucked off. "He lived, didn't he?" Santee said. "I don't see what has you so upset."

"Rufus is my pard," Simmons said harshly. "And he'll never be the same again because of you. The sawbones says he can't hardly feed or dress himself no more."

"So that's what this is about?" Santee shoved the drunk from him. "All those gray hairs and you don't have the brains of a jackass." Dismissing Simmons with a wave of contempt, he turned to the counter. "You're not worth the bother, you old buzzard. Say you didn't mean those words, and I'll let you go home in one piece."

"I meant what I said."

"You only think you did, you ornery son of a bitch," Santee said, placing his hands on the edge of the bar. He had been in a good mood when he entered, but being reminded of his father had spoiled it. And now he felt a familiar tightening in

9

his innards that told him he was on the verge of exploding. The only thing that held him in check was his promise to his boss to take it easy while in town.

Art Simmons glared but said nothing. He stepped over to an empty chair and leaned on it, as if for support, muttering under his breath the whole while. Suddenly, he gripped the chair in both spindly hands, whipped it on high, and whirled, intending to smash it down on the gunman's head.

The drunk moved with surprising speed. To some of those witnessing the incident it appeared as if Santee would have his head caved in. But they failed to take into account his reputation for being as quick as a striking rattler, a reputation he proved was well deserved by spinning, drawing, and firing all in the blink of an eye. Art Simmons rocked backward, a neat hole high on his chest, the chair falling with a crash. He touched the entry hole, his face blank with amazement.

"A pitiful case of slow, old-timer," Santee said coldly, and fired again. This time he deliberately aimed low, putting a shot into the drunk's gut.

Simmons clutched his stomach and staggered into a table. Clutching it for support, he blinked up at the gunman and opened his mouth to hurl a last, defiant oath.

Santee chuckled as he squeezed off a third shot. The slug ripped into the drunk's tongue, shearing it off and boring into his throat. Spitting and coughing blood, Simmons slowly sank onto the table, then slid off onto the floor. By the time he thudded down, he was dead.

"I guess no one ever told him that the bigger the mouth, the better it looks shut," Santee joked, swirling his hand at the acrid cloud of gunsmoke hovering before him. He quickly replaced the spent cartridges in his Colt and was just twirling the ivory-handled pistol into his holster when heavy footsteps sounded outside and the sturdy frame of Marshal Tom Crane filled the entrance. "Howdy, Tom!" Santee called cheerfully.

Tucson's top lawman advanced slowly, scowling, the bartender dogging his heels. Crane stood over Art Simmons and stroked his waxed mustache. "Damn it all, Santee. You've gone too far this time. This man never carries an iron."

"It was still self-defense," Santee said. "Just ask anyone. He tried to brain me with a chair."

The marshal surveyed the patrons and several nodded. Sighing, Crane faced the gunman. "I don't suppose it occurred to you to wing him instead of filling him full of lead?"

"Sorry. No," Santee said. "I have this rule I live by. Any hombre who tries to put windows in my skull ends his days pushin' up daisies."

Crane addressed the barkeep. "Will, see that the body is taken to the undertaker's. Tell him I'll be down directly." Motioning at the gunman, Crane led the way outdoors. A crowd was gathering. Crane shouldered his way through and went two blocks to the mouth of an alley where they could talk without being overheard. Pivoting, he jabbed a finger into Santee's chest and growled, "What the hell are you trying to do? Cost me my badge? Miles gave me his word that you'd behave from now on."

"I didn't start it."

"But you sure as hell finished it, didn't you?" Crane slapped his thigh in frustration, then scoured the street to make certain no one was approaching. "Sometimes I wonder if the money Miles pays me to make sure his gunnies stay out of the calaboose shouldn't be twice as much."

"Spare me your bellyachin'," Santee said. "You have a sweet deal going here and you know it." Brazenly he tapped the lawman's badge. "If it hadn't been for Miles Gillett you wouldn't be wearin' that tin star. I'd say that being at his beck and call has fattened your poke considerably."

"Maybe so," Crane agreed, "but the headaches caused by hotheads like you are enough to drive a man to drink." Draping an arm on the gunman's shoulders, he lowered his voice. "I want you to mount up and head for the Triangle G—"

"Why should I?" Santee said defensively. "I had my heart set on kickin' up my heels later and maybe beddin' one of the doves over at Walker's."

"Another time," Crane said.

"Think again," Santee said. He would have walked off, but the marshal grasped an arm and pushed him into the alley, where they had complete privacy.

"You listen to me, you dunderhead, and you listen sharp," Crane snapped. "Every time you unshuck that hardware of yours, it costs me. The rate you're going, I won't have this job after next year, not unless I can convince the folks hereabouts that I'm doing as fine a job as any man living could."

"I wonder what they'd say if they knew about the arrangement you have with Gillett," Santee said, just to agitate the lawman. "Most likely they'd tar and feather you and run you out of town on a rail."

"Or invite me to a necktie social," Crane said. "But none of that will happen if I can keep a lid on the gunplay. That's where you come in. Miles told me I could count on you to cooperate."

"But why do I have to leave? The night is still young."

"So everyone will think I ran you out for shooting

12

Simmons," Crane admitted. "It'll make me look good in their eyes."

Santee shook his head. There was a lively filly by the name of Missy he was determined to see, no matter what. Crane would have to work out his own problems.

The marshal lowered his arm, his features hardening. "Suit yourself. But don't blame me if Miles gets upset when I tell him."

Indecision set in. The last thing Santee wanted to do was anger his employer, who was not noted for having a charitable disposition. And he well remembered how stern Gillett had been the day before when telling him to behave himself in Tucson in the future—or else.

Crane started to stalk off.

"Hold on, Tom. Don't leave in a huff," Santee said earnestly. His fertile mind had already seen a way of turning the situation to his advantage, and he went on, "I was just givin' you a hard time for the hell of it. I'll do like you want, but you owe me, and I'm one gent who always collects on his favors."

"I'm obliged," Crane said, smiling. "I'll be sure to tell Gillett that you weren't to blame for Simmons." Touching the brim of his hat, he departed.

Billy Santee grinned as he strolled toward the stable. Not bad for one night, he thought. He'd blown out the lamp of a worthless old yak and gotten the town marshal in his debt. And later, when the town quieted down, he'd sneak back in and pay Missy a visit and dumb Tom Crane would never be the wiser.

Not a bad night at all.

Chapter Two

Delgadito the Apache was mad. Had anyone been sitting next to him on his lofty perch overlooking a remote sanctuary high in the Chiricahua Mountains, however, he would not have known it. For Delgadito the Apache did not wear his emotions on his sleeve, as whites were wont to do. No, his features were as inscrutable as the smooth stone cliff against which he leaned.

But if there had been a way to peer into the depths of Delgadito's turbulent soul, an onlooker would have recoiled at the raging cauldron of volcanic fury boiling there. Delgadito wanted to kill, to reach out and seize the object of his wrath and slowly twist the man's neck until the eyes went blank and the tongue protruded.

White Apache! Delgadito fumed, absently fingering the hilt of his keen knife. *You have turned my plan against me and you must die!*

14

Delgadito gazed with fiery dark eyes down upon the five men in the valley below. Four were fellow Apaches, the fifth the white-eye who had unwittingly thwarted him. How could such a thing have happened after all his careful plotting? To him, no less, a warrior highly respected for his ability at *na-tse-kes*, the deep thinking that was the hallmark of a great Apache.

Seated there under the blistering sun, Delgadito reviewed the sequence of events in his mind's eye, trying to find where he had gone wrong, where he had lost control of the whirlwind that had caught him in its grasp.

Everything had begun with the lynching, as White Apache called it. Delgadito had seen a group of whites hang another from a tree limb, and when the riders had departed, he had quickly ordered the dangling victim cut down.

Through sheer force of will, that man, Clay Taggart, had lived. At first Delgadito had thought to use Taggart to arrange a truce with the American Army, which had been in relentless pursuit of his renegade band. But that hope had been dashed when scalp hunters from Mexico raided the camp and slew practically every last man, woman, and child. Only five warriors had escaped. Plus Clay Taggart.

As if that tragedy had not been enough for any man to endure, as if the *Gans* themselves had turned against him, Delgadito had to endure the added shame of knowing that the only reason he survived the massacre was because Clay Taggart had risked all to save him. He owed his life to one of the despicable white-eyes he despised!

So much had happened so swiftly after that. Delgadito had taken Taggart with him high into the mountains and during their long journey started to teach the white-eye his tongue while trying to master the strange language of the whites. When the other survivors had shown up, he had cleverly conspired to have them accept Taggart's reluctant leadership in a series of raids on the men responsible for the lynching.

They had all balked at first, especially Fiero. They had demanded to know why they should risk their lives to help one white-eye seek revenge on other white-eyes. For the plunder, for many guns and horses, Delgadito had countered. Still some of them had been unwilling, and it had taken all of his considerable skill to manipulate them into going along with the idea.

There was a reason Delgadito had gone to so much trouble. Since the others would not allow him to lead the band after the slaughter, he had conspired to control them through the white-eye.

His plan had been simple. Since White Apache viewed him as a friend and relied on his judgment in making decisions, the others would come to see that he was the guiding influence in the success of their raids, and as a result, he would regain some of the standing he had lost.

The next step had required a daring strike into northern Mexico. Again led by White Apache, they had gone after the scalp hunters who had wiped out their families and friends. It had been Delgadito's intention to slay Blue Cap, the leader of the butchers. In doing so he would have restored himself almost fully to the good graces of his fellows.

But everything had gone wrong once they were south of the border. White Apache had done well— too well. Taggart had freed Fiero, Ponce, and Amarillo after they were caught by Blue Cap, and later had slain Blue Cap, himself. Instead of

Delgadito earning their praise and esteem, White Apache had garnered it.

And now that they were back at their mountain retreat, the others were treating White Apache as one of them. No, worse. They had come to respect him, to trust him. They looked to him for leadership, as they had once looked to Delgadito.

It was infuriating.

Delgadito wanted to roar with rage, but he held his tongue and rose. As he stood there simmering with frustration, he was suddenly struck by a remarkable fact. From that height the five men on the canyon floor all looked the same. They all had long, dark hair. They all wore long-sleeved shirts, breechcloths, and high moccasins. They all had cartridge belts slanted across their chests or waists. To all intents and purposes, there were five Apaches down there, not four and a white man.

The sight was profoundly disturbing. Until that very moment Delgadito had not quite realized how completely Clay Taggart had taken to Apache ways.

Fresh, raw rage pumped through Delgadito's veins. His standing in the tribe meant everything to him. It was the source of his pride, his secret joy. He liked being widely admired and having less experienced warriors flock to him for advice and instruction. Now all that was denied him and there was only one person he could blame—himself.

He was the one who had saved Clay Taggart. He was the one who had taken Taggart under his wing and taught Taggart the the *Shis-Inday* ways. He was the one who foolishly thought he could use Taggart for his own ends and then discard the white fool later.

Delgadito headed down the cliff with the agility of a mountain goat. Halfway down he paused to let his blood cool. It would not do to the let the others know his true feelings. For a *Shis-Inday* to show such emotional weakness would be inexcusable. He must accept things as they were for the time being. He must bide his time until an opportunity presented itself to dispose of Clay Taggart in such a way that the others would never suspect the resentment he had harbored.

By the time Delgadito stepped onto the canyon floor he was his normal self again. He strolled over to where the five men were talking about their recent adventures in Sonora.

Fiero, always the most alert, looked up first and asked, "Any sign of them yet?"

"No," Delgadito said.

"Where could they be?" Fiero wondered in a typically gruff fashion. "Palacio told Amarillo it would be five sleeps, but tonight it will be seven."

"You know Palacio," Cuchillo Negro said. Next to Delgadito, he was the deepest thinker of the group, the one who saw under the surface of things to their hidden meanings, the quiet one whose words counted more because each was spoken with care. As he made his comment, he absently touched a hand to his chest above the wound he had suffered in Sonora. It still bothered him but not enough to keep him from being up and about.

"What does that mean?" Fiero wanted to know. The firebrand of the tribe, he was noted for his ferocity in battle and for always being too hasty in speaking his mind.

"It means," Amarillo said, "that he is showing his contempt for us by keeping us waiting." Always the most cautious of them all, he added, "Even though he insults us, we must not take offense. This is our chance to mend the break, and we should do everything in our power to make him welcome."

"I agree," said Ponce, the youngest, who yearned for the companionship of others his age, particularly that of a certain young woman.

Delgadito sat cross-legged and stared at the party who had ruined his well-laid scheme. "And what does *Lickoyee-shis-inday* say?"

Clay Taggart, the man called White Apache, squared his broad shoulders as he regarded the ring of warriors with his penetrating blue eyes. He knew how much the meeting meant to them, and he wanted to do everything in his power to bring about the result they desired. It was the least he could do after everything they had done for him. "I say you should make Palacio welcome, smoke the pipe together, and listen to what he has to say. Later you can decide whether to accept his terms."

"He will want us to grovel," Fiero said in disgust. "And I grovel to no man."

"You do not know that for certain," Clay said in his lightly accented Apache. He had been working hard in recent weeks to master the tongue and was proud that he could speak it with a fluency few white men shared. "If he is wise, he will know you have suffered enough. For the good of the whole tribe it is best to let you mingle with your people from time to time. Surely, he will not hold your war on our common enemy against you."

Delgadito had listened in disguised amazement. Taggart, he reflected, had offered exactly the same advice he would have given. Even more interesting was the way in which Taggart had referred to their white oppressors.

"One does not mention Palacio and wisdom in the same breath," Cuchillo Negro said.

"Then he is not fit to be leader of the Chiricahuas,"

Clay said frankly. "I am surprised you would pick such a man to guide your footsteps."

"He was not picked," Cuchillo Negro clarified. "His father was a chief, and his father before him."

Clay merely grunted, Indian fashion. There were two ways to attain a position of leadership among the Apaches, or the *Shis-Inday*, as they called themselves. One was to earn it by proving superior ability, the other was to have it bestowed by virtue of a bloodline. He had only been among them a short time, but already he'd learned that those who had to work to earn high regard made better chiefs than those who had come by it easily.

"Do not let Palacio hear you talk this way," Amarillo warned. "He is very quick to anger if someone so much as hints that he is not a good leader."

The more Clay heard, the lower his opinion of Palacio became, and he had yet to even meet the warrior. Sighing, he stared into the distance. Why was he getting so worked up over it? The internal problems of the Apaches were really none of his business. He was becoming softheaded to think they cared about his opinion one way or the other. Uppermost in his mind, at all times, should be that he was white and they weren't. No matter how friendly they acted, in their eyes he was still an enemy. Delgadito had told him so many times.

Still, Clay had been forgetting his proper place among them quite a lot lately. After so many weeks of living with the band, of fighting by their side, of hunting and eating and sleeping together, there were times when he thought of himself as one of them, without even being aware that he was doing so.

And who could blame him? The Apaches, Delgadito most notably, had treated him better than his own kind. It wasn't Apaches who had betrayed him. It wasn't Apaches who had tracked him down and left him for dead at the end of a rope. And it wasn't a rich Apache who had plotted to take his woman, his ranch, and his very life.

Clay scanned the five swarthy faces and suppressed a self-conscious grin. Who would ever have figured that one day he'd consider five Apaches to be some of the most likable hombres he'd ever met? Every last one of them, even the hot-tempered Fiero, would do to ride the river with, and it galled him that most of his kind rated them as the scum of the earth.

Suddenly Clay realized Delgadito had addressed him. "What was that?" he asked in English. The warrior liked to practice every chance he got, and Clay was more than willing to oblige Delgadito since Clay reckoned that he owed the Apache his life several times over.

"Someone else should keep watch. It is your time, I think."

"That it is," Clay said, rising. They had been taking turns standing guard over the entrance, watchful as hawks, not only for other Apaches, but for the cavalry and anyone else who might be out for Clay's hide. Picking up his Winchester, Clay hiked southward. A shadow fastened itself at his side.

"I will go along," Delgadito said.

Grateful for the company, Clay commented, "That's right neighborly of you."

"Neighborly?" Delgadito repeated the new word, rolling it on his tongue as he might an unusual morsel of food.

"Friendly," Clay explained, translating in Apache, "*Nejeunee.*"

"You Americans make much of having friends,"

21

Delgadito said, saying each word slowly, choosing them with care as he always did. He had to labor hard at English but he was making swift strides. "Everyone you meet, you want to like them and for them to like you. If someone does not like you, you are upset and feel there is something wrong with you." He shook his head in reproach. "Too many of you have your brains in a whirl."

"The Apaches do not place as much stock in friendships, I've noticed."

"There you are very wrong," Delgadito corrected him. "We value our few true friends highly. But we are smart enough to know that no one person can be the friend of all others, so we pick our close friends after much thought. And when we make an offer of friendship, we bind ourselves by giving a gift and smoking a pipe."

"I'd like that."

"What?" Delgadito said, not certain what part was being referred to.

"I'd be honored if some day you would smoke a pipe and share a gift with me."

That was the farthest thing from Delgadito's mind, but he smiled and said, "Name the day and we shall do it." He saw Taggart beam like a small boy just given a lizard to torture, and he had to turn away so the white-eye would not detect the mirth that racked him.

Clay was touched by the offer. It was yet another example of the kindness the Apaches had extended him, yet another reason why he believed the terrible stories about the tribe were nothing more than tall tales. For years he'd been led to think that if he were ever caught by Apaches he'd wind up staked live on an ant hill with his gut sliced open and his scalp gone. Yet, the only warrior who had ever tried to

22

harm him was Fiero and that had been more the result of a misunderstanding than anything else.

The thought prompted Clay to say, "Delgadito, there's something gnawing at my innards."

"You have swallowed a live snake?"

"No, no. Nothing like that, pard," Clay said. "It's this business about the *Shis-Inday* always thinking of outsiders as their enemies."

"What of it?" Delgadito responded. From infancy he had been taught that very thing, along with the two cardinal rules of the Chiricahuas: Steal without being caught and kill without being slain.

"Do Cuchillo Negro and the others still think of me that way? After all we've been through?"

The appeal in Taggart's voice startled Delgadito. No matter how much he learned about the whites, no matter how much time he spent in the company of White Apache, he could not get used to their childlike attitudes. "It matters that much to you?" he said.

"It matters greatly," Clay confessed.

"No man can know another man's heart. You must ask them how they feel." Delgadito saw sadness etch Taggart's face and mulled over its meaning as they hiked to a cliff wall near the valley entrance and began climbing. He had to keep in mind that the white-eye was cut off from his own kind, that the five warriors in their band were the only companions Clay Taggart had had for quite some time. Perhaps it was only natural for *Lickoyee-shis-inday* to regard them as more than mere enemies.

For Clay's part, he was thinking about the sequence of violent events that had resulted in his adopting Apache ways and marveling at how it had all turned out. Once he had been like most Arizonans and hated Apaches simply because they

23

were Indians, because they were different. Now, having learned that deep down they were a lot like himself, his hatred had evaporated, and he found himself liking them more and more as the days went by.

It took several minutes to scale the heights. When Clay finally stood on a ledge no wider than his shoulders and stared down at the ground far below, he smiled at his accomplishment. Most whites would have been afraid to try such a feat. Six months ago, he would have felt the same. Now he could scale the sheerest cliffs with an ease that astounded him.

Delgadito reached the ledge moments later and stood a few feet from Taggart. He, too, gazed downward, but not to compliment himself on his climbing ability. Rather, he was imagining the shape White Apache's body would be in after a fall from that high up. All it would take was a slight nudge at just the right moment and the thorn in his side would be gone.

Clay shifted to survey the stark Chiricahua Mountains, admiring their rugged beauty as he never had before. Previously, when delivering cattle to the reservation or on those other rare occasions when he had visited the remote region, he had thought of the mountains as he had thought of most Arizona landscape—arid, harsh, and foreboding. He'd been wrong, though. When seen through the eyes of someone who was growing to know them intimately, the Chiricahuas had a personality all their own, a raw splendor unique among Arizona mountains. Small wonder the Chiricahua Apaches were so passionately devoted to their homeland. Small wonder the tribe had fiercely resisted the white invaders at every turn.

Delgadito took a casual step closer to Taggart.

He peered down at the spot where the rest of the warriors were sitting and was pleased to find that a tree screened them from sight. No one would see if he gave Taggart a push. He could claim the white-eye slipped and the others would accept him at his word because they all knew White Apache was as agile as a pregnant cow.

"I reckon I understand," Clay said softly.

Delgadito looked at him.

"I always figured you Apaches were a bunch of miserable savages who were only interested in butchering helpless whites, but now I see there was more to it. You were also protecting your land."

"This country was ours from long ago," Delgadito said. He neglected to bring up that defending their land was only part of the reason they fought the whites. From as far back as any Apache could remember the six tribes had lived to raid and to plunder. The Zunis, the Pueblos, the Pimas, the Maricopas, the Spanish and others had all paid dearly in order that the Apaches might flourish.

"I know what it means to have your land taken away from you," Clay mused. "Miles Gillett has stolen my ranch right out from under me." He bowed his head, feeling unbridled fury gush up within him. "That, and the woman I love."

"We rub out Gillett soon," Delgadito said, to keep Taggart talking while he inched ever closer.

"No, I'd rather save that bastard for last," Clay said. "First we'll blow out the lamps of the rest of that damn posse, just like we did with Jacoby and Prost." Both of his hands clenched so tightly that his knuckles turned white. "All ten of them will pay! Marshal Crane, Bitmer, Moritz, that gunny Santee, every last one!"

There was no denying Taggart's thirst for vengeance. It was enough to give Delgadito pause, to remind him of his earlier scheme to use the white-eye to destroy more Americans and, in the process, regain his standing in the tribe. Then he thought of the unexpected influence Taggart had earned among his fellows, and he firmed his heart to the task confronting him.

"We ought to go on another raid soon," Clay was saying. Thoughtfully, he scratched his chin. "Let me see. The next one should be Harvey Denton. I've never been to his spread, but I know right where it is."

Delgadito took another step. He was now within arm's length of the unsuspecting white.

"Denton has more hands than Jacoby and Prost had, but they shouldn't be a problem if we scout the area first," Clay went on, lost in reflection. "It won't take us more than a week to get there and probably ten days back because we'll have so many horses to—."

Shutting the words from his mind, Delgadito slowly raised his right arm, extending his hand toward Taggart's vulnerable back. He glanced into the valley again to verify none of the other *Shis-Inday* was watching. With his fingertips poised next to the white-eye's shoulder blade, he was all set to shove when, unbidden, memories of the time Taggart had saved his life filled Delgadito's head.

"We'll have to be on our guard for the cavalry," Clay was saying, his attention glued to the nearly invisible trail that led into the retreat from a rocky, desolate canyon. "The army must have beefed up their patrols after our attacks. I wouldn't be surprised if they're offering bounty money to the first of their Indian scouts who locates our hideout."

Racked by rare doubt, Delgadito still could not bring himself to do what must be done. Was he growing weak? he wondered. If so, he was no longer fit to be a chief, and he might as well leap from the cliff himself.

"Yes, sir," Clay declared. "You have the honor of being the most sought-after Indian in the entire Southwest."

At any other time, Delgadito would have been flattered, but at that moment, all he wanted to do was what he should have done weeks earlier. Bunching his shoulder muscles, he banished his doubt, drew back his arm, and lunged, at Taggart.

Chapter Three

The devilish leer on Billy Santee's face was ample testimony to the success of his night spent in Missy's willing arms. As he trotted toward the Triangle G, he swore he could still feel the soft touch of her mouth on his and the taut swell of her lush body as she moved in rhythm to his ardent thrusts. "That gal could turn a Bible-thumper into a sinner so fast his head would swim," he told his bay.

Commotion in the corral adjacent to the stable caught Santee's eye, and he angled in that direction. A dozen punchers were seated on the fence watching Jennings, the bronc buster, work a new animal.

Santee rode right up to the corral and slid from the bay onto the high rail. Several of the cowboys called his name in greeting.

"The boss has been looking for you all morning," said Red. "Where you been?"

"As if we can't guess," said Poteet, jabbing Red

28

with an elbow. "Look at that lipstick all over his face."

Automatically Santee brushed a sleeve across his mouth. On hearing their peels of laughter, he knew they had hoodwinked him, and while he wouldn't abide such treatment by strangers, these were men he considered pards, so he joined in the mirth.

Just then the bronco tried to chin the moon, and Jennings went flying to land in a humiliated heap by a post. Everyone cackled.

"Serves you right!" Santee chimed in. "You shouldn't climb on if you can't stay on, butter butt! Hell, I could do better than you!"

Hoots and catcalls added to the din. Jennings rose and slapped his hat against his shirt to remove some of the dust. "Think you can do better?" he challenged Santee. "Put your money where your brag is. I've got ten dollars that says you can't stay on him longer than two minutes."

Santee suddenly became the focus of attention. He studied the bronc and could tell the mustang was a mean one just by the way it pranced defiantly in the center of the corral. Any sensible man would have declined rather than risk busted bones, but not Santee. The young gunman had never turned down a challenge in his entire life, and he considered himself too old to start. "You're on, mister!" he cried.

A flurry of betting took place; men were exchanging bills and coins and giving odds on exactly how long they figured Santee would last.

Climbing into the corral, Santee unbuckled his crossed gunbelts and handed the heavy hardware up to Red. "If I get my head stove in, these are yours," he said.

The mustang lifted its head and cocked an eye at

Santee as he warily advanced. Its sides heaved from its exertions, and the reins dangled to the ground. Santee pulled his hat down, then crouched to grab the reins. No sooner did his hand close on them than the mustang pulled backward. He had to hold on tight. The horse jerked, twisting its head, trying to break loose.

"Give him a kiss!" someone hooted. "Maybe that'll tame him!"

Santee waited for the mustang to quiet enough so he could sidle nearer. The horse snorted, shaking as if with a cold chill. "Be still another second, you mangy cayuse," Santee taunted, "and I'll teach you who's boss."

Without warning Santee seized the animal's ear and gave it a sharp twist, distracting it long enough for him to vault onto the bronc saddle, which was specially made with built-in swells, a wide, undercut fork, and a deep-dish cantle. His bottom hardly came to rest when the mustang exploded into action, showing it was a regular pile driver.

A jolt nearly tore Santee's spine out, then he buckled down and clamped his legs tight, whipping and bending with the motion of the horse. To say it was a beast with a bellyful of bedsprings was an understatement.

"Ride 'em, Santee!" Red shouted.

That was easier said than done. Santee forgot to clamp his teeth and nearly lost a few on coming down from the clouds. The corral and the men on the fence were a constant blur as the mustang leaped and whirled and bucked.

Santee had never worked as a buster but he'd had to deal with a few contrary horses in his time and knew the basics of staying on when his mount wanted otherwise. He let himself relax, the better to absorb the punishment he was receiving, and in sheer spite, raked the rowels on his spurs into the mustang's sweaty flesh.

The bronc shot off the ground as if blasted from a cannon and came down too close to the fence to keep from smashing into it. Santee rocked and nearly fell. He would have grabbed for the apple, except that it was the habit of rank greenhorns. Shifting his weight to counter the tilt of the mustang's back, he clung on with his knees as the horse spun and made like a jackrabbit.

All the hands were shouting at once, but Santee had no idea what they were saying. He'd tried to keep track of the time but had lost count almost immediately. An abrupt whirl caught him unawares, and he felt himself slip to the left. Again, he tried to counter. Gravity interfered, and before he could straighten, the ground rushed up to meet him and intense pain lanced his left side.

Rowdy guffaws broke out. Santee pushed to his hands and knees, winded by the fall. Instead of laughing with them, a burning anger rose in his gorge, an anger that blazed like a red sun when he looked up and saw the mustang romping in triumph around the corral.

Slowly, he stood. Slowly, he walked up to Red and retrieved his gunbelts. And slowly, he turned on a boot heel, drew one of his pistols, and shot the mustang in the forehead.

Stunned silence ensued. The hands gawked at the thrashing horse. Jennings sputtered and aimlessly waved his arms. But no one uttered a word of protest.

Santee strapped on his six-guns, then nonchalantly went over to the horse. "I don't like being beaten," he said before kicking the animal in the mouth. Adjusting his neckerchief, he left the corral, making for the huge white house perched on top of a low hill to the south of the stable. He could have ridden, but he needed to let his blood cool down and walking always cleared his head.

The ornate columns on the front porch hid the man standing a few feet from the front door until Santee was almost upon him. On spying the hawkish figure, who wore a high-crowned sombrero and fancy Mexican garb, Santee drew up short.

"*Buenos dias,*" said Surgio Vasquez.

Santee merely nodded. He had never been one to dislike greasers on general principle, as did many of the punchers, but he did dislike Vasquez. The Mexican had an uppity air that Santee found galling. And all because Vasquez happened to be the best damn tracker on both sides of the border and his services were highly valued by Miles Gillett.

"I was on my way to find you," Vasquez said. "*El patron* is most unhappy that you were not back by dawn."

"I got held up," Santee said, and immediately regretted explaining himself to someone who was just another hired hand. "Lead the way."

Vasquez knocked twice. They were admitted by a servant and escorted to the sitting room, where the richest rancher in the Southwest and his lovely wife were enjoying a cup of coffee and the morning sun.

Miles Gillett was a formidable presence. More than anything else, he resembled a walking slab of mountain, as he turned from a glittering window and strode ponderously over to an easy chair beside his wife's. Incongruously, he held his coffee cup in a dainty fashion, his little finger pointing in the air. "Greetings, gentlemen," he said in his deep voice, as he sank down.

"Mornin' boss," Santee said.

"Is it indeed?" Gillett retorted, locking a steely stare on the gunman. "Closer to noon by my reckoning. I take it you were in town again last night?"

"A man has to have some fun every now and then," Santee said lamely. He did not like the tone the rancher used, but he was not about to say anything that would make Gillett angrier than he already was.

The truth be told, Miles Gillett was the only person on the face of the planet that Billy Santee feared. Not because the rancher was better with a six-gun. Gillett never carried one. No, Santee feared Gillett because there was something about the huge man, a sense of raw, wild power, so potent that Santee could feel it whenever they were close. Like now.

"I'm the first to agree a man needs to sow some oats on occasion," Gillett was saying with a teasing wink at Lilly, "but in your case it seems to be a nightly occasion. You head for town early and get back late. Half the time you're not around when I need you." Gillett lowered his coffee cup to his big lap. "And I don't pay top dollar to someone who isn't dependable."

Santee fidgeted. "I'm loyal to the brand, and you know it," he argued meekly.

"Correction, William," Gillett said. He was also the only person on the face of the planet who always used Santee's given name. "My punchers are loyal to the brand. Gunnies like you stick by their employers only so long as the money keeps coming. If something were to happen, and I couldn't keep paying you, you'd lose no time at all saddling up and going to look for work elsewhere."

Since there was no disputing the truth, Santee held his tongue.

"But we got off the subject," Gillett continued. "From here on out I want you to keep me posted of your exact whereabouts at all times. I have reason to believe an attempt will be made on my life before too long, and when it comes, I need to be ready."

"Who would be addlepated enough to try to put you under?" Santee asked, and chuckled at the crazy notion.

"Have you forgotten about Clay Taggart so soon?"

"One measly loco renegade won't give you no trouble, Mr. Gillett."

The rancher pursed his lips and regarded the gunman as he might an ignorant child who had made a ridiculous statement. "That measly renegade, as you call him, has already killed Jacoby and Prost. He's riding with a band of Apaches now, and that makes him ten times more dangerous than he ever was alone."

Santee hitched at his gunbelts. "I can handle him without working up a sweat."

Gillett looked at his wife, who tittered, then set his cup on a table and folded his hands. "You never cease to amaze me, William. Always looking at the bright side is a trait to be admired, but in your case, you're ignoring reality. Clay Taggart might not have fourteen notches on his guns like you do, yet even so, he's still one of the fastest men in Arizona, and a dead shot to boot."

"I've never met anyone I couldn't take," Santee said matter-of-factly, with a deliberate glance at Vasquez. The Mexican had a rep as a gun hand himself, his nickel-plated Colt boasting seven notches.

"You'll have a chance to prove your mettle sooner than you think," Gillett said. Standing, he moved to the east wall which was decorated with a large map of the territory. "Notice anything?" he asked.

Santee walked over. Near as he could tell, there was nothing unusual about it. Tucson was clearly marked. East of the town was the San Pedro River. Farther east lay the Dragoon Mountains, beyond them the Chiricahuas. He was about to shake his head when he noticed two tiny blue pins stuck in the map not far from Tucson. "What are those?"

"One is Jacoby's spread, the other is Prost's. Anything about them catch your eye?"

"They're a pretty shade of blue," Santee said without thinking.

"Not the pins, you dunderhead. The location of the two ranches."

Long ago, Santee had decided never to strain his brain more than was absolutely necessary to get through the day with a minimum of fuss. No one had ever accused him of being a deep thinker, and situations like this annoyed him to no end. Not wanting to appear stupid, he studied the pins long and hard, trying to figure out what Gillett thought was so important, until a brainstorm occurred to him. "Each ranch is a bit closer to town," he said.

"So which ranch will be hit next?"

Santee pondered. Twelve men had been on that posse, four of them ranchers. With Jacoby and Prost dead, that left Denton and Bitmer. "Harve lives the farthest out," he mentioned.

"Excellent." Gillett scanned the map, then tapped the spot where Denton's ranch would be. "My hunch is that Taggart will attack Denton soon. I've already had a long talk with Harve, and he's taking steps to give Taggart a suitable welcome."

"Why tell me all this?"

"Because Harve will need help. I want you to pick

out eight leather slappers and light a shuck for his spread at first light. You're to stay there until I send for you."

"But it could be days before Taggart shows his hand," Santee said, thinking of Missy.

"Weeks maybe," Gillett said. "I don't give a damn how long it is, you're not to budge from Denton's until I'm sure Taggart has changed his pattern." He paused. "Do you savvy, mister?"

"I savvy," Santee grumbled.

Miles Gillett returned to his easy chair. "Make no mistake. I want Taggart and his red devils to buck out in smoke. Fail to make wolf meat of them, and you'll get me riled." Gillett's hooded eyes were like those of a coiled serpent. "And I don't reckon you want me riled, do you?"

"No, sir."

Assuming all had been said, Santee went to leave.

"One more thing."

"Boss?"

"Vasquez is going with you."

The gunman tried to hide his resentment. "We don't need him taggin' along."

"I beg to differ. You might find a tracker handy, and you know damn well that Surgio is the best there is at what he does."

"I can manage by my lonesome," Santee insisted.

Gillett leaned back and made a tepee of his fingers. "Are you much of a tracker, William?"

"Middling, I suppose."

"But not as good as Surgio?"

"No," Santee was loathe to confess.

"And how are you at bronc busting?"

The unexpected query put Santee on his guard. "About the same," he answered.

"So you're not good enough to be paid to break stock?"

"No."

"Then kindly explain to me why the hell I looked out my window a while ago to see what all the ruckus was down at the corral, and lo and behold, I saw you on the new mustang."

The rancher had put Santee on the spot. Embarrassed, the gunman made a show of being interested in the map. "There was a little bet as to how long I could stay on," he explained, and let it go at that.

"Was it part of the bet to shoot the mustang when you were done?"

"I got a mite flustered after that mangy gut-twister flung me away, and I lost my head there for a minute."

"Short-trigger men with short tempers cause more problems than they solve," Gillett said sternly. "Get a rein on yours, or else."

"I'll do my best." Santee headed for the door. Out of the corner of his eye, he glimpsed Surgio Vasquez grinning, and it took all the self-control he could muster not to pull his iron then and there.

"One more thing," the rancher called.

"I pay for the mustang?" Santee guessed.

"Next payday it will be deducted from what you have coming," Gillett said. He shook his head in annoyance as the gunman and the tracker left; then he heard his wife cluck like an irate hen.

"Honestly, Miles. You would be better off if you sent that boy packing. He's brought more aggravation down on your head than all the rest of your men combined."

"Ordinarily, I'd agree," Gillett said. "But that young man is pure hell with the hide off. For the right money he'd brace his own mother, and smile while squeezing the trigger."

"He makes my skin crawl," Lilly objected. "Those eyes of his are as cold as a winter's day."

"His kind are always that way," Gillett replied. "Santee is a rarity, a born killer, a man with no conscience, no scruples whatsoever. Killing is the same to him as breathing and eating."

"Do you really think he can stop Clay?"

"Not by himself. He's not smart enough to be a match for Taggart. Vasquez, however, is the canniest Mex around. No one can outfox him. So, between the two of them, I hope to put a stop to the White Apache, before he shows up on our doorstep."

"We should have finished him when we had the chance."

"I know. But don't fret, my dear. I never make the same mistake twice."

Outside the house, something was happening that would have a profound bearing on Miles Gillett's scheme. Billy Santee had halted and spun toward a surprised Surgio Vasquez, his clawed hands inches from his six-shooters.

"You might be able to track bees in a blizzard, but if you ever laugh at me behind my back again, I'll put some pills into you before you can so much as blink."

The tracker took the rebuke in stride. He was accustomed to the gunman's outbursts and was under strict orders to bend over backward, if need be, to keep Santee in line. "You sure are as techy as a teased snake, Senor Billy," he said amiably, using a figure of speech favored by the Anglo cowboys. To his consternation, Santee reddened and hunched forward as if to draw.

"No one calls me by my first name! It's Santee to you and don't you forget it!"

"What does it matter?" Vasquez asked innocently.

"Just never you mind!" Santee hissed. His whole body tensed; then he glanced at the sitting room windows, scowled, and pivoted to storm toward the corral.

Vasquez tactfully veered toward the bunkhouse. He couldn't help but wonder if his employer wasn't demanding the impossible. Riding roughshod on Billy Santee was akin to sitting on a lit powder keg; there was no telling when either might go off.

At times like this, Vasquez longed to be back in Mexico with his family and friends. He never quite felt at home in Arizona, though he had been there almost eight years. A lot of it had to do with the attitude of the many Americans who looked down their noses at anyone not of the same race, the same culture. He despised them as much as they despised him, perhaps more so.

Had it not been for an unfortunate bit of gunplay that resulted in the death of two *soldados*, Vasquez knew he would be living the good life in Sonora, perhaps tracking for one of the wealthy landowners there.

Since childhood, Vasquez had liked to read sign, an interest sparked by his grandfather who had learned the art when young from a friendly Indian. The old man had taken him out into the hills, almost as soon as he could walk, to teach him all about the various types of prints and how to tell whether a track was one day or ten days old. He'd learned how to determine gait, stride, height, weight, and sometimes the gender, by the size, depth, and angle of the impressions in the soil. Even in his early teens he had been widely recognized as the most skilled tracker in all northern Mexico.

Vasquez thought of his grandfather now and felt melancholy. The old man had been slain by Apaches, as had Vasquez's brother and cousin. The three had been part of a small *conducta* caught in a mountain pass by a roving band and promised safe passage if they would lay down their arms to show their peaceful intentions. The fool of a wagon master had agreed. Hardly had the men disarmed themselves than the Apaches pulled out their knives and war clubs and went to work with sadistic glee. The women and children were taken captive: the men were tied upside down to wagon wheels, and fires were lit under their heads.

As a result, Vasquez hated Apaches even more than he did most *Americanos*. Any opportunity to hunt them down, he took. This new job held added appeal because Gillett had promised him a large bonus if he brought back Taggart's head, swinging from a pole.

Vasquez needed the money. A frugal man, except where his personal appearance was involved, he had saved a hefty sum over the years. With the bonus thrown in he might have enough to bribe certain officials in Sonora into letting him return in safety. He would be able to see his aged parents again and to hold his dear sister in his arms.

At the bunkhouse door Vasquez paused to gaze at the corral. Santee was leading his mount into the stable. There went the fly in the ointment, as the Americans might say. Unpredictable as a grizzly, Santee might spoil the whole plan if his temper reared at the wrong time.

Vasquez wasn't about to let that happen. He would do whatever he could to put an end to the so-called

White Apache, and if circumstances dictated putting an end to Billy Santee, then that was precisely what he would do. He could always make it look like an accident.

Humming to himself, Surgio Vasquez went inside.

Chapter Four

There are those who would say that Clay Taggart lived a charmed life. Certainly, the events that led up to the bloodiest reign of terror in Arizona's early history would lend support to their view. Lynched by vigilantes, he was spared from certain death by bloodthirsty Apaches. Trapped by scalp hunters in northern Mexico, he narrowly escaped to fight on.

And on this day, as Delgadito the Chiricahua lunged at Clay Taggart's broad back to push Taggart to his death, that same mysterious hand of fate was at work again. For a fraction of an instant before Delgadito surged forward, ·Clay spotted movement in the canyon leading to their sanctuary and shifted to get a better view. As he did, two things happened. His right foot slid too close to the edge of the ledge and the brittle earth gave way under his weight, while simultaneously, he felt something brush against his right arm.

Gravity carried Clay over the edge. For a frantic second he hung half-suspended in midair, his arms flailing. Then he did the only thing he could do under the circumstances; he twisted and grabbed for Delgadito to keep from plummeting to his death.

For one of the few times ever, Delgadito was taken completely unawares. Startled by the white-eye's unexpected action, he reacted instinctively, holding on tightly to keep Taggart from falling, just so he wouldn't be pulled to his own death, thereby doing the exact opposite of what he had planned. Instead of shoving White Apache to certain doom, he had saved White Apache's life by yanking the white man back onto the ledge. So swiftly did it all take place that they were standing in safety side by side before either of them had time to think about what had happened.

Clay grinned self-consciously and said, "Much obliged, partner. That was a mite too close for my liking."

Delgadito could only stare at his own hands in disbelief.

"I owe you again," Clay went on. "And somehow I aim to find a way to repay you." He clapped the warrior on the arm and laughed. "We make quite a pair, don't we? You watch my back, I'll watch yours, and we just might wind up seeing old age after all."

The Apache glanced up, furious at the silly white-eye for daring to think he truly cared whether Taggart lived or not. In his anger he was all set to finish the job he had started when he, too, spied movement below and saw several of the figures gazing up at them.

"Palacio?" Clay asked in Apache.

"Palacio," Delgadito growled, not only because

he disliked the leader, but also because Palacio's untimely arrival had spoiled his chance to destroy Taggart.

"You really do hate him, don't you? Maybe you'd better let the others do the talking. You might say something that'll get his dander up and ruin the whole deal."

"A man who can not control his tongue is no man at all," Delgadito said gruffly, and turned to descend.

Clay did likewise, first checking that his twin Colts were securely wedged under the top of his breechcloth and that his Winchester hung securely by its leather sling across his back. In addition to the guns, he had a Bowie knife on his right hip, a dagger tucked inside the top of his right moccasin, and a throwing knife tucked inside his left moccasin. He was a walking arsenal, and glad to be one, since an Apache's life often depended on his weapons.

Delgadito gave a yip to alert the others to Palacio's arrival and hurried so he could rejoin them before the chief's band came through the defile. He had already shut the incident on the ledge from his mind. Brooding over it would serve no purpose, and there would always be another day.

Clay had likewise forgotten about it in his nervousness over the impending get-together. He had never met Palacio, never met any of the warriors who were attending, and he was more than a little worried over how they would treat him. Even though these were Apaches who had accepted reservation life, at heart most Apaches despised their white conquerors. Would they try to kill him as Fiero had done that time?

Once on firm footing Clay hurried to a bare clearing at the base of a knoll, where Delgadito and the others had taken seats facing the entrance. All except Ponce, who was making a fire. Beside Delgadito rested a large pipe and a pouch of precious tobacco.

Clay glanced at the defile and saw the first of the warriors materialize. His stomach did flip-flops. Hastening to the clearing, he paused, debating where to sit.

Delgadito solved the problem by indicating a spot next to him.

"I've never been to one of these powwows before," Clay mentioned, sinking cross-legged to the ground. "Are there any rules I should know?"

"Rules?" Delgadito repeated, trying to recall if he had heard that word before.

"Things to do. Things not to do."

"Only not to speak unless you are called on," Delgadito said. "Palacio or someone else will talk for his side. I talk for ours."

A full dozen warriors were now in the hidden valley, advancing on foot in single file. At their head was the first, and only, fat Apache Clay had ever seen. The man fancied himself, judging from his strut as he walked and the colorful attire he wore—a yellow headband, a bright red shirt, and leggings adorned with rows of red and blue beads. This dandy halted a yard in front of Delgadito and declared in an uncommonly high-pitched voice, "I come as a friend."

"We greet you as friends."

"Smoke with us and we will hear your words."

The fat Apache was surprisingly supple, as he demonstrated by his fluid motion as he sat. His rifle went across his ample thighs, and he gave each of the outcasts a steady look. Clay, he ignored.

A bad sign, Clay reflected, made worse because

the fat one had to be Palacio. His right hand held so that his fingers brushed the butt of one of his pistols; he kept his features impassive in order not to betray his thoughts. The other Apaches, he observed, did not share their chief's lack of interest. Each and every one scrutinized him.

Delgadito filled the pipe and lit it. He offered the stem to Palacio, who puffed solemnly, then smoked it himself and passed it to his right. One by one, the Apaches participated, and when all were done with the token symbol of their peaceful intentions, Delgadito set the pipe aside and said, "Now to the matter that has brought you here."

"Your messenger did not have much to say on the subject," Palacio said, "but I can guess. Tell me your desire, my brother."

"We grow lonely up here. We want to be able to move among our people now and then."

"I speak with the heart of feeling when I say that I would like to help you," Palacio replied. "But you must understand that you have brought this upon your own heads."

Clay saw Fiero frown and Cuchillo Negro bow his head.

Delgadito was a rock. "We are the first to admit, Palacio, that we should never have abandoned reservation life and gone to live in Mexico. I am to blame, and I alone, since I was the one who convinced the others to go with me. I was the one who promised them we would live as our ancestors did in the old days, free as the eagle with no one to tell us how we must dress or behave."

"I am sad for my brother," Palacio said, but his face did not show any sadness. "When I heard of Blue Cap's raid on your camp and the loss of all your women and children, I became like a woman

46

and wanted to shed tears for the many lost lives."
But neither Palacio's tone nor his manner confirmed
the torment he claimed to have endured. "I wanted
to go to the reservation agent and urge him to let
my brothers live in peace once again."

"But you did not," Delgadito said.

Palacio never missed a beat. "The time for words
is long past, old friend. Too many Americans and
Nakai-yes have fallen to your rifle and knife for them
to smoke the pipe with you." He leaned forward and
said in reproach, "You chose your path, and you
must live with the consequences."

Clay felt sorry for Delgadito. His friend had held
high hopes for the meeting, and it was not going
well at all. He was inclined to speak in Delgadito's
defense, but doing so would be a breach of Apache
etiquette, so he held his peace.

"It is true we all live according to the paths we
have picked," Delgadito said after some reflection.
"Yet is it not also true that we may change our paths
at any time?"

"I respect your wishes but sometimes we go too
far on one path to turn back or to go another
way."

"We would simply like to walk among our own
kind again," Delgadito said wearily.

"I cannot give my approval. If you were caught,
the army would throw you in the stone wickiup
with iron bars. You would be left to rot or sent
to the land of many swamps. And that would be
your business. But our people would be made to
suffer on account of you. The white-eyes would cut
back on our rations as punishment for sheltering
you."

"We would come and go without being caught."

"The white-eyes you can fool, yes, but not the

Shis-Inday, who now scout for the army and the reservation police. They would hear of your visits and hunt you down."

Silence fell. Clay knew there was nothing Delgadito could say that would change Palacio's mind. They must go on living as outcasts for the rest of their lives, shunned by the very ones they sought to free. "It's just not fair," he muttered in English, and when he looked up, he was shocked to discover everyone staring at him.

"What is not fair, Clay Taggart?" Palacio asked in clipped English.

"You speak my tongue?" Clay said. "And you know who I am?"

"I was one of the smart ones who learned your tongue when the first white-eyes came to our land. I also speak the tongue of the *Nakai-yes* and the Maricopas," Palacio boasted. "As for you, who among the *Shis-Inday* has not heard of Lickoyee-shis-inday?"

"I had no idea I was so well known."

The fat Apache glanced at Delgadito and reverted to his own tongue. "It should not surprise you to hear that warriors laugh at you behind your back because you have taken this white fool into your band."

Clay should have kept quiet, but he never had been able to abide insults, no matter who did the insulting. In crisp, precise Apache, he snapped, "Who are you to call me a fool? At least I stand by my friends when they are in trouble, which is more than can be said about you."

The remark was directed at Palacio, yet it was another, younger warrior who sprang to his feet and whipped a rifle to his shoulder. "You will keep quiet, dog, when your betters are talking."

"Show me one of you who is my better and I will," Clay retorted.

"Die, white-eye, so that I may have many horses," the young warrior barked. He sighted down the barrel as he slipped his forefinger through the trigger guard.

Clay didn't wait to learn what would happen next. His right arm flashed up and out, and his Colt banged once. The bullet struck the Apache in the shoulder, knocking the man backward and causing him to drop the rifle. In a twinkling, all the warriors were on their feet, some in Palacio's party with their weapons leveled at Clay. To his amazement he wasn't the only one pointing a gun at the chief's followers. Fiero and Cuchillo Negro both had their rifles trained and were ready to fire.

Bloodshed loomed a heartbeat away. At that junction, Palacio and Delgadito rose, their arms upraised, and together called for everyone to stay calm and to lower their guns. Reluctantly, the Apaches complied.

Loathe to leave himself defenseless, Clay dropped his hand to his side but held on to the six-shooter and cocked the hammer.

The wounded Apache had sunk to his knees and was doubled over in pain while another inspected his shoulder.

"What have you done, White Apache?" Delgadito whispered urgently to Clay. "We are in much trouble now."

"Was I supposed to sit there and let him rub me out?"

"You should not have talked."

"Would you let someone call you a fool?"

"No," Delgadito admitted. And while he appeared as upset as the rest by the dispute, secretly he was

49

greatly pleased. It had not been his idea to send a messenger to Palacio. He had not been one of those who wanted to venture down to the reservation on occasion and live among the tame Apaches, as the whites called them. No, it had been Amarillo and Ponce who had proposed the idea and Cuchillo Negro who had suggested giving it a try, although Cuchillo Negro was too wise not to have foreseen the predictable outcome.

Now Delgadito gazed on the tense scene and mused that he should thank Taggart for playing right into his hands. In more ways than one, as it turned out, when moments later a stocky warrior advanced and said something into Palacio's ear. The chief then called for quiet and made an announcement.

"Chivari will see his family again. The white-eye's bullet did not cause a wound unto death." Palacio glared at Taggart. "But a terrible wrong has been done, a wrong that demands justice! And since Chivari is in no condition to satisfy his honor, his brother, Pedro Azul, has taken this thing on himself. The shame is on their house and, as such, he can issue a formal challenge."

"No!" Fiero cried. "He does not know our ways. He would be at a disadvantage."

"He calls himself White Apache now, does he not?" Palacio disputed him. "He lives in our mountains, dresses as we do. In every respect he has become *Shis-Inday*. If that is his wish, then he must live by Apache law. And our law says that one who is wronged may challenge the one who has wronged him in a fight to the death."

"The law of the knife," Cuchillo Negro said softly.

Clay had been listening attentively. As the full

implications hit him, he wished he had listened to Delgadito and kept his big mouth shut. So what if he felt Palacio to be a stiff-necked ass. Apache doings were none of his business. Or—and here a new thought dazzled his brain—were they? "What do I do?" he asked.

Delgadito did not answer right away. He was happier than he had been in weeks since now he would not need to bother with disposing of Taggart. Pedro Azul would do it for him. Acting highly concerned, he said, "You must accept the challenge or all Apaches will say *Lickoyee-shis-inday* is a coward."

"We fight with knives, I take it?"

"Yes."

"Until one of us is hurt?"

"Until one of you is dead."

The disclosure gave Clay food for thought. "And if I win? What then?"

"You earn much respect."

"That's all?"

Delgadito looked at Clay and answered in his own tongue. "For a warrior, what else is there?"

Until that moment Clay hadn't given the matter much thought. The truth would have been obvious if he had opened his eyes to it. The Apaches did, in fact, base their relations on mutual respect for one another, not on the silly values the whites did. His own kind rated others by the amount of money they had and how powerful they were. Comparing the two, he decided the Apaches had a more honest way of doing things. "All right, pard." Out came his Bowie. "Let's get it over with."

"Not this very moment," Delgadito said. "It must be done according to custom. You not fight until tomorrow."

"What am I supposed to do until then?" Clay asked irritably, displeased at having to wait so long.

"Prepare."

"How?"

"Any way you want." Delgadito watched as Chivari, supported by Pedro Azul, made for the spring. Several others tagged along. "Talk to your white God. Paint your body. Do that which makes you strong, that which brings you good medicine."

"White men don't believe in that nonsense."

"Maybe time you start." Lips compressed, Delgadito walked off.

Clay knew he had offended the warrior and went to follow to offer his apology. Suddenly Fiero appeared, blocking his path.

"Are you skilled with a knife?" the firebrand inquired without ceremony.

"I fought Blue Cap with one," Clay reminded him.

"But are you skilled?" Fiero persisted, stressing the last word.

"I can get by when I have to."

"Come." Wheeling, the warrior strode westward toward a stand of fir trees.

"Where are we going?"

"I will teach you how Apaches fight with knives," Fiero said. "There are many tricks you must learn if you are to survive the challenge. Pedro Azul is very crafty with blades."

"You'd do this for me?" Clay marveled, recollecting that at one time Fiero hated all whites, including himself, with a raging passion.

Unknown to Clay, Fiero was thinking that very thing. No one was more confounded by his change of heart than he was himself, and he was all the more upset because it had claimed him like a thief in the night, insinuating itself without his being aware, so that one night he had gone to bed detesting the entire white race and the next morning he had gazed on White Apache with new vision that told him this particular white-eye was not such a bad person. "You saved me from the *Nakai-yes*," he said, since that was as good a reason as any and the only one that halfway justified his new outlook. "You gave me *pesh-e-gar*," he added, hefting his rifle.

The shade under the trees was refreshing. Fiero leaned his rifle against a trunk bordering a clearing, stripped to the waist, and drew his gleaming butcher knife. "Come, White Apache. We see how you do."

Feeling self-conscious, Clay placed his Winchester next to the warrior's, palmed the Bowie, and cautiously advanced, not quite sure what to expect. It occurred to him that this could all be a ruse on Fiero's part to stick eight inches of metal between his ribs when he relaxed his guard, a notion he dismissed as a product of his suspicious nature. Fiero might have the fiery temperament his name implied, and be pure Apache through and through, but Fiero was also a man of honor.

"Expose little of your body to your enemy," the firebrand was telling him. To demonstrate, Fiero bent at the waist and balanced lightly on his feet. He had reduced his size by a third and could now dart either right or left, forward or backward, with supreme ease. "You try."

Clay coiled in imitation of the warrior.

Fiero grunted, then nodded at his knife. "Always hold the blade down so your enemy can not tell which way you will strike." Again he demonstrated by flicking his butcher knife this way and that, always returning it to the original position afterward.

Once more Clay did as he was instructed. He would rather have held the Bowie in front of him, blade extended, to ward off his foe's thrusts, a preference he did not mention so as not to annoy his new teacher.

"Now we hone your skill," Fiero declared. He promptly closed, stabbing at Clay's legs so fast Clay barely had time to parry and dance aside.

"Careful," Clay objected. "That was too close."

"Pedro Azul will come closer."

For the next half an hour Clay Taggart was put through his paces by a master knife fighter. It gave him a whole new appreciation for his deliverance during their first encounter, when a timely fall down a slope had been all that saved Clay from Fiero's blade. And it left Clay drenched with sweat, craving a visit to the spring.

"Remember all I have taught you and you might live," Fiero said, in the act of slipping his knife into its beaded sheath.

"Do you want to know the truth?" Clay responded. "I would gladly forget all about fighting if Pedro Azul could be persuaded to change his mind."

"That will not happen," Fiero said. "Pedro Azul wants your blood for his brother's. It is the way of the *Shis-Inday*."

"My people call it taking an eye for an eye," Clay revealed.

Fiero grinned. "At last. Some white words that are not nonsense."

The pair walked side by side from the first, parting when Clay angled to the spring where the two brothers and five other warriors were seated. The looks they bestowed on him were enough to provoke nightmares in children. Kneeling, he dipped a hand in the cool water and gulped thirstily until Pedro

Azul abruptly rose and came over.

"I will kill you tomorrow, white-eye."

"You will try," Clay amended.

The warrior's dark eyes took Clay's measure. "Before we were forced onto the reservation I slew many of your kind. Babies are harder to kill."

"I must take your word for it," Clay said, standing and taking a step back to give himself room to maneuver. "White men never harm babies. Only weakling and cowards do."

"Are you calling me a weakling and a coward?" Pedro Azul rasped.

"If you have slain babies, Yes."

The stocky warrior hissed and placed a hand on the hilt of his knife.

Chapter Five

There were no friendly Apaches nearby. Clay was on his own, confronted by the furious brother of the brave he had wounded and with five more hostile warriors close by, all armed. He saw Pedro Azul begin to pull the butcher knife and automatically braced to fill his hand with a Colt.

"No, brother!" Chivari cried from his resting place at the base of a large boulder. Wincing, he pushed onto an elbow. "The challenge has been issued. We must do this according to custom."

No other appeal could have been so persuasive. Apaches were creatures of custom; disputes, marriages, warfare, every single activity had to be done in a certain way. Pedro Azul would have liked to carve the haughty white-eye into a hundred pieces right there, but he knew the proper time would be during the formal duel. So, restraining his wrath, he contented himself with a verbal barb. "We will get as many horses for you this way as another."

The comment jarred Clay's memory; Chivari had mentioned the same thing prior to taking aim. "Another warrior has offered you horses to take my life?"

"What Apache would be bothered?" Pedro Azul rejoined. "No, *Lickoyee-shis-inday*, it is your own kind who will pay a high price to the one who brings you in."

"Who will? The army? The reservation agent?"

"Find out for yourself, if you live through the day tomorrow," Pedro Azul baited him. Sneering, the Chiricahua walked to his fellows, and one by one they showed their disdain by turning their backs on him.

Clay hardly noticed. He slouched off, depressed by the alarming, but not entirely unexpected, news. A while back he had been involved in a skirmish with a cavalry patrol in which the soldiers had discovered he was a white man. It stood to reason the army would be interested in him. Evidently, they didn't care whether he was brought in alive—or dead.

The rest of the day Clay spent off by his lonesome, high on a crag only eagles or mountain sheep could reach. He had weighty issues to ponder, a future to chart, and all depended on the outcome of the fight. He reached decisions that would impact not only his life but the lives of every man, woman, and child in Arizona, northern Mexico, and western Texas. Later he would look back on this day as the crucial turning point in his life, although he had no inkling of its importance at the time.

That night, after a light meal of antelope, Clay sat by himself under a rock overhang, a blanket wrapped around his shoulders. Footsteps heralded a shadowy shape that paused in the darkness.

"I would share words with you, White Apache."

Clay had expected Delgadito or perhaps Fiero. Mystified, he responded, "You are welcome to sit with me, Cuchillo Negro."

Black Knife, the name meant in English. The quiet one. The thinker. The one who saw much but disclosed little of what he saw. Ducking under the overhang, he sat.

"What brings you to see me?" Clay asked. Never in the months he had been with the band had he had a man-to-man chat with this one. Yet, Clay felt closer to Cuchillo Negro than to any of the others except Delgadito. Why that was he could not say.

"Our bullets have killed the same enemies."

"This is so," Clay said.

"We have eaten the same animal, drunk from the same spring."

"Many times," Clay confirmed, sensing he must pay close attention.

"When Delgadito wanted to make you a member of our band, I was not the one who loudly objected."

"True."

"When Delgadito let you lead us on our raid into Mexico, I fought by your side."

Clay's ears perked up. Had he understood rightly? He distinctly recalled Delgadito planting the idea that the others had wanted him to lead. "Are you saying Delgadito could have led if he wanted to?"

"I say no such thing," Cuchillo Negro said. "I simply give voice to the truth."

Puzzled, Clay said, "What other truths does my red brother care to share?"

"Has White Apache ever stood near the top of a mountain peak when the clouds are low?"

58

The unusual query intensified Clay's curiosity. "Several times," he replied.

"And what did White Apache see?"

"Clouds. What else?"

"Did he see the land under the clouds, the hills and valleys and rivers?"

"How could I when the clouds hid them?"

Cuchillo Negro gazed into the distance. "Like those clouds, that which we see often hides something else beneath the surface. Things are not always as they seem. Men are not always as they appear to us. Their words may have one meaning, their actions another, their innermost thoughts a third."

"Can you give me more details?"

"I have already revealed too much." Cuchillo Negro stood and blended into the night without saying anything else.

Clay was left more perplexed than before. He suspected that Black Knife had given him a subtle warning, but he had no idea what the warning implied. The very thought of casting any sort of suspicion on Delgadito, who had treated him kindly from the first day they met, went against his grain. And even if he were right about the accusation, he saw no basis for it. Delgadito had never harmed him in word or deed.

The quarter moon was well on its downward arc when Clay Taggart spread out his blankets near the embers of the fire and, with a sigh, reclined on his back. By all rights he should be sleeping, should be conserving his energy for the knife fight. Yet try as he might he was unable to doze off. His mind raced more rapidly than a runaway stage, his blood boiled with excitement.

In the wee hours of the morning, Clay finally

drifted into an undisturbed slumber. Bright sunshine warming his eyelids awakened him, and he sat up, blinking in dismay at finding the sun an hour into the sky. Across from him sat Fiero diligently attaching a leather hide to a wooden framework.

"You greet the day late, White Apache," remarked the firebrand. "Your nerves must be made of iron to let you sleep so long on the day a challenge must be answered."

Afraid he had slept past the appointed time and shamed himself in the eyes of the band, Clay shoved the blanket from him and exclaimed, "The fight!"

"Is not for a while yet," Fiero said. "The circle has been set up and soon the shields will be done." He held out the object he had been working on. "We had to use antelope skin since there are no oxen within two days' travel."

Shaking his head to dispel lingering tendrils of drowsiness, Clay said, "No one told me that we'd use shields." Yawning, he stretched, then balanced on his knees. "It is good to hear. I will be able to protect myself from his blade."

"A shield can protect, yes, but it can also hide," Fiero pointed out. "A clever fighter sometimes conceals his knife behind his shield so his foe can not predict his movements."

"Thanks, friend. I will remember it." Clay headed for the spring and noticed the Apaches had divided themselves into two groups. Delgadito and company were off to the left, while Palacio's bigger group sat to the north. The challenge had widened the rift between the two factions, so that now neither wanted anything to do with the other.

Clay's sympathy went to the outcasts. To his way of thinking it wasn't unreasonable for them to want to mingle with their people again, and he begrudged

Palacio the right to turn them down.

Several mouthfuls of the crystal clear water did wonders to revitalize Clay. He was rising when a hand fell on his left shoulder.

"Are you ready, White Apache?"

"As ready as I'll ever be, I reckon," Clay answered Delgadito. He stared at the warrior closely, thinking of Cuchillo Negro's baffling warning. In the light of the new day, with his friend standing right there in front of him, it seemed more senseless than ever.

"When the sun is there," Delgadito pointed, "the fight will begin."

Clay patted his Bowie. "Do I get to use my own knife?"

"You may use any knife you want." Delgadito squatted to cup water to his mouth. After drinking, he smacked his lips and looked up at the white-eye. Oddly, he was experiencing no great joy at the prospect of Taggart being slain. For as surely as the day turned to night and the night to day in an endless cycle, White Apache would meet his death at the hands of Pedro Azul, one of the best knife fighters in the tribe.

"Have you ever been challenged?" Clay inquired.

"Twice, both when I was much younger," Delgadito said. "No one ever wanted to challenge me again after that day."

"You fought them both at the same time?"

"No. One after the other. That was back when I had two wives and my first wife's brothers did not like that I had set my second wife above her and made her do all the work. She complained to them, and they complained to me, and when I told them I would do as I pleased, they became angry." Delgadito peered through the haze of time and commented, "Their challenge was stupid. My affairs were my own."

Clay remembered that Delgadito had only one wife when they met. "Was that she who nursed me back to health?"

"No. After I killed her brothers, she ran off and starved herself to death in the mountains. The woman I had favored died later of disease. You saw my third wife." Delgadito stopped, surprised he was revealing so many personal details. Such matters were better locked up deep inside and reflected on in private.

Glancing around to insure no other Apaches were watching, Clay placed a hand on Delgadito's arm and said sincerely, "No matter what happens today I want you to know I'm right grateful for all you've done for me. I speak from the heart when I say that you're one of the best pards I've ever had."

Delgadito simply stared as White Apache walked off. Once again, he was bothered by a tug of affection for the white man, a tug he suppressed with hard effort. It should make no difference that Taggart had saved his life. It should not matter that they had been through many hardships together and lived as true *Shis-Inday* should live. Taggart was spoiling his carefully laid plan to regain a position of leadership in the Chiricahuas and, accordingly, must be destroyed.

Over by the fire, White Apache was rolling up his blankets, when Fiero approached bearing the antelope-hide shield and several long leather strips.

"It is time to make ready."

Clay was directed to strip to his breechcloth and moccasins. He had to sit and hold out his left arm while Fiero ceremoniously bound the shield to his elbow and wrist. As the warrior worked, he imparted critical advice.

"A blade can pierce the hide. Do not try to stop a direct stab straight on. Use it so"—Fiero made a sweeping gesture—"to deflect his knife."

"I will," Clay said.

"It is not necessary or wise to get too close to him. Stay just out of his reach and when an opening presents itself, strike with the speed of a rattlesnake."

"I'll do my best."

"Some men have weaknesses that can be taken advantage of," Fiero continued. "Pedro Azul does not. He attacks with skill and defends with skill. Rarely does he make a mistake." Fiero looked at Clay. "If I knew how to defeat him, I would tell you."

"You have already done more than I had any right to expect."

"But not enough. You saved my life in Mexico, and that is a debt I can only repay in kind."

A circle thirty feet in diameter had been trampled in the high grass. Around it the Apaches gathered, Palacio on the south side, Delgadito to the north.

Pedro Azul strode into the ring as a gladiator of old striding into an arena, smiling smugly in his supreme confidence in his ability. Bronzed sinews rippling, he held his head high for the benefit of his admiring friends and made a few passes with his long butcher knife to loosen his arm for combat.

By contrast, Clay Taggart looked as somber as living death as he entered the circle and stood regulating his breathing. His pulse drummed madly. It was all he could do to keep his presence of mind. He tried to disregard the spiteful glares of Palacio's people but could not.

No one imparted last minute instructions. No one told them to begin. Pedro Azul started the fight by streaking across the grass to strike, adopting the role of aggressor, his knife glittering in the sunlight.

Clay had been so engrossed in composing himself that he nearly missed seeing the charge. He had his eyes on the ground, not on his adversary as they should have been. On hearing the patter of footfalls, he raised his head and his shield at the same time and, by accident, blocked the first swing. Then, darting to the right, he retreated under an onslaught that few could have withstood.

Whoops and yells broke out as the Apaches cheered their favorites. The shouts of Pedro Azul's backers nearly drowned out the few who were roaring to inspire Clay.

When it comes to a fight to the death, no amount of thinking can prepare a person for actually being in that fight. Death seems remote from a distance but is horrifyingly real when it comes calling at the door. Clay Taggart had thought he was ready, but he was not. Fear coursed through his veins, a chilling fear that he might die in the next few moments. Fear turned his soul to ice; fear made him less than he was. But it was also fear that set his blood to pumping even faster and fear that lent speed to his limbs to back-pedal so swiftly the Apache was unable to deal a killing blow. Indeed, the warrior had a hard time keeping up.

Clay Taggart had made one circuit of the circle. Then, suddenly, he stopped. Shame crept over him as he realized he had given rein to abject cowardice. He stood his ground, his fear vanishing, replaced by guilt and the calming influence of his inner manhood. In that twinkling of time, he took stock of himself and found the inner strength that every man must find to be worthy of the brand.

Pedro Azul misunderstood. He'd seen the terror in the white man's eyes and counted his victory as already won. When White Apache stopped, Pedro Azul thought that the white-eye was too afraid to move a muscle. Teeth bared, he dashed forward and delivered an overhand swing that would have split his foe's face like an overripe gourd had it landed.

Only it didn't. Clay Taggart saw the blade sweeping toward him and did exactly as Fiero had advised. He drove the shield at a slant into the warrior's forearm and deflected the blow. Then, leaping clear, he circled the Apache, his knife at his side, the shield held high.

Taken aback by this unexpected resistance, Pedro Azul blunted an impulse to recklessly spring on the accursed white-eye. There was something new about White Apache—a new, firm set to his jaw and a blazing defiance in his eyes. Pedro Azul did not know what had brought about the change, but he did know that he must exercise care. He was facing a brand new foe.

There is a paradox in confronting death. In that moment, when a person stands on the verge of the great unknown, he feels more alive than he ever has before. Clay Taggart felt that way as he countered a series of blows, either with his shield or his knife. He tingled from head to toe. His hearing was so acute he heard the swish of the warrior's blade. His sense of smell was so keen he inhaled the odor of the Apache's sweat. And when he moved, he felt as if his arms and legs were liquid fire. Graceful, powerful, unstoppable. He was all these, and more.

Pedro Azul became more cautious. He thrust and slashed more precisely, never overextending himself and never leaving an opening that could prove fatal. His whipcord body bending and flowing to the demands of the moment, he sought to break through White Apache's guard and end the fight quickly.

Clay concentrated on staying alive until he recognized the mistake he was making. A man whose only interest is warding off blows can hardly deliver a killing blow himself. He was delaying the inevitable, no more. To win he must be as aggressive as his adversary. He must attack, not only defend.

Seconds later, first blood went to Clay. Pedro Azul jabbed at his groin and Clay slammed the shield into the warrior's wrist to swat the knife aside. In that same moment, Clay also pivoted and speared his Bowie high, going for the heart but scoring on the shoulder as the Apache ducked and skipped away.

Palacio and the rest of the reservation Apaches fell silent; Delgadito and the outcasts found new voice.

None was more shocked than Pedro Azul. Blood flowing down his torso, he moved to the edge of the clearing. The white-eye let him go, giving him the opportunity to examine the long, inch-deep wound. The tactic White Apache employed had been masterly, just the kind Pedro Azul often used. There could be no doubt now. He wasn't up against an inferior. He was fighting an equal.

When the two men closed again, there was a marked difference. The white man and the warrior fought with mutual respect for each other's prowess. They did not strike for the mere sake of striking but chose their stabs and parries carefully. There were fewer blows, less wasted movement.

On the sidelines, two men looked on with vastly different reactions.

Palacio could not believe his eyes. He had expected the fight to end in the first few seconds. No one wielded a knife like Pedro Azul, yet this white dog was holding his own.

Pedro Azul had to win. The Great White Father, himself, would be greatly pleased when the body was brought in. The reservation agent had said so.

Fully a moon ago the word had gone out. The Americans wanted this man badly, so badly they were offering a large price for his head. It had been the bounty, and not any presumed insult, that had prompted Chivari to try and shoot him. It had been the bounty, and not Chivari's wound, that had influenced Pedro Azul to issue the challenge.

The brothers were simply less prudent than the rest of Palacio's warriors. Three-fourths would have gladly slain the white cur were it not for the fact White Apache was under the protection of Delgadito who had a formidable reputation. Hardly less so was Fiero's, and Palacio had seen with his own eyes how Fiero treated the white man as a friend. Fiero, who had hated whites from the day he was born. Fiero, who had once vowed he would let maggots eat him alive before he would ever say to a white man, "*Nejeunee*." Neither Palacio nor his followers dared court the wrath of the two warriors by killing the white-eye outright.

Now, watching Pedro Azul feint and cut, the chief chafed with impatience for the duel to end, with Pedro Azul victorious. The warrior would earn the bounty being offered, and Palacio would garner a reward, too, in the form of the goodwill of the agent and the army commander, which would bring him more influence at tribal council meetings.

Across the clearing, Delgadito was also concerned about his influence among his people. The more popular White Apache became with the other outcasts, the less Delgadito's opinion would matter.

And if, as Delgadito foresaw, their raids were so successful that younger braves flocked to join them, Delgadito would just be one of many instead of the leader.

At the same time, Delgadito was bothered by a conscience he rarely acknowledged. Clay Taggart trusted him implicitly, after all. The white-eye would gladly sacrifice his own life for Delgadito's, in return for all Delgadito had done for him. And Delgadito could not say that about anyone else he had ever known. Not even his father or his brother since Apaches regarded such self-sacrifice as the height of folly.

It was this thought, more than any other, that sprouted the germ in Delgadito's mind which, in time, would blossom into a partnership the likes of which the Southwest had never seen before or since.

Meanwhile, in the center of the trampled grass, Clay Taggart fought on with no thoughts in his head save one: staying alive. When Pedro Azul lanced the knife at his midsection, he drove his shield downward, keeping the blade at bay. His Bowie arced at the warrior's neck but the neck was gone when the Bowie arrived.

Fatigue gnawed at Clay's shoulders. When the butcher knife leaped at his chest, he got the shield up just in time. Evidently, Pedro Azul had been waiting for that exact moment because he sprang, smashing the shield away with a bunched forearm and stabbing at Clay's right wrist in an attempt to disarm him.

The blade seared into Clay's flesh, not deep, but deep enough to sting terribly and draw blood. In reflex, Clay jerked his arm back, exposing his right side.

Pedro Azul, grinning, lifted his knife for the next, lethal stroke. He counted on Clay being unable to block his swing with either his knife or his shield. What he did not count on was that Clay would not bother to block but would attack instead.

Since Clay realized he couldn't stop his foe's knife arm, he instantly drove his shield at the only other target he had, Pedro Azul's chest. The tough hide rammed into the warrior, throwing Pedro Azul off balance, rocking him on one heel with his right arm upraised and his own shield out to one side.

Moving in a blur, Clay Taggart sliced the Bowie into Pedro Azul's stomach. Once, twice, and again—and on the third stab, the warrior tilted his head to the heavens and screeched a death wail that echoed off the cliffs and peaks and floated down around the heads of the onlooking Apaches, the majority of whom now fixed flinty stares on the slayer of their champion.

Chapter Six

Clay Taggart would be the first to admit he had a temper. As a boy he had gotten into hot water time and again with his folks because he let his temperament get the better of him. Every time his parents turned around, it seemed, he was embroiled in another scrape. His mother had always sadly shaken her head and told him he'd wind up at the gates of Hell if he didn't mend his ways. His father, usually sterner, had surprised the boy by saying that he understood since he had the same affliction.

Of late, that temper had seldom shown itself, in part because Clay had felt more content than he could recollect ever feeling, and in large measure because Apaches went out of their way to avoid antagonizing members of their own band and the five outcasts had come to regard him as one of their own, whether they were all willing to admit it or not.

But now, as Clay saw the flush of hatred on the faces of many of Palacio's followers, and in particular, the open dislike Palacio's features expressed, his old temper returned with a vengeance. He had not been the one who brought a rifle to bear at the powwow! He had not been the one who issued a formal challenge! How dare Palacio look at him that way!

Clay advanced on the reservation warriors, bloody knife clutched at waist level. "Anyone else want to challenge me?" he demanded harshly. "Anyone else want to die at the hands of the White Apache!" Straight at Palacio he strode, fury transforming his features into a feral mask.

The chief was dumbstruck by the startling change in *Lickoyee-shis-inday.* It was as if a savage spirit had taken possession of the white-eye; he wanted no part of this madman coming toward him.

Plus, unknown to Clay Taggart, Palacio had not engaged in personal combat for several years. That, combined with the idleness of reservation life, which had made him soft and flabby, meant Palacio was so out of shape that he knew he'd be slaughtered by the enraged American.

So, as Clay moved forward, Palacio retreated, his palms held outward. "No one else wants to challenge you!" he exclaimed. "Remember we came in peace!"

Clay heard the words but they failed to register. He was thinking of how the chief had called him a fool and belittled Delgadito for befriending him. "Fool, am I?" he roared, waving the dripping Bowie in an arc. "We'll see who's the jackass here, you son of a bitch!"

Palacio backed up farther, barely able to hide his fear, and several of his warriors closed in to defend him.

Once again violence threatened to break out.

Clay was less than six feet from the chief when calloused hands gripped his arm and held fast. Automatically, he went to yank free, then saw that Delgadito was the one holding him and that Fiero, Cuchillo Negro, Ponce and Amarillo were on either side, all armed and ready to fight, if need be.

"No, White Apache," Delgadito said quietly in English. "This is not right time, not right place."

"Let me go," Clay said, his fuming gaze boring into Palacio. "He isn't fit to lead your people! I'll carve out his heart and feed it to the buzzards! Then you can be chief!"

Palacio had never beheld such blatant rage on another human being before. For a *Shis-Inday* such lack of self-control would be unthinkable. He feared that Taggart was so incensed the white-eye would instigate a bloodbath by attacking him, so he appealed to Delgadito by saying, "We smoked the pipe together. Does it mean nothing to you?"

Delgadito stepped between Clay and Palacio, his left hand against Taggart's straining chest.

"You and I will die if you do not control him," Palacio said.

There was no disputing that fact. Every last warrior was primed to erupt into violence at the slightest provocation. Turning, Delgadito gripped Taggart by both shoulders and shook him, hard. "You must listen, my friend!" he declared. "This is not the Apache way."

"So?" Clay growled.

"So you live as *Shis-Inday* now, eh? You must live by our rules."

The haze of blood lust that was clouding Clay's mind began to clear. He saw the stormy countenances of Palacio's followers, saw their cocked rifles and nocked bows and poised lances, and the light of reason returned. His companions were greatly outnumbered. A battle would result in their slaughter, and their blood would be on his hands. With an effort, he shook himself and slowly lowered the Bowie. "Fair enough, pard," he said. "I owe you not to cause a ruckus."

Delgadito confronted Palacio. "You were right about one thing. I was a fool, but not for letting *Lickoyee-shis-inday* join my band. I was a fool for thinking we could mend the break between us. How can the wolf lie with the sheep? You have chosen your path, I have chosen mine. And we each must live with our decisions." He gestured at Pedro Azul. "Take your dead and go."

Palacio only had to nod, and two warriors moved to collect the body. "I am sorry it ended like this," he lied.

"Do not be. In the end you will see that I was right. There can never be lasting peace between the whites and Apaches, not so long as they treat us like they treat their cattle."

"We get by. They feed us and clothe us."

"But never enough. Our children are always hungry, our women wear torn clothes." Delgadito remembered something and pivoted to point northward where several dozen horses grazed on the lush grass at the end of the valley. "One favor I would ask. We have stolen many horses in our raids, enough to feed many mouths. Take them when you go and see that they are given to those in need."

"I cannot," Palacio said.

"Or will not?" Delgadito challenged.

"Cannot. Or are you unaware the white-eyes mark their animals so there is never any question of ownership? They can tell at a glance whether a horse has been stolen." Palacio nodded northward. "Were we to take them back and the marks be seen, we would be punished."

"So you will let our people go hungry because you are afraid of the whites," Delgadito said, not without malice.

Palacio had his limits. He would tolerate only so much; his Apache nature asserted itself. "I am not the one who led women and children from the reservation, where they were safe. I am not the one responsible for them being butchered by scalp hunters."

Of all the things Palacio could have said, this was the worst. Delgadito was stung to the core of his being although he never betrayed as much. From that moment on, he enshrined Palacio in his breast as his most bitter enemy and vowed to gain sweet revenge one day. To his lips came only one word, "True." A word that gave no inkling of his feelings.

Nodding curtly, Palacio lumbered off with his band in tow, the pair bearing the dead warrior at the rear. Chivari looked back once at Clay, an unspoken threat crackling in the air.

None of the outcasts spoke until the last of the chief's men was gone. Then it was Ponce who said, "That is the end of it. We are on our own."

"Wagh!" Fiero said. "Was there ever any doubt we were not? The fat one would sooner lie in a den of rattlesnakes than have anything to do with us. He is a disgrace to all Apaches. He should have been born white."

"I was hoping—" Ponce said, and did not complete his statement. Head bowed, the young warrior walked away.

"The warpath is always hardest on the young," Amarillo mentioned, then sighed. "But I did want to see my sister and her family once more."

"What is stopping you?" Delgadito said. "We are not bound by Palacio's will. We tried being open with him, but he has closed his mind to any thoughts that do not agree with his." Delgadito gestured in disgust. "*Shis-Inday* are born free men. No one has ever had the right to tell us how we should live. We can do as we please. If we want to visit our relatives or friends, we will."

"Palacio will not like it," Cuchillo Negro said.

"I spit on him," Delgadito said, spitting on the ground.

Unnoticed by the Apaches, Clay had squatted and was wiping his Bowie clean on the grass. "I do not know about the rest of you," he remarked, "but I am in the mood for another raid."

"A fine idea," Delgadito agreed, since the activity would take their minds off the meeting and serve to remind them of the sacrifice they were making for the good of all Chiricahuas. Their cause might be hopeless, yet as long as breath remained, they must never give in to those who had broken the spirit of their people. "Tonight we hold a *cha-ja-la*. Tomorrow we make war." He glanced at Taggart and inquired in English, "What is the name of the other rancher who helped hang you?"

"Harvey Denton," Clay grinned. "He doesn't know it yet, but he's in for one hell of a surprise."

The White Apache was wrong.

At that very moment Harvey Denton, a brusque bulldog of a man whose wide frame housed two hundred pounds of solid muscle, stood at the head of a polished mahogany table in his spacious ranch southeast of Tucson and jerked a lit cigar from his mouth to jab it at Billy Santee. "Is your boss plumb loco? Ten gunnies is all he sends? We're talking Apaches here!"

An amused Santee leaned back in his chair and hooked his boot heels on the table, nicking the edge with a spur. "Don't have a fit, Harve. Mr. Gillett knows what he's doing."

Denton came around to stand beside the gunman. "I don't care if you are hell on wheels. Get those damn high heels off my furniture, or so help me, I'll have my boys skin you alive."

Across the table Surgio Vasquez smiled. Harve Denton was afraid of no man, and his hands were as loyal to the brand as an outfit could be. If Santee bucked the rancher, there'd be fireworks, which Vasquez, for one, would be delighted to see. He wouldn't lift a finger to interfere if Denton's punchers took it into their heads to beat the cocky gunfighter to a pulp. Secretly, he'd cheer them on.

Santee, however, just chuckled and let his boots thud to the floor. "Lord, you're gettin' high-strung in your old age!"

"You would be, too, if half the damned Apache nation was out for your blood," Denton declared.

"If there were that many don't you reckon the army would be out in force?" Santee said, shaking his head. "No, accordin' to Mr. Gillett, there ain't but a half-dozen of the red devils involved. Them and that turncoat Taggart."

"Even so, he should have sent a few extra," Denton stated. "I've fought Apaches before. I know how tricky they can be, how they can sneak right into a man's house and slit his throat while his wife, lying next to him, never hears a sound."

"Speakin' of which," Santee said, "where is Mrs. Denton? I wouldn't mind helpin' myself to some of her tasty apple pie."

"Packed her off to Tucson, so she wouldn't be in danger."

Vasquez rested his elbows in front of him. "A wise decision, Senor Denton. This Taggart is ruthless."

"He's scum," Denton said. "I never thought I'd live to see the day when a white man would ride with a pack of miserable Apaches. When we catch him we should do to him what those mangy Injuns have been doing to our kind for years."

Vasquez pushed back his sombrero. "My employer wanted me to assure you he will do all in his power to help you. That is why he sent us." He paused. "Tell me. How many hands do you have?"

"Fifteen."

"That give us twenty-six guns, if they will all fight."

A rangy cowpoke leaning against the far wall stiffened. "What's that supposed to mean, mister? There ain't a one of us who wouldn't lay down his life for Harve and Priscilla. They're decent folks and have always treated us right."

"I meant no insult," Vasquez said tactfully. "The reputation of the Box D hands is well-known."

The rancher stalked to his chair. "What I want to know is how we're going to stop this so-called White Apache, and stop him for good. If Miles is right and I'm next on his list, it's our responsibility to make sure Taggart's rampage ends here."

"There are several ways to proceed, senor," Vasquez said. "We can try to figure out which way they will come and set up an ambush—"

"To hell with that notion," Santee scoffed. "In case you haven't noticed, Vasquez, Arizona is a huge territory. We couldn't cover all the ways here if we had the Fifth Cavalry to help out. Besides which, Apaches ain't partial to stickin' to trails."

"He's right," Denton said.

"I was about to point out the same thing," Vasquez said stiffly, peeved at being treated like a greenhorn by the gunman.

Santee gave a light laugh. "Who died and put you in charge? The boss picked me as I recollect."

"We're to work together," Vasquez reminded him.

"You're both wrong," Denton interjected. "This is my spread, my life we're talking about. I'm in charge of this here operation and if either of you don't like it, skedaddle back to Miles right this minute."

"No one is tryin' to steal your thunder, Harve," Santee said, although, in truth, it bothered him to have to take orders from someone he hadn't hired out to.

"Good." Denton removed his cigar again. "Now the way I see it, we have to set a foolproof trap for these red varmints. From what Miles heard, Taggart and his pet Injuns snuck into Jacoby's and Prost's homes and killed them right there. I figure we can use that to our advantage."

"How?" Santee asked.

The rancher elaborated. At the conclusion, he folded his arms and ventured, "What do you boys think?"

"You're an hombre after my own heart," Santee said, chuckling. "They won't be able to Indian up on us no matter how they try. Why, there won't be one of those polecats left alive."

"I like your idea too, senor," Vasquez said. And he really did. There was little risk to the men and scant chance of anything going awry. He could almost feel his bonus bulging in his pocket.

"The only question is how long we have to wait before they show up," Denton remarked. "I can't keep my hands on night duty for too long. The ranch work won't get done." His attention drifted to the rangy cowpoke. "Bart, I want a skeleton crew riding day herd until further notice."

"Yes, sir."

"And tomorrow I want you to take the buckboard into town and stock up on ammunition. While you're at it, fetch home a few more Winchesters."

Billy Santee gleefully smacked the table. "It'll be like shootin' paper targets in a shootin' gallery! Too bad I can't add notches for no-account redskins."

Many miles away Clay Taggart was busy gathering wood for the bonfire to be built for the war dance, when Delgadito appeared.

"We must talk, White Apache."

"About the way I acted up today?"

"About the raid."

"What's there to palaver about? Who leads? Hell, if you want to, go right ahead. I never feel comfortable being head man anyway."

Delgadito had another subject in mind but the mention of leadership struck a profound chord. "This Apache thinks you joke with him. Most men would be happy having others do as they say."

"Maybe so," Clay said, while picking up a suitable broken branch. "But every herd has a few contrary steers who like to go their own way." Which was true to a point, but only partly applied to Clay. Deep down he would have to confess that he did like having five fearless warriors at his beck and call. It was akin to having the power of life and death over everyone in Arizona since, at a word from the him, the Apaches would attack anyone he chose. But he owed too much to Delgadito to hog the top spot if Delgadito wanted it.

"Why you not feel comfortable?" the warrior wanted to learn.

"Because it's like having a tenderfoot lead a pack of salty dogs on a roundup."

"I do not understand."

Stopping, Clay said, "Compared to you, I know next to nothing about living off the land. You can hunt better than I can, fish better, track better. You know which plants are good to eat, which aren't. When you have to you can move as quietly as a ghost. And your senses are a heck of a lot sharper than mine. Add to all that the fact you know more ways to kill a person than I can even think of, you can see why having me lead is a lot like having the cart lead the horse."

"You are too hard on yourself," Delgadito said, picking his words with care. "*Lickoyee-shis-inday* is much better than he thinks."

"I appreciate the compliment but it just ain't so," Clay disputed him. "If you're partial to leading, be my guest."

"No," Delgadito said. "The others picked you. They like you. They say you do good job."

Cuchillo Negro's statement came back to Clay. "Are you sure they didn't pick me because you told them to?"

"My words would fall on deaf ears," Delgadito lied with a straight face. "They no longer do as I say, not since the massacre. They not trust me anymore. Say my judgment bad."

"I can set them right if you want," Clay proposed. "You'll do to ride the river with in any man's book."

"Riding the river is good?"

"Very good."

80

Warrior Born

Although Delgadito was at a loss to explain the connection, he accepted Taggart's word and went on to the matter that had brought him over. "Do you remember our first raid together?"

"How could I forget? Jacoby was the first bastard to pay for lynching me."

"But you changed your mind about killing him. You were going to let him live after all we had gone through to get you into his—" Delgadito stopped, about to say lodge. "Into his house."

"I wasn't thinking straight," Clay excused his conduct. "Jacoby and Prost were the only two members of the posse I knew halfway well. We used to drink together, play cards on occasion. Rubbing them out wasn't easy."

"And this time? This Denton? You change your mind about him, too?"

"I see what you're getting at," Clay said. "You're worried I'm a mite paperbacked, that I don't have the backbone to do what has to be done." He shook his head. "Well, don't you fret none, pard. This time will be different. Harve Denton and I never did see eye to eye. He's a pushy cuss, likes to boss folks around. And I've never been one to take a shove without shoving back."

"So you kill this one no problem?"

"You bet your life I will. I could understand Jacoby and Prost turning on me because they were plumb scared of Gillett. But Denton isn't scared of no man. He didn't have to help string me up if he didn't want to."

The fire in the white-eye's tone was unmistakable. Delgadito grunted. "This is good to hear. When a man has enemies, he should kill them and be done with it." Looking down, he spotted a solitary beetle scuttling across the ground. Grinning, he planted

81

his foot on top of the insect and heard the distinct crunch. "Like so."

That night the Apaches stripped to their breechcloths and painted their bodies, each according to his personal taste. Then they gathered at the fire for their war dance, a ritual they went through prior to every raid, a dance designed to bring them good medicine while on the warpath and to insure that each and every one of them returned safely.

Clay Taggart had witnessed one of these dances before. He'd marveled at their lithe, flowing movements, and felt his blood pulse to the beat of their drum and the rasp of their rattles. He had felt strongly tempted to join them but had held back for fear of violating a tribal taboo.

This night was different. As the Apaches formed a circle around the fire, they were joined by a white man dressed as they were, his body painted with long white stripes that lent him an eerie aspect in the flickering firelight. No one objected. No one chided him for overstepping the bounds of custom. They accepted him as one of their own.

Overhead a full moon beamed down on the barbaric scene. The fire was allowed to blaze high because it was a special occasion and they were safe in their sanctuary. Amarillo beat his drum skillfully, the tempo hard, driving, intoxicating. Ponce and Fiero shook rattles in perfect rhythm.

Their agile bodies glistening, their muscular legs stomping in regular cadence, the warriors wound in a precise pattern. As a ritual, the dance had to be done just so, and each man knew his part. They spun and whooped and chanted, building to a frenzy, showing by their actions how they would slay the many foes they would face.

And foremost among them, whooping the loudest

and leaping the highest, dancing the hardest of them all, was *Lickoyee-shis-inday,* the White Apache. He did not feel awkward or out of place because he was a white man. He did not feel silly taking part in a custom his people had branded primitive. On the contrary, White Apache reveled in the celebration. He thrilled to the movements, embracing the dance heart and soul.

To all intents and appearance, there were not five Apaches and one white man taking part that night. There were six Apaches.

Chapter Seven

Apaches usually conducted their raids on foot. To greenhorns the idea seemed ridiculous until they learned that full-grown warriors could cover seventy-five miles in a single day and do it faster than horses.

Clay Taggart didn't share the Apache preference for foot travel. The months he had spent in their company had hardened his body to the point where he was in superb physical shape, the best condition of his whole life. Yet he still found keeping up with Delgadito and company to be trying and tiring.

So, on this third raid in the vicinity of Tucson, Clay decided to take mounts. Fiero and Ponce grumbled but had to go along with the idea since they wanted Clay to lead.

Astride a fine zebra dun, the White Apache led his small band from their remote retreat. They rode out of the depths of the Chiricahua Mountains, northward through Apache Pass, then westward to the Dragoons, stopping at Dragoon Springs a whole night to refresh their horses and themselves. It was twenty-eight miles from the springs to the San Pedro River, which they reached before noon of the next day.

Clay would have liked to lay low in the dense manzanita until nightfall and then go on, but they were now in country where they might encounter whites at any time and his Apache companions had an aversion to fighting at night—an aversion he had been working hard to make them overcome.

Consequently, after a short stop to water their mounts, the band was on the go again, sticking to rough country where cover was readily available. Once they saw a column of smoke in the distance which they wisely skirted. Another time they saw several wagons lumbering southward toward a common crossing at the San Pedro. Fiero was all for killing the muleskinners and taking whatever plunder the wagons contained, but Clay reminded him they had business elsewhere, and if they attacked now and somehow the alarm should spread, the man they had come to kill would be forewarned.

As it turned out, Clay had decided wisely because not ten miles farther on they spied a cavalry patrol and immediately sought shelter in the heavy brush. Amarillo went alone to spy on the patrol and was to report back right away if the troopers were coming in their direction. When he finally showed, it was to relay the news that the patrol had ridden southward and would not cut their trail.

From here on out Clay proceeded cautiously. He had been in the area before but only a few times; his own ranch was much farther north. He knew the Box D lay in a spacious, verdant valley about thirty-five miles from Tucson. If he could locate Webber Creek, he could follow it into the valley, but he was unable to recollect the exact location of the creek.

A chaparral-covered rise gave Clay a vantage point from which to survey the countryside. Pinpointing the creek was child's play; any year-round ribbon of water in that arid land was bordered by trees nearly its entire length. The creek turned out to be southwest of their position.

Once there, Clay entered a small forest of mesquite and secreted their horses in a suitable clearing. They double-checked their rifles and pistols, tightened their moccasins and adjusted their headbands, and were off, gliding like antelope toward the valley.

Clay was in the forefront, doing his best to move quietly. Every so often a twig would crackle under his feet, and he would flinch in embarrassment knowing full well the Apaches never made such blunders. But then, they had a lifetime of experience. He was just learning.

Presently, Clay detected the rattle of wagon wheels and motioned for his band to seek cover. Snaking toward the noise on his hands and knees, he parted high weeds and discovered a rutted dirt road that wound through the mesquite. A buckboard occupied by two cowboys was headed into the valley. They were joking and laughing. Green canvas had been spread over the bed, no doubt to screen their cargo from the blistering sun.

On an impulse, Clay moved closer to the road and shadowed the punchers. They were as rock headed as he had once been and were paying no attention to the vegetation around them.

"—that Carlotta is some woman, Bart," the

smallest of the hands was saying. "The next time we go into Tucson, I figure on askin' for her hand in marriage."

"Has the sun baked your brain?" the rangy Bart responded. "You can do better than her, Tom."

"What the hell is that supposed to mean?"

Bart gave the reins a halfhearted flick. "I don't rightly know how to put this other than to come right out and say what we both know to be true." His pause was perfect. "Carlotta is a whore."

"If'n we wasn't pards I'd shoot you."

"What are you so techy about?" Bart demanded.

"Carlotta ain't no whore."

"I don't know what else you'd call it when a woman has taken money from half the male population hankering for the privilege of lifting her petticoats."

"So what? People change."

"Not her."

"What makes you so all-fired sure, Mister-Knows-Everything?"

The wagon covered a dozen feet before Bart answered. "Don't it strike you as peculiar that a gal as enthusiastic about her work as Carlotta would be ready to call it quits?"

"Enthusiastic how?"

"Don't you recollect that time she took on five punchers at once just to prove she could?"

"One time."

"And the night she bet fifty bucks she could handle more men in one hour than any other gal there?"

"She was drunk."

"And the week that convention came to town and she wasn't off her back once?"

"Shut up, Bart. You're depressin' me."

"Sorry pard. You'll feel better when your hangover goes away."

"Hope so. And Bart?"

"What?"

"The next time I come up with one of these harebrained notions, you have my permission to wallop me over the head as hard as you can with a singletree."

"Will do. But I reckon the boss won't like having his singletree bent."

Clay stopped shadowing them, convinced he was wasting his time. They were a harmless pair of cowhands, not worth bothering, and he hoped they wouldn't get in his way when he went after Harve Denton.

The Apaches flanked him. Clay motioned and trotted deeper into the valley, angling to the north, away from the road. Rolling grassland soon replaced the mesquite. Snaking into the grass, he avoided clusters of cattle as he made his way toward structures a mile off. Occasionally, a cow would lift its head from grazing to watch them go by. He only saw one bull which he diligently bypassed.

Stealth required they move slowly. Brilliant hues of pink and yellow blazed in the western sky, heralding sunset, when at last they came to a stand of oaks and crept to the far side for a better view of the buildings.

The Bar D was typical of Arizona ranches. A house, stable, and bunkhouse formed a triangle separated by a corral and a neatly tilled lawn boasting two long flower beds that spoke of the hands of Mrs. Denton. On seeing them, Clay jerked as if stung, then glanced at the Apaches.

"You hurt?" Delgadito asked.

"I just thought of something," Clay said. "I don't want her harmed."

"Who?"

"Harve Denton's wife. She had no hand in her husband's deed, so she's to be spared."

Delgadito stared in dismay at the white-eye. Despite their talk days ago, Clay Taggart was still as weak as ever. The white-eye had the head for the life of an Apache, but not the heart. Women and children were fair game in war. They were enemies just as much as their men. Had Taggart so soon forgotten the massacre at the hollow, where the scalp hunters slew Apache women and children with sadistic glee? "She is your enemy," he tried to explain. "If we see her, we should treat her the same as her husband."

"No," Clay said emphatically. "Unless she's fixing to blow your head off, you're not to touch a hair on her head." Switching to the Apache tongue, he relayed the same instructions. Fiero looked at him as if he had gone mad. Ponce puffed his cheeks and exhaled loudly like an irate chipmunk. And Cuchillo Negro cocked his head, studying Clay as he might a rare curiosity.

"Any young ones here?" Delgadito asked, certain White Apache would not want them harmed, either.

"Not to my knowledge," Clay said. "But if we find any, the same rule applies."

"Rules. Always rules," Delgadito said with marked disgust. "Why are you whites so fond of being told what to do? Why can you not *live*."

Whatever reply Clay was going to make was forestalled when three riders appeared in the adjoining pasture. Flattening, the Apaches watched the cowpokes, their weapons ready for instant use.

Clay abruptly realized these were the first punchers he had seen. It struck him as a bit odd. The Bar D was a big spread and by rights there should be ten to twenty hands abroad. He figured most were off rounding up cattle farther down the valley or else busy with some other chore, and he dismissed the discrepancy as unimportant.

Another decision had to be made. With nightfall so close, Clay either had to convince the Apaches to ignore their taboo on night raids or go on alone. He'd finish off Denton, then return to assist in stealing as much of the horse stock as they could manage. Twice before he'd been able to convince the warriors to raid after dark, and he probably could have done so now, but all the talk about Mrs. Denton and children had made him leery of a mishap. It would be safer, he reasoned, to sneak into the house by himself. The Apaches could wait right where they were.

"One of us should go with you," Delgadito objected on being told.

"I will," Amarillo offered.

Clay was inclined to refuse but knew he could not without offending them. "All right. As soon as the sun sets we go in."

Half an hour later the three riders came back, making for the bunkhouse. There had been no activity anywhere in all that time, which Clay thought odd. Having owned a ranch himself, the daily routine was familiar. Toward evening the punchers converged from all parts of the spread to wash up for supper. The clang of the triangle would cause a mass rush to the table, and they would gorge themselves to bursting. Over at the house the rancher and his family would sit down to a more sedate meal, and afterward the husband

and wife would retire to the cool comfort of their rocking chairs on the front porch. But there was none of that here.

In the back of Clay's mind, something stirred. A vague feeling of unease that he tried to shake but couldn't. There had to be a logical explanation, he assured himself. Perhaps the Dentons were gone, spending time in Tucson. If so, they undoubtedly took most of the hands with them as a treat since to a cowpoke a night spent in town was a night spent in heaven.

Gradually, the light faded. Twilight claimed the landscape, then a veil of darkness. Lights came on in the bunkhouse. Shortly thereafter, a single lantern flared to life in the ranch house.

So there was someone home, Clay mused. He would wait until all the lights went out, allow another half an hour to insure they were all sound asleep, and make his move.

Toward midnight the time arrived. Clay signalled to Amarillo and crept from concealment, stalking through the grass on a beeline for the stable.

No moon brightened the pasture. Clay paused often to look, listen, and test the air with his nose as the Apaches regularly did, even though his sense of smell was much worse than theirs. He counted on Amarillo warning him of any dangers that he failed to discern.

Close to twenty horses packed into the corral, far more than Clay expected. Many were dozing. Only a few bothered to lift their heads as Clay and the warrior crawled along the base of the corral to the stable doors, which were closed. Rising on tiptoe, Clay threw the huge bar and cracked the near door a few inches, so he could peak inside. The gloom did not prevent him from seeing that every stall contained a horse.

Clay was puzzled. The hands would not have left their individual mounts behind if they'd gone into Tucson. Fewer horses should be present, not more than usual. Closing the door, he crouch-walked to Amarillo and dropped to one knee. "You stay," he whispered in Apache. "I will go in alone."

"Is that wise?" the cautious warrior asked. "You might need help if this white-eye fights back as did the other two."

Common sense confirmed Amarillo had cause for concern, but Clay hesitated. He wanted to prove to Delgadito, and perhaps to himself as well, that he could tend to Harve Denton without weakening as he had with the others. "I can take care of this on my own."

"As you wish, *Lickoyee-shis-inday*."

A last glance at the corral and Clay was off, sprinting to an oak tree and from there to a flower bed. The fragrant scent of roses caught his attention. He surveyed the white-frame house, about to dash to the closest corner, when an image registered in his brain, the fleeting image of a shadowy shape at one of the windows. It was gone so quickly that he wondered if his eyes had been playing tricks on him.

Clay went prone and waited to see if the figure would reappear. He assumed that someone had gotten up for a drink of water and just happened to look out. Since clusters of tall flowers screened him, he doubted he had been spotted.

A minute went by without a hint of movement inside. Reassured, Clay snaked to a tree, careful to keep the wide trunk between him and the window. A low branch afforded the means of ascending to a fork shrouded by foliage. Here he sat, listening intently, attuning his mind to the night.

Of all the Apache traits that Clay admired, patience was high on his list. They were masters at the art of ambush and could lie totally still for an incredibly long time in order to surprise game or an enemy. Patience, Delgadito had instructed him, was the key to survival in the wild. A person who had it would never starve, never be taken by surprise.

Clay exercised his patience now. Content to sit until certain the coast was clear, he rested his rifle across his legs and leaned back, his legs dangling. He happened to notice that a stout higher limb projected awfully close to a second floor window, which gave him an idea. After a suitable interval had passed, he climbed to the limb, slung the rifle over his back, and moved hand over hand toward the house.

The limb sagged and creaked and, for a moment, Clay feared it might break. Keeping his body still, he let the swaying subside, then inched outward. In the dark, he had misjudged the distance; the window was four feet from the branch, almost beyond reach. He had to hang by one arm, move his body in pendulum fashion, and lunge to grab hold of the sill. For a precarious few seconds gravity threatened to tear him loose. Whipping his hips, he practically hurled himself at the window and caught hold with his other hand.

Body flush with the side of the house, Clay strained to lift his right leg high enough to hook his heel on the edge of the eaves. Getting the other foot up there took the same amount of effort. A hard shove and a mad scramble put him belly down next to the window. From here he could pull on the lowest sash bar to find out if it was latched.

Soundlessly the window slid up. Clay put an ear to the opening and listened again. When confident silence reigned within, and he had not been heard, he twisted, looped a leg around the side jamb, and slid into Harve Denton's house. No sooner did his feet touch the floor than he bounded to the right and unlimbered the Winchester.

The room was small and smelled faintly of jasmine. Clay found shelves on either side crammed with quilts, blankets, and assorted knickknacks. In the center sat a sewing machine, beside it a chair and a bench bearing folded clothes and other articles.

Mrs. Denton's sewing room, Clay figured, tiptoeing to the door, which hung open a crack. He pressed an eye to the opening and instantly recoiled. Two men were walking down a hall toward him! He hugged a corner, his finger on the trigger of the Winchester.

"—the damn fuss was for nothing!" a gruff voice said quietly. "There was no one out there!"

"Fritz probably saw a cat and thought it was an Apache," said the other one.

"Fritz is an idiot. One more false alarm from him and the boss is liable to bust his fool head wide open."

Clay saw the door swing suddenly inward. Both men entered, the taller grumbling about having had to run downstairs for no good reason. The second man saw the open window and stopped.

"What the hell! Didn't we leave that closed?"

"We sure as blazes did. Then how—"

Their backs were to Clay. He took a long stride and brought the stock of his rifle smashing down on the taller man's temple, flooring the cowboy on the spot.

The second puncher spun, hand stabbing for a six-shooter riding high on his right hip. His fingers were curling on the smooth butt when the stock caught him full on the jaw, crunching his teeth together. He staggered into the sewing machine, toppling it to the floor with a tremendous crash.

Downstairs, shouts arose. From somewhere on the same floor a man bellowed, "What the hell was that noise? An Injun could hear it a mile off!"

A short dash brought Clay to the window. He did not need to be a genius to deduce that Harve Denton had set a trap for him, and that if he didn't light a shuck for the chaparral he'd likely take a lead plum or be the guest of honor at a necktie social.

Lifting a leg out, Clay slid over the sill, and was about to leap to the limb, when the heavy tread of boot heels announced the arrival of a third puncher who stood framed in the doorway gawking at the two men on the floor. That moment of shock cost the man dearly, for Clay already had his rifle leveled when the puncher went to fill his hand.

The first blast of the Winchester drove the puncher into the hall. The second blast slammed him against the wall. Arms limp, the man slid to the floor, leaving a dark stain in his wake.

Yells, curses, and the drum of boots on the stairs goaded Clay into slinging the rifle over his shoulder, bunching his leg muscles, and jumping. He caught hold of the limb, felt it bend steeply under his weight, then heard a loud crack. A sickening sensation in his gut, he fell, shoving the limb from him and vainly flailing his arms to right himself, so he would land on his feet. Instead he smacked down on his side, the jolt jarring every bone and causing pinwheels of light to dance before his eyes.

Too stunned to move, Clay braced for the searing

impact of multiple slugs. The thunderous din of
gunfire erupted, and he involuntarily flinched, only
to realize seconds later the shots were not being
directed at him. Sluggishly, he rose on an elbow
and blinked, clearing his vision.

Clay was at the base of the wall, within yards
of a window through which several rifle barrels
protruded. Lead and smoke spat from each, as well
as from the guns at other ground floor windows,
pouring a swarm of lethal hail into the darkness.

Thinking the Apaches had come to his aid, Clay
scanned the yard. There was no return fire from
anywhere, leading him to suspect that the men in the
house had panicked on hearing the shots upstairs
and started firing at shadows. Cowboys were notorious for having an abiding fear of Apaches.

Clay had to get out of there before the punchers
rushed outside, but he dared not try to cross the
yard with bullets flying so thick and fast. Turning, he crawled rapidly toward the corner on the
assumption Denton's men were concentrating their
fire on one side of the house alone.

A chorus of rifle fire showed otherwise. Clay
stared at the rifles cracking with regular cadence
and thought of the horses filling the corral and the
stable. Now he knew why there had been so many.

At the very corner there were no windows. Clay
slowly stood, his back scraping the house. In front
of him were trees, then a low hedge. At a lull in
the shooting he bolted, weaving as he ran, and
he had passed the first tree and was nearly to
the second when someone bellowed, "There's one
of the bastards!" and a ragged volley blistered the
very air around him.

Clay dived and rolled to the right. Something
stung his left arm. Bees buzzed overhead. He

gained the shelter of the tree and listened to wood splintering as slug after slug tore into the trunk. When the firing slackened, he raced to the next oak. The hedge was now twenty feet away. Adjacent to it was a pasture and, in the pasture, several stacks of hay. As Clay looked, those stacks moved, breaking apart to disgorge men armed with rifles.

Men who came straight in his direction.

Chapter Eight

The trap had been cunningly laid. A dozen or more men had waited in the house, covering all four sides, ready to converge at any point once an alarm was sounded. Freshly mown hay had been stacked at various points to conceal additional riflemen. And for all Clay knew, more men might have been lurking in the stable. He cursed under his breath for being the biggest jackass in all of Arizona as he ducked low and darted to the hedge.

"Spread out!" commanded someone in the pasture. "But not too far. We can't let them get past us."

Clay cocked his rifle and peered through the thin branches and leaves at the aproaching figures. Denton's men believed an entire Apache band was pinned down. Thank God he'd left Delgadito and the rest in the stand, otherwise there would have been.

Four men now stood about eight yards out, spaced ten feet apart. They concentrated on the yard, scouring the flower beds and trees and hedges.

Easing the barrel of his Winchester into the hedge, Clay pointed it at one of the cowhands. Fixing a precise bead was impossible, but at that range he did not have to be precise. He simply centered the barrel on the man's torso and fired.

The puncher collapsed. His pards instantly cut loose, firing wildly since they had no idea where the shot had come from. Clay swiveled, putting a slug into a second man, who tottered rearward and sprawled onto his back. The last two did not have the gumption for a stand-up fight, not exposed as they were. They retreated toward the hay mounds, levering off rounds as fast as they could work their Winchesters.

Clay pulled his rifle out of the hedge and sprinted to his left, keeping low, his elbow scraping against the tips of branches. Some of the men inside were still shooting, but they were unable to distinguish his form against the dark background of the hedge.

Somewhere a door slammed. Clay realized the gunmen were venturing outdoors. He had to reach the corral before they spotted him. Then, somehow, he and Amarillo must make it to the stand of trees where the others waited. Getting there wouldn't be easy, but it was their only hope.

A flurry of gunfire broke out near the stable. Clay rose high enough to see the corral and was aghast at spotting Amarillo out in the open. The warrior was fleeing across the pasture to escape a half-dozen men who had emerged from the stable. They had seen him, and even as Clay looked on, they opened fire, stitching the dirt around him with miniature geysers.

Amarillo had almost gained the high grass. He flung himself forward, his arms outstretched, and was midair when bullets cored his hurtling body from back to front. Jerking from each shot, Amarillo arched his spine but did not cry out. He crumpled, landing in a disjointed heap, his legs twitching.

The killers cheered in delight and raced toward him.

Cold rage gripped Clay's soul. He had never been as close to Amarillo as he was to Delgadito, but still he had regarded the Indian more as a friend than an enemy. Vaulting the hedge, he pounded after the punchers responsible, heedless of shots directed at him from different quarters.

Amarillo had risen on one elbow in an attempt to crawl into the grass. He saw the white-eyes bearing down on him and sought his rifle but it was out of reach. Drawing a knife, he twisted, striking at the first cowboy who reached him. The blade buried in the man's leg, eliciting a screech.

Three rifles roared in unison. Amarillo wore a snarl of defiance as the slugs ripped into his head, a snarl that stayed locked on his features as he sagged lifelessly to the ground.

Clay was beside himself with fury. He slung the Winchester on the fly and filled his hands with his twin Colts in a cross draw. One of the cowpokes heard him, glanced around, and tried to bring a rifle into play. Clay shot the man in the eye.

Two more spun at the gunshots, their Winchesters slanted downward instead of level, as they should be. Clay stroked each trigger once, bucking the pair out in gunsmoke. Only three were left, the two responsible for killing Amarillo and the man with the knife wound. All three were gathered around the Apache's supine corpse. They saw Clay coming.

Two snapped their rifles high; the wounded man released his and made a stab for a pistol, his speed uncanny. Had Clay not had his six-shooters out, the man would easily have gunned him down first.

But as it was, Clay shot before any of them, blasting his pistols simultaneously, three times apiece. The trio were hit in their chests, each reacting differently. One toppled, one staggered a few feet before falling, and the third, the one who was wounded, roared like a berserk grizzly as his knees buckled and he caved to the earth.

A loud beating in Clay's ears was matched by the explosive beat of gunshots coming from the yard. He lingered for a fleeting look at Amarillo, then barreled into the grass and fled across the pasture in bounds worthy of an antelope. Ranch hands were in pursuit, but so far behind, he was confident he would escape, until the nicker of horses let him know that some of Denton's men were mounting at the corral.

Outrunning a galloping horse was impossible, even for a full-blooded Apache. But Clay ran as never before. When a man's life is on the verge of being blown out, he does what he must to stay alive, even if he knows his efforts will be in vain.

The stand of trees materialized. Clay gauged the distance, then checked behind him to gauge the gap between himself and the four riders. They would be on him well shy of the oaks. Lashing their horses, guns unlimbered, they swept across the field intent on doing to Clay what he had done to their friends.

Thirty feet from the stand Clay halted, turned, and knelt to make a smaller target of himself. He extended both pistols at the lead rider, a burly cowboy with a revolver in hand.

The night cracked with gunfire, but not Clay's

own. From the trees came rifle fire that peppered the onrushing horsemen and their mounts. In a whirl of legs and tails attended by strident neighs, the horses went down, spilling the cowboys from their saddles.

Clay did not wait to see if any were alive. He bolted into the stand and halted beside the four Apaches, fingers flying as he reloaded his six-guns.

"Amarillo?" Delgadito asked.

"*Yah-ik-tee,*" Clay answered, which was Apache for "he is not present." Apaches never mentioned that a friend was dead, a taboo stemming from their belief in ghosts. Instead, they used figures of speech to say the same thing.

"He will be missed," Delgadito responded.

And that was all any of them had to say. They did not treat death as whites did. There would be no public mourning, no remembrance of any kind.

"The white-eyes come in force," Fiero commented eagerly, gazing at the field. "Let us stand and fight! We can slay many before they kill us."

"Why waste our lives when we can live to kill again?" Cuchillo Negro said. Always the most practical, he began to hasten off.

"We must go," Delgadito agreed.

Clay was content to jog in their wake. The forest of mesquite was a long way off, and he knew they would be lucky to reach it without losing anyone else. He tried not to dwell on Amarillo's fate; deep down he felt responsible since the Apaches would not have been there if they weren't helping him settle a blood debt.

Most troubling of all, the Apaches might feel the same way. Clay worried they would hold the death against him and refuse to help him any more. To lose a warrior on a raid was regarded as a terrible calamity, and the one leading the band on such an occasion lost valuable standing in the tribe. Since he'd been the leader, he was accountable.

Strung out in single file, the warriors ate up the distance at a steady pace. Clay twisted repeatedly, seeking sign of Denton's hands. Lanterns flashed at the ranch house and stable, and the breeze brought the faint noise of a great deal of commotion, but as yet, not one cowboy showed himself past the trees.

Half a mile had been covered when Clay saw dozens of lights bobbing back and forth, spreading outward from the buildings. The punchers sped toward the stand, evidently assuming the Apaches were still hidden there. A few fired rashly into the oaks, wasting ammunition.

The warriors broke into an out-and-out sprint, their goal the mesquite, now visible as a murky band far off. Clay brought up the rear, doing the best he could but still unable to match their speed. Gradually, he fell behind, a few yards initially, then more than a dozen. None of the warriors noticed, and he was not about to advertise his weakness by giving a yell. He would forge on and catch them eventually.

Suddenly the thunder of hoofs sounded to Clay's right. Slowing, he brought the Winchester up, seeking the silhouette of a rider. But where there should be a lean black figure atop a horse he saw a bulky black outline that bore down on him with all the subtlety of a steam engine.

Clay didn't need moonlight or a lantern to identify the creature. It was a bull! A thousand pounds of solid muscle housing a temperament charitably described as irritable. And this specimen was clearly on the rampage, angered by the intruders in its domain.

Clay went to take a hasty bead, but the gigantic brute was on him in a twinkling, moving with astounding speed for something so huge and heavy. Outswept curved horns glinted dully in the starlight as the bull's massive head lowered for the killing sweep.

Taking a step to the left, Clay flung himself prone and heard the bull go rumbling by, so close it seemed as if the ground itself shook. He scrambled erect and saw the bull wheel. Turning, he fled for his life, an eye on the monster barreling toward him.

The bull was only feet away when Clay repeated his tactic of throwing himself aside. This time he was a bit slower than before and he paid dearly for his sloth. A horn caught him on the side, gouging a shallow groove along his ribs, the impact throwing him head over heels.

Clay came down on his back, his breath whooshing from his lungs. Disoriented, he lay still, hoping against hope the bull wouldn't see him or pick up his scent. Near at hand, the grass rustled, and there were heavy thuds.

The bull was hunting for him.

Rolling onto his stomach, Clay craned his neck. The behemoth plowed along off to the right, grunting and snorting in a bovine tantrum. Clay crouched, pivoted, and skulked in the opposite direction. He had gone a considerable way, and was feeling fairly confident he had eluded the bull, when hooves drummed—directly ahead..

Clay froze, amazed the bull had been able to get in front of him without his knowing it. He reared high enough to see, and what he saw sent a ripple of consternation down his spine. In his rush to get away from the bull he had blundered badly. When he should have been heading to the southeast to reach the mesquite, all the time he had been heading to the northwest, toward the ranch buildings. And closing in on him were a long line of punchers, every other man bearing a lantern held high to illuminate the field.

Flattening, Clay scrambled into the thickest patch of grass in his vicinity. The bull was all but forgotten now, in the face of this greater danger. Because one of the lantern bearers was heading uncomfortably close to his position, Clay crept to the left in order to get beyond the circle of pale light.

"Anything yet?" called a stern voice well behind the riders.

"Nothin', boss," answered a puncher Clay recognized as the tall man named Bart, from the buckboard.

"Keep searching. They couldn't have gotten away this fast."

Farther down the line someone piped up with, "They're Apaches, ain't they?"

Clay came to a point midway between Bart and another hand. Bart held the lantern and slowly swung it from side to side, a cocked six-shooter resting on his thigh. Like the rest, he would shoot at anything that moved.

Lying on his stomach, rifle on his chest, Clay commenced bending grasses over his body. His movements were unhurried, silent. His eyes flicked from Bart to the other hand, who wore a wide-brimmed black hat, packed a pair of ivory-handled pistols, and favored big silver spurs. Something about him set Clay's nerves to jangling, causing him to remember that horrible day when the posse had strung him up. In particular, he recalled a certain smirking gunman who had roped him, then dragged him for miles across the burning desert. He could still feel the stinging bite of every cactus needle and the razor slice of every sliver of rock.

That rider was Billy Santee!

Clay impulsively gripped the Winchester and would have shot the young gunny right that moment if the act would not have been sure-fire suicide. To savor sweet revenge he must stay alive. He eased his thumb off the hammer, frowning.

Santee's presence added a new element to the situation. Santee worked for Gillett, and it was a safe bet that the gun shark would not be there without Gillett's knowledge and approval. That meant Gillett was the one who had guessed where Clay would strike next and had acted accordingly. It also revealed where the extra men came from. They must be some of Gillett's hired guns, not run-of-the-mill cowhands.

Fresh hatred rose in Clay's gorge, releasing bitter bile in his mouth. To be outfoxed was one thing, to be outfoxed by the son of a bitch he had sworn to kill was like rubbing salt on an old wound. No matter how Clay schemed, Gillett was always one step ahead of him.

Santee and Bart were almost abreast of Clay, only thirty feet separating them. Clay could see the lantern light glinting off their hoglegs and the oval silver pieces adorning the gunman's gunbelts as clear as day. He could see their eyes darting right and left, a tenseness in their coiled frames.

Without warning, the night was rent by a crashing sound. Billy Santee moved like liquid lightning, clearing leather with ambidextrous precision and firing four shots so swiftly it was impossible to tell one from the other. Nervous trigger fingers all along the line twitched in accord, booming a fusillade that ended in a piercing bawl.

"Stop firing, you yacks!" snapped a strapping man, who appeared at the center of the line. It was Harve Denton, himself, and he was livid. "That's old Scarface you just shot!"

Clay dared not turn his head to see for himself, but he didn't have to. It couldn't have happened to a nicer animal.

"How the hell was I supposed to know?" Santee was arguing. "All I saw was something comin' at us."

"One of my prize bulls!" Denton snarled. "Wait until Gillett hears about this!" Applying a quirt, he rode westward, missing Clay by mere feet. The gunmen and cowpokes closed in to see for themselves and were reminded of the task at hand by Denton's outraged order. "Back in line, damn it! The White Apache and his cutthroat friends are still out here somewhere, remember?"

The reminder brought guns up in a flash, the men looking every which way.

So far no one had spotted Clay. But he feared that might change as Billy Santee advanced. The gunman had the instincts of an animal.

Clay made a point to observe Santee out of the corner of one eye rather than stare right at him. The Apaches believed that a person could sense when someone was gazing at him long and hard, and accordingly, Delgadito had taught Clay to avoid doing so at close range.

Abruptly, Santee stiffened and peered at the surrounding ground. A gleaming Colt in each hand, he twisted from side to side, resembling a coiled spring about to explode into action.

Meanwhile, Bart also advanced, the light from his lantern streaming forward as he rode.

Clay squinted as the glow enveloped the thin

blanket of grass covering him. The flimsy covering was all that stood between him and certain death. The rest of Denton's small army were so close that if anyone spotted him, he'd be gunned down before he could run five feet.

The young gunman unexpectedly reined up ten feet away. As Clay had suspected, Santee had a gut feeling that something was not quite right. Santee couldn't isolate the reason, but he figured there must be an Apache nearby. Rising in the stirrups, he concentrated on thicker patches of grass where one of the crafty redskins might be hiding. He searched to his right, then swiveled to his left.

"Santee! You comin' or do we leave you behind?"

The line of riders was moving onward. Annoyed, Santee hesitated. He wanted to cover the area thoroughly, but he didn't care to be left there alone. Not that Apaches scared him. They simply didn't fight fair. "I'm comin'," he grumbled, telling himself his suspicion was all in his head.

Two yards away Clay Taggart let a tiny breath out through his nose. Immobile as a rock, he didn't twitch until the sounds of the horsemen had faded into the night. Then he rose, the stems rustling ever so slightly.

Now what do I do? Clay mused. His enemies were heading toward the mouth of the valley, the very direction he had to go to reach the mesquite. Trying to sneak past them was too risky a proposition. His gaze idly roamed the ranch and settled on the buildings.

Odds were that Denton had most, or all, of the men taking part in the hunt. The ranch itself might be temporarily deserted, and there was bound to be a spare horse or two left behind.

Smiling at his cleverness, Clay dogtrotted toward

the rear of the stable, which lay plunged in gloom. Lanterns shone at various points; the front of the house, the bunkhouse, and on a post at the corral. No figures were moving about, but Clay had learned long ago never to take anything for granted.

A low snort drew Clay up short. From the south hustled a large black form. Clay, thinking it was another bull, took aim. Just when he was ready to fire, the animal veered off, and Clay was able to see that it was a cow, with a calf tagging along.

Steadying his nerves, Clay silently stalked close enough to the stable to hear voices inside. On elbows and knees, he snaked to the corner. The voices were louder, but he still couldn't make out the words being spoken. Crawling to the closed rear door, he pressed an ear to the gap at the bottom and heard a low curse.

"All these good men done in by those damn butchers!" someone declared.

"If I had my way," said another, "I'd wipe the red vermin out. I'd exterminate every last man, woman, and child."

A third person made a comment, a man with a decided Spanish accent. "They do what they have to. We do what we have to."

"What the hell does that mean, Vasquez?" demanded the first man.

Clay's interest perked. *Vasquez.* Another name from the lynch party. Everyone in Tucson had heard of Surgio Vasquez, the finest tracker on either side of the border, the man who Miles Gillet had hired to track Clay down for the posse.

The Mexican was answering. "Apaches are born fighters, Senor Roarke. They live to make war. And so long as they live, there will be those who refuse to accept reservation life, who will demand our blood for the land taken from them—"

"All the more reason to rub them all out," Roarke spat. "Keeping them lousy redskins on a reservation is a waste of tax dollars."

"And the government wastes enough as it is," said the third man.

There was a shuffling sound, and when the three men next spoke, they were much nearer.

"What I don't savvy," said Roarke, "is this White Apache. How could any white man ride with Apaches? He must be plumb loco."

"It's more than being crazy as a loon," remarked the other. "He's just rotten to the core. Didn't you hear about him trying to rape Mrs. Gillett? And she's the kindest, sweetest, most decent woman in the territory. Why, I hear she wouldn't harm a fly if it was crawling on her nose."

"That Taggart will get his pretty soon," Roarke predicted. "There isn't a white man in this neck of the country that wouldn't shoot him on sight. And not just for the reward money, either."

"A thousand dollars is a lot."

"After this it'll be five thousand," Roarke said.

Surgio Vasquez spoke with a keen edge. "It will, won't it?"

"Hell, yes," Roarke responded. "The more killing and stealing Taggart does, the higher the reward will go. If he lasts a year I reckon his head will be worth a fortune."

"A fortune," Vasquez repeated.

Clay still listened but his mind was in a whirl. A thousand dollars bounty on his head! That was more than had been offered for Ben Johnson, the most notorious man in the territory. Every money-hungry gunman around would be after his skin. They'd hound him mercilessly, maybe even go into the Dragoons after him, in violation of the treaty. Suddenly a few words caught his ear.

"—tend to Nature's call. Be back in three shakes of a lamb's tail."

Footsteps scuffed the dirt floor. Clay looked up at the latch and heard a metallic rasp as a hand gripped the other end and pushed.

Chapter Nine

Clay Taggart's mind and body were so superbly coordinated that the instant he heard the latch move his finely honed muscles exploded into motion. Shoulders rippling, he shoved off the ground, putting his back to the wall, as the door swung outward and came within an inch of slamming into his face.

Clay fingered the trigger of his Winchester and listened to the cowboy walk off into the field. A shadow suddenly filled the crack between the door and the frame, and there was the flare of a match being struck. Clay smelled acrid smoke.

"So how come you ain't out there with Harve and them, Vasquez?" Roarke inquired from inside. "You being such a good tracker and all."

Vásquez puffed on his cigarrillo. "Only a man with a death wish dares to overtake Apaches when they are in their element." He took another drag. "Besides, tracking in the dark is slow business. At first light I will take the trail, and by noon, I will have brought them to bay."

"Too bad the reward goes to the hombre who makes wolf meat of the White Apache, and not to you for doing all the tracking."

"I did not think of that," Vasquez said.

"Course, knowing Harve as I do," Roarke said, "he'll probably hog the bounty for himself. He's a greedy man. But don't ever say I told you so or I'll flat-out lie. Denton ain't one to cross, not if you want to stay healthy."

Surgio Vasquez stared at the glowing end of his cigarrillo, pondering. He did not like the idea of someone else benefiting from the work he did, especially when not one of the gunmen or cowhands could get close enough to Taggart to draw a bead without his help. And if one of them brought Taggart down, Vasquez would be out both the government bounty and Gillett's promised bonus.

Then there was this matter of the government reward. Earning a thousand dollars was well and good but could not compare to earning five thousand. Or perhaps ten thousand. Vasquez smiled, anticipating all he could do with so much money.

"I hope Morgan gets back with the sawbones soon," Roarke mentioned. "Those poor bastards in the house are hurt real bad."

"At least they are alive," Vasquez said.

"How many Apaches you figure were out there? Ten? Twenty, maybe?"

"Two."

"Quit pulling my leg. There had to be more. Two couldn't have killed all these men and wounded all those others."

"The one who came into the house did most of the

killing. The one by the stable was more interested in saving his hide."

"Think it was him in the house? The White Apache?"

"If so, he is more Apache than white. He is truly worthy of his new name."

On that note their talk ended. The third man returned, Vasquez went in, and the man pulled the door closed behind them.

Clay quickly got out of there. Originally, he'd figured on sneaking into the stable to steal a horse since the corral was illuminated by lantern light, but now he hurried around the end of the building and crept toward the corral fence. The last twenty yards were covered on his stomach.

Two horses stood near the lantern, the only mounts left. From under the bottom rail Clay studied them, picking a sorrel as the better animal. Slinging the rifle, he started to slide into the corral when the stable door opened wider and out stepped Surgio Vasquez, still smoking.

The Mexican adjusted his sombrero, then walked toward the ranch house.

Clay waited to see if Roarke and the other man would emerge, but neither did. Applying both hands to the rail for leverage, he propelled himself past the fence. Both horses saw him and the black mare shied.

"Hush," Clay whispered. "No one is fixing to hurt you." Hearing English, he deduced, would calm them down since English was the language they were accustomed to. "I'm a friend."

The trouble was, while Clay sounded white, he looked and smelled like an Apache and the two horses accepted the evidence of their eyes over their ears. The black moved flush with the rails and nickered. The sorrel stayed where it was but stamped a front hoof.

"All I want is to ride you," Clay said simply for something to say. Edging forward, he glanced at the house, then froze.

Vasquez had stopped and turned around.

Miles away, Delgadito followed Cuchillo Negro deeper into the night. His features were calm to the point of being impassive, yet inwardly, he was in turmoil. Amarillo, his friend, had died. Amarillo, one of the few who had been loyal to him from the beginning, who had sided with him against Palacio and the weaklings who licked the boots of the white invaders.

Delgadito had few friends. The loss of any one of them was a grievous loss, especially now with his band slaughtered and his leadership in question. Soon word would reach the reservation Apaches and the young warriors would say among themselves, "Delgadito is bad medicine. Only a fool would ride with him."

The sole solace Delgadito could take was in the knowledge *Lickoyee-shis-inday* had led this raid, not him. The blame fell squarely on White Apache's shoulders. Now, the others would see that Taggart was not fit to be leader. They would turn to Delgadito for guidance, as they always had. Amarillo's loss would not be in vain.

The clearing where the horses had been left appeared. Delgadito crossed to his animal, swung up, and lifted the reins.

"Wait," Cuchillo Negro said. "Where is White Apache?"

Fiero, the last to show, looked back. "I thought he was behind me all this time."

"Remember the shots we heard?" Ponce mentioned. "Maybe the white-eyes killed him too."

"I will go look for him," Fiero announced.

"No," Delgadito said curtly, forgetting himself. "White Apache, if still alive, is on his own. He knew how it would be." The *Gans* had been kind. At last, Delgadito was rid of the white nuisance, and he wanted to leave it that way.

"Since when do the *Shis-Inday* desert their own?" Fiero challenged. "You are the one who has done more than any other to make him one of us, yet now you will not lift a finger when he might be lying out there wounded?"

A twinge of temper made Delgadito say, "We lost Amarillo because of him. Let him share Amarillo's fate if that is the will of *Yusn*."

"You do as you want," Fiero said. "I do as I want. I am going." A single step was all he took, though, when an unusual sight riveted him in place.

Off through the mesquite faint lights could be seen, bobbing and flitting like so many golden insects.

"The white-eyes have found us," Ponce declared.

"No," Cuchillo Negro said. "See how they move in many different directions? They still hunt us, but they have no idea where we are. We must leave quickly, or they will."

Nothing could have pleased Delgadito more. Circumstance had conspired to accomplish what all his scheming could not. "We should hide until morning and then try to find White Apache."

"And do not forget Amarillo," Cuchillo Negro said. "We must recover his body, if we can, in order to lay him to rest as he should be."

All of them shared the sentiment. Proper burial was a grave matter. It was the Apache custom most shrouded in secrecy, the one outsiders were never allowed to see, the one Apaches never spoke of to anyone other than Apaches.

"Let us go," Cuchillo Negro coaxed, jabbing his heels into the flanks of his steed.

The band trotted eastward, the reluctant Fiero bringing up the rear. No one else saw the scowl of disapproval he wore at being compelled to flee from craven whites.

Nor did anyone notice the rare grin on Delgadito. Exultant that at last he was rid of the White Apache and able to regain the trust of his fellow warriors, he yearned to whoop for joy. But that was not the Apache way, so he rode on silently, thinking, in his own tongue, the Apache equivalent of "Good riddance!"

At that precise moment, the man Delgadito wanted to see rubbed out was crouched inside Harve Denton's corral, a hand resting on a Colt, primed to unlimber his hardware in a blaze of lead, if he was discovered. And that was a very real possibility since Surgio Vasquez was retracing his steps and staring intently at the horses.

Clay locked his gaze on them too. Should one of the animals act up again Vasquez would be even more suspicious and might just shout an alarm. Clay touched his thumb to the hammer of his six-shooter and waited like a sidewinder coiled to strike.

Vasquez was indeed suspicious. He'd heard a horse nicker, as if in fright, but now both were simply standing there, looking off into the darkness. Stopping, he scanned the pasture flanking the stable but saw nothing out of the ordinary. Since he had been around horses from the age of six, he well knew their skittish dispositions. A playful rabbit or the hoot of an owl might have spooked the pair in the corral. With a shrug, he turned and strolled on to the house.

The second the front door closed behind the Mexican, the White Apache padded to the sorrel, rubbed its neck a few times, and slid onto its warm back. Thankfully, the horse showed no fright. Clay prodded it over to the gate, worked the bar by bending far down, and gave a shove. Before him was the yard and the house, which he skirted by riding to the left.

Just then voices sounded, and Roarke and the other cowhand came out of the stable, recoiling in shock on spying the presumed Indian in the act of stealing one of their employer's animals.

"What the hell!" Roarke roared.

"It's one of them!" squealed his partner.

Both men dug for their blue lightnings.

Clay Taggart had twisted sharply at the first syllable. As they drew, so did he, and they were the ones who suffered from a bad case of slow. Clay sent a slug ripping into the squealer, a gut shot that doubled the puncher over.

Roarke was bringing his pistol up when Clay shot twice. The bullets caught Roarke in the throat and spun him around. Sputtering crimson, he staggered, gunplay forgotten in the face of his mortal wound.

At the house, shouts rent the air. Clay brought the sorrel to a gallop, fleeing around the same hedge he had hidden behind earlier. Almost immediately, he discovered that something was wrong. The sorrel moved with an awkward, broken gait. Bending low again, he saw the right foreleg was the cause, and he mentally cursed his stupidity. He should have realized the horse had been left behind for a reason. It was going lame.

Clay had no choice but to flag the animal onward. He had to get out of there before Vasquez organized pursuit. Passing several trees, he bore southward, acting on the assumption that Vasquez would count on him heading northeast, to the mouth of the valley.

Within a quarter mile, the sorrel limped so badly Clay had to rein up. Dismounting, he felt the leg carefully, then set it down in disgust.

"Some days nothing goes right," he complained. Giving the horse a pat, he hiked on, listening for the telltale drum of hooves. Nor was he disappointed. In the distance, riders were galloping to the northeast, just as he had figured they would. He chuckled at how easily he had outwitted them.

A new element was abruptly added. The sorrel let out a series of strident whinnies, one right after the other, without letup.

Clay froze, dreading the result. He could still see the sorrel and would have shot it if he could do so without any risk of the shot being heard. As near as he could determine the riders had not heard the sorrel—yet. Gripping his rifle securely, he sprinted across the field, his destination distant black humps, in reality a line of rolling hills.

Presently, Clay realized the night had fallen quiet except for the sorrel. "Damn critter!" he snapped. Bearing credence to his anger, the sound of the riders resumed, but they had changed direction and were coming toward the sorrel. Toward him.

Clay flowed over the ground as would a bounding panther, his dark hair flying in the wind, his moccasins making as little noise as would a field mouse. A harried glance revealed one of the riders had lit a lantern. But that was all right. He'd left few tracks, not enough for a man to read. A typical cowboy, anyway. Surgio Vasquez was a whole other story.

Had Clay been next to the Mexican, he would have seen his anxiety justified. Vasquez was the one with the lantern, on the ground near the sorrel, kneeling to better see the faint impressions left by the Indian they were after. Apaches were noted for being light on their feet and rarely leaving tracks, but this one, Vasquez saw, had been careless. He found a partial print, then the entire outline of the left sole on a patch of bare earth. A low hiss issued through his parted teeth.

"What is it?" asked one of the five punchers with him.

"Not what. Who," Vasquez said. "It's him."

"Who?"

"Blanco Apache."

"Blanco?"

"White, Griffen. It is the White Apache himself," Vasquez clarified, taking his reins in hand. "He is smart, this one. He doubled back to lose Senor Denton and the rest. And he would have gotten away, if not for Roarke and Charley."

Griffen stroked his scruffy beard. "You don't say. There's a heap of money on this turncoat's head. I'm all for going after him."

"Me, too," said another. "One of us might be lucky enough to drop him."

"What I couldn't do with a thousand dollars!" declared a third.

Vasquez regarded them with concealed contempt. Americanos had more courage than brains, and where money was involved, more greed than common sense. "That works both ways," he commented.

"What does?" Griffen asked.

"At the same time we are hunting him, he might

take it into his head to hunt us." Vaquez paused. "Do you want to be riding around in the dark when you might find yourself right in his gun sights?"

Griffen was an older hand, a puncher who had worked for Harve Denton since the founding of the Box D. Like most cowpokes his age, he had a little money salted away for a rainy day, and like most, he dreamed of having more, his hope pinned to one day winning big at one of the weekly five-card stud games in town and having enough to tide him through his later years without having to fret where the next meal would come from. So, in reply to the tracker, he said, "For that much money I'd trail the Devil into Hell."

Vasquez gestured southward. "Be my guest. He's heading for the Rosita Hills and should reach them by dawn."

"You aren't coming?" inquired a beefy man in a surly manner.

"I like living, Terrill," Vasquez said, hooking a boot in a stirrup. Swinging into the saddle, he grinned and said, "Adios, amigos. Good hunting."

"Now hold on," Griffen said. "Didn't your boss, Gillett, send you to lend Harve a hand?"

"Sí," Vasquez admitted.

"Gillett wants this White Apache bad, I hear," Griffen said.

"He does. So?"

"So why is it you've done next to nothing since you got here? You wouldn't go with Harve and them because you claimed they were wasting their time, and now you won't go with us because you're scared you might be shot. It seems to me that your boss is going to be mighty mad when he hears how his great tracker has a yel—" Griffen choked off his final words and blanched, for Surgio Vasquez's hand had swooped close to the fancy notched pistol low on his hip.

"Have a care, amigo. You were about to say something that would have gotten you killed."

Griffen had heard of Vasquez's skill, rumored to be second only to Billy Santee's. Griffen was a fair hand with a six-gun, himself, but nowhere near as talented as those two. "I didn't mean no insult," he said amiably. "I was just trying to make the point that if you don't tag along, your boss might be a mite upset with you."

Vasquez slowly lowered his arm though his blood boiled. He was slow to anger except when his courage was called into question, and the notches on his six-shooter were ample evidence of the consequences when people thought him less of a man than he was.

The tracker did not want to go with the hands. They were being stupid, and stupidity cost lives. Yet he had to concede that the hairy Griffen had a point. His employer might not agree with his reasoning; he might hold it against him. And of late, Miles Gillett had dealt harshly with anyone who failed to do his job.

"Ahhh, we don't need Vasquez," Terrill was informing the others. "There's five of us, ain't there? We can handle this Taggart feller by ourselves."

Griffen nodded. "I'm game. How about the rest of you? Lane, Edwards, Hanks? Are you with us, or not?"

"To the finish," said Hanks, a cowboy bearing a nasty scar on his left cheek courtesy of a Comanche lance. "I'm not fond of Injuns nohow."

"Like a steer, I can try," Edwards said.

Lane simply nodded.

"Then let's punch the breeze and get this over

with," Griffen stated. He glanced at the Mexican. "Do us a favor and tell Mr. Denton, when you see him, that we'll be back with the White Apache's hair, or we won't be back at all."

"He will have to find out some other way," Vasquez said, blowing out the lantern and giving it to Edwards. "I'm going with you." He did not like the way Griffen grinned at him, but he held his peace as the five cowhands took up the chase and lashed his own mount into following. He had no interest in leading. Experience had taught him that Apaches picked off those in the front of an enemy party first, thinking that the leaders would be at the front, and once they were disposed of, the rest would become too confused to fight effectively. Typical Apache brilliance.

Vasquez tugged his sombrero down low, then loosened his pistol in its holster. He could feel the boot knife he carried rubbing against his right ankle. And in his saddle scabbard was a .56-caliber Spencer, a new seven-shot model, as accurate as any Winchester ever made. Armed to the teeth as he was, he somehow suspected it still wouldn't be enough. Bullets were no match for savvy, and the craftiness of Apaches was legendary. He could only hope this White Apache hadn't gone completely Indian, or he might never see Mexico again.

Meanwhile Clay Taggart ran on across the benighted Arizona landscape. He was in full stride, running as Delgadito had taught him, breathing in deeply and exhaling smoothly through his nose, not his mouth. He had seen the lantern snuffed out, and although he had too wide a lead to hear any pursuing horses, he guessed the punchers were after him and refused to slacken his pace.

Jake McMasters

The hills had grown from black mounds to resemble a miniature mountain range. Clay figured he had half a mile to go, and he would be able to lose himself in the uninhabited region bordering the valley. The only hurdle he must overcome was outrunning the cowpokes. And Vasquez. He must never forget about Vasquez, who could track like an Apache and knew Apache ways. Vasquez mattered the most. Outthink him, Clay mused, and he would come out on top. Fail, and he'd be sprouting daisies come Spring.

The throaty snarl of a cougar wafted from the hills. There had been a time when Clay would have given one of the big cats a wide berth, but that was before his confidence in his own ability had grown under Delgadito's tutelage. He no longer feared the wilderness, as he once had. Not when he could live off the land anywhere, at any time. Not when his senses were so much sharper than they had been, and the odds of his being caught unawares, by man or beast, were so slim.

The rumble of hooves intruded on Clay's reverie. He looked back but, as yet, could not see them. The nearest hill reared five hundred yards off; so close, yet so far. Could he do it?

Exerting himself to his limits, Clay flew. His own speed amazed him. The grueling months of constant hardship he had spent with the Apaches had worked wonders on his sinews and stamina. He felt as if he could run for another hour or two without any trouble whatsoever.

Horses were faster, though. Clay looked once more and spotted vague forms at the limits of his vision. They were forty or fifty yards east of him and would miss him, unless they fanned out.

Suddenly the unforeseen occurred. The earth

seemed to give way under Clay, and he tread on air while falling like a rock. Too late he realized he had blundered onto an arroyo. His waving arms clipped a bush. His body smashed into another bush, tumbling him end over end down a steep slope littered with dry bush. His descent was halted by a boulder.

Excruciating pain lanced through Clay like a red-hot knife. He sprawled facedown, glad he had not split open his fool head. Luck had been with him.

Or had it?

Vasquez and the cowboys out for his blood were racing along the rim of the arroyo toward him.

Chapter Ten

The White Apache struggled to his knees beside the boulder at the base of the slope and unslung his rifle. He remembered the lessons Delgadito had imparted, remembered that the key to Apache stealth was an uncanny ability to blend into the background so perfectly they appeared part of the terrain itself. Accordingly, lying on his side, he molded himself to the shape of the boulder, hugging the rough surface with the Winchester pinned in front of him.

In moments the riders arrived, traveling past the point where Clay had fallen and drawing rein a dozen feet off.

"You must of been hearing things, Terrill," someone said after a bit.

"There was a noise, I tell you," argued the man with keen ears.

"What kind?"

"Hard to say, Griffen," Terrill said. "Sort of like

126

rocks clattering and a crackling sound."

"How could you hear anything over the sound of our own horses?" wondered another man.

"I did, damn it," Terrill snapped. "And the next one who brands me a liar is going to regret it."

A voice marked by a Spanish accent chimed in. "Calm down. No one would think of doing that." A horse stomped a hoof. "I would suggest we keep looking, companeros. Sitting here we are easy targets, no?"

Clay didn't move until the racket the horses made died in the distance and quiet reclaimed the night. Peeling himself from the boulder, he stood and winced when pain speared through his left ankle. He took a few tentative steps, testing his leg. Evidently, he had strained a muscle in the fall. The injury was aggravating but not severe enough to slow him down.

Gritting his teeth, Clay climbed to the south rim. The hills were so close he imagined he could reach out and touch them. Rifle in hand he jogged forward. Half of the five hundred yards had fallen behind him when the breeze brought news of the riders. They were coming back, and from the sound of things they appeared to be on the same side of the arroyo as he was.

The ground here was flat and barren. There was no grass in which to hide, no weeds or trees or underbrush. Clay went prone, cheek to the earth, head pointed at the oncoming horses. They were even closer to the arroyo and would miss him if they didn't alter course. But they did.

Clay saw the six men swing toward the hills. But their new direction would bring them uncomfortably near, so near they'd undoubtedly spot him.

With the insight came action. Clay leapt to his feet and bolted.

"There he is!" a man bellowed.

Gunfire boomed. Deadly hornets buzzed on either hand, one stinging Clay on the left arm but not deep enough to draw blood. Excitement had caused the riders to shoot in haste, a mistake they would swiftly remedy. He had to discourage them, and to that end he whirled, jerked the rifle to his shoulder, and cut loose with three rapid shots.

The Box D men were caught flat-footed. In their greed, they had raced toward their quarry without regard for their own safety. All but one. Surgio Vasquez had held back, unwilling to throw his life away, no matter how much money was involved. He saw the White Apache move with astounding speed, saw Taggart spin and Taggart's rifle flare red. Edward's horse crashed down; then the rest scattered.

Vasquez galloped to the west. Once he lost sight of everyone else, including the White Apache, he guided his mount southward, moving parallel to Taggart, and slowed to a walk so Taggart wouldn't hear him.

Unknown to the tracker, Clay did. The rest had fled back to the arroyo so there was just this one still after him. Vasquez probably, he suspected, and angled to the east, shutting his sore ankle from his mind. Before long, sparse brush rose before him, indicating he was almost to the hills. On seeing a welcome slope, he smiled and plunged into the murky soup at its base.

Clay halted to listen. He no longer heard the lone rider to the west. For the time being he was safe. Whether his pursuers gave up depended on how badly they wanted him, or the bounty. He replaced the cartridges he'd used, turned his back on the valley, and forged on.

At that selfsame moment, Surgio Vasquez arrived on the opposite side of the same hill. Shucking his Spencer, he slid off and led his horse by the reins along a winding route deeper into the stark region. After passing a half-dozen hills, he forked leather and made for the top of the one to his left. Below him the slope was dotted with pinon trees. Eastward rolled more hills, blending into the far horizon.

Vasquez sought any hint of movement. He had the White Apache all to himself now, and he did not intend to let the opportunity go by. All the money would be his, the thousand from the government and the five hundred from Gillett. His only regret was that the price on the White Apache wasn't higher.

The tracker deduced that Taggart was somewhere to the south of him. All he needed was a fleeting glimpse to pinpoint the renegade's position and he would close in at his leisure, relying on tracks once dawn broke.

A pale streak prompted Vasquez to lean forward, eyes glued to the spot. He had found the gringo, several hundred yards to the southeast moving across a low slope. Lifting the reins, Vasquez took himself lower, pronto, to keep from being seen. Once on level ground, he held his horse to a brisk walk, so as not to overtake his quarry prematurely. He wondered how the Americanos were faring and hoped they would go back to the Box D and leave the tracking to a professional.

Vasquez would have been unhappy had he witnessed the scene at the arroyo. A heated dispute had arisen. The cowpoke named Edwards was jabbing a finger at Griffen. "Like hell you can't take me along!

129

You could if you wanted to. Just let me ride double. I can take turns with each one of you."

"It'd slow us down too much," Griffen objected.

"And every minute counts," Terrill added. "All this squabbling is giving Taggart time to get away." He nodded toward Edwards's dead horse. "It ain't our fault your claybank took a slug."

"I want to be in on the finish," Edwards insisted. "I want a chance to earn the bounty."

"Sorry," Griffen said.

Edwards tried a different tack. "You can't just ride off and leave me here with Apaches roamin' the valley! I'd be afoot and it's miles to the ranch."

"The sorrel is back yonder," Griffen brought up. "Catch it, and it might hold up until you get back."

"Might," Edwards spat.

"The best we can do, pard," Terrill said.

Edwards glared after them, flooded with wrath until the cough of a cougar reminded him where he was. Stooping, he heaved his saddle over his shoulder and trudged into the darkness. "I hope to hell they turn that traitor into a sieve," he fumed.

The traitor in question was a mile and a half from the arroyo and thinking he was in the clear. Clay had not heard anyone dogging him since he lost the solitary rider. His foot hurt worse the farther he went, and he decided to find a sheltered spot to rest. As luck would have it, he came on a hill where long ago part of the slope had buckled, leaving a jumbled maze of boulders and huge earthen clods. He meandered into these: a flat boulder gave him a spot to sit.

The ankle was sore to the touch. Clay drew his Bowie knife and sliced off a wide strip from the bottom of his shirt. This he looped around the ankle and tied tight. It wasn't much, but the extra support might help reduce the swelling.

Going on, Clay reflected on whether he should try to find the Apaches or go all the way to their secret retreat in the Dragoons. If the band wasn't there when he arrived, they were bound to show up eventually. Or there was a third alternative.

For the first time in many weeks, Clay was completely on his own. He could do as he pleased, go anywhere he wanted. How about Mexico? he queried himself. No one knew him. He'd be able to lose himself in the throngs, start over in a new line of work. Best of all, federal jurisdiction stopped at the border. The government couldn't bring him to trial for his White Apache escapades without the cooperation of the Mexican government. And for the right price, it was rumored, any government official could be bought.

Or Clay could shuck the whole Southwest and head for another part of the country. Montana, perhaps, where there was so much land and so few people. Or Idaho, where a man could lose himself forever. Or California, where life was carefree and the sun shined three hundred and sixty-three days of the year.

The thought was appealing. Then Clay thought about Miles and Lilly Gillett, about Lilly's treachery and how Miles stole his ranch out from under him. He would have to forego his revenge if he left, and that was something he would never do. They had to pay for what they had done, and pay with their lives.

Once again, unchecked rage boiled within Clay, and for the next ten minutes, he hiked on oblivious to his surroundings, reviewing the events over and over. It was an error a full-blooded Apache would never make, an error he realized on hearing the far

131

off clink of a horseshoe on stone.

Someone was following him. Clay went up the hill on his right, ascending some forty feet. From behind a pinon, he searched for sign of his shadow but could find no one. Lying in ambush appealed to him, but there might be more than one, and he was not inclined to tangle with them just yet. He'd rather pick a better time and place, particularly if Surgio Vasquez was among them.

His ankle protesting, Clay broke into the tireless dogtrot of the *Shis-Inday*. There were times, like now, when he felt as much Apache as white. And the longer he stayed among the Apaches, the less he thought about his white past, about his folks and his ranch and everything he had once deemed important. None of it mattered anymore. Nothing did, except being on the warpath against Gillett and the posse members. Against his own kind.

Suddenly, Clay had the feeling he was being watched. He glanced around, chiding himself for having the overwrought nerves of a ten year old, and involuntarily caught his breath in his throat on seeing several spectral forms on the hill to his right. They were men on foot, near naked men running in single file. They were Indians.

Clay slowed, his first impulse to call out to them. Then he realized they couldn't be Apaches, not the way they were dressed. And they couldn't be friendly, or they would have made their presence known already. For them to be skulking along the way they were did not bode well, at all.

Racing to the north into a gap between a pair of identical hills, Clay glued one eye behind him. Whoever they were, they didn't give chase. Forty yards from where he'd turned, Clay stopped and waited. The seconds crawled by with agonizing slowness, and still no one showed.

Hoping he had lost them, Clay resumed his eastward trek. A nagging pinprick of apprehension goaded him into maintaining his top speed for much longer than he should have, so that when he finally halted, he was winded from the exertion.

At an open space separating a rocky hill from a grassy one, Clay faced around, the Winchester at his waist. He didn't wait long this time, and when convinced there was no danger, he pivoted to depart.

The three Indians stood fifteen feet away.

Clay stiffened, starting to bring up the rifle when he saw they were making no move to use their weapons. One held a lance, two others had bows, but both were slung over their bronzed shoulders. He recovered sufficiently to hide his surprise, his pride bothered at being taken unawares.

"We greet you in peace," said the man holding the lance in Apache dialect, his atrocious accent proof of his infrequent use of the tongue.

Clay studied them, trying to identify them from their clothing and hairstyle. They weren't Comanches; he was certain of that. Comanches never went anywhere unless on horseback. Nor were they Navahos. They could be Maricopas. Or they could be Pimas. And that was bad news because both tribes hated Apaches. "I greet you the same," he responded.

"I am Corn Flower," disclosed the talker. "How are you known?"

There was no hesitation on Clay's part. "*Lickoyee-shis-inday.*"

Corn Flower relayed the information to his companions, then bent his mouth in the semblance of a friendly smile. "White Apache. We have heard of you."

"You have?" Clay said, unable to smother his consternation. For the first time, the full extent of his notoriety was fully impressed upon him. Being wanted by the law and the military was no surprise in light of Gillett having learned his identity. Being known by Palacio and the reservation Apaches was also only natural since any news important to the tribe was soon spread from one end of the reservation to the other. But this, being heard of by members of a tribe with which he'd had no dealings, was downright staggering.

"Your name is on many lips these days," Corn Flower said. "They say you are a white man who has become Apache. They say you are wanted by your own kind for killing other whites in the Apache fashion. They say you are a formidable man."

Clay let the flattery go without comment.

"We are on our way back to our village." Corn Flower continued. "We had camped for the night on a hill so we could see if anyone came near us. Shots woke us. And then we saw you."

"And followed me," Clay said.

"From the hill you appeared to be Apache. We wanted to learn if there were more and if you were hunting us."

The excuse made sense as far as it went. "To which tribe do you belong?" Clay asked.

"We are Lipans."

Such an atrocious lie was laughable but Clay wasn't in the mood. Lipans were much like Apaches in their dress and customs. They resembled one another so closely that some whites believed the Lipans were a branch of the same tribe. The Apaches, themselves, considered the Lipans brothers in spirit, but not true *Shis-Inday.*

"We are friends to all Apaches," Corn Flower compounded his deceit.

"And to all whites?" Clay inquired.

"Lipans are special friends to white-eyes," Corn Flower said. "Every Indian knows it is bad medicine to harm one."

But not one wanted by the law, Clay mused. The bounty would go to whomever killed him, red or white. Pedro Azul and his brother had tried. And he wouldn't put it past these Pimas or Maricopas to try, either. "Now that you know I am not Apache you can go on your way," he said.

"You would not like our company?"

"Where I walk, I walk alone."

"Not entirely alone. There are men after you."

"How many?"

Corn Flower made a show of thinking a moment. "We counted eight, *Lickoyee-shis-inday.*"

Which was two more than Clay had seen, and one of those had taken a wicked spill. No, the warrior was lying again. And Clay could guess why. So, now he had to decide whether to let the trio tag along, where they would be under his nose the whole time, or to brush them off and have them come at him from out of the dark, when he least expected them to pounce. "Will you help me if I am attacked?" he asked, knowing the answer he would get before it came.

"Of course. Lipans always stand ready to help their brothers, the Apaches."

"Come then," Clay said, motioning for them to fall into step to one side. Unknown to them he had the Winchester cocked and he kept it that way as they headed out in a ragged line, bearing on his original easterly course.

It made Clay uncomfortable to have three hostile

Indians jogging within arm's reach. They played their part well, casually ignoring him, hiding the vile intent lurking in their hearts. Rarely did they so much as glance at him.

The charade went on until a half an hour before dawn. The hills dwindled both in number and size. Clay picked the last high one he could see and climbed to the flat crown for a panoramic view of the countryside. By now the sky was light enough for him to spot any riders, even those a long way off, but there were none.

"They gave up," Corn Flower commented.

"Or they are behind a hill or in a gulch," Clay said. "We will wait here awhile."

The bogus Lipan relayed the news to his equally bogus fellows, and all three sat or squatted, none of the bowmen so much as touching their bows.

"I am curious, White Apache," Corn Flower said.

"About what?" Clay had stepped to the right a few yards and knelt, his body aligned so the trio were always in sight.

"Why you have given up white ways for Apache ways. This has never been done before."

"It seemed like the right thing to do at the time," Clay said softly in English.

"What?"

"There are many reasons a man does what he does and some of them can only make sense to that man."

"Your words are true," Corn Flower conceded, and promptly tried another subject. "Your own kind hate you for what you have done. Does this bother you?"

"White men like to throw stones at those they cannot understand."

"Throw stones?"

136

Now Clay changed the topic. "Where did you hear all this about me?"

"From a trader named Decker who comes to our people once each moon. We are a poor people and do not have many fine blankets like the Pimas or bracelets and necklaces like the Pueblos, so Decker offers us many goods for a night with our women."

Clay thoughtfully pursed his lips. Corn Flower, by admitting they weren't Pimas, had inadvertently revealed who they truly were: Maricopas. Both Pimas and Maricopas had similar builds in that the men of both tribes were barrel chested, with narrow shoulders, long trunks and arms, and bow legs. Since they weren't Pimas, these men, built as they were, had to be the other. And it fit what little he knew about them. Both tribes lived in permanent villages and tilled the soil extensively. They were as warlike as the Apaches or the Comanches, but neither had they given up the notion of war entirely, particularly the Maricopas, who were noted for their ferocity in battle. As a rule, the two tribes enjoyed peaceful relations with Americans. But there had been a few incidents, always involving Maricopas, that had blemished their record.

"You have Apache wife yet?" Corn Flower inquired.

Such a question was the last Clay would have expected. "No," he responded curtly. "Apache women do not marry white-eyes." He paused. "Where did you learn to speak the Apache tongue so well?"

"When I was little the Apaches stole me on a raid. Until my twelfth winter, I was raised by them and learned all their ways. Then one day some American soldiers fought our band and captured many of us.

When they learned I had been taken, they sent me back to my own people." His chest puffed out. "Now I am a big man in my tribe because I can do many things an Apache can do but others cannot."

It was no secret that the Pimas and Maricopas believed the Apaches were endowed with superhuman abilities, and Clay had no trouble imagining how a devious man like Corn Flower could turn that to his advantage.

"I have men who follow me," Corn Flower boasted, pointing at his companions. "Others also." In his excitement, he so forgot himself that he did not keep up the pretense of being a Lipan. "We are not content to sit in our lodges smoking pipes while our women wait on our every need. No, we want to live as our people lived long ago, as warriors! We want to strike fear into our enemies and show them that we are as powerful as Apaches." A bloodthirsty gleam lit Corn Flower's eyes, and he wagged his lance excitedly. "Soon the old men will be put in their proper place, and we will be the ones who lead our people. And I will be over all the rest."

"You have big plans," Clay said. And he saw how he fit into those plans. Corn Flower would be considered a mighty man indeed, if he were the one who slew the infamous White Apache. Young braves would flock to him in droves. Corn Flower would achieve his heart's desire in half the time it would otherwise take.

"Great men plan big," the Maricopa amended, smacking his wide chest.

"I am glad you are here to help me," Clay flattered him. "The white-eyes will lose many lives if they try to kill us."

Grinning enigmatically, Corn Flower grunted, then spoke in a low voice to the other two. Their faces gave nothing away but their muscles tensed.

Clay was holding the Winchester across his thighs, the barrel drooping, but slanted toward the warriors. Braced for a rush, he watched them carefully, ready for anything—or so he thought.

"Look!" Corn Flower cried, rising and pointing westward. "The Americans come!"

Despite himself, Clay automatically looked and realized he had fallen for a ruse as old as the hill on which he knelt when the three Maricopas uttered piercing shrieks and sprang.

Chapter Eleven

An angry Billy Santee wheeled his horse, glared balefully at the nervous men staring back, and lowered his quicksilver hands close to his expensive Colts. "We can't give up yet!" he barked. "I ain't ready to call it quits!"

"Be reasonable, Santee," the lanky Bart said. "We never did find their trail. And the sun will be up soon."

"We'll be able to spot them now." Santee refused to bow to public opinion. "I say we stay out all day if we have to."

"We're tired and hungry," Bart mentioned. "We wouldn't be worth a plugged nickel if we did find the vermin."

"My boss gave me a job to do and I aim to do it," Santee stubbornly announced. "Since I can't do it alone, I'll put a lead pill into the first son of a bitch who calls it quits."

"You'll do no such thing!" Said Harve Denton, who had sat silently listening to the heated exchange long enough. "As you'll recollect, I'm in charge here. Miles told you to work for me. And I'm saying we head for the Box D and rest up tonight in case those filthy red devils come back."

"They won't show their faces again, and you know it," Santee said in disgust. Gillett was going to be awful displeased, he knew, on learning they had muddled things up. But he might be able to direct Gillett's wrath elsewhere—at Denton, for instance—if he could rightfully claim that he'd been overridden all the time and that Denton's carelessness had resulted in the Apaches skedaddling.

"We can't hunt them down if we're exhausted," the rancher declared. "We're heading back, and that's final."

"Whatever you say," Santee said, and puzzled everyone by chuckling at his private joke. He fell in beside Bart, relishing the attention. The riders to the right of him swung off a few yards, giving him more room, and that made him laugh harder, which in turn caused the entire outfit to regard him as if he'd gone loco.

Soon the sun rose. Santee peered along the back trail, anticipating the arrival of Surgio Vasquez. The uppity Mex had refused to tag along last night, claiming he could track better once daylight arrived. Santee hadn't bothered to debate the point because he'd been cocksure he would be the one claiming the White Apache's head as his trophy before the night was done.

Santee had no intention of letting Vasquez steal his thunder. If the Mexican went tracking, Santee would go with him. If Vasquez objected, Santee would prod him into slapping leather and demonstrate that he, Santee, was the fastest damn gun shark in Arizona.

But the morning hours dragged on, and Surgio Vasquez did not appear. Santee fretted that Vasquez had found tracks and was right that minute closing in on the Apaches. He fidgeted in the saddle the rest of the ride. When the buildings came into sight, he raked his spurs against his flagging horse and galloped to the stable, where two punchers stood smoking. "Where's that no-account greaser?"

"Who?" one said blankly.

"You know who the hell I mean. Vasquez."

"I wouldn't call him a greaser to his face if I were you," the hand remarked sarcastically. "He's a bad man to cross."

Santee leaned down, baring his teeth as would a mountain lion about to bite. "And you reckon I'm not?"

The Box D puncher swallowed and nervously glanced at the gunman's waist. "Hell, everybody in Arizona knows you're a regular curly wolf. Everybody!"

"You'd do good to remember that," Santee said. "Now where is he?"

"Rode out last night with Griffen and a bunch of the boys," stated the other cowpoke. "Seems that one of those rotten Apaches snuck in here and stole a horse right out of the corral."

"What?" Santee said, agitated by the notion of Vasquez succeeding where he had failed.

"True enough," said the man. "The savage lit a shuck but it didn't do him no good 'cause the sorrel he stole had a bum leg. Appears the boys caught up with him, and he shot a horse out from under Edwards, who moseyed in about an hour ago—"

"Vasquez!" Santee hissed. "Where's he?"

"Still out yonder," answered the first hand, jabbing a finger to the south. "Him and the rest ain't back yet. Edwards says they were fixin' to hunt that Apache down no matter how long it took."

"Be worth it, too," the other Box D man said.

"How do you figure?" Santee demanded.

"Edwards told us they were lucky as sin. That Injun who stole the sorrel—"

"Yes, yes," Santee said impatiently.

"Why, it's none other than the White Apache."

Billy Santee was off his horse in a flash, lightning dancing on his brow. "I want me a new horse," he ordered crisply, "and I want it five minutes ago."

Elsewhere, much earlier, the man who had most galled Billy Santee was crouched beside a stretch of bare earth, his nose to the musty soil, his eyes raking the surface for the tiniest of lines and smudge marks.

Surgio Vasquez was upset. He was not one to buck the odds, and the odds had just increased dramatically against him. Hunting the White Apache had been perilous enough. Hunting four Indians, by himself, was the same as asking to have his hair lifted.

Where had they come from? Vasquez reflected. *Which tribe did they belong to?* The moccasin pattern definitely wasn't Apache or Lipan or Comanche or Yuma. His best guess was that the newcomers belonged to one of the more peaceful agricultural tribes in the region, yet if that was the case, why had they linked up with the White Apache? Did Taggart know them? Unlikely, since as far as Vasquez knew, Taggart's only dealings with Indians had been delivering beef to the Chiricahua reservation.

That, in itself, was telling. Vasquez sometimes speculated on whether Taggart had struck up friendships with several of the warriors back then, and whether those friendships accounted for the Chiricahuas saving Taggart from being lynched.

Why else would the Apaches have done it? They hated whites almost as much as they hated Mexicans. A Chiricahua would as soon spare the life of an Americano as have his daughter marry a Sonoran scalp hunter.

There were so many mysteries about this strange white man, who now lived as an Apache. Why would anyone forsake their way of life and their own kind to live among his enemies *as* an enemy? No Mexican would ever do such a thing.

Vasquez stepped into the saddle and rode on but much slower than before. He settled the Spencer in his lap. Soon the sun would peek above the horizon, and he would be able to make better time, but not too much better if he wanted to avoid being bushwhacked.

Had the choice been his, the tracker would have turned around and headed for the ranch. But the decision had been stripped from him by two factors over which he had no control. The first was the fury of Miles Gillett should he fail. The second was the chance to beat out Billy Santee, to rub in the gunman's nose the fact that he was better than the gunman. And not even Vasquez could say which factor influenced him more.

The promise of dawn painted the sky pink. Birds awakened to warble their morning litany. A few lizards, early risers, moved sluggishly abroad, awaiting the sun's warmth on their bodies so that they would regain their strength and be able to scamper about with dazzling speed in search of insects.

Warrior Born

Surgio Vasquez shifted to relieve a kink in his back and was raising a hand to scratch the stubble sprouting on his chin when he faintly heard the piercing shriek of war whoops followed by the blast of a gunshot.

Lilly Gillett paused before the full-length mirror in the plush corridor of her home to admire herself. Her luxurious hair shone, her full body shaped the contours of her dress just right. She was an eyeful, as men might say, and proud of it. Hips swaying, she sashayed into the sitting room where her husband sat reading the latest newspaper from Tucson. "Shouldn't we have heard something by now?" she inquired.

"Not yet, dearest," rumbled his voice from behind the uplifted pages. "Be patient. This sort of thing takes time."

"I don't like the waiting," Lilly confessed, prowling to the window where she admired the splendid vista of the eminent dawn. The two of them always rose an hour before sunrise. She had never been an early bird herself, but it was a habit with Miles, a habit she enjoyed sharing since he was most amorous in the mornings. Every day started the same way, with half an hour of intimate, frenzied lovemaking, the sort she had only dreamed about when younger, the sort that left a woman limp with satisfaction and grinning wickedly.

"It's the female disposition," Miles commented. "Women always want everything done right away."

"Men are no different," Lilly responded, miffed. She never liked it when her husband treated her as if she were a little girl instead of a mature woman. Patronizing, they called it, and it made her see red.

The newspaper crumbled noisily, and Miles looked at her. "Now don't start," he chided. "I know that tone, but I wasn't being insulting. Men and woman have different traits, is all. We both have our failings."

"To hear you talk sometimes, a body would think you didn't have any," Lilly sniped.

"Have I ever claimed to be perfect?" Miles retorted. "I reckon no one knows better than me what weaknesses I have. But where most men are ignorant of theirs, I recognize mine and control them." He smoothed the papers. "Most of the time."

"When have you not?"

"When I had that damnable Taggart in my grasp and I let him slip away."

Turning, Lilly went over and gently squeezed his wide shoulder. Under her fingers rippled sinews of steel. "That was hardly your fault, my love."

"Wrong," Gillet said bitterly. "I had him right in the palm of my hand. I could have crushed him like this." Extending an arm, he slowly bunched his thick fingers. "But I wanted the bastard to suffer first. I wanted him to grovel, to beg me to put him out of his misery." He sighed. "I was too bloodthirsty for my own good."

Lilly stroked the brooding man's brow. How unlike Clay, her first lover, was this great hulk of a genius who was in the act of carving out a ranching empire that would one day rival the biggest spreads in Texas. During those quiet early morning moments when they lay clasped in each other's arms, he had often confided his innermost longings, his secret goals. The day would come when her man would be the single most powerful person in Arizona. And she would be right at his side, hobnobbing with senators and bankers and others of their ilk. Money, power, and prestige would all be theirs; the prospect made her giddy. "Live and learn," she said to soothe him. "I don't blame you one bit for what happened. If it had been up to me, I would have done the same thing."

Gillett patted her knuckles. "That's one of the reasons I was so attracted to you, my dear. You're the only woman I've ever met who is as ruthless as I am."

"And loves it just as much."

Laughing, Gillett pulled her down onto his lap and cupped her exquisitely chiseled chin in his mighty paw of a hand. "The way I figure, we're a match made in heaven."

"Or somewhere a bit lower," Lilly tittered.

Gillett mashed his lips to hers and molded her willing flesh to his. When they parted they were both flushed, breathing heavily.

"Care to retire to the bedroom for a second helping?" Lilly teased.

"Gladly," Gillett said, "were it not for a previous commitment in Tucson."

"You have to go all the way into town?"

"Can't be helped," Gillett idly stroked her hair while staring out the window. "Jeffers has found a legal chink in Old Man Binder's armor."

Lilly wriggled in delight. "He really thinks we can take the property right out from under Binder's nose?"

Gillett nodded. "And if Jeffers says we can, we can bank on it. That law wrangler of mine is the most devious son of a bitch around. He has a real nose for loopholes."

"We should keep a good man like him on the payroll at all costs. I do hope we pay him enough so he won't take his shingle elsewhere," Lilly joked.

"Never fear on that account," Gillett said.

"Why not?"

Before Gillett could explain, there was a polite rap at the door and a man called out, "My apologies, sir. A rider has just delivered a message from Mr. Denton."

"Fetch it in," Gillett commanded, giving his wife a push to her feet. She primped herself as the door swung in and their manservant brought over an envelope.

"The rider is awaiting a reply," Partridge said.

Harve Denton's distinctive scrawl always reminded Gillett of the tracks of a beheaded chicken. His lips moved slightly as he read, then he slapped the note against the arms of his chair and cursed.

"What is it?" Lilly was all interest.

"That fool Denton couldn't catch a dead hog. And I sent him my best men to help out!"

"Clay got away?"

"Not yet. But I'm not one for letting grass grow under me." In his annoyance Gillett tore the note to shreds, then tossed the pieces onto the floor. "Tell the rider to have my men sent home once Vasquez and Santee show up."

"Will do, sir," Partridge said, then hurried out.

"What will you do if they fail?" Lilly probed.

"Put the next step into motion," Gillett said. "And this time I'm not leaving anything to chance. This time the buzzards will feast on Clay Taggart's rotting flesh."

"I can hardly wait."

Many miles to the southeast of the Triangle G, a small band of Apaches stood in a ravine arguing in a rare heated fashion. At the center of the storm of harsh words was Delgadito, brawny arms folded across his muscular chest, his head uplifted at an arrogant angle. "I have said all I am going to say."

Fiero paced back and forth nearby. "I cannot follow your trail anymore. First you befriend the white-eye and tell us we must accept him as one of our own, and when we finally do, you tell us we are too friendly and would have us turn our backs on him in his time of need."

"A warrior must be able to look after himself," Delgadito said. "*Lickoyee-shis-inday* lives as one of us now, true. But he must prove he is worthy."

"So that is it," Fiero said. "You are testing him."

"Yes," Delgadito responded, and saw Cuchillo Negro scowl and turn away.

"Why did you not say so from the beginning?" Fiero snapped. "Then I would have understood."

"And I," Ponce said.

"Must a man explain all his thoughts?" Delgadito criticized them. "I myself brought the white-eye to our *kunh-gan-hay. Shee-dah!* I alone."

"We all know this," Fiero said.

"Then you should know I have the right to decide his fate," Delgadito stated.

"*To-dah!*"

The sharp "No!" fixed all eyes on the speaker, Cuchillo Negro, who so rarely raised his voice that Fiero and Ponce were startled. But not Delgadito. He suspected Cuchillo Negro's motivation and said, "You disagree, my brother?"

"I disagree," Cuchillo Negro said flatly.

"Would you share your reason?"

Cuchillo Negro waited before answering, and when he did, he began by addressing questions at no one in particular. "Since the beginning of time the *Shis-Inday* have gone on many raids, have they not?"

"Yes," Delgadito said.

"They have taken many captives, brought back many women and children."

"We all know this."

"What was done with those captives? Did we kill them?" Cuchillo Negro concentrated on the firebrand and the young warrior. "*To-dah*. We took the women as wives and the young ones as our own, to be raised in the Apache way. And when the children grew, they were *Shis-Inday* from head to toe. They looked on themselves as Apaches, and we looked on them as Apaches."

"Why bring this up?" Ponce broke in.

"You would not think of saying to one of them, 'Yes, we made you Apache, but you do not have the right to decide your fate. We can throw your life away when we want, as we want.' You would not do such a thing because every *Shis-Inday* has the right to decide his or her own life according to his or her own wishes."

"This is so," Fiero said.

"When we open our arms to others, we do not open them halfway," Cuchillo Negro elaborated. "Either they become Apache or they do not, and those who do are one of us."

"You have said it," Fiero agreed.

"Then why do we have one standard for the captives we take and another for *Lickoyee-shis-inday?* He has been among us many sleeps now, learning to be as we are. Our eyes have seen his progress. We have seen how hard he works."

Delgadito's active brain had already guessed where his friend's words were leading. He could see the others were being influenced, and it upset him that the warrior he most trusted was doing this to him.

"So, I say White Apache has the right to decide his own fate." Cuchillo Negro concluded. "He has earned this right as surely as anyone else adopted by our people. For us to desert him now, after he has saved all our lives at least once, is to prove the lies of the whites who say Apaches are without worth."

Neither Fiero nor Ponce had ever heard Cuchillo Negro say so much at one time. That, combined with his sincerity, doubly impressed upon them his appeal. Together, they regarded Delgadito critically, and Fiero said, "We cannot doubt the words of our brother. White Apache is one of us in spirit. White Apache has gone on raids with us and has risked himself for us many times, even when we did not ask. When he first came among us, no one hated him more than I did. But now I see he is good medicine. He has earned the right to be a warrior."

Delgadito never liked to be opposed, and this time rankled worse than ever before because it was Cuchillo Negro who had betrayed him. Since he could not trust his tongue to stay still, he stormed off, going up the side of the ravine for a look at the buildings in the valley below.

During the hours between midnight and the warbling of the first birds, the Apaches had doubled back on themselves, a time-honored tactic that saw them concealed due north of the Bar D before daylight.

From that distance, the men moving about appeared twice the size of ants. Yet even so, Delgadito's hawkish vision picked out the four cowboys bearing a stiff corpse into the pasture west of the stable. A large pile of brush and wood had previously been piled there.

Cupping a hand to his mouth, Delgadito yipped, as would a young coyote, bringing the others on the run. They took one look and stared grimly at the unfolding tableau.

"Amarillo should be buried in the old way," Cuchillo Negro said resentfully.

They all watched as the body was roughly tossed onto the pile. One of the cowboys stepped up close, sunlight gleaming off a slender blade; then he stepped back, waving something in his right hand.

"I will kill ten white-eyes for this," Fiero vowed.

More hands converged. Some people walked from the house. A can was brought out, and its contents were splashed over the body; then another cowboy lit a match and tossed it.

As the flames leaped high, the spirits of the four Apaches sank. Their faces were transformed into copper masks of stony outrage. For that moment in time, they were fully united in thought and purpose, their previous dissent forgotten. They beheld ravening flames devour one of their own, in violation of sacred Apache tradition, and an answering fire filled their eyes.

"And these are White Apache's people," Delgadito noted. "The man all of you would side with was reared in treachery, bred to exterminate the *Shis-Inday* to the last person."

"They are different," Cuchillo Negro said.

"Are they?" Delgadito said. "Does a leopard change its spots? A skunk its stripe? As White Apache was, so he shall ever be, and in the end any of us who puts his trust in him will pay a steep price for being so gullible."

None of them had a reply. Nor did they need to answer. Delgadito knew by their expressions that he had rekindled doubt in their minds, and from doubt it was a short step to mistrust, dislike, and violence.

Some of the Box D punchers were laughing and skipping around as if having a grand old time. One threw clods of dirt at the corpse. Another drew a pistol and fired four shots into it.

"When I kill those ten, I will cut their hearts out while they are still alive!" Fiero said.

Delgadito could not resist a final barb. "And you would have one of them live among us?" The sullen silence that greeted his question made him want to smile.

Chapter Twelve

The Maricopas had White Apache dead to rights.
Corn Flower's trick had given them the edge they
needed to dispatch the white-eye before he could
snap off a shot. Weapons raised, they swooped down
on their intended victim.

Clay Taggart knew a moment of bone-chilling
dread, in which he was certain his life was over.
Surging erect, attempting to bring the Winchester
into play, he saw a lance and two glittering knives
flashing toward him.

Just when it seemed the blades and tapered point
were about to plunge into Clay's torso, his left foot,
balanced precariously on the top edge of the slope,
gave out from under him as the earth crumbled
away. Clay fell. The lance swished harmlessly past
his chest; then he was on his back, sliding downward
with the Maricopas baying behind him like a pack
of wolves in frenzied pursuit.

An earthen knob brought Clay up with a lurch. Swiftly, he tried to rise, but the foremost warrior, one of the knife wielders, was almost on him. He wedged the rifle against his thigh, angled the barrel and stroked the trigger.

At the retort, the Maricopa did a backward somersault, slamming down so hard a bone broke with a resounding crack. The others, undeterred, bounded down the hill for the kill.

Clay worked the lever but had it only halfway when Corn Flower reached him. The barbed tip of the deadly lance rushed at his neck. Driving the Winchester upward, Clay deflected the spear, giving him room to land a roundhouse punch on the jaw that sent Corn Flower staggering to one side.

But no sooner did one foe fall than another was there to take his place. The third warrior vented a bestial snarl and slashed his blade in a short, precise stroke.

A flick of the Winchester spared Clay's life awhile longer. The knife clipped the stock, chipping off a sliver of wood. In retaliation, Clay swung the barrel into the warrior's stomach, bending the man in half. A chop forced the Maricopa to his knees.

Clay trained the rifle on the warrior's head to finish the man off when, from out of nowhere, leaped a screeching banshee in the form of Corn Flower. The lance scored a narrow groove along Clay's side as the two men crashed together; then they were tumbling, locked nose to nose as they fell and slid over a score of feet.

Corn Flower lost his lance, Clay his Winchester. Shoving apart and standing, the Maricopa went for his knife, White Apache for a Colt. Clay was a second faster, but as the six-shooter leveled, the knife slapped into it, swatting the revolver aside as the hammer fell. The slug went wild, whining off a rock, and before Clay could fire again Corn Flower hurtled into him, stabbing at his throat.

Clay twisted his neck aside, felt the side of the blade touch his skin. He let the impact bowl him over, and as he fell, he grabbed hold of the warrior's neck with his free hand and jammed both feet into the Maricopa's chest. On hitting the ground he heaved, sending Corn Flower sailing like an ungainly bird.

The warrior Clay has slugged with the rifle was up and charging, hatred animating his features. Clay spun and fanned the Colt three times. Three holes sprouted on the warrior's right side, and the man crashed to earth lifeless.

Only Corn Flower, who lay groaning on his stomach, left arm bent at an unnatural angle, was left. Clay walked down and gave the Maricopa a nudge with his toe. Corn Flower groaned louder, blinked a few times, and glanced up, terror overcoming him.

"Do not kill me!"

Clay responded in Apache, saying, "You are good for nothing!" Contempt and anger combined to drive his foot into the man's cheek.

Corn Flower was flipped onto his side, blood flowing from the newly created gash. "Spare me!" he wailed, clutching the wound.

"Spare a liar? Spare a hater of Apaches?" Clay tapped the Colt on the Maricopa's brow. "For what you tried to do to me, I will kill you slowly, Apache style."

"I plead with you," Corn Flower said. "I cannot take pain."

"But you are the one who lived with the *Shis-Inday*," Clay said. "The one who learned their ways. The one with such great medicine."

"I spoke with two tongues!"

"Before I am done you will not have one," Clay pledged, and reached for his Bowie. In doing so, his gaze lifted to the west, and what he saw made him dash to his Winchester and make rapidly off around the hill.

Corn Flower, dumfounded, watched the White Apache leave. Leaning on his left hand, he sat up, marveling at his deliverance. He would live! And when his people heard of his clash, they would hold him in higher esteem than ever before, for only the very bravest of men would dare confront the white traitor.

Hoof beats alerted Corn Flower to a small group of riders racing madly toward him. He saw they were white-eyes, four in all. Corn Flower was relieved because his tribe was on friendly terms with the Americans. They might help set his broken bone and give him some food before sending him on his way. Waving his arm, he shouted in his own tongue. Needlessly, as it turned out, since they had already spotted him and were thundering up the slope in a swirl of dust.

"Friends!" Corn Flower called, one of the few English words he knew.

The four riders stopped and sat contemplating the Maricopas. Corn Flower addressed them but was totally ignored.

"He can't be far ahead," Griffen guessed.

"We keep goin', then," Hanks said.

"What about these vermin?" Lane asked.

"Scalps are scalps in my book," Terrill said. "There's always a buyer somewhere." Gripping his saddle horn, he slid down. "You fellas go on. I'll catch up."

Griffen also dismounted. "No. We stick together

157

in case there are any more red bastards around."

Their conversation was not understood by Corn Flower. He assumed the white-eyes were talking about him, assumed they were walking toward him to help him, so he beamed and said in his own tongue, "I hope you understand enough to know that I will be forever grateful. And if you would be so kind as to take me to my village, I will have my people hold a celebration in your honor with all the meat and corn you can eat and all the women you can bed."

"What in the hell is this buck chatterin' about?" Terrill asked as he took up position in front of the Maricopa.

"Beats me," Griffen said. "He probably don't know himself."

Corn Flower smiled wider. He was feeling generous toward these simpletons who had unwittingly saved him, so he went on, "When I become chief, I will remember your deed and give orders to spare your lives if you should ever be captured."

"Windy cuss, ain't he?" Evans quipped.

"Figures," Griffen said. "If they ain't trying to gut you, they're trying to talk you to death." He moved to the right of the warrior. "Let's get this over with."

Corn Flower held up his good arm. "Help me," he said, and was shocked when the bearded man on his right and the skinny man on his left seized him by the elbows. Sheer agony coursed through him as he was roughly thrown flat and knees were placed on his shoulders to pin him in place. "No! No!" he screeched. "What are you doing?" Then he saw the hefty one pull a slender knife from a boot and comprehension froze his blood but not his mouth. Terrified, he threw back his head and screamed.

The wind had picked up since sunrise, whipping

among the hills and out over the flatland to the east. It carried the scream far and wide, brought every quavering note of mortal anguish to the ears of the White Apache and caused him to sprint a shade faster.

Clay made no effort to hide his tracks. The cowboys were too close for him to waste precious minutes, plus he figured Surgio Vasquez was with them and knew the wily tracker wouldn't be fooled for a second.

More important to Clay was finding a spot to make a stand, somewhere he could defend himself against superior odds. The problem was the lay of the land. Trees were few, and brush thin. Now, when he wanted to find an arroyo, there was none.

Clay glanced repeatedly at the high hill, thinking the cowboys would appear near the crown. He had gone half a mile and was well out in open country when he spied a dust cloud at the base of the very last hill. They were almost upon him, and he had nowhere to hide!

A shallow depression offered the only haven. No more than a wind-worn rut flanked by dry weeds, it was deep enough for Clay to throw himself down flat and still be below the level of the arid plain. He resisted the urge to take a peek and pressed his ear to the soil, listening to the rumble of onrushing hooves. They came closer, steadily closer, until he could feel the ground tremble. Then, they abruptly stopped, and he heard voices.

"Where the hell did he go?"

"I don't see him nowhere."

"Maybe he lit off north or south."

"Let's divide up. We can cover more ground that way."

"No," said someone sternly. "We stick together like I've been saying."

The horses bore southward and presently Clay stood to observe their dust disappearing in the haze. Apparently, he'd been wrong. Vasquez wasn't with them. He resumed his easterly jog, hopeful he might escape after all.

Not long after sunrise, the heat climbed. The day promised to be another scorcher. When once Clay would have frowned at the thought, he now accepted the weather as a matter of course. When once the heat ate at him like a red-hot knife, his hardened body now absorbed it without weakening.

Shimmering invisible bands danced on the horizon. Sweat poured down Clay's body; only his headband was keeping it from getting into his eyes. He remembered to reload the Colt and inserted a round into the chamber of the Winchester.

Clay thought about the bounty on his head. From the sound of things, practically everyone in the Southwest had heard of him. He wouldn't be able to go within five hundred yards of a town or he'd be blown to smithereens. There might even be wanted posters. Marshal Tom Crane had a reputation for being thorough.

Thinking of the lawman reminded Clay of Miles Gillett, and he unconsciously lifted a hand to his throat, to the spot where, months ago, a searing rope had nearly strangled the life from him. He wondered how Gillett had known to set a trap for him at Denton's, then wanted to kick his own backside when he realized the pattern was as obvious as an udder on a cow to anyone with the brains of a turnip.

Clay resolved to be more careful in the future. Ten members of that posse were as yet unaccounted for.

To complete his revenge, he must live long enough to finish the job. From now on, he would pick his targets at random and never fall into a set pattern anyone could detect. He had to be as wily as a coyote, as vicious as a sidewinder.

As if by design, an odd rustling sound alerted Clay to a large specimen, about ten feet off, slithering northward in a unique manner. At the rate he and the creature were traveling, they would surely cross paths. So, in order to avoid the rattler, Clay stopped and hunkered down, barely aware of the sun blistering his exposed skin.

At that instant, the cowboys returned. Clay saw them strung out in a line to the south, coming slowly toward him, riding back and forth as they scoured the plain. He looked for somewhere to hide, but this time there was no convenient depression. A few assorted cactus plants and a wealth of weeds—that was all.

Clay moved toward a high saguaro, forgetting about the sidewinder until the crackling rattle of its tail warned him he had blundered too close. Glancing down, he blinked on seeing the snake within a foot of his moccasins, coiled and ready to strike.

To move was to court death. Clay froze, looking from the rattlesnake to the cowboys and back again, willing the sidewinder to go about its business so he could take cover before he was seen. The reptile showed no such inclination. Rattling furiously, it glared at Clay's legs; it was ready to sink its wicked fangs into them if they so much as twitched.

The Box D hands drew nearer. Three were clustered to the west. But the fourth had strayed eastward and was much too close to Clay for comfort. The puncher was concentrating on the brush in his immediate area or Clay would have already been spotted.

Clay felt sweat trickle down his forehead, felt a salty drop seep into his right eye. His natural impulse was to blink but he controlled it, leery of the consequences. His eye would just have to sting. Any motion, however minor, would be all the incentive the sidewinder needed.

By this time, the cowboy was close enough for Clay to see his fingers as he drummed them on his leg. The rider was on the far side of the saguaro, his head bent. Suddenly, the puncher straightened, uttered an oath, and used his spurs while shouting at the top of his lungs.

"Here! Over here! I've found him!"

So many things happened so swiftly. The cowboy swerved around the saguaro, slapping leather as he did, clearing a Colt in a fluid sweep. The sidewinder, drawn by the thump of hooves, twisted toward the oncoming horse. And Clay, acting on pure reflex, leaped forward, gripped the rattler by the tail, and hurled the snake at the rider.

The smug smile the ranch hand had worn changed to a yelp of horror. He yanked on his reins to turn his mount and had begun to swing wide when the sidewinder struck him on the shoulder. Instinctively, he swatted at the rattler with both hands, but in doing so, he released the reins and his horse, spooked by the noise of those whirring rattles, bucked. Once was enough. The puncher became airborne, flying in an arc that ended on top of the saguaro.

Clay had taken only a single step when the horse shot past him. He took another lunging stride and threw himself at the saddle, catching hold of the apple with his left hand. There was a brutal wrench, and he was torn off his feet, nearly suffering a dislocated shoulder. Exercising all his strength he pulled, scrambling atop the animal before he lost his purchase.

At last, Clay had a horse under him, but it was too panic-stricken to obey tugs on the reins or the pressure of his legs. Clay tried. How he tried. But the horse was still in full flight after a quarter of a mile, and was heading for the ranch!

Clay leaned back and hauled on the reins, throwing his whole weight into it. The horse fought him, teeth bared, snorting and jerking its head. He was able to slow the animal to a trot but could not force it to stop.

To the rear a rifle banged, then a second.

Twisting, Clay saw that two of the hands had given chase while the third had stopped to tend the man who had slammed into the cactus. The two had shucked their rifles and were firing at random, a waste of ammunition as far as Clay was concerned since only the most expert of marksmen could hit the broad side of a barn from horseback.

As if to prove Clay wrong, his horse suddenly whinnied and buckled, slinging him from the saddle. He had a fleeting vision of dry brush; then he was rolling end over end, limbs askew, until brought up short by a scruffy mesquite growing in the middle of nowhere.

Shrugging off the effects, Clay rose onto one knee and turned. The horse was on its side, wheezing and coughing blood, while the cowboys were angling wide to flank him, both reloading at a full gallop.

Clay took a hasty bead on the beefy man to his right and fired. The rifleman threw both hands into the air, then oozed from the saddle as if his bones had been rendered mush.

A quick swivel to the left and Clay had the other

puncher in his sights. But not for long. The second man knew a trick often practiced by Indians, and as Clay aimed, the man slid onto the opposite side of his mount. All Clay could see was the cowboy's boot and forearm.

The cowboy intended to move in closer, then shoot at Clay from under the neck of his horse. It was a tactic that would have worked on most white men. Clay Taggart, however, knew Indian ways better than most. In some respects, he had become more Indian than white. So, when confronted by the puncher's clever ploy, he did as an Apache would do: he shot the man in the foot.

There was a shriek of agony as the man lost his hold and thudded onto the hard earth. The horse kept on going, leaving its rider lying out in the open, unprotected.

Clay went to finish off his enemy, but the hand had plenty of fight left. A bullet nearly clipped off part of Clay's ear. Diving, Clay squirmed behind the solitary mesquite and squirmed past it since its slender branches wouldn't stop a rain of lead. A wise move, as it turned out, since the cowboy peppered the mesquite the very next second.

Jumping erect, Clay imitated a roadrunner, weaving toward the haven offered by nearby saguaros. Slugs bored into the soil on either side of him, several missing by the width of a cat's whiskers. The puncher's rifle went empty as Clay flung himself flat.

Since a man could never know how many shots he'd need at any given time, Clay availed himself of the brief respite to reload. The Box D hand was no longer where Clay had last seen him. Thanks to a thin trail of blood that led into a growth of wispy grass, figuring out where he'd gone wasn't difficult.

Clay edged through the cactus, never exposing himself, waiting for the cowboy to make the first mistake. From out of the blue a bullet smacked into a cactus next to him, sending bits flying. Going prone, he searched the plain and caught glimpses of the third gunman and the one who had fallen on the saguaro. Both were stealthily moving toward him from different directions.

Now Clay had three enemies to worry about. To make matters worse, the stand he was in measured no more than ten feet in diameter, which did not give him much room to maneuver. Much as he wanted to, he couldn't make a break for it; they'd cut him down before he went five yards.

From behind a thick cactus, Clay settled the Winchester's front sight on one of the stalking punchers, a tall man sporting a bushy beard. When the cowboy darted into the open, Clay stroked the trigger. The man went down but was still alive seeking cover behind a small boulder.

In angry response, the three Box D men cut loose, blasting shot after shot, raking the stand from top to bottom and side to side.

Clay could only kiss the ground, his hands protectively shielding his head. Pieces of cactus sprayed down on him. Slugs bit into the dirt. Something stung his elbow. Moments later, all three punchers had emptied their rifles, and Clay seized the opportunity to sling the Winchester over his back, draw both Colts, and rise, bursting from cover.

The wounded man in the grass was caught in the act of feeding cartridges into his gun. He glanced up in surprise and tossed the rifle down to make a play for his six-shooter.

Both of Clay's pistols boomed. The wounded man melted, his face blank as a slate. Pivoting, Clay saw the other two, one upright and firing as he advanced, the other behind the boulder, working a rifle lever.

Clay planted both legs and took them on in a stand-up gunfight, shooting calmly, cooly. The first rule of a shootout: shots must never be rushed. It was akin to committing suicide. The man who came out on top was invariably the man who had kept his head while all those around him had lost theirs.

These cowboys proved the rule. They blazed away indiscriminately, relying on the volume of their gunfire to accomplish what the quality of their marksmanship could not.

Clay dropped the bearded hombre with a dead center shot to the man's left eye. He felled the second cowboy with a pair of shots to the chest. Then, he strode over to insure they were wolf meat. The second hand moved feebly and stared at him through slitted eyes.

"Bastard!" The growl was barely audible.

"You made your bed," Clay said.

"They'll get you," breathed the cowboy. "Pretty soon the whole territory will be after your mangy hide. You won't last out the year, traitor."

"You won't last five minutes."

Turning scarlet, the man lashed out with a leg, trying to rake Clay with a spur. The attempt was more than his punctured body could take. Gurgling deep in his throat, he stiffened, clawed at his chest, then died.

"Adios," Clay said. He stooped to collect the man's guns but stiffened on hearing an approaching horse. In the distance, a single rider galloped from the west. Another cowboy, Clay mused. Another fool letting greed get the better of him.

Clay stepped to a prickly pear and squatted. Resting the tip of the barrel on one of the arms, he mentally measured the range and tested the wind. The stock was warm to his cheek, the trigger cool to the touch. He aimed with marked deliberation, and when he felt confident, he fired. His intent was to bring down the rider, but at that range any error, however slight, was enough to throw a bullet well wide of the mark. In this case, the horse crashed down, and neither the animal nor the man moved again.

Where there was one, there might be others, and Clay had no wish to tangle with more Box D hands. Forgetting about the guns, he moved slowly toward the sole horse still in the vicinity. Its reins were caught in a jumping cactus, otherwise it would have hightailed it toward the ranch like the rest.

Clay gingerly pried the reins free and vaulted into the saddle. The horse made a halfhearted attempt to throw him, but Clay showed it who was boss, and it calmed down. Gazing once at the bodies sprawled on the baking plain, Clay Taggart rode to the southeast, his bronzed figure gradually shrinking in size until it vanished in the shimmering haze.

Hours later, miles away, another man saw a figure coming toward him from out of the haze, and his right hand swooped to one of his ivory-handled Colts. On studying the toiling form, the rider smirked and galloped to intercept him.

Surgio Vasquez, a heavy saddle over his left shoulder, a rifle in his right hand, slowed and squinted, his face beaded with perspiration, his shirt soaked. He licked his dry lips and frowned. "Come to gloat, Santee?"

Billy Santee chuckled. "Who, me? Hell no, pard," he answered. "I thought you might need a helpin' hand."

"From you, no."

"Techy, ain't we?" Santee rose in the stirrups and put on a great show of scanning every which way. "Lose that cayuse of yours?"

"Not that it is any business of yours, but he was shot out from under me," Vasquez said, shuffling on.

"The White Apache?"

"The White Apache."

The young gunman let his mount fall into step beside the tracker. "And Denton's men?"

"Dead. All dead."

"The White Apache bed them down too?"

Vasquez nodded. "And some Maricopas I found."

"Injuns too?" Santee cackled and slapped his thigh. "Damn, if this Taggart isn't a man after my own heart! He must like to kill almost as much as I do!" A thought struck him and he sobered, afraid his thunder had been stolen. "He is still alive, I take it?"

"Sí."

Santee's face creased in a contented grin. "All's well that ends well, I reckon."

Although Vasquez was too tired from having lugged his saddle for over an hour to expend more breath talking, he had to ask, "Has the sun fried your brain? Our boss will be very upset with us, and you know how he can be."

"'Tain't our fault. Denton planned the ambush, not us. He'll have to account for everything." Santee removed his hat to mop his brow with a sleeve. "You tried your best. I tried mine. Mr. Gillett won't hold it against us."

"I wish I had your faith in human nature," Vasquez said sourly.

"There's only one thing in this whole world I put

faith in," Santee said, and he gave his pistols a pat. "These. They ain't never failed me yet."

"One day you will meet someone faster. Everyone does, sooner or later."

"Maybe so, but I'm not going to lose sleep over it. Life is for livin'." Santee nodded at the tracker's saddle. "Are you sure I can't fetch you a new horse? Must be all of ten miles to the ranch yet."

Vasquez stopped. "You would do that for me?"

"Hell, I'm in such a good mood, I'd help anybody," Santee replied. Laughing gaily, he trotted northward.

At that same moment in time, elsewhere, another person was in comparable spirits, which in itself was not remarkable except that this other person was a stoic Apache.

Delgadito the Chiricahua sat on a flat rock beside a tranquil spring and munched on a piece of rabbit meat. Many sleeps had passed since last he felt so good about things. And he owed it all to Clay Taggart. Or, rather, to the white-eye's death. With the White Apache gone, Delgadito was now free to take up the leadership of his band again. He must first convince them he was worthy, but he was confident a way would present itself.

From across the small spring, Ponce broke the silence. "What will we do when we reach the Dragoons? Go on as before?"

"There is no other path for us," Cuchillo Negro said. "Palacio will not let us mingle with our people."

"He cannot stop us!" Fiero said.

"The army can. And I would not put it past Palacio

to whisper in the right ears that we are back on the reservation," Cuchillo Negro remarked.

"We should have let *Lickoyee-shis-inday* kill him," Fiero declared, bestowing a meaningful look on Delgadito.

In too fine a fettle to let himself be bothered by the implication, Delgadito commented cryptically, "There were other chiefs before Palacio. There will be other chiefs after him."

"Do you intend to challenge him?" Ponce asked.

"He is too clever to give me cause," Delgadito said. "To give any of us cause." He noticed one of their horses staring at the undergrowth, and he did the same but saw only a sparrow perched on a limb. "No, to dispose of Palacio we must be as clever as he is."

"You plan to kill him, then?" Ponce pressed.

"Who is to say how *Yusn* will guide our steps?" Delgadito hedged. "I only know that the backs of our people are bent by the yoke of the whites. I know they must be freed and allowed to roam this land as in days of old. We are the *Shis-Inday*, Men of the Woods, not Men of the Desert."

"You always talk well," Fiero said, "but the time is past for talk." Pausing, he looked at each of them in turn. "No band can be effective unless it has a leader. Who will lead us now that White Apache is gone?"

Here was the opportunity Delgadito had waited for. He opened his mouth to say that of them all he had the most leadership experience, and as such, he should be given another chance to prove himself, when suddenly the alert horse nickered and out of the vegetation came a lone rider whose lake-blue eyes lit with warmth on seeing them.

"White Apache!" Cuchillo Negro said. "We believed you were dead."

"The white-eyes are poor shots," Clay Taggart said, dismounting. He was glad to be among them again but did not show it, according to their way. His happiness was tempered, though, by the loss of Amarillo, which he feared they would hold against him.

Predictably, the four warriors gave no hint of their feelings.

Cuchillo Negro was secretly pleased at the turn of events. Of late he had grown to respect the white man, and the more he did, the more he disliked seeing the unsuspecting Taggart manipulated by Delgadito.

Fiero was elated for all of five seconds, until he remembered the fate Amarillo had suffered and recalled Delgadito's words concerning the treacherous nature of all white-eyes. And to think he had helped Taggart against Pedro Azul!

Ponce was the only one who did not care much one way or the other. He liked the white-eye, but he would not display his affection in public. And since learning Delgadito was distrustful of the American he had twice the reason to remain aloof.

Of all the Apaches, only Delgadito burned with passion, but not that of friendship. He pulsed with burning resentment at being thwarted again, and it required all his self-control to stop from leaping up and burying his knife in Taggart's heart. Since it would not do to have the white man suspect his true feelings, he said, "Welcome back, *Lickoyee-shis-inday.*"

"Thank you," Clay said, stepping to the spring. The lack of friendly overtures upset him, confirming, in his mind, that they were angered by the loss

of Amarillo. To gauge their feelings he prompted,
"Glad to see me again?"

Delgadito the Chiricahua looked White Apache
straight in the eye and said earnestly, "You have
no idea how much this means to me." He beckoned.
"Come. Join us. We have a future to plan."

QUICK KILLER

Prologue

His name was Chawn-clizzay and he was an Apache. In the language of his people the name meant "goat," and it certainly fit him this day as he scaled the high wall of a rocky gorge with the graceful ease and marvelous agility of a mountain goat. Overhead, the scorching summer sun blistered the arid Arizona landscape. The air was as still as death; not so much as a single leaf stirred anywhere.

Corded muscles rippling, Chawn-clizzay came to a wide shelf and stopped to check his back trail. He knew someone was back there, knew someone had been trailing him for half a day, yet he had not been able to catch more than one brief glimpse of the one shadowing him. And while Chawn-clizzay would never admit as much to another warrior, he had grown very worried.

Apaches were masters at moving stealthily and avoiding detection, able to rove the countryside without leaving a trace of their passing. It was said they were virtual ghosts, unseen and unheard until they cared to be. Like all men in his tribe, Chawn-clizzay had been schooled at a very early age in the art of being a living specter.

Yet now Chawn-clizzay's skill was doing him little good, and he could not understand why. When he first became aware of the man in the red headband, he had tried every trick he knew to shake the mysterious stalker. He had stuck to the rockiest, hardest ground, avoided skylines and open slopes, doubled back on himself several times, and more. To no avail. His pursuer had never lost the scent, never once been fooled. Of that he was certain.

What kind of man was he up against? Chawn-clizzay wondered as he scoured the jagged mouth of the gorge far below. He had no doubt the man had come to kill him for the bounty being offered by the white-eyes. Although he could not say exactly how he knew, he did.

Chawn-clizzay recalled his one glimpse, earlier that day, when he had stopped to quench his thirst. He had risen, wiped his mouth with his sleeve, and idly scanned the nearby rimrock. And there the man had been, brazenly standing in the open, his rifle glinting in the bright sunlight. Chawn-clizzay had been so surprised that he had gaped in disbelief until the lean figure in buckskins had melted into the shadows.

Many times over in the next several hours Chawn-clizzay had wondered why the man had done what he did, particularly when it would have been so easy for the stranger to pick him off from a distance. It was almost as if a challenge had been issued, as if the man wanted Chawn-clizzay to know he was being hunted so that he would have a fighting chance. But that was a ridiculous idea. No known enemy fought his people on their own terms because the Apaches won every time. They were the best at what they did, and justifiably proud of their prowess.

Chawn-clizzay's pondering was interrupted by a hint of motion several hundred yards away. Riveted to the cluster of boulders in question, he tucked his rifle to his shoulder and waited with a patience born of long practice for the hunter to show himself. Time dragged by, but the man in buckskins didn't appear.

Chawn-clizzay snorted like an angry buffalo, pivoted on his heel, and resumed scaling the wall. Presently he gained the top, and from this new vantage point he surveyed the gorge from end to end. No flash of red or brown gave the presence of the stalker away. He began to wonder if perhaps he wasn't behaving like a small child and letting his imagination play tricks on him. Or maybe he was simply mistaken. Most likely the stranger had gone elsewhere.

A barren switchback brought Chawn-clizzay to a tableland dominated by yucca. He broke into a tireless dogtrot so he could reach the Chiricahua Mountains that much sooner. As with most full-grown warriors, he was capable of covering seventy miles in a single day. Since he only had twenty miles to go to reach his destination, by nightfall he would be with his family. The thought brought a rare smile to his lips.

For over twenty minutes Chawn-clizzay ran eastward, until he detected movement out of the corner of his left eye. He looked around, expecting to see wrens or sparrows off in the brush. To his utter consternation, he saw the man in the red headband.

The stranger was over a hundred yards off, jogging on a parallel course. And he was staring right at Chawn-clizzay and grinning!

Chawn-clizzay broke stride and slowed, but only for an instant. Darting to the right, he plunged deeper into the yucca, weaving this way and that as openings presented themselves. When he had gone fifty feet he slanted to the left and crouched. Cocking his Winchester, he strained his ears to hear the telltale rustle of vegetation sure to give the stalker away. But all he heard was the faint whisper of the northwesterly breeze that had cropped up.

When half-an-hour had gone by and nothing happened, Chawn-clizzay bore to the south in a wide loop that would bring him out on the east side of the tableland. He was more troubled now than ever. The man in buckskins seemed to be playing some sort of strange game with him. Even worse, the man seemed to be his equal at woodcraft, for somehow the stranger had been able to scale the gorge and keep up with him without being detected.

Chawn-clizzay wondered if his pursuer were an Apache. He hadn't gotten a close enough look to see the man's features, but he had noticed the man's hair, which was cut short instead of being allowed to grow to the shoulders, or longer, as was Apache custom.

A clearing appeared. Chawn-clizzay mistakenly went straight across it rather than going around. He was halfway to the other side when he belatedly registered a hawkish form poised among the yucca to the north. Spinning, he brought his rifle to bear, but he did not yet have the gun level when thunder peeled and an invisible hammer slammed into his chest. Dimly, he felt himself hit the ground. There was a ticklish sensation as blood gushed from the wound, splattering on his neck. He tried to rise but his body refused to obey his mental commands.

Suddenly the man wearing the red cloth headband loomed above him. Chawn-clizzay saw a stern, almost cruel face, half-white, half-Indian. The dark eyes fixed on his were as cold as ice.

"You were careless, Chawn-clizzay," the man spoke in flawless Apache. "You should have known they would send me sooner or later."

Chawn-clizzay licked his unexpectedly dry lips and forced his mouth to move. "Who—?"

"Tats-ah-das-ay-go."

At last all was clear. Chawn-clizzay thought of his devoted wife and young son and prayed *Yusn* would grant him the strength to draw his knife and thrust. Just once was all it would take. He attempted to move his hand and had to choke back intense frustration when his arm wouldn't budge. Moments later his suffering was cut short by an inky veil that enveloped his mind. The last sight he beheld was the killer's countenance creasing in the same grin as before, only now he realized it wasn't a grin, after all. It was a smug, triumphant smirk.

Then everything went black.

Chapter One

About the same time that the Apache named Chawn-clizzay breathed his last, another man was taking a deep breath to fill his lungs with air. Clay Taggart stood perched on a flat boulder on the bank of a narrow stream situated high in the remote, rugged Chiricahuas. Below him the stream widened into a murky pool not quite five feet deep.

Taggart stepped to the edge of the boulder, extended his arms, and dived. Cool water encased him in a velvety cocoon, all the more welcome because it afforded great relief from the burning sun. As his fingers brushed the muddy bottom, he arched his spine and whipped upward, cleaving the surface smoothly. Exhaling, he tread water and allowed himself to relax.

This was the first dip Taggart had taken in months, ever since a fluke of fate had resulted in his being taken in by a band of renegade Chiricahua Apaches.

Quick Killer

The *Shis-Inday*, they called themselves. The men of the woods. And now, should any of his old acquaintances see him, they would rightfully think he had gone Injun, as the saying went.

Taggart's dark hair was worn Apache style and hung to his shoulders in a shaggy mane. His skin had been bronzed a coppery hue, the soles of his feet coated with callouses. Except for his striking lake-blue eyes, he was the perfect picture of a robust, full-blooded Apache. And of late he had even begun to think like one, which bothered Taggart immensely.

Mere months ago, he had been a moderately successful rancher living not far from Tucson. Today, he was hiding out on the vast Chiricahua reservation, a wanted man, sought by the army and civilian authorities alike, despised by whites and most Apaches. How, he wondered, could so much have gone so wrong so rapidly?

The answer was as plain as the nose on Clay's face: Miles Gillett. It was the wealthy rancher who had seen fit to frame Clay in order to get his greedy hands on Clay's ranch. It was Gillett who had to shoulder the blame for the lynch party that left Clay for dead. And it was Gillett who was indirectly accountable for the bloody revenge Clay had taken on those who nearly hung him.

Suddenly, Clay had the feeling he wasn't alone. Swiveling in the water, he scoured both banks. Months ago he wouldn't have spied a thing out of the ordinary. But the many weeks he'd spent among the *Shis-Inday* had sharpened his senses to the point where he immediately saw the vague outline of a man crouched in the high grass. Acting as if he hadn't noticed, he swam leisurely to shore, to the strip of gravel where he had left his clothes and weapons.

11

Clay casually wiped his hands on grass and reached for his breechcloth. But instead of picking it up, he snatched his Winchester and took a running dive into the grass, rolling and flattening on his stomach as he landed. He leveled the rifle and worked the lever to feed a new cartridge into the chamber.

Fifteen yards off, the man abruptly stood. He was a handsome Apache with the weathered features typical of his kind, a rifle clasped in the crook of his left elbow. He made no move to employ the gun. Instead, he raised his other arm in greeting and said a single word, "*Nejeunee.*"

Clay slowly stood and eased the hammer down on his Winchester. "Friend," he said in response. His Apache was far from perfect, but he had the satisfaction of knowing he spoke it better than most other whites and was improving all the time. "I am pleased to see you, Cuchillo Negro. It has been seven sleeps since any of you have so much as spoken to me."

The Apache came forward, his inscrutable visage providing no clues as to the reason for his unforeseen visit. "It is time we talked, Lickoyee-shis-inday."

White Apache. The name had been bestowed on Clay by another warrior, the one responsible for saving him from the lynch party, a man Clay had assumed was a staunch friend until recently. "I will gladly hear your words. Wait a moment," he responded. In no time, he donned his breechcloth, shirt, and knee-high moccasins. Around his waist he strapped a pair of matching Colts in twin holsters. From the back of one dangled a large butcher knife. Twin bandoleers crisscrossed his chest. "Now I am ready."

Quick Killer

Cuchillo Negro stepped to a majestic willow and sat with his back to the wide trunk. Had Clay Taggart been able to peer into the warrior's mind, he would have been amazed to find that Cuchillo Negro was greatly concerned about his welfare. The two of them had never been all that close, so it would have interested Clay greatly to learn that Cuchillo Negro thought quite highly of him, but for a reason Clay would never have suspected.

Cuchillo Negro stared at Clay as he took a seat, then the warrior picked his statements carefully. "We have hunted together, skinned the same deer together."

"This is true," Clay acknowledged. He knew enough of Apache ways to realize that something of the utmost importance had brought the warrior to him, and he was eager to learn its nature. Ever since the band had returned from their last raid, the four warriors had virtually shunned him. Their cold attitude had bothered him initially, until he concluded they were upset because a fifth warrior, Amarillo, had been slain fighting his enemies.

"We drank from the same spring, slept beside the same fire."

"This too is true."

"Never once have I spoken in anger to you, like Fiero. Never once have I tried to make you follow my path instead of your own, like Delgadito."

"True," Clay said, while inwardly he filed the reference to Delgadito away for future consideration.

"So would you say we are brothers, White Apache?"

The question confused Clay. Given the history of the *Shis-Inday*, it was rare for them to regard outsiders as brothers. They had fought the Spanish when the Spaniards first came to the New World.

They had raided into Mexico as the whim moved them. They had resisted the influx of whites into their domain and lost a costly clash with the United States. To top it all off, they were even in a state of perpetual war with most other tribes.

Clay had spent months in the company of the renegade band that had saved him, and he'd gotten to know the five stalwart warriors fairly well. For the most part, the Apaches had never been more friendly than they had to be, the lone exception being Delgadito, the former leader who had lost his right to lead when his band was slaughtered by scalp hunters.

As for the others, there was Fiero, the firebrand who lusted for war as some men lusted for women. The youngest was Ponce, so eager to make his mark according to the time-honored Apache ways of stealing and killing. The fourth had been Amarillo. And here sat the fifth, Cuchillo Negro, the one who always held his own council, the one who spoke the least but whose influence always held great weight, the one who had always seemed so aloof. Yet he referred to Clay as he would his best friend.

To Clay, it made no sense. But he answered, "Yes, I would say we are brothers. After all we have been through together."

"Brothers listen to brothers," Cuchillo Negro said. Then he did an odd thing. He tilted his head and glanced upward. "Do you see the high limbs being rustled by the breeze?"

"Yes," Clay said.

"So can I. Yet we cannot see the breeze itself. No man can." Cuchillo Negro paused. "The thoughts of men are much like the wind. We can see the actions that come about as a result of thoughts, but we cannot see the thoughts themselves. Would you agree?"

Completely puzzled, Clay replied, "As always, you speak with a straight tongue."

"Sometimes the wind is so strong that it pushes against us, trying to move us against our will. Has this ever happened to you, Lickoyee-shis-inday?"

"Sometimes," Clay admitted. He figured the warrior would elaborate but Cuchillo Negro sat gazing at the treetops for the next couple of minutes, his knit brow indicating he was lost in reflection. Clay would have liked to quiz him at length but that wasn't the Apache way. Men spoke their peace at their own pace. To pry was to court their anger.

While the custom frequently bothered Clay, he admired the Apaches for their laconic natures. It was a welcome change from white society. There were no snoops or busybodies to contend with, no town gossips who had nothing better to do with their lives than spread the latest malicious rumors concerning people they hardly knew. In the Apache scheme of things, everyone was expected to mind their own business.

Cuchillo Negro cleared his throat. Unknown to Clay Taggart, inwardly he was in great turmoil. Meddling in the affairs of two others was strictly taboo, yet he couldn't bring himself to sit back and do nothing while the white-eye was being manipulated by Delgadito. Since White Apache had been accepted into the band, and had risked his life on their behalf on more than one occasion, Cuchillo Negro felt it only right that the white man be treated with the respect due all, not as a puppet in another's quest for power and prestige. But he had to be careful. He risked antagonizing Delgadito. Cuchillo Negro knew he had already overstepped the line that separated friendly advice from intentional meddling. Delgadito would be entirely justified in challenging him to formal, ritual combat if he found out. "Have you ever noticed that sometimes branches are broken by strong wind?"

"Yes," Clay said, at a loss to know how the remark applied to him. He was taken aback when the warrior abruptly rose.

"Take care, Lickoyee-shis-inday that the wind does not break you." Cuchillo Negro turned and walked off, and soon he was lost among the cottonwoods.

Frowning, Clay stood and hiked westward. This made twice that Cuchillo Negro had implied he couldn't trust Delgadito. The first time he had dismissed the notion as preposterous. After all, it had been Delgadito who saved him from being hung, Delgadito who later had gone to great lengths to safeguard his life. Surely, he had reasoned, Delgadito wouldn't have invested so much time and energy in his welfare unless Delgadito genuinely cared.

But now Clay wasn't so certain. Delgadito hadn't been quite as friendly during the week or so leading up to Amarillo's death. And since then Delgadito had wanted nothing to do with him, hardly the act of a staunch friend. Perhaps Cuchillo Negro had been right all along. Perhaps Delgadito had used him as some sort of puppet to suit a purpose Clay had yet to divine.

A flock of sparrows winged from a thicket on Clay's left, breaking his concentration. He passed on by and crossed a wide meadow. Several grazing horses glanced at him, then resumed eating.

After the last raid the Apaches hadn't returned to Warm Springs, the sanctuary they usually used, but to another isolated retreat hidden high in the Chiricahuas. Sweet Grass, they called it, because of the abundant forage to be found. The warriors had set up camp in a sheltered nook at the base of a high cliff. Clay had stayed with them the first week, until their cold treatment influenced him to seek a spot elsewhere. On a bench that straddled the lower slope of a mountain he'd found a suitable spot.

Several times during his climb Clay paused to survey the valley. Bathed in sunshine, the green of the verdant vegetation and the blue of the sinuous stream lent the scene the aspect of a literal Eden. Over half-a-mile away, a few stray tendrils of smoke wafted skyward.

Clay came to the bench and walked to his lean-to. He knelt, opened a pouch, and removed a couple of strips of venison jerky he had made himself. As he munched, he dwelled on the same problem that had confronted him for days, the issue of what to do next. Should he stay among the Apaches where he clearly wasn't wanted, or should he leave the territory for parts unknown? Venturing to Tucson or any of his other old haunts was akin to committing suicide since he was wanted by both the U.S. Army and the civil authorities. To complicate matters, a large bounty had been put on his head, dead or alive, a certain lure for every bounty hunter and money-hungry kid west of the Pecos.

Clay had always been a loner, always kept pretty much to himself, but he'd never figured on ending his days a complete outcast. He had a few close friends, a very few. He'd very much like to see them again, but he dared not. Once he traveled beyond the boundaries of the reservation, his life wouldn't be worth a plugged nickel. Not that it was worth any more in the reservation. He'd already made an enemy of Palacio, an influential warrior, and he wouldn't be at all surprised if Palacio sent someone to rub him out.

As if on cue, a jay higher on the mountain squawked in alarm. It was the kind of cry jays only voiced when they were extremely upset, either by the presence of a roving predator or intruding humans. And all the members of the band were down in the valley.

Clay cocked his head and listened intently. There might be a bear or mountain lion abroad, or perhaps even a rare jaguar. Delgadito had told him that many years ago jaguars were quite numerous in the Chiricahuas, but the spotted cats had almost died out shortly after the coming of the Spaniards.

Finishing his first piece of jerky, Clay went to bite into another when a squirrel erupted in a fit of irate chattering, in about the same vicinity as the jay. His curiosity was aroused. Stuffing the jerky back in the pouch, he grabbed his Winchester and padded into the ponderosa pines. The carpet of yielding needles underneath enabled him to move as silently as his shadow.

There had been a time when Clay Taggart wouldn't have bothered investigating. Back in his ranching days he had paid little attention to the cries of wild animals. Where Nature was concerned, he had been like a babe in the woods. Ironically, though, he'd always assumed he knew just about all there was to know about wilderness survival. Fortunately, his stint with the Apaches had disabused him of such idiocy.

To fully understand the ways of the wild, a person had to live in the wild. To fully appreciate the rhythms of the wildlife, a person had to experience those rhythms firsthand. The Apaches were adept at living off the land because in a sense they were as much a part of the land as the animals they shared the land with. They were at home in the mountains, on the plains, or in the deserts. The land was in their blood, one might say.

The same could not be said to an equal degree of Clay Taggart, but he had learned a whole new appreciation for Nature and had learned to relate to the multitude of creatures inhabiting Nature's domains. They were no longer simply dumb brutes put on Earth for humankind to exterminate at will. They lived, they breathed, they did things for a reason. Just as the jay and the squirrel must have done.

Both had fallen silent, so Clay had no means of pinpointing their exact locations. He slowed, searching the slopes above. If he saw a mountain lion, he'd take a shot. Apaches were especially fond of lion meat. A fresh kill would make a dandy gift to offer Delgadito and the others in the hope of mending fences. But if he saw a bear, he wouldn't fire unless his life was in peril. Apaches had high regard for bears, something Clay had learned only after coming to live among them. Bears were their wise brothers, as they put it, and no Apache would ever eat the flesh of a brother.

The forest was quiet, unnaturally so. There should be birds singing, insects buzzing, the chattering of chipmunks and squirrels. The silence had an ominous feel about it, like the lull before a storm.

Clay halted beside a pine and squatted. As Delgadito had taught him, he gazed through the brush at knee level, where the moving legs of large animals and men would be most obvious. Though he looked and looked, he saw nothing other than undergrowth.

As the minutes dragged by and nothing happened, Clay decided that whatever had agitated the wildlife had probably drifted elsewhere. He stood and turned, then realized the forest continued to be as still as a tomb.

Seconds later, the faint snap of a twig reached Clay's ears. Promptly ducking low, he moved warily in the direction the sound came from, diligently placing his feet with consummate care. He held the Winchester low to the ground so stray shafts of sunlight wouldn't glint off the metal and give him away.

Clay went forty yards without finding whatever had busted the twig. It could have been a deer, even a raccoon, but his gut instinct told him otherwise. He veered to the right, past a patch of briars. Suddenly, a section rustled. Automatically, he brought the rifle to bear, but held his fire when a rabbit hopped into the open. The second it saw him, it bounded off in prodigious leaps, making enough noise to alert every predator within hundreds of feet.

Clay dashed to a patch of scrub brush and flattened. Doing as he'd been instructed by Delgadito, he quickly covered as much of himself as he could with fallen limbs and leaves so that he would blend in with the background. Then he laid motionless, awaiting developments.

Less than a minute elapsed when something moved deep in the woods. A stocky form flitted across the ground toward the briars, halting among a packed growth of ponderosas a dozen yards away, where it vanished as if sucked down into the very earth.

Clay wasn't fooled. Moving only his eyes, he probed the forest for others, and when none appeared he focused on the strip of ground between the briars and the ponderosas, certain that was where the man would show himself again. Even though he knew it would happen, he was surprised when the heavily built Indian sprang up like a sprouting plant not eight feet from his hiding place.

It was an Apache, but one Clay had never seen before. The newcomer wore buckskin leggings and high moccasins. His chest was like that of a bronze sculpture, his sinews rippling as he moved. The man sniffed the air, then bent to see into the depth of the briars. Satisfied no one lurked within, the warrior straightened, put a hand to his lips, and twittered in perfect imitation of a mountain bluebird, a series of *terr-terr-terr* cries that would have fooled Clay into thinking they were the genuine article had Clay not seen the man make them.

Two more Apaches popped up from out of nowhere. One was skinny, a jagged scar on the left side of his chest. The other wore a faded blue army jacket with a torn sleeve. All three converged and huddled to consult in whispers.

Clay caught just a few snatches of meaningless words. The warrior sporting the scar glanced in his direction and he involuntarily tensed, dreading discovery. The last time he'd encountered an unknown Apache, the man had tried to kill him. But there was no outcry. The warrior's gaze drifted beyond him and around to the north.

At a gesture from the Apache wearing the jacket, the three men jogged off down the slope.

To ensure he wasn't spotted, Clay stayed put until they were out of sight. Rising, he hastened in their wake, anxious to learn the reason they were there. His best guess was that they were friends of the warriors in Delgadito's band. Yet, if that were the case, why were they sneaking into the valley instead of entering through the gap to the south? Had they been sent by Palacio to dispose of him?

Caution kept Clay a prudent distance back. Occasionally, he glimpsed the three Apaches as they glided downward. They came to the bench and right away saw the lean-to. He crept to a weed choked knob that afforded a clear view and watched them rummage through his meager belongings. The stocky one had the audacity to take a stick of his jerky.

Downward the trio went, to the edge of the meadow. Rather than cross, they went around, and Clay observed them test the breeze to guarantee they stayed downwind of the horses. They were leaving nothing to chance.

Clay became more troubled the farther the three warriors went. Friends of Delgadito's would hardly need to employ the degree of stealth being exercised by the newcomers. But maybe, he reflected, they weren't sure Delgadito was there so they were exercising typical Apache vigilance.

The warrior in the blue shirt took the lead. They slowed to a cat-walk shortly thereafter, spreading out as they drew within sight of the cliff.

Clay hung back, in a quandary over the right thing to do. He could fire a few shots to alert Delgadito, or he could bide his time and avoid making a fool of himself should the trio prove friendly. He choose the latter.

All four members of the renegade band were in camp. A low fire blazed, the wood crackling loud enough to be heard in the surrounding trees. Delgadito, Fiero, and Ponce were gambling with a deck of cards stolen from a ranch the band had raided several months ago, while Cuchillo Negro looked on without much interest.

Clay saw the three new Apaches lower themselves to the ground and crawl. His brain shrieked a strident warning that they must be enemies, but once again logic intervened and he persuaded himself the trio had indeed been sent by Palacio and were seeking him. Naturally, they wouldn't show themselves until they found their quarry.

Thus convinced, Clay didn't interfere when the one in the blue coat stopped behind a bush and parted the branches. He didn't move a muscle when the warrior poked a rifle through the opening. But when he saw the man take a steady bead on Delgadito and touch a thumb to the hammer, he knew beyond a shadow of a doubt that his first hunch had been the right one and the three newcomers were up to no good. Unfortunately, he had no time to fire warning shots, no time to do anything other than what he did; namely, to rear erect and charge the warrior about to fire.

Chapter Two

He came down out of Apache Pass with a pack animal in tow and made for Fort Bowie using the Tucson-Mesilla road. Clad in buckskins, his short hair crowned by a red headband, he was little different in appearance from the many friendly Indians and breeds who used the road on a regular basis. But there was something about this man that drew uneasy looks from other travelers and compelled those in his path to move quickly aside to grant him passage. Perhaps his sharply hawkish features were to blame, or his hard as flint eyes, or maybe the latent suggestion of a severely cruel disposition that shrouded him like a dark cloud.

Tats-ah-das-ay-go made no attempt to hide his disdain for those who moved out of his way. To his way of thinking, they were all weak and worthless, little better than human sheep who quaked at the presence of a wolf in their midst. Even the white-eyes gave him a wide berth, confirming his belief in his own superiority.

Most of those Tats-ah-das-ay-go passed noticed the burden his pack animal carried and flinched at the sight. A few crossed themselves or muttered hasty prayers.

Tats-ah-das-ay-go knew they were afraid and was pleased. He liked nothing better than to inspire terror since it served to enhance his reputation, which in turn made his job easier in the long run. By nightfall, news of his latest success would have spread far and wide, and when he went into town people would point at him behind his back and whisper to one another.

As well they should. Tats-ah-das-ay-go was proud of his accomplishment. He was the best there was at what he did, as the fourteen renegades rotting in the ground confirmed. Not for nothing was he the highest paid scout, tracker and hunter in all of Arizona.

A dust cloud rose in the far distance. Tats-ah-das-ay-go's dark eyes narrowed, reading details few others could. He knew it was a cavalry patrol long before the patrol spotted him. When the officer at the head of the column raised a gloved hand to halt the soldiers, Tats-ah-das-ay-go reined up.

"Hello, Quick Killer," said Captain Gerald Forester, a tough veteran of the Apache campaigns and one of the few officers who bothered to give the Fifth Cavalry scouts the time of day.

Quick Killer gave a curt nod.

"Is that who I think it is?" the officer asked.

"Chawn-clizzay."

"He give you any trouble?"

"You joke, white-eye," Quick Killer said indignantly. "None are as good as Tats-ah-das-ay-go. They are all easy."

"Including Delgadito?" Captain Forester responded, and grinned when the halfbreed flashed crimson with anger. It was common knowledge around the fort that twice Quick Killer had gone after Delgadito and each time returned empty-handed.

"His luck cannot hold out forever. I will get him one day. *Shee-dah.*"

"Then you'd better hurry," Captain Forester said, "or Nah-kah-yen will beat you to it."

Quick Killer was suddenly all interest. "What do you say?"

"Haven't you heard? Colonel Reynolds gave permission for Nah-kah-yen and two other scouts to hunt Delgadito's band down. They left the fort pretty near a week ago and headed deep into the Chiricahuas. Nah-kah-yen has probably lifted Delgadito's hair by now."

Raw resentment ate at Quick Killer's innards like a scorching acid. Nah-kah-yen was the only scout whose record came anywhere near matching his, and an abiding rivalry had sprung up between the two of them. Each was determined to outshine the other. Should Nah-kah-yen bring Delgadito to bay, it would diminish Quick Killer's standing tremendously.

"Nah-kah-yen *no vale nada,*" he spat without thinking.

"That's your opinion," Captain Forester said. "The colonel thinks right highly of him."

"Nah-kah-yen will fail," Quick Killer said, but his tone lacked confidence. For all his dislike of the Tonto, and despite what he said in public, he had to admit that Nah-kah-yen was extremely skilled. "If anyone brings in Delgadito, it will be me."

The officer removed his hat to brush dust from the brim. "Maybe it will. Nah-kah-yen might have bitten off more than he can chew this time around."

"I do not follow your trail."

"Haven't you heard? Word had drifted down from the Adjutant General's office that the turncoat we're after, the one called the White Apache, is riding with Delgadito. The two of them combined could be more than Nah-kah-yen can handle." Forester jammed the hat back on. "Well, enough dawdling. I have a patrol to make." He waved his arm and led his troops westward at a trot.

Quick Killer rode off, breathing shallow so as not to inhale the choking dust. Once clear of the cloud he swiftly brought his bay to a gallop, motivated by a sudden eagerness to have a talk with the colonel. He didn't slow down until the hill on which the fort was located hove into view.

The sentries and gate guards knew Quick Killer on sight so he was admitted without a fuss. He rode straight to the hitching post in front of the post headquarters. As he looped the reins, the door opened and out strode a burly sergeant whose bristly mustache seemed to stretch from ear to ear.

"Well, well, well. If it ain't the high and mighty Quick Killer," Sergeant Joe McKinn said. "Didn't expect you back for another week or better. Chawnclizzay must not have put up much of a scrap."

Quick Killer made no reply. He was not one to accord respect to those who showed him none, and he had a particular dislike for the sergeant who took advantage of every occasion to insult him. He stepped toward the doorway but the noncom barred his path.

"Where do you reckon you're going, scout?"

"I must talk to colonel."

"Do you have an appointment? Reynolds is a busy man. We can't be interrupting his work every time someone gets a hair to stop on by. Especially breeds."

The sergeant would never know how close he came to having his throat slit. Quick Killer's hand started to drift toward the hilt of his knife, but he stopped himself in time. To give in to his fury would result in his being branded a renegade, just like those he hunted for a living. The shame would be almost more than he could bear. "I must see colonel," he insisted.

"Run along and get drunk on *tiswin*. I'll pass on the word and let you know when he's free."

"I must," Quick Killer said. He went to go around but McKinn grabbed the front of his shirt.

"Didn't you hear me, breed? I told you to get lost."

Again Quick Killer's anger nearly got the better of him. He was on the verge of lashing out when a stern voice intruded from within the building.

"What the hell is the meaning of this, Sergeant? Release that man this instant."

McKinn let go and snapped to attention as 'a young officer appeared. A recent arrival to the fort and fresh out of the academy, Lieutenant James Petersen clasped his hands behind his rigid back and gave the noncom a withering look. "Correct me if I'm in error, Sergeant, but isn't this man one of our regular scouts?"

"Yes, sir," McKinn growled.

"Which means he's on the army's payroll, the same as we are. Which puts him on the same side as us, doesn't it?"

"Yes, sir," McKinn answered. He wanted to plant a boot on his own backside for not remembering the junior officer had been conversing with the orderly moments ago. In his estimation, Petersen was too damn green to be serving a hitch on the frontier. The man knew virtually nothing about Indians, and even less about Apaches and breeds.

"Then kindly explain to me why you felt it necessary to treat him the way you did?" Petersen demanded. As the newest officer at the post, he had been looking for a chance to put the arrogant know-it-all noncom in his place and this was the perfect opportunity. "It's hard enough, I understand, to enlist Apaches willing to fight against their own kind, without you scaring them off."

"There's more to it than that, sir," McKinn stubbornly held his ground. "If we don't put these bastards in their place, they get all uppity on us."

Petersen smiled smugly. "I had no idea you were such an expert on Indian affairs. Maybe I should contact the War Department and advise them to consult with you before making future decisions." He dismissed the sergeant with a wave. "Run along, mister, before I have you up on report. Unless, of course, you'd rather go on giving me guff and spend the rest of the day jogging around the parade ground while carrying a fifty-pound rock."

Quick Killer did not let his delight at the noncom's comeuppance show. He watched McKinn huff off, then straightened to impress the junior officer and said in his best English, "Please, sir. It is very important I speak to the colonel."

Lieutenant Petersen had been about to return indoors. The cause of the disturbance had not been all that important to him except as a means to teach the sergeant a lesson. Now he regarded the man before him with a mixture of curiosity and scarcely suppressed contempt. For all his talk about the need to treat the scouts decently, secretly he rated them as akin to intelligent animals trained to perform on command. "Does it involve a matter of life and death?" he asked, half sarcastically.

The scout took him literally. "Yes, sir."

"It does?" Petersen scratched his smooth chin, then motioned. "Come on in, then, and I'll see if the colonel will talk to you."

At Quick Killer's entrance the orderly behind the desk gave a start and commenced to rise out of his chair.

"At ease, Private," Petersen said. "I'll handle this."

The door to the office stood ajar. The lieutenant knocked, was bid to enter, and went in. Quick Killer heard the gruff voice of the commanding white-eye raised in irritation. He paid no attention to the gawking orderly but stood as if carved from wood.

"All right, you can go in," Petersen said on reappearing, and lowered his voice. "But don't take much of the colonel's valuable time. He has important duties to attend to."

How well Quick Killer recalled Reynold's white hair and mustache, a rarity among whites and Indians. Knowing that the white-eyes were fond of puffing out their chests and squaring their shoulders whenever they were in the colonel's presence, he did the same. "Thank you for seeing me," he said.

"Quick Killer, isn't it?" Reynolds said, setting down the ink pen he had been writing with. "I remember you from that wagon train business. Horrible, truly horrible."

Quick Killer recalled the eight Mexican traders who had been found the previous year. They had been on their way to Tucson from Chihuahua when they were ambushed in Coyote Canyon, very near the fort. The Apaches had been in such a hurry to take their plunder and leave that they hadn't bothered to mutilate their victims as they ordinarily did.

Quick Killer

Instead they had hung the Mexicans upside down over roaring fires. The stench had been awful, but Quick Killer would hardly call the deaths horrible compared to some he had seen.

"What can I do for you?" Colonel Reynolds asked.

"I learn you send Nah-kah-yen or Keen Sighted as you call him, after Delgadito."

Reynolds propped both elbows on his desk and cupped his hands. "It was Captain Parmalee who submitted the request. All I did was concur with his proposal. Why? How does this pertain to you?"

Quick Killer hid his annoyance at the revelation. He should have suspected that it had been Parmalee, since Parmalee always had liked Nah-kah-yen better. All fourteen scouts had learned to accept the favoritism as a fact of life, but it still galled him. "I want to kill Delgadito myself."

The colonel blinked, glanced at the lieutenant, and cleared his throat. "You know as well as I do that Captain Parmalee is in charge of the scouts. If you have a complaint, I suggest you take it up with him."

Quick Killer thought fast. "I come to you because men say you fair with Indian. Men say you can be trusted." He paused, disliking the need to act like a cur begging for food at the feet of its master but seeing no other way to get his heart's desire. "You know Delgadito is worst renegade of all. You know how many he has killed. It is time someone stop him. And I am the one."

"I have been kept informed of your outstanding record," Colonel Reynolds said, "and I dare say no one is better qualified to hunt Delgadito down. But I also recollect that you went after him before and failed to bring him in."

"I will this time," Quick Killer vowed.

"Maybe so. But, as I've stressed, it's not my place to decide. There is such a thing as a chain of command in the U.S. Army. I realize it's not a concept you can comprehend, but it means you must go to Captain Parmalee first and he will relay any pertinent requests to me. The disposition of the scouts is in his hands. You'll have to talk to him if you think you're being treated unfairly."

Severely disappointed, Quick Killer said, "He not listen."

"Do you want to file a formal complaint?" the colonel asked impatiently.

"No," Quick Killer said, knowing it would be a waste of his time.

"Fine. Is there anything else?"

"No." Rotating on a heel, Quick Killer left before his simmering resentment showed. He had been stupid to expect fair treatment from the white-eyes. They looked down their noses on all who were not of their race, on Mexicans and Indians and blacks, but most especially on those of mixed ancestry like himself. The only thing that could be said in their favor was that they were no different from those they despised. Mexicans and Indians and blacks also looked down on his kind.

It was a heavy burden for any set of shoulders to bear, and Quick Killer had been doing so for twenty-nine years. He had been constantly mistreated from the day he was old enough to stand until the day he killed for the very first time. And what a glorious day that had been! Just thinking about it sent a tingle of excitement coursing down his spine, for slaying that Navaho had taught Quick Killer a remarkable truth that had served him in good stead ever since: People treated those whom they feared with respect. Not genuine respect born of high esteem, but respect bred by the very oldest of human instincts, self-preservation. He had discovered that those who formerly poked fun at him tread lightly if they believed their lives might be forfeit if they did not. How sweet life had become! he reflected. On the day that Navaho died, he had been reborn.

"Hey, buck! Are you fixing to grow roots there, or can I mosey on by?"

Quick Killer glanced up at the gruff hail and was annoyed to find he had blundered into the middle of the rutted track the wagons took from the sutler's store to the gate. The muleskinner bellowing at him was an older man he knew but whose name he couldn't remember. He moved out of the way and the wagon rattled on by.

Swiftly, Quick Killer made his way to the small building housing the office of the Chief of Scouts, as the army styled their liaison with the warriors who had volunteered to so serve. Parmalee insisted that all his scouts knock before entering, but this day Quick Killer didn't bother.

The captain was caught by surprise. He sat in his chair, his feet propped on his desk, a half-empty flask tipped to his lips. As the door swung wide, he hastily lowered the bottle out of sight and swung his feet to the floor. "What the hell!" he blurted. "What do you think you're doing, barging in here like this?"

Quick Killer halted in front of the desk and shifted his rifle from his left hand to his right. He did not rant and rave as whites would have done. He simply stared.

"Tats-ah-das-ay-go," Captain Vincent Parmalee said, slightly slurring the syllables. He had taken the time to learn the Indian names of all the scouts, not because he cared a damn about them, but because the army claimed it was a means of establishing a working rapport. Had it been Parmalee's choice, he would have had nothing to do with the lot of them. To him, they were filthy, ignorant savages, hardly better than the renegades they hunted.

Parmalee resented them not only for who and what they were, but because he had been picked against his will to serve as the officer in charge. He had objected strenuously, to no avail. None other than General George Cook himself had decided that it took an Apache to catch an Apache. And Colonel Reynolds, in implementing the program, had chosen the only officer who had ever spent any time among them. It had been Parmalee's misfortune to have spent several months prior to his enlistment working on a boundary commission that had dealings with the Mimbres. He'd pointed out to the colonel that he had hardly spoken three words to an Apache the entire time, but that hadn't mattered. Reynolds had made his choice, and the decision had been final.

Now Parmalee looked into the smoldering eyes of the one scout he secretly feared and put on a blustery front. "The next time you want to see me, Tats-ah-das-ay-go, by damn you'd better show some courtesy and knock first. You wouldn't want me entering your lodge without permission, would you?"

Quick Killer stayed silent, his contempt knowing no bounds. He could practically smell the white-eye's fright, and it insulted him to think that he had to work under such a weakling.

Parmalee licked his thin lips, then casually jammed the cork back into his flask and slid the whiskey into a drawer. "Now that we've settled your rudeness, would you mind telling me what the devil has you in such high dudgeon?" He paused, gazing through the doorway at the headquarters building. "Oh. I see. You've brought back Chawn-clizzay already. You're to be commended for a job well done."

"Not job I want," Quick Killer said.

"Oh?" Parmalee had regained his composure and assumed the superior air he always put on around the scouts. "Now I get it. You've heard about Nah-kah-yen."

"I should go after Delgadito. Not him."

"As I recollect, you had your chance and failed."

"Delgadito not like other Apaches. He much smarter, clever like a fox."

"Smarter than you, at any rate," Captain Parmalee said. "But just so you'll know, all things being equal, I doubt Nah-kah-yen will do much better than you did. But he has an edge."

"Edge?"

"Yep. He's been wanting to go after Delgadito for months, but I kept putting him off, telling him that he'd be wasting a lot of effort for nothing. The Chiricahua and Dragoon mountains cover a hell of a lot of territory. It'd be like looking for a needle in a haystack." He hooked his fingers behind his head. "But Nah-kah-yen is a persistent cuss. He came up with a brainstorm that might enable him to do what no else has done."

"What is brainstorm?" Quick Killer wanted to know.

"An idea. A bright idea." Parmalee chuckled. "Since Nah-kah-yen knew he couldn't get at Delgadito directly, he started nosing around the reservation, trying to find out who else was in the band. At first no one would give him the time of day, but then someone let it slip that a young buck named Ponce is one of those who rides with

Delgadito. Later, Nah-kah-yen learned that Ponce is partial to sneaking into one of the villages now and then to see his sweetheart."

Quick Killer's face didn't show the shame he felt at not having thought of the idea before his rival. He had taken it for granted that no one would turn the renegades in and never made the attempt.

"So how could I refuse when Nah-kah-yen asked me for permission to go after the band? It's the best lead we've had in years. We might even be able to kill two birds with one stone."

"The White Apache?"

"You've heard, have you?" Parmalee nodded. "Yet another reason for me to let Nah-kah-yen have a try. Command has made a priority out of this Taggart character. They want him, want him badly. More than they want Delgadito."

Here was information of some consequence and Quick Killer filed it for future consideration. "That why they pay large bounty?"

"You're learning. It'll be quite a feather in Nah-kah-yen's cap if he kills both Delgadito and Clay Taggart." Parmalee began sorting through a stack of papers. "As for you, I have another job you might like."

"I want Delgadito and this Lickoyee-shis-inday."

"We've just been all through that," Parmalee said irritably. He pulled out a sheet and studied it. "Here's the man I want you to try to find. His name is Chipota—"

"The Lipan," Quick Killer said with a measure of disgust.

"Don't sound so put out. He's been raiding for four months now, and he recently stole a shipment of flour and other foodstuffs bound for Fort Grant."

"I not become scout to fight men who steal food

for families," Quick Killer protested.

"You don't have the luxury of choosing who you go after and who you don't," Captain Parmalee reminded him. "Technically, we're not even supposed to let you kill these renegades. That should be our job. But it's a hell of a sight better all around if we give you boys a free reign. You get the job done with a minimum of fuss and everyone's happy." He set the paper aside. "Just so the Eastern press doesn't find out. Those damned bleeding heart journalists would have a field day at our expense."

Quick Killer turned and walked to the entrance, stopping when the officer said his name.

"One more thing. I don't want you getting any notions about going after Delgadito yourself. So help me, if I find you've disobeyed a direct order, I'll have you up on charges so fast your head will swim."

Without saying a word, Quick Killer went out, closing the door quietly behind him. It took all of his self-control not to slam it. Striding toward his horse, he pondered the setback. Gradually, a sly smile spread across his bronzed features. Yes, he would go after Chipota the Lipan, who raided the country to the north. But in order to deceive Chipota, who might have spies everywhere, he would have to take a roundabout trail getting there. The way he saw it, the wisest thing to do was to swing around to the southwest and circle until he reached Lipan country. And if, in so doing, he just happened to cut through the heart of the Chiricahua and Dragoon mountains, that was sheer coincidence.

Quick Killer didn't care what Captain Parmalee said. The threat of being disciplined held no weight with him. All that mattered was being the best. All that concerned him was his reputation. Delgadito—and the so-called White Apache—would be his, and no one else's.

Chapter Three

Had the warrior in the blue coat fired at the very second he sighted down his barrel at Delgadito, the lives of many innocents would have been spared. But the man hesitated to be sure of his shot, and in doing so he drastically altered the destiny of Arizona, for the worse.

For in those fleeting seconds of delay, Clay Taggart had time to leap to his feet and charge while venting an Apache war whoop and jamming his Winchester to his right shoulder. He snapped off a round, but the warrior in the blue coat spun at the same instant and the slug tore into the ground inches from the man's torso. Then Clay angled behind a tree to weather the return fire. But there was none. Peeking out, he was astonished to see the three warriors retreating northward as rapidly as their legs could carry them.

The undergrowth crackled and the four renegades appeared, rifles at the ready. Delgadito, Cuchillo

Negro, Fiero, and Ponce looked around for the source of the commotion they had heard. Clay immediately revealed himself, pointed at the fleeing men, and yelled in the Apache tongue, "They were going to shoot Delgadito."

With a yip the bloodthirsty Fiero was off in pursuit, bounding like a tawny cougar after panicked antelope, the jagged scar on his brow flushed scarlet from the excitement. Among a race that prided itself on its warlike qualities, he was the most warlike of all Chiricahuas. Fiero lived for the thrill of combat, for the pounding of his blood in his veins, for the fresh scent of the spilled blood of enemies in his nostrils. He was always at the forefront of every clash, spurred by his unbridled ferocity.

Second after the firebrand ran Ponce, the youngest member. Ponce, who had joined Delgadito to earn recognition and honor as a warrior, had of late begun to entertain doubts about the leader he had once thought the greatest of all. The slaughter of their fellows by scalp hunters had greatly shaken his confidence in Delgadito's ability, shaken it so badly that recently Ponce had toyed with the notion of abandoning the life of a renegade for life on the reservation. Despite his feelings, when his companions were threatened he was quick to spring to their defense.

Last to join the chase were Delgadito and Cuchillo Negro, the former the tallest of the four and next to Fiero the most superbly muscled. He presently pulled ahead of his companion and was in turn overtaken by the White Apache.

Clay Taggart looked at Delgadito, thinking that after so many days of being given the cold shoulder he had at last regained Delgadito's respect by saving the Apache's life. But the warrior didn't so much as glance around. And moments later a shot reminded him that he had to concentrate on the matter at hand if he intended to live long enough to smooth relations.

The fleeing trio had halted. Clay saw them seek cover behind pines and he dived for the ground as they commenced firing with a vengeance. The rest of the band did the same, Fiero the first one on their side to cut loose from behind a boulder.

Lead whizzed over Clay's head, clipping needles off the low branch of a tree. He fixed a bead on the stocky one who had taken his jerky but the man ducked back before he could squeeze the trigger. The exchange lasted less than a minute. Then the three ambushers broke and resumed their flight.

Once again Fiero led the pack of pursuers, whooping lustily and firing at random. Clay marveled at the hothead's audacity, for Fiero took risks more sensible men wouldn't take in a million years.

But Fiero didn't see it that way. He took calculated gambles, nothing more. He was a master at reading the intention of an adversary by the man's posture and reacting with his lightning swift reflexes before his life was put in serious jeopardy. Already he had observed that the warrior in the blue coat was the leader of the three strangers, and that whenever that warrior looked back and scowled, all three were certain to fire a volley seconds later. Now the warrior in blue did just that, and Fiero fell flat. Their bullets zinged harmlessly past.

Clay had crouched behind a log. He braced the Winchester barrel on top and once more tried to get the stocky brave in his sights. As before, the elusive threesome wheeled and sped off as he touched his finger to the trigger. Their shoot-and-run tactic was proving successful in that they had gained a wider lead. Afraid that they would escape, Clay poured on the speed.

There had been a time not long ago when Clay Taggart would have been left in the dust in a foot race with Apaches. But the months spent among them had steeled his sinews to a degree he never would have believed possible. Wilderness living had that effect on a man. Either he hardened, or he died. There was no place in the wild for the weak and the lazy.

Clay could jog for half a day without tiring. He could go two days without water, three without food. He had learned to ride for twenty-four hours at a stretch and not need sleep. He had become so much like an Apache that the other members of the band had regarded him as one of their own until Amarillo's death. And, oddly, he liked the change.

The fleeing warriors came to a glade and bore to the right. Both the stocky Apache and the man in the coat inadvertently pulled ahead of the third warrior when he paused to reload his rifle.

Snapping his Winchester up, Clay stroked the trigger a hair before Fiero and Delgadito. Their enemy staggered backward, clutched his chest, and toppled like a felled tree. Both the stocky one and blue coat stopped, but only momentarily. They plunged onward when they realized their friend was beyond help.

Apaches weren't prone to giving their lives needlessly for their fellows. Warriors who did so were branded fools and seldom spoken of highly unless they had been mortally wounded when they made the sacrifice. In such instances, since they already had nothing to lose, they would fight with a desperate fury, sometimes keeping an entire company of soldiers at bay while their people made good their escape.

The Apache attitude stemmed from the two main precepts of their existence: to steal without being caught, and to kill without being slain. To these ends the men were trained from infancy. Obtaining plunder and conducting warfare were all that interested them. And it went without saying that in order to enjoy plundering and killing, they had to be alive.

Fiero was the first to reach the fallen warrior. Hardly slowing, he nevertheless bashed the man's head with the stock of his rifle to ensure the warrior was dead.

Clay stayed abreast of Delgadito. He saw the Apache glance at their slain foe but observed no flicker of recognition. Meanwhile, the stocky warrior and blue coat had stopped pausing to fire every so often and were in full flight. The pair had changed direction, bearing to the northwest. Clay suspected they were making for their horses.

No one whooped or yipped, not even Fiero. The race was conducted in somber silence, with each man driving himself to his limit. The fleeing twosome no longer gained any ground, nor did Clay and his companions gain any. Through the woods to the north edge of the meadow the chase progressed, and it was here that luck favored the renegades.

Grazing nearby were a dozen horses. The man wearing the army coat went by without a second look, but the stocky warrior darted toward the animals. He lunged at a sorrel, caught hold of its mane, and went to swing up when the horse caught his strange scent and pranced skittishly to one side. Holding on, the stocky warrior ran awkwardly beside it, trying not to lose his footing. Abruptly, the horse spun, throwing the man off-balance. He stumbled and fell to his knees, his rifle flying from his hand. Frantically he reached for it, but it was beyond his grasp.

Fiero hurtled through the air and slammed into the stocky warrior, knocking the man flat. Quickly, the stocky Apache pushed to his knees, his knife flashing from its sheath. Fiero swung his Winchester, striking the gleaming blade and batting it aside. He then pivoted, ramming the muzzle into the other warrior's stomach. The stocky Apache doubled over but recovered almost immediately and flung himself to the left as Fiero went to strike him on the head.

Fiero intended to take the man alive. There were questions that had to be answered, and Fiero was a master at persuading captives to talk. He leveled his rifle and prepared to shoot, to wound, not to kill.

Suddenly a shot rang out to Fiero's rear. A hole blossomed in the center of the stocky warrior's broad chest. He looked down at the blood oozing forth, then snarled at Fiero. Fiero put a slug in the warrior's head.

Ponce ran up, beaming in triumph. "I shot him first," the younger man boasted.

Fiero had to resist an urge to lash out. "You did fine," he said sarcastically. "Now all we have to do is learn how to talk to dead men and we will know who sent him and why."

In a burst of insight Ponce understood the reason his companion was so upset. He felt like a chastened child for having fired, and he was about to explain that in the excitement of the chase he had simply gotten carried away when the White Apache and Delgadito passed them and Fiero dashed in their wake.

Clay had gained the lead. He could see the warrior in the army coat dozens of feet ahead on the timbered slope, still running smoothly with no evidence of being fatigued. Whoever the man was, he knew how to pace himself and had the stamina of a mustang. Clay fell into a steady rhythm, avoiding obstacles and thickets where necessary. The warrior came to the bench and bolted past the lean-to.

Breaking into the open, Clay pumped his legs for all they were worth. Behind him pounded Fiero and the others, each eager to be the first to get his hands on their enemy. Clay was determined not to let them outstrip him. He would do it himself, thereby demonstrating once again that he was worthy of being one of their number.

The slope steadily steepened. Clay ran on the balls of his feet, digging them in for better traction. Several times he had clear shots but didn't avail himself of the opportunities. He'd seen Fiero's expression when Ponce shot the stocky warrior and knew they needed the last one alive.

The man fleeing for his life knew it too. He glanced over his shoulder repeatedly, and when he discovered that the White Apache was narrowing the gap, he pushed himself recklessly.

Clay had one thing in his favor. He knew the vicinity better, had trekked the length and breadth of the canyon. He knew the slope they were climbing eventually flattened out on a high ridge. It was there, he figured, the three warriors had tied their mounts.

The man in the army coat might have made it if not for another fluke of fate. A maze of thorny brush barred his ascent so he cut to the left. In so doing, he encountered a handful of downed saplings uprooted during a storm. Normally he would have negotiated them with ease, but today he was in such a hurry that he misjudged a step and his foot caught on one. He crashed down, throwing out his arms to catch himself.

Clay had the chance he needed. He took three more long steps and leaped, his Winchester angled on high for a stroke that would have knocked the warrior out had it landed. But the Apache was a credit to his tribe. He rose on one knee and whirled just as Clay pounced. Their bodies collided and together they tumbled down the slope.

They rolled over a dozen feet, until Clay's shoulder smashed into a tree trunk. At that juncture a knife magically materialized in the warrior's hand, and Clay used the Winchester to deflect a stab to the throat. Racked by pain, he pushed upright barely in time to keep the Apache from burying the knife in his chest. The warrior swung again, striking the barrel, and Clay's finger accidentally tightened on the trigger.

The Winchester blasted.

To Clay's dismay, he saw the slug catch the warrior high in the shoulder and lift the man off his feet. The Apache fell against a small ponderosa, his knife falling from nerveless fingers. Game to the last, the warrior got his other hand under him and began to rise.

Piercing whoops heralded the arrival of Fiero and Ponce. They bowled the other Apache over and Fiero wound up astride his chest. In seconds they had battered him near senseless and roughly jerked him erect.

Fiero looked at the bleeding wound, then at Clay. "You are as bad as Ponce, Lickoyee-shis-inday," he commented. "We needed one alive."

Quick Killer

"I know, friend," Clay answered, using the word intentionally. While initially Fiero had hated him and despised having him in the band, at the time of Amarillo's death Fiero had come to accept the fact and been acting downright friendly on occasion. "My rifle went off by accident."

"There are no accidents. Only mistakes made by those who are too careless for their own good."

Clay was inclined to debate the point. But the nape of his neck abruptly prickled as if from a heat rash, and at the same time the two Apaches glanced up and over his head at someone behind him. Fearing there might have been a fourth ambusher no one had noticed, he spun to find Delgadito watching them.

"Take him to our camp, Fiero. We will get the answers we need there."

As always, Delgadito's features were the most inscrutable of all. Rarely could anyone read his thoughts. Clay Taggart would have given anything to know what was going through the former leader's mind. Yet had he known, he would have been shocked. For at that precise instant Delgadito, the Apache, was reflecting on how unfortunate it was that Taggart had survived the fight. In his cold heart Delgadito harbored an unquenchable thirst for revenge on the man who had spoiled his carefully laid plan to regain a role of trust and prestige in the Chiricahua tribe.

Once Delgadito had been a widely respected warrior. Once other warriors had flocked to join him on raids, had reveled in his victories and delighted in their share of the spoils taken. Once his name had been bandied about in the same breath as that of Mangus Colorado, Cochise, and Gokhlayeh. Then disaster had struck.

Delgadito had refused to bow to the white man's rule and fled into Mexico with a large number of followers. Scalp hunters drove them back across the border and later took them by surprise, slaughtering warriors, women, and children as if they were sheep. Only Delgadito and five others had survived.

For Delgadito, it would have been better had he died with the rest. He not only lost his wife, his relatives, and most of his friends, but he lost something he considered more precious. He lost his standing among the Chiricahuas. Where before he was regarded as a man of powerful medicine, now he was widely viewed as bad medicine, as someone the *Gans* had turned against and brought to ruin. No one wanted anything to do with him.

Delgadito had refused to give up hope. He had always prided himself on being adept at *na-tse-kes*, at the deep thinking that distinguished the common warrior from the great one. All Apaches of note were highly regarded for this virtue, and he had honed his skill to a degree seldom known.

He had schemed to have the white-eye he had jokingly named White Apache lead his small band on raids against those who had left Taggart for dead, dangling from a tree limb. He had hoped that a series of successful raids would go a long way toward changing the minds of his people. And he had intended, once White Apache outlived his usefulness, to reassume the leadership role rightfully his.

But everything that could go wrong had gone wrong. The *Nakai-hey* had captured Fiero, Ponce, and Amarillo, and it was White Apache who freed them. The scalp hunter responsible for the massacre of their band had given chase, and it was White Apache who tracked the butcher down and slew him.

Incredibly, Delgadito's few remaining followers turned to the white-eye for leadership, for the guidance they had formerly sought from Delgadito. White Apache's name became known among the Chiricahuas and other tribes, and everywhere it was mentioned in a more favorable light than Delgadito's.

Delgadito had seen the last wisps of power fading from his fingers as if they were tendrils of fading smoke. And the man he blamed, the man he wanted to destroy, was Clay Taggart. To that end, he was trying to poison the hearts of Fiero, Ponce, and Cuchillo Negro against the white-eye. To that end, he had blamed Amarillo's death on White Apache's bad medicine.

Now, as Taggart stood looking hopefully at him, Delgadito turned on his heel and followed Fiero and Ponce down the mountainside. Cuchillo Negro awaited them below and fell into step next to him.

"You did not run very fast," Delgadito said in tactful reproach.

"The last I knew, a *Shis-Inday* could run as fast as he pleased."

Delgadito cast a frown at the only man he regarded as a true friend. "Why must you twist my words all the time of late? Why has your heart grown so bitter toward me?"

"Lickoyee-shis-inday."

"What sorcery has he worked to turn you against me?"

"I am not against you so much as I am for him."

"You speak in riddles."

Cuchillo Negro pointed at the captive. "White Apache saved your life, yet still you seek to take his."

"Can you read another man's thoughts then?"

49

"Yours," Cuchillo Negro stated flatly. "I know you as I know myself. I know the trails your thoughts take, the secrets you share with no one else."

"Do you?" Delgadito tried to say with scorn that wasn't there. "One with so much power should be a medicine man, not a simple warrior."

"You hurl words as if they were rocks, yet you do not deny what I have said."

Delgadito slowed because he did not want anyone to overhear the next part of their conversation. Fiero and Ponce were yards off, hurrying onward. A look back showed White Apache sulking far behind. "I would speak straight tongue with you, my brother."

"My ears have always been open to Delgadito."

"Tell me why. The plain truth, nothing else."

Cuchillo Negro walked in silence for a bit, and seldom had Delgadito's nerves been so on edge. At last the former sighed. "The truth it will be, and it is truth born of our boyhoods together, of the many hunts we went on, the many grand times we had practicing the skills we would use when we became men. It is truth born of the manhood we have shared, of the many battles we have fought, the many hardships we have endured."

"What truth?" Delgadito said, scarcely able to conceal his impatience.

"The truth of your mistake."

"You promised you would speak with a straight tongue."

The warrior the Mexicans called Black Knife locked his gaze on Delgadito. "In all the winters we have known each other, I can count the mistakes you have made on one hand." He held up one finger. "And it is in this matter of the white-eye you took under your wing in order to soar among the clouds once again. You make a mistake in that you cannot see the good he can do not only for you but for all our people, the good only he could achieve because he is who he is. You make a mistake because you are thinking only of yourself. Think of the welfare of the entire tribe and you will see the wisdom of my words. I have walked with the bear. I know."

For once Delgadito was utterly confused. "You call that straight tongue? Of what possible good can this miserable white eye be to the Chiricahuas?"

"You have eyes but you do not see."

"See what?"

"That he can do for us what we have been unable to do for ourselves." Cuchillo Negro halted. "White Apache can free the Chiricahuas from the white man's yoke."

Chapter Four

The building was as brown and stark as the land on which it sat. A hovel, really, situated in the middle of a vast nowhere, with heaps of refuse piled out back and scruffy mongrels out front sniffing at the heels of everyone who entered.

And a lot of people did visit through the course of an average day, the majority Apaches from the reservation who broke the law to warm their bellies with the firewater to which they were addicted. The authorities knew about the hovel, and the man who ran it, but they made no attempt to put him out of business. In the army's opinion, drunken Indians were little threat, so the Apaches were permitted to inebriate themselves with unofficial sanction.

Much to the delight of Santiago Pasqual, the owner of the run-down saloon. Half Mexican, half Cibeque Apache, and all greed, he made his living selling watered down whiskey to the gullible reservation braves and hoarding the profits for his eventual move to Sonora where he planned to buy a large estate and live out his later years in comfort.

There was little actual work involved. Santiago poured drinks, wiped tables, and had his woman make *burritos*, *tacos*, or *enchiladas* for those of his customers who arrived hungry. It was fortunate for her she liked to cook because Santiago kept her at the stove twelve hours a day.

Occasionally there was trouble. Drunks were always cantankerous, and Santiago sometimes had to pull his scattergun out from under the bar and remind whoever was raising cane that buckshot meant burying. Usually the shotgun quieted them down. If not—well, he'd had to shoot a few over the years but there had never been a problem with the law. The ones he shot were always Apaches or breeds like himself.

On this day, Santiago leaned on the counter and idly observed the fourteen men scattered about the room. Three were playing cards in a dark corner. Two others were talking in low tones. Most simply sat staring with glazed eyes at the filthy walls, their precious bottles clutched in front of them.

Suddenly a shadow filled the doorway and Santiago glanced to his left, mildly surprised that someone had ridden up without him hearing. The figure was backlit by the sun, his face in dark shadow, and for a few moments Santiago was unable to distinguish more than a buckskin clad frame and a red headband. Then the man entered, a rifle held in the crook of an elbow, and all activity in the saloon ceased.

Santiago stiffened and gulped, his mouth going dry in the blink of an eye. Goose bumps broke out all over him as the newcomer walked to the bar and regarded him as he might a sidewinder about to strike. Santiago coughed to get his throat to work and said in greeting, "Tats-ah-das-ay-go. *Hola, amigo.*"

"I am not your friend," Quick Killer responded in flawless Spanish as he placed his .44-40 on the bar with a resounding thud that made several in the room jump.

"To what do I owe this honor?" Santiago asked, refusing to take insult since to do so would result in his death. "It has been six or seven months since you stopped by last."

Quick Killer surveyed the premises with disgust. "And nothing has changed, I see."

"Would you like a drink?" Santiago inquired to change the subject. He leaned on his elbows and spoke softly. "To show you I am not the bastard you seem to think, I will give you a bottle of my best. On the house."

"I did not come to this pigpen to slake my thirst," Quick Killer said indignantly. "I need information."

"And you think I can supply it? My humble self is flattered." Santiago gave his most ingratiating smile, a smile that always worked to pacify belligerent Americanos. It was his way of groveling without actually bending his knees, a way of showing he was as harmless as a fly. But this time it failed to impress. A hand of solid steel snaked out and pulled him halfway across the counter.

"Your humble self will not live out the day if you don't stop acting like the jackass you are and tell me what I need to know."

"Anything," Santiago said, embarrassed at being manhandled with all his customers looking on. "Please, Tats-as-das-ay-go. I did not mean to offend you."

Quick Killer let go and Pasqual slid back and

straightened. "Delgadito," the scout said.

"Again?" Santiago declared without thinking and hastily went on when the scout's hand moved toward him. "I can tell you no more than I did the last time!" He twisted, plucked a bottle of rye from a shelf, and poured himself a large glass. "Surely you heard about the raid? How Blue Cap wiped out nearly all of Delgadito's band? He has few friends left and no living relatives that I know of. So he never visits any of the villages. Never."

"What about those who ride with him?"

Santiago froze in the act of lifting the glass, then set it down so hard the rye splashed onto his hand. "They are hardly acquaintances of mine," he hedged.

"Still, you have heard things. You always hear things."

"Not this—," Santiago began, but stopped when the scout lifted a hand.

"Don't lie to me, dog. I know that Nah-kah-yen came to see you and that you gave him information about one of those who rides with Delgadito."

"Who told you such a thing?" Santiago responded, still stalling in the hope of scheming a way to turn the situation to his benefit. He didn't relish the prospect of having to give away something for nothing.

"None of your business," Quick Killer said. "Now tell me about Ponce and leave nothing out or I'll be back to visit you after I'm done in the mountains. And you wouldn't want that."

Santiago put his head closer to the other man's. "Have a heart, will you? Information is sometimes worth more than liquor. Nah-kah-yen paid me thirty dollars for the news I had learned. What will you give?"

"Something much more valuable than thirty dollars."

"Oh? What?"

"Your life."

One look into those snake-like eyes convinced Santiago that it was no empty threat. Sighing in frustration, he whispered, "All right. I will confide in you because I like you. But you must promise never to tell anyone where you obtained the information. Should Ponce hear, or anyone close to him, I would be in great danger."

"Do you really think I would tell a soul?"

"No," Santiago admitted. It was common knowledge that the only company Quick Killer kept was his own.

"Then start talking."

Santiago looked about to verify the drunks and card players were not paying any attention to him. "Several weeks ago a man came in. Old Coletto. Do you know him?"

"No."

"He stops by only now and then. Usually he hardly says a word, but this time I couldn't get him to shut his mouth." Santiago paused. "I think I gave him straight whiskey by mistake."

"Get to the point."

"While he was sobbing over the many sorrows in his life, he mentioned that his granddaughter was seeing a warrior who rode with Delgadito. He was quite proud of the fact. Claimed it was a man named Ponce, and went on and on about how Ponce was a credit to the Chiricahuas because he refused to give in to the white-eyes, and how if he was younger he'd be right out there with them and—"

"Where do I find this Coletto?"

"Palacio's village. He lives by himself. His wife died two winters ago and he hasn't been the same since."

"Who else have you told this to?"

"Only Nah-kah-yen."

Quick Killer grunted and picked up his .44-40. "You will forget I was here. You will forget ever talking to me. You will forget Coletto paid you a visit. And you have never heard the name Ponce before. *Comprende?*"

"*Si. En este asunto me lavo las manos.*"

"You do well to wash your hands of it," Quick Killer said. Turning, he silently departed, with nary a ripple of the air to mark his passage.

Santiago Pasqual shivered as if it were icy cold and hastily gulped the rye down, savoring the burning sensation that warmed his throat and stomach. His larcenous nature prompted him to wonder how he might make a dollar or two off the scout's visit. There were a few people who would pay for the news, not the least of whom were Ponce's own family. But another shiver reminded him of the inevitable consequences should Quick Killer find out about his treachery. He filled the glass, then stared at the entrance. No, he decided, it would be smarter to check his impulse to make a dollar or two and let events play themselves out without his interference. He'd live longer that way. A lot longer.

Clay Taggart sat under his lean-to, staring into the crackling flames of the small fire he had started an hour ago, shortly after sundown. A glowing ember made a slight popping sound and reminded him of the noise made when Nah-kah-yen's fingers were broken one by one. Before his mind's eye flashed unbidden the long torture the scout had endured, the torture Clay had witnessed from grisly start to gory finish. He should have turned away, he reflected. Or, at the very least, he should have protested the barbaric acts the Apaches committed, yet he'd sat there and done nothing.

It was hard to say which upset Clay more. The torture, or the fact he hadn't felt the least bit upset about it. Never once had he felt queasy, never once had the atrocities bothered him. Not when the scout's lips were peeled from his face, not when Fiero chopped the man's toes off, not when Nah-kah-yen's abdomen was sliced open and his intestines pulled out. Yet, only a few months ago, Clay would have been sick to his stomach on seeing such savagery.

Clay leaned back and thoughtfully regarded the sparkling stars. What in the world was happening to him? he wondered. Had he gone plumb loco? Had living with the Apaches changed him that much in such a short time?

Nothing made sense anymore. Clay shook his head, recollecting a saying his grandpa had been fond of: Life was too ridiculous for words. And Clay had a feeling that it was going to get a lot worse before it got better.

The next second Clay had a different feeling, that of being watched. Without being obvious he placed his right hand on his rifle and drifted his gaze along the bench. He saw no one and chalked it up to a case of bad nerves until a shadow detached itself from the darkness.

Delgadito stepped into the flickering rosy light and halted. "May I join you, Lickoyee-shis-inday?" he asked.

Flabbergasted, Clay nevertheless collected his wits and beckoned. "You are welcome at my fire any time," he said. For the life of him he couldn't explain the warrior's visit, and he sat tense with expectation as the Apache hunkered down and switched to English.

"What you think of scout?"

"He got his due, I reckon," Clay said.

"You speak with straight tongue?"

"Yes," Clay answered, and repeated it louder, realizing he truly did believe justice had been served. "Those three varmints tried to bushwhack us. If I hadn't spotted them, all four of us would be pushing up flowers come spring. They got what was coming to them, sure enough."

Delgadito looked down at the ground. "You save my life, White Apache. I treat you bad and you save my life."

Clay wouldn't have been more shocked had Delgadito announced he'd repented of his misdeeds and wanted to turn himself over to the army. "Hell, partner. You haven't been treating me that badly."

"I have," Delgadito insisted. "There is much I must say to you to set things right."

"I'm listening," Clay said. In all the time he'd been with the renegades, he'd never heard a single warrior apologize for anything. For Delgadito to do so meant more to him than he cared to concede because he was more attached to the Apache than he cared to admit. He'd been flattering himself that the two of them were made from the same leather, and then Delgadito had up and yanked the rug out from under him. Maybe, he mused, the Apache had come to his senses.

Ironically, Delgadito was thinking the exact same thing, but his motives were far different than Clay suspected. His fruitful talk with Cuchillo Negro had persuaded him that he had indeed made a mistake, which he was about to rectify. So, folding his brawny hands in his lap, he began in his own tongue. "Do you understand good medicine and bad medicine, Lickoyee-shis-inday?"

"I believe I do," Clay said.

"When a warrior dies on a raid it is considered very bad medicine. We do not go near the place where he dies ever again." Delgadito picked up a stick and poked it in the fire. "Losing Amarillo was bad medicine. Because we lost him on a raid to wipe out your enemies, we blamed you for his death."

"I did all I could—" Clay started to object, but let it drop when the warrior resumed.

"We know you did not want him to die. We know you planned your raids carefully, as a *Shis-Inday* always should. But we blamed you anyway," Delgadito said. "To understand, you must see the world through our eyes. You must think like we think, believe as we believe."

"I am trying," Clay stated.

"You were born a white-eye. We should not blame you for that since none of us has control over such matters. But when you first came among us, we naturally saw you as an outsider. Your ways were not our ways and our ways were not yours."

Clay merely nodded. Apaches were reared to regard everyone not of their tribe as an enemy, and given the suffering they had endured at the hands of the Spaniards, Mexicans, and later his own kind, their outlook couldn't be faulted.

"Even after you had ridden with us on raids, we did not think of you as one of us. You were still the *Americano*. You were still not to be trusted." Delgadito tossed a stick into the flames. "Then you saved the others from the *Nakai-hey* and killed Blue Cap. You worked hard to learn our ways, to speak our tongue."

"Very hard," Clay threw in.

"And for a while we thought of you as one of us and all was well. But old habits die hard. When

Amarillo died, we again saw you as an outsider. We wanted nothing to do with you."

"And now?" Clay asked hopefully.

"Now I am here to say that our fire is your fire. We would like you to be one of us again. We want you to lead us on more raids."

"What?" Clay exclaimed, dazzled by his good fortune. With the Apaches once again under his thumb, he could continue his campaign of vengeance against the posse members who had strung him up and the man who had put them up to it, Miles Gillett. He was so elated that for a span of seconds he forgot about Cuchillo Negro's warning. On remembering, he eyed Delgadito suspiciously. "What is in this for you?"

The question surprised the warrior. Never before had the white-eye presumed to question his motives, which had secretly amazed and amused him. Apaches learned early on to never take anything for granted, to always look for the underlying reasons behind the actions of others. Delgadito believed that Lickoyee-shis-inday was too trusting for his own good. Perhaps, at last, he mused, the white-eye had learned not to trust anyone. "You know the thoughts of your kind better than we do. With you leading us, we will outsmart them at every turn. We will kill many whites and take much plunder."

"And what if another warrior dies?" Clay asked. "Do I take the blame again?"

"No. All that concerns us is the fight to rid ourselves of those who invaded our country and herded our people onto the reservation. Many sleeps ago we took an oath to resist with our lives, if need be, and that is what we will do."

"I see," Clay said.

But Delgadito had only detailed part of the reason. The warrior hadn't gone into his personal agenda, into the new long range plan he had to regain his leadership role. Nor did Delgadito see fit to mention the part Cuchillo Negro wanted Clay to play in reviving the flagging spirit of the entire Chiricahua tribe.

"I don't mind telling you, pard, that I'm right pleased at how things have turned out," Clay said good-naturedly in English. "I figured we'd never smoke the peace pipe and was set to light a shuck for parts unknown."

"Now we are friends again?"

"We sure are," Clay declared. "Now that we've mended fences, we can get on about the business of seeing that those vermin who made me the guest of honor at their necktie social pay for what they did." He saw the Apache smile and assumed it was with pleasure at having mended fences.

Actually, Delgadito was showing his derision at how easy it had been to manipulate Clay. During his short stay on the reservation, Delgadito had learned about the strange eagerness of the whites to readily forgive those who did them wrong. The trait ran contrary to all that Apaches believed, and he had been unable to comprehend how any people could pride themselves on exhibiting such weakness. But since they did, and since any and every weakness of an enemy was to be exploited, he had learned to take advantage of their stupidity.

"When do you want to go on the next raid?" Clay asked.

"When you are ready," Delgadito said.

"I'm ready now. We can head out at first light if it's all right with you." Clay chuckled in anticipation. "The next no-account on my list is a gent named

Jack Bitmer. We can be at his spread in three days. He has a sizeable herd of thoroughbreds, and some cattle besides if we want to go to all the trouble of driving them back to the reservation."

"We will see."

Clay touched a finger to his coffee pot. "The Arbuckle's about done. Care for a cup?"

Delgadito was more inclined to return to his fellow warriors, but his mouth seemed to have a will of its own. "I stay."

Rummaging in a pouch, Clay produced his battered tin cup and filled it. "Here. After you." He sat back as the warrior sipped loudly. "I've been doing a lot of thinking the past few days and I've got some notions worth sharing."

"My ears are open."

"Having lived with you a spell, I'm beginning to see that the Apaches and I have a lot in common."

"You think so?"

"Look at the facts," Clay said. "I had my ranch stolen out from under me by a greedy *hombre* who wants me dead. The Chiricahuas had their freedom stripped from them by a whole passel of greedy politicians who think the only good Apache is a dead one."

The similarity hadn't occurred to Delgadito and he remarked as much.

"There's more," Clay stated. "I'm now a wanted man because I had the gumption to fight for what is mine. You and the rest of your band are all wanted men because you had the grit to fight for what is yours."

"We are much the same," Delgadito conceded, the comparison sparking a new train of thought.

"I'm not done yet," Clay said. "I reckon I speak for both of us when I say that I'm not about to give up while a breath of life remains in my body."

"You do."

"So since we have so much in common, doesn't it make a heap of sense for us to work together to help one another get what we want?"

Delgadito took another swallow. He suspected where their conversation was leading and couldn't believe how smoothly things were working out. "We help you kill your enemies," he said.

"For which I'm grateful as can be," Clay said. "That's why I gave you a hand rubbing out Blue Cap. But you've helped me more than I've helped you, and I've always been a firm believer in paying my debts in full."

"Meaning?"

"Meaning there has to be more I can do on your behalf. I don't exactly know how, but I bet if you give it some thought you can come up with a few ideas."

"Maybe we can," Delgadito said, and it was all he could do not to yip in triumph. The white-eye had played right into their hands.

"I'm serious," Clay asserted. "I can be of big help to you. I spent a lot of time at the different forts when I delivered beef to the army. I know how they operate, and I think I can help you beat them at their own game." He watched a moth flit past. "Since I'm white, if I'm careful I could probably mingle among them without anyone being the wiser and learn all sorts of important information."

"You have this well thought out, Lickoyee-shis-inday."

"You're damn right I do. Since the law and the army have seen fit to brand me an outlaw and a renegade, I guess I might as well live up to the lies they're spreading about me. The Taggart clan has never backed down from a scrape yet and I'm not about to break the family tradition." Clay stared somberly into the night. "The White Apache, I'm called. Well, that suits me just fine. From here on out I'm going to be the wildest, fiercest, meanest, damned Apache anyone has ever seen. By the time I'm done, they'll tremble in their boots at the mention of my name."

Chapter Five

The village of Palacio had quieted for the night when Quick Killer made his move. From before sunset until close to midnight he crouched in the chaparral and observed all that transpired. He saw children playing, women working on skins and cooking and gossiping. He watched warriors gamble, clean their rifles, sharpen their knives. No one had the slightest idea he was there, not the deer hunters he had crept past high in the rocks, not the dogs that were unable to detect his scent because he had smeared himself with horse dung, and certainly not the reservation warriors who had lost their razor edge from too much soft living.

Quick Killer had nothing but contempt for reservation Indians. They were pale imitations of the men they had once been, the course of their lives set by their white masters. He held the renegades he tracked down in higher regard than he did these pathetic prisoners of their own cowardice.

When the last of the men had entered their wicki-ups, Quick Killer edged closer to the village. There were dozens of dwellings but only one housing an old man who lived by himself. Quick Killer had made doubly certain, memorizing all the comings and goings of everyone.

The old man had picked well. His wickiup was situated at the base of a knoll in a secluded spot that afforded shade in the day and protection from the wind at night. The interior was dark.

Quick Killer glided like a panther to the end of the brush, then moved swiftly to the wall of the conical structure. Circling around to the front, he pointed his rifle at the entrance and said softly in Apache, "Coletto, come out."

There was a rustling noise and the wizened features of the aged warrior appeared. "Who calls me?"

"Tats-ah-das-ay-go."

The old man recoiled, then seemed to see the Winchester for the first time. "What does Quick Killer want with me?"

"Ponce."

"I know no one by that name."

Quick Killer slid closer so that the rifle muzzle almost touched Coletto's wide nose. "Allow me to refresh your memory. He is the young man who pays your granddaughter visits. The same young man who rides with Delgadito."

"And it is Delgadito you really want." Coletto frowned. "I have heard many stories about you, scout. They say a man must have a death wish to cross you. But I tell you now that I will not say anything."

"You care for this Ponce that much?"

"I hardly know him. It is Delgadito I think of. He is the last true *Shis-Inday*."

The disclosure unsettled Quick Killer. He had intended to barter Ponce's life for the information he needed. "So you will not tell me in which lodge I can find your granddaughter?"

"Never."

"You are wrong, old one," Quick Killer said, and slammed the .44-40 against the venerable warrior's head twice in such swift succession the rifle was a blur. Coletto fell from sight. Quick Killer took a moment to scan the village and verify no one had seen, then he drew his long hunting knife and slipped within.

For the next two hours little stirred in the village of Palacio. Once a mongrel strayed by Coletto's wickiup and lifted its head on smelling the tangy scent of blood. It padded to the opening, sniffing loudly, and it was still sniffing when an iron hand flashed out and grabbed it by the scruff of the throat while at the same instant a dripping knife was plunged between its ribs three times. The animal went limp and was dragged inside.

Presently Quick Killer reappeared. He stared at a particular dwelling a while, turned, and melted into the chaparral. A circuitous route brought him to the trail the women took every morning on their way to the spring for water. He hiked to the pool, a distance of forty yards, and drank his full. A convenient thicket provided the cover he needed, and he sat down in the middle of it to wait. A few hours before dawn he lowered his chin to his chest and slept, awakening when the first pale streaks of pink framed the eastern horizon.

Soon the early risers came, mostly married women who had husbands and children to feed. The younger, single women came later, usually in pairs or threes, chattering gaily. Quick Killer studied them, seeking one wearing a red shawl, and half an hour after sunrise she came, with one other. He listened closely and heard her name. Ko-do. It meant Firefly.

The two women knelt to fill their clay water jars. Another woman was just leaving. Quick Killer didn't move until she was gone around a bend, then he rose, slipped from the brush, and was behind the two young ones before either suspected. The friend of Ko-do's started to look up. Quick Killer buried his knife between her shoulder blades, then smashed the hilt against Ko-do's chin as she whirled.

Swiftly Quick Killer dropped to his right knee, slid the knife into its beaded sheath, and slung the unconscious maiden over his shoulder as if she were a sack of grain. He checked the trail as he picked up his rifle. No one else had shown yet but it was only a matter of minutes.

Quick Killer hastened into the brush, making for the high ground where he had left his calico. For hundreds of feet he walked on solid rock. Once at the horse, he laid Ko-do over its back and mounted. From the vicinity of the spring issued a screech attended by loud shouts, and he knew that within a short while there would be Chiricahuas scouring every square inch of undergrowth for a mile around.

Lifting the reins, Quick Killer jabbed his heels and galloped down into a ravine that brought him to a lowland plain covered with mesquite. He rode on until the sun was straight overhead. In a narrow gorge he drew rein and roughly dumped the woman on the ground. She stirred, moaning faintly.

Dismounting, Quick Killer ground-hitched the calico and squatted beside Ko-do. He admired her rosy lips, noted the fullness promised by the fit of her clothes. And he reflected that rarely had a manhunt brought him so much pleasure.

Many miles away another man was equally pleased by a turn of events. Clay Taggart rode beside Delgadito at the head of the renegade band, heading westward toward the San Pedro River. He was glad to have been accepted by the Apaches again, and gladder still that he could continue his vendetta against those who had wronged him.

So far Clay had accounted for two of the twelve posse members. That left ten men who were going to die, eleven counting Miles Gillett, the cagey mastermind who had framed him for murder and stolen the woman he had once loved.

Clay planned to save Gillett for last. He wanted the bastard to know what was coming, to experience the same gnawing helplessness that Clay had felt as the noose was tightened around his neck. For as long as Clay lived he would never forget that awful ordeal, in particular that terrible moment when his fiery lungs had been fit to burst and his vision had dimmed to black as he balanced on the brink of oblivion. It was the spur that pricked his conscience every time he dared think about turning back from the vengeance trail. It was his single greatest motivation in life.

The chestnut gave a snort and pricked its ears. Clay immediately scoured the landscape but saw no cause for alarm. He complimented himself on being able to convince the Apaches into using horses instead of going afoot as they were accustomed to doing when on raids. Granted, on foot they could exercise greater stealth and would leave fewer tracks. But what they lost in that regard they made up for in being able to go faster and covering more ground at a single stretch. Plus, they could make meals of their mounts should game prove scarce.

Suddenly, Clay's chestnut nickered lightly. Clay saw Delgadito give it a sharp glance, reminding him that Apaches wouldn't abide a noisy horse. Any animal that loved to hear itself neigh invariably wound up simmering in a stew pot. He leaned forward to throttle the chestnut so it wouldn't whinny again when his nose registered the faint odor of wood smoke.

All the Apaches drew rein at the selfsame moment Clay did. The sluggish wind blew toward them from the northwest, across the arid plain they were crossing. Except for scattered islands of scrub trees and waving strands of dry grass, there was scant cover, certainly not enough to hide a camp or a fire. He looked at the warriors and found them looking at him. "Cuchillo Negro," he said.

The lean warrior swung down, handed the reins to Ponce, and sped off across the plain. In seconds he had blended into the land, becoming invisible.

Clay never tired of marveling at the uncanny ability of his companions. No matter how hard he tried, he couldn't duplicate all their feats although he came close in more regards than most. To kill the time, he turned to Delgadito and whispered in Apache, "It is good to be on the war path again."

The warrior grunted. "You are more *Shis-Inday* than you think," he said softly. "Maybe your mother stole you from an Apache woman when you were a baby."

That was the first and only joke Clay had ever heard Delgadito make, and he was so taken aback he nearly blundered and laughed aloud. Instead, he caught himself and whispered in English, "The longer I ride with you, the more I like it. I don't mind confessing it's got me a mite worried."

"Why worry?" Delgadito responded. "You like Apaches, you stay with Apaches. Always welcome."

"I'm obliged, pard," Clay said, and meant it, but at the same time he was mystified by the warrior's complete change in attitude. One day Delgadito wouldn't have anything to do with him, the next Delgadito acted as if they were best friends. There was no explaining the *Shis-Inday* sometimes.

The next five minutes were spent in alert silence. Finally Cuchillo Negro popped up beside a hedgehog cactus. He jogged to the group and reported. "There are three hairy white-eyes camped in a gully. They have extra horses, and many packs of furs."

"Poachers," Clay deduced. Ever since the U.S. government signed a treaty with the Chiricahuas, the area embracing the Dragoon and Chiricahua Mountains was exclusively theirs. No whites were to hunt or trap anywhere within the reservation boundaries. But the treaty hadn't stopped poachers from helping themselves to the land's bounty whenever they were of a mind. To Delgadito, he said in English, "They must be on their way to Tucson to sell their hides. They probably only travel at night to avoid army patrols, and right now they're lying low until dark. What do you reckon we should do?"

Delgadito acted surprised. "We all agreed that you should lead us. So lead, Lickoyee-shis-inday."

Clay was inclined to suggest they should ride on and avoid the trappers until it occurred to him that here was a chance to show the warriors he meant what he had said about siding with them in their war on those determined to destroy their kind. The poachers had no business killing animals the Apaches needed to feed and clothe themselves. Maybe, he mused, he should make an object lesson of this bunch so others would think twice before trespassing on Apache territory. He faced the others. "We will kill these whites and take everything they own."

The reactions of the four warriors differed. Delgadito was immensely pleased. Cuchillo Negro was too, but it also bothered him a trifle that White Apache was so readily falling into the pattern they wanted. Ponce hefted his rifle, eager to hone his fighting skills. And Fiero gazed on White Apache as if setting eyes for the first time on a kindred spirit.

"Leave your horses here," Clay ordered. "When we are in position, wait for my signal. Use your knives, not your guns. This must be quiet work."

The gully cut the plain from north to south. Twenty yards wide, it afforded the perfect spot to hide. Had the trappers not become hungry and started a fire to roast their meal, they would have been safe.

From the west rim Clay peered down at the three burly specimens and their haul. One was busy skinning a rabbit, the other two were puffing on pipes and talking. Piled against the east wall were twelves bound bales of beaver, cougar, and fox plews.

"—wait to get my share," a pipe smoker was saying in a low voice. "I'm fixin' to head for New Orleans and have me a grand time."

"Why go so blamed far?" asked the other. "What does New Orleans have that Denver and St. Louis don't?"

"Women. Droves of easy women sashaying their wares right there in the street."

"Hell, Denver and St. Louis have more fallen doves than you can shake a stick at. And they're a far sight closer."

"Don't care, Eb. I'm partial to New Orleans. Spent a lot of time there when I was sprout. You ain't lived until you've taken in the sights that wicked city has to offer."

"I'll take your word for it," Eb said. "Me, I'm heading for St. Louie, as I like to call it. Got me an old gal there who can wrap her legs around a man and not let go for a month of Sundays."

"Sure she'll recollect you after all this while?"

"Hell, yes," Eb said. "She don't get many gentleman callers as handsome as me."

"But I bet the others smell better."

The poachers chuckled.

On the rim, Clay hesitated to give the signal. It had been easy to pronounce judgment on the trappers when he hadn't set eyes on them. But now there they were: living, breathing human beings—white men like himself, men who must have kin somewhere, relatives who would mourn their loss. How could he rub them out with a gesture? Then he thought of his promise to the Apaches, and how much taking his revenge on Miles Gillett meant to him. His mouth a somber slit, he waved his rifle once.

The poachers never had a prayer. The four Apaches swooped into the gully like ferocious birds of prey, pouncing on the startled trappers before they could bring a rifle or pistol into play. Ponce and Cuchillo Negro closed on Eb, who clawed at a Colt as two knives ripped into his flesh. Fiero took the other poacher, his blade slicing to the hilt in the man's throat as the trapper foolishly tried to grab his arm.

Quick Killer

Delgadito jumped on the man working on the rabbit. Since the poacher already had a knife in hand, he was able to leap erect and defend himself. He parried Delgadito's first few thrusts while frantically back-pedaling. Unfortunately for him, he neglected to keep an eye on the ground and didn't notice a saddle until his foot caught in it and he went down. Delgadito was on him in a twinkling, his knife sinking deep, not once but four times.

And just like that it was over. The three trappers lay in spreading puddles of blood, one motionless in death, another twitching convulsively, and Eb wheezing raggedly as tiny red geysers pumped from his chest.

Clay rose and walked to the bottom. He stood over Eb, saw the trapper's eyes widen.

"Your eyes! They're blue!" Eb erupted in a coughing fit, and when it subsided, said, "You're the one we heard about, aren't you? The White Apache?"

"I am," Clay admitted.

"How can you do this to white folk?" Eb asked. "How—" Whatever else he was going to say was lost to posterity when the poacher went limp, expiring his last in a long, loud breath.

The Apaches had already started stripping weapons from the dead, and Ponce was busy collecting the horses. Oblivious to them, Clay Taggart stared at Eb, trying to come to terms with the question the trapper had posed. On an impulse he leaned down and snatched Eb's hat, an old brown woolsey of the sort worn by prospectors, with the front brim folded up at a rakish angle and one side sloped from the crown to the brim. Clay couldn't say what prompted him to put the hat on.

Delgadito had seen and came over. "What you want with that?" he asked in English.

"I don't rightly know," Clay admitted.

"Hats for white-eyes, not a *Shis-Inday*."

"But I'm the *White* Apache, remember?" Clay said, and to avoid debating the matter further he pointed at the plunder and asked, "What do you suggest we do with all this stuff? We could cache the spoils but we can't very well leave the horses here until we come back this way next."

"One of us must take plunder to Sweet Grass."

"Who?"

"You are leader," Delgadito reminded him yet again.

Clay debated whom to pick. It couldn't be Delgadito since he didn't feel confident enough to handle the others without Delgadito's support. Cuchillo Negro was reliable so far as he knew, but he'd rather have Black Knife with him. Fiero was too hotheaded to be let loose on his own; there was no telling what the firebrand might do. All of which made his decision a simple one. "Ponce," he said in Apache, "will you take the trappers' belongings and animals to Sweet Grass and watch over them until we return?" He half expected an argument since Ponce was so keen on earning merit in warfare. To his surprise, the young warrior did not appear the least bothered. In fact, based on Ponce's expression, Clay suspected he was strangely pleased by the request.

"I will be glad to do so, White Apache."

Fiero was admiring a Colt he had taken from the poacher he slew. "You will miss out on all the fighting," he mentioned.

"There will always be more," Ponce said, and occupied himself gathering the possessions lying about.

Gratified that his decision had not been challenged, Clay climbed from the gully and headed toward the horses. He didn't look back to see if the rest followed. He just naturally took it for granted they would.

Delgadito was the first to catch up. "You do well, White Apache" he remarked in English.

"I reckon I'm getting the hang of being the cock-a-doodle do."

"The what?"

"The big sugar. The one who reads the Scriptures. The leader."

"Some yes, some no."

"I don't savvy."

"You ask Ponce to take plunder back."

"So? Should I have asked someone else?"

"Not that. *Shis-Inday* leader not ask. *Shis-Inday* leader tell."

"I thought Apaches were too independent to take orders. I didn't want to start barking commands at Fiero or someone else and have them turn on me."

"Most time *Shis-Inday* not take orders. In war we do. Always have war chief."

"Am I to take it that I'm the war chief of this outfit?"

"No. You White Apache. You special."

"Thanks, I think."

Once they were mounted, Clay bore to the north-west. They rode hard until an hour before sunset, at which time he led the Apaches in among manzanita to rest their animals. He had brought a pouch filled with jerky and shared it with the others. The warriors squatted on their haunches. He sat with his back to the cherry-red bark of one of the short trees and pushed his new hat back on his head. "I can't wait to see the look on Jack Bitmer's face when I bury my knife in his belly," he told Delgadito.

"How many others be ranchers?" the warrior asked.

"Denton and Socher. The rest of the men I'm after are gunnies, cowhands, and drifters."

"And marshal."

Clay hadn't forgotten about Tucson's top lawdog. Marshal Tom Crane was his name, and he was a cat's-paw controlled by Miles Gillett. Clay would never forgive Crane for the unsavory part the lawman had played in the lynching. In his estimation, when lawmen went around breaking the law there was no law, and it was time for ordinary folks to take matters into their own hands. Just like he was going to do.

Until late that night the band pressed on. Clay was so anxious to reach Bitmer's spread that he would have gone on until dawn, but common sense warned him not to. He slept lightly, as he always did on the trail, yet in spite of that he was up well before first light, feeling refreshed and raring to go. It was another example of the drastic change that had come over him since he'd been living as an Apache. During his ranching days he'd slept out many a night and always awoke the next morning suffering stiff muscles and tight joints.

Because Bitmer's ranch lay well to the north of Tucson, Clay bore in that direction. Toward the middle of the morning he guessed they were close to the road that connected Tucson to Mesilla far to the east, and he slowed the chestnut to a walk. Cavalry patrols traveled the road regularly to safeguard the steady stream of pilgrims using it, so he had to be careful not to blunder into one. Sometimes, as he'd learned the hard way, those patrols included Apache scouts who were every bit the equal of their renegade counterparts.

Clay was winding among dense brush when the rattle of wagon wheels carried to his ears through the hot, dry air. Reining up, he tied his animal and announced quietly, "I will go check. When you hear me whistle, bring my horse."

Keeping low, Clay advanced until he saw the dusty roadway ahead. A large saguaro stood close by it, and he quickly crawled into its shadow for a clear view in both directions. He thought he would see a farmer or rancher or perhaps a trader but instead spied two figures in a buckboard. And that wasn't all.

Escorting the buckboard was a full detachment of United States Cavalry.

Chapter Six

The Chiricahua maiden named Ko-do came awake
with a start. She automatically sat up and fearfully
glanced around, not knowing what to expect. The
last thing she remembered was seeing her dearest
friend collapse with blood spurting from a back
wound, and then something had smashed her on
the jaw. Now, she set eyes on a dark stranger in
buckskins who was in the act of removing the short
moccasins he wore in order to replace them with a
different pair lying on the ground beside him.

"At last," the stranger said in her tongue. "Have a
nice rest?"

Ko-do went to stand and discovered to her dismay
that her ankles were bound. She reached for the
rope but a low hiss from the stranger froze her
midway.

"I would not do that, sweet Ko-do, unless you
cannot wait to die."

Quick Killer

Struggling to control the panic that threatened to overwhelm her, Ko-do swept their surroundings. They were in a rocky gorge close to a small spring. High overhead a lone buzzard circled as if waiting for a meal. A lump formed in her throat and she had to swallow before she could speak. "Who are you? What do you want with me?"

"I am called Quick Killer," the man said with exaggerated pride. "Perhaps you have heard of me?"

"No," Ko-do said.

The man grinned. "Then my reputation is not as widespread as I flattered myself to believe." He removed the second of the two short moccasins. "I am a scout, pretty one. A very special scout. The white-eyes pay me to track down renegades and ask no questions if I bring the renegades back slung over a horse. At the moment I am after Delgadito and the *Americano* known as the White Apache."

"What does this have to do with me?" Ko-do bluffed, knowing full well the answer.

"Please, woman. Do not insult me or I will make your end so painful you will plead with me to end your misery." Quick Killer lifted one of the knee-high moccasins at his side and began squirming a foot into it.

"Do the whites pay you to kill women?" Ko-do snapped, her fertile mind racing as she tried to scheme a way out of her predicament.

"No," Quick Killer said. "But what they do not know cannot hurt me." He commenced lacing up the moccasin.

"My people will know. They will report what you have done to the reservation agent and soldiers will come after you."

Quick Killer fixed her with a sneer. "How silly you are. Do you think I would be so careless?" He

81

patted the short moccasins he had just removed. "These are Comanche. They belonged to a warrior I killed several winters ago. I wore them when I took you so that the men of your village will think a Comanche was to blame." He resumed lacing. "Your tribe and their tribe have been at war forever. It is nothing new for a warrior from one to steal a woman from another." Quick Killer grinned again and touched the knee-high moccasin he had just put on. "These are Chiricahua-made. I bought them from a Chiricahua scout at Fort Bowie before coming to the reservation. If any men from your tribe see my tracks now, they will think I am one of their own."

Ko-do saw her abductor in a whole new horrific light. She wriggled her legs to test her bonds and realized she could not possibly escape with him right there.

"The secret to staying alive in a world filled with enemies is to always be one step ahead of them," Quick Killer lectured her. "I have lived as long as I have only because I am never caught unprepared."

"My father and grandfather will find you. Nothing will keep them from tracking you down."

"Again you talk like a child and not a mature woman," Quick Killer said while putting on the other knee-high. "I took great pains to hide my trail. Your father will lead a search party but he will never find us." The scout paused. "As for Coletto, he has gone to meet his ancestors."

The shock drained the blood from Ko-do's fair face. "You killed my grandfather?" she asked, aghast.

"I needed to know your name and what you looked like. Old Coletto did not want to tell me, but after I had skinned him down to his waist he changed his mind."

"You are worse than the Comanches!" Ko-do said, her grief dominating her. Without thinking, she added, "It's true what they say! Breeds like you are no better than animals! You live to torture and kill!"

The words were scarcely out of the maiden's mouth when Quick Killer was on her. He hit her twice, knocking her flat, her lips mashed and bleeding. "For that, bitch," he growled, "you will suffer far worse than the old one did."

"I do not care!" Ko-do blustered. "I will never tell you what you want to know!"

Quick Killer composed himself and sat on a nearby boulder. "Is Ponce that important to you? Do you love him so much you would endure pain such as you have never known in a stupid attempt to save him?"

"Ponce is going to take me for his wife soon. He has grown tired of the war path."

"Is that the lie he told just so he could fondle you?" Quick Killer said in contempt. "How could you believe him? Ponce is an Apache and Apaches live for war. I know, because my father was a White Mountain Apache."

Ko-do found the strength to prop herself on an elbow. "You waste your words, breed. I will not fall for your trick. Nothing you can say will convince me that Ponce does not love me." She gingerly touched her lower lip and felt the pulped flesh. "As for Ponce being Apache, almost all Apache men have given up the war path for reservation life. He will be doing no differently than they do."

"Then he is less of a man than I thought," Quick Killer said. He gazed almost wistfully at the distant horizon. "You might find this hard to accept, girl, but I admire men like Delgadito, men willing to fight for their freedom. Men who live according to the old ways. Men who will never give in to the *Americanos*."

"Yet you hunt them for the *Americanos!*"

Quick Killer regarded her sadly. "If I did not hunt them, I would be one of them. Do you understand?"

Ko-do was thoroughly confused. She was terribly scared and hurting but she refused to give her tormenter the satisfaction of seeing her cry or show weakness in any other respect. "All I understand is that you are a mad dog who kills his brothers in the name of those who are our enemies. Or maybe you are a coward at heart, too afraid to fight the whites yourself so you kill those who are braver than you."

The scout's gaze hardened. "Stupidity runs in your family, I see." He sighed. "Very well. Enough talk. Tell me where Delgadito's band is hiding out."

"Ponce has never told me," Ko-do declared, her heart fluttering in her chest like that of a panicked bird.

"You are a poor liar. Young lovers never keep secrets from one another."

"Delgadito made Ponce pledge never to reveal the locations of their camps."

Quick Killer rose. "I tire of this game, woman. I want the information and I want it now." He rested his hand on the hilt of his knife. "The choice is yours. Fast or slow. Which will it be?"

Ko-do was no fool. Until the white-eyes forced her people to adopt to reservation life, she had lived under the constant threat of attack by their many enemies. She had witnessed a raid by Navahos in which many Apaches had been slain; she had seen wounded warriors brought back to die. Violence and death had been a daily part of Apache life. So she knew the full consequences of her act when she squared her slender shoulders and announced, "Do with me what you will. I will not betray Ponce."

"We will see," Quick Killer said harshly as he slowly drew the knife and leaned over her. "Yes, we will most certainly see."

At the very moment that the woman who loved Ponce with all her heart saw a gleaming blade dip toward her body, the young warrior was on his way to Sweet Grass, a string of stolen horses laden with plunder strung out behind him.

Ponce was quite happy at the turn of events. He hadn't said anything to the others yet, but he had been pondering the merits of quitting the band and settling down ever since meeting a certain *ninya* in Palacio's village. At one time he would have banished such a thought from his head the instant it blossomed. He would have told himself women were unimportant in the Apache scheme of things. Ko-do though, was different. Try as he might he was unable to get her out of his mind.

Ponce knew that all men went through a similar period in their lives. From his father and his father's father he had learned that one day he would look on a woman and see her differently than he ever had any other female. As a boy and young man he had secretly scoffed when they mentioned it. His sole interest was in becoming the best warrior he could be, a man worthy of respect, perhaps a tribal leader one day.

So Ponce had been all the more surprised after he was introduced to Ko-do and could not stop thinking about her. She had become an obsession, and he knew he wouldn't be satisfied until she shared his wickiup.

Apache custom in affairs of the heart was clear-cut. A man interested in taking a woman to wife must tie his horse outside her father's lodge. If the woman left the animal standing there neglected for four days, it meant she wasn't interested. If, however, she fed the horse, took it to water, and tied it in front of her suitor's wickiup, it meant she had accepted.

Ponce intended to try his luck the next time he visited Palacio's village. He already knew Ko-do cared for him but he couldn't keep a tight knot of tension from forming in his gut every time he thought about putting her to the test. More than one warrior who believed he had a woman's heart in the palm of his hand was later shamed and made an object of ridicule when his poor horse was left to suffer thirst and hunger. Ponce didn't want that to befall him.

So preoccupied was the young warrior that he failed to note the slight swirl of dust to the southwest until it had grown in size to resemble a pale tornado. When he did spot it, he slowed, his brow knit in consternation.

A large body of horsemen were heading his way.

Only for a few seconds did Ponce stare at the cloud. Reining sharply to the left, he made for thick brush, tugging furiously on the lead rope to goad the string of horses into faster motion. He glanced over his shoulder at the wisps of dust his animals were raising and hoped the oncoming party wouldn't notice.

Ponce had no idea who the riders were but of one fact he could be sure; they wouldn't be friendly. Chiricahuas were restricted to the reservation so it was unlikely they were warriors from his own tribe. He suspected it was an army patrol. And if the soldiers spotted him, he wouldn't live out the day.

Quick Killer

Once in the brush, Ponce tied the lead rope to a limb, swung down, and dashed to the edge of the vegetation. He flattened behind a bush, his keen eyes roving the choking cloud until figures materialized, Indians in breechcloths and painted for war. They were Navahos, bitter enemies of the Chiricahuas.

Ponce counted eleven in all. They were riding westward, herding several dozen head of horses between them. Warriors returning from a raid, Ponce deduced. He stayed perfectly still, watching the main body go by. A few warriors rode behind the herd to urge the animals on. And fifty yards back rode a solitary brave whose job it was to keep an eye on their back trail. This man was the only one who had not yet passed by when one of the horses Ponce had secreted let out with a loud neigh.

The Navaho drew rein and glanced at the brush, then at the herd. The man started toward Ponce, but stopped, evidently uncertain whether the whinny had issued from the brush or the herd. He might have gone on had the horse in the brush not decided to let out with another cry. The Navaho worked the lever on his rifle and slowly advanced.

Ponce glanced at the retreating war party. So far none of the other warriors had noticed their companion was missing. Crawling backwards, he moved deeper into the growth and concealed himself in a stand of high brown grass.

The Navaho reached the brush and soundlessly slid to the ground. Holding the rifle at his waist, he padded toward the hidden horses, his lively eyes darting to and fro. He was in his middle years, an experienced warrior who would not be easily subdued.

Ponce let go of his rifle and drew his knife. He would rather use the gun but a shot would bring the rest. The Navaho had crouched and was working from shrub to shrub. Ponce saw that the man would miss his hiding place and go by about ten feet to the left. He twisted, placing the knife close to his chest, his legs coiling under him.

Suddenly the Navaho halted and made a three hundred and sixty degree turn. He suspected something but saw nothing. More slowly than ever, he went on.

Ponce was coiled to spring. He didn't like having to cover so much distance but it couldn't be helped. The Navaho spied the stolen horses and crouched low to study them.

Rising, Ponce hurtled at the Navaho's back. He knew the warrior would hear him, knew the man would whirl, but he counted on his speed to get him there before the Navaho fired and his speed was equal to the occasion. He slammed into the warrior like a human battering ram. They both went down, the Navaho losing the rifle, Ponce almost losing his knife.

Ponce slashed, tearing into his enemy's leg but not deeply. Swift as a cat, the Navaho rose to his knees and whipped out his own blade. Ponce had to throw himself to the right as the warrior stabbed at his throat. He cut low, into the Navaho's other leg, which didn't stop the Navaho from lancing a blow at his shoulder. He felt the steel bite, felt blood seep out.

A push and a hop brought Ponce erect. The Navaho was just as quick and the two of them circled, seeking an opening. Ponce lunged high; the Navaho countered low. Neither scored but it was close both times.

In the back of Ponce's mind was the nagging thought that the other Navahos might soon miss the one he fought and ride back to investigate. He had to dispatch his adversary swiftly but the Navaho was a formidable fighter, wary and skilled.

As if to prove Ponce right, the Navaho feinted, spearing his blade at Ponce's groin. Ponce automatically blocked the blade with his own. The Navaho was expecting that and simply reversed direction, swinging at Ponce's chest. By mere chance the knife slipped between the young Apache's torso and his arm, nicking his ribs.

Ponce retreated to give himself more room. He noticed a smug smile on the Navaho but didn't let it anger him. At an early age Chiricahua boys were taught that the key to winning in battle was to keep a clear head. Anger clouded judgment, dulled reflexes.

The Navaho abruptly glanced westward and opened his mouth to yell, an unexpected tactic, all the more so because it would never have occurred to Ponce to do the same. Apaches were staunch believers in fighting their own battles. Even when unevenly matched, rarely would a Chiricahua call for aid.

But being caught off guard didn't stop Ponce from acting. As the first sound started to issue from the Navaho's mouth, Ponce launched a savage attack, swinging in wide, controlled strokes that forced the Navaho to devote his whole attention to staying alive, the shout momentarily dying in his throat.

Ponce deliberately pressed the Navaho as hard as he could. The warrior retreated under the onslaught, their knives ringing together as they thrust and blocked with ferocious intensity. Had their ages been more equal, had the Navaho been as young as Ponce, the outcome would have been decided in the first few moments with Ponce the victor. Navahos were formidable fighters in their own right, but man for man they were no match for the scourges of the Southwest.

This certain Navaho lost his smug smile and fought with renewed tenacity. He tried a flurry of cuts that would have slain most antagonists. His inability to deliver a fatal blow made him reckless, made him careless, so that when he came to the rim of a shallow basin he failed to notice it until his left heel slipped out from under him and he toppled backwards.

Ponce took a single step and leaped, his knife raised high as he came down on top of the scrambling Navaho. The warrior twisted and tried to spear Ponce in the belly but Ponce hit him before he could. Together they went down, Ponce sinking his blade in the other's shoulder.

The Navaho scrambled backward. Ponce went after him and sliced open the man's shin. Bending at the waist, the Navaho attempted to cleave Ponce's head from his shoulders but Ponce ducked underneath the Navaho's flashing arm and drove his knife into the man's armpit. Stiffening, the Navaho then slumped and endeavored to feebly crawl off. Ponce ripped out his knife, pounced on the Navaho's chest, and finished their conflict with a thrust to the heart.

Ponce's temples pounded as he slowly rose. The fight had taken more out of him than it should have, and he stood there a few moments catching his breath. Then he remembered the Navaho's horse.

Whirling, Ponce shoved his knife into its sheath and ran to the patch of grass to retrieve his rifle. From there he jogged to the edge of the brush. Hundreds of yards to the west the dust cloud swirled. As yet, there was no sign of other warriors. He moved toward the Navaho's sorrel and reached for the dragging reins. The horse snorted, jerked its head away, and went to dash off. Ponce leaped, clutched the rope, and held on tight. His scent agitated the sorrel even more and he had to grip the reins with both hands to keep from being yanked off his feet.

Ponce had to quiet the horse quickly. He grabbed for its mane but the animal wrenched to the right and the reins nearly slipped from his grasp. Taking a short jump, he looped his right arm over the animal's neck and planted his feet firmly to show it who was the master. The sorrel, though, had ideas of its own and started to trot westward.

Ponce hauled on the horse's neck with all his might, causing the animal to veer into the brush. It went less than a dozen yards, then halted and tried to shake Ponce off. Since every moment of delay increased the danger, and since he already had more than enough horses to handle on the long ride to Sweet Grass, Ponce was in no frame of mind to go easy on the sorrel. He tried one last time to force it to stand still and failed.

Suddenly stepping back, Ponce whipped out his knife again and slit the animal's throat. The sorrel nickered as blood spewed from its throttle. It took a few steps toward the plain, then halted, wheezing noisily. Ponce slipped in close and opened the jugular groove with a deft slash. His forearms became sticky with crimson spray so he squatted and wiped them dry on the ground.

Standing, Ponce ran to where the Navaho had dropped the rifle. He looked back once and saw the sorrel sink to its front knees, its chest and legs a bright scarlet. It didn't take long to find the gun, and in short order Ponce was astride his horse and hastening eastward with the long string in tow.

Everything depended on how soon the war party realized one of its own had gone missing. Ponce pushed hard, heedless of the many sharp branches and leaves that tore at him and the animals. There was no time to think about erasing their tracks. He must put a lot of distance behind him.

The stolen stock slowed Ponce down but he wouldn't consider abandoning them. To Apaches horses were tokens of wealth; the more a man owned, the higher his public esteem. Ponce already had a sizeable herd thanks to the many raids led by Lickoyee-shis-inday, and before he quit the band he hoped to have twenty or more.

For the remainder of the day Ponce traveled across some of the most rugged country in Arizona. The searing heat had little effect on him but it readily tired the sweating horses. Twice he had to stop and beat flagging animals with sticks to keep them going.

Nightfall came and went. Ponce rode on until close to midnight. He would have gone longer but by then all the horses were flagging badly so he stopped in a sheltered ravine where there was grass for grazing. He took up a post on the rim and allowed himself to doze.

The first tinge of pink in the eastern sky found Ponce on horseback, hurrying to reach the Chiricahuas before the day was done.

The Dragoon and Chiricahua Mountains had long been the stronghold of the Chiricahua Apaches. Time and again they had expelled outsiders who dared to claim the land as their own. First it had been haughty Spaniards intent on educating the Apaches in the one true faith. Then it had been Mexicans, who came to mine for copper and other precious metals. Finally, the Apaches had clashed with relative newcomers to the region, the Americans, who asserted a right to the land because they had beaten the Mexicans in a great war.

Ponce would never accept the American claim. The Chiricahuas were his home. He'd rather fight and die, if need be, for the land that meant so much to him. Now he scoured the horizon with eager eyes for his first glimpse of the range he knew like he did the back of his hand. The mountains where he would be safe.

At the sanctuary known as Sweet Grass.

Chapter Seven

Clay Taggart's first impulse on seeing the cavalry escort was to vault erect and flee. He wouldn't have gotten five feet before the troopers spotted him, and realizing that, he did the next best thing. Picking up handfuls of dirt, he covered his legs and sprinkled some on his back. Then he put his head as close to the saguaro as he dared, tucked his arms close to its base, and went as rigid as a rock.

The buckboard moved at a snail's pace. Both occupants wore suits and bowlers. Beside them rode a captain in a dusty uniform who was listening to the older of the pair.

"—damned nice of you, Forester, to ride with us the rest of the way. Not that we'd need the protection. We haven't seen a lousy Apache the whole trip."

"That doesn't mean they're not around, Mr. Walters," the captain responded.

Quick Killer

"Then why haven't they ambushed us?"

"If you had lived in Tucson longer, you'd know the answer," Captain Forester said. "Apaches only attack when it's in their best interests. Nine times out of ten they do it for the spoils." He gestured at the buckboard. "They don't have any use for wagons, so they'd likely figure the two of you weren't worth the bother."

"But wouldn't they want to lift our hair?"

"Not necessarily, sir," the officer said. "Apaches aren't like the Sioux and Cheyenne and other Plains tribes. They don't count coup, and as a rule they don't do much scalping. It has to do with their beliefs about the dead."

"I don't follow you," Walter said.

"Apaches want nothing to do with those who have died. When one of them passes on, right away the body is wrapped in a blanket and buried at a secret location, then all the deceased's belongings and wickiup are burned." Forester scratched at the stubble on his chin. "If a warrior takes a scalp, he has to go through a long purification process before he can keep it. Most think it's not worth the bother."

"Where did you learn so much about their heathen ways?"

"From the scouts at Fort Bowie. Some of them are Apache."

"I must say, I never thought when I left Illinois that—"

Distance and the rattle of accoutrements on the cavalry mounts prevented Clay from hearing the rest. He saw tired trooper after tired trooper go by, and only after the last quartet had disappeared to the east did he rise and rejoin the Chiricahuas.

Once across the road, Clay struck to the northwest. The band came on scattered ranches and gave

95

them a wide berth. Occasionally, they encountered roving herds of cattle in which the Apaches showed no interest. They preferred horseflesh to beef and only resorted to stealing cows when there was a shortage of horses.

Clay couldn't wait to reach the spread of the man he was going to kill. He imagined the horrified look Jack Bitmer would wear when they came face to face, and relished the thought of making Bitmer's death an agonizing one. So distracted did he become by his daydreams that he didn't hear voices wafting over a hill to their left until Delgadito leaned over and slapped him on the arm to get his attention.

Instantly drawing rein, Clay cocked his head. The words were in English but too faint to make out. He handed his reins to Delgadito and went up the slope on foot, dropping prone near the crest.

Below lay a sprawling valley filled with everything from young calves to old bulls. A dozen cowboys were busy steer roping and branding. Clay had done the same countless times on his own ranch, and for a minute nostalgia provoked a deep sadness over the turn of events that had deprived him of the way of life he'd known and loved.

Some cowboys were born to the saddle. Others learned to cherish the work by becoming a puncher through circumstance. Whichever was the case, once they were a charter member of the cow crowd they'd rather die than do anything else for a living. Something about the feel of a dependable horse between a man's legs, about the creak and smell of saddle leather and the carefree life of the open range, got into a man's blood and never went away.

The yip of a puncher closing in on a running steer near the base of the hill caused Clay to duck down. He heard the thud of hoofs as the steer thundered up the slope with the cowhand on its tail. Scooting downward on his hands and knees, he rose just as the steer pounded over the top. The animal slanted to the right. And then came the cowboy, astonishment as plain as day on his face, reining up in alarm and giving voice to a bellow that must have been heard clear back to Tucson.

"Injuns! Injuns! Everybody, there's Injuns here!"

Clay had no desire to shoot the man. He turned to run as the puncher's hand dropped to a flashy Colt. A rifle cracked, and the cowboy tumbled backward.

Bounding like a jackrabbit, Clay reached the bottom and swung onto his horse. A chorus of incensed cries told him the rest of the hands were on the fly toward the hill, so without delay he reined the chestnut and galloped due south. The Apaches fell in behind him.

Clay looked back as the hands crested the hill. They hardly paused at the body. Palming their hardware and pulling out rifles, they flew after the band. Clay bent low, riding for his life, the wind whipping his hair. If he had his druthers, he'd rather be chased by the cavalry or other Indians or anyone except a passel of riled punchers. Cowboys were not only superb horsemen from having spent every day from dawn to dusk in the saddle, they were a lot more persistent than the army would be when one of their own bought the farm. They were pure hell with the hide off and as fearless as Apaches.

Scattered shots broke out, none drawing blood. Clay swept around another hill and rode like the wind across barren flatland, the Apaches staying even with him, the four of them forming a ragged line. Rifle fire fueled their flight. Clay glanced at the Chiricahuas and wondered what they were thinking.

At that moment, their thoughts were varied.

Fiero was filled with disgust at being made to run from a pack of lowly white-eyes. He was disappointed in Lickoyee-shis-inday, who had shown such promise in wiping out the poachers. He would much rather have dug in and fought. The odds meant nothing to him. Many times he'd faced far greater and survived.

Cuchillo Negro, on the other hand, approved highly of White Apache's leadership. True to Apache custom, he would rather run away to fight another day than let himself be senselessly slaughtered. His only complaint was that White Apache had been preoccupied the past few miles instead of fully alert as a *Shis-Inday* should be.

Delgadito had mixed feelings. He still didn't like being overshadowed by another, especially an *Americano*, but he no longer resented it so strongly. Not now that Cuchillo Negro had shown him the way to excite the entire Chiricahua nation into breaking the fetters of their white conquerors. All it would take was a series of successful raids, enough to convince his people that the White Apache was a man of powerful medicine. They would see a white-eye who was on their side, see that those who rode with him slew whites with impunity, and they would come to realize that Americans were not the invincible foes most Chiricahuas believed. More and more warriors would flock to join the band. Eventually they would drive the whites from their land, and when that was done, Delgadito would assume the leadership so long denied him and take his rightful place as war chief of the tribe.

Unaware of all this, Clay vaulted a narrow gully on the fly. While in midair a bullet tugged at his new hat. Several others buzzed close overhead. It seemed the cowboys were more interested in bringing him down than they were any of the warriors, and he knew why. Everyone in the territory had heard of the White Apache and of the bounty being offered for his corpse, no questions asked.

In an ironic switch, the Apaches rode silently while the cowboys whooped in bloodthirsty glee. None of the Chiricahuas wasted ammo by returning fire although several times Fiero began to lift his rifle as if to do so.

The open flatland gave way to a forest of saguaro that stretched for as far as the eye could see to the southwest. Clay would rather have run naked through a briar patch than attempt to lose the cowboys among the giant cactuses, but he had no choice. Into their midst he plunged, weaving and winding as openings presented themselves, doing his best to spare himself and the chestnut from harm where the saguaros were packed close together.

Slugs ripped into the cactus on either side, sending pieces flying. Something stung Clay's left cheek, cutting deep. A glance revealed the cowboys had fanned out to enter the saguaro at different points. Some were closer than others, and all were finding it hard to use their guns accurately with so many cactuses intervening.

Clay saw one puncher swing in behind him and cut loose with a pistol. The shots came much too close for comfort, so Clay shifted, leveling his Winchester. The cowboy panicked and slanted to the right, reining so abruptly his animal was unable to make the turn smoothly and plowed into a tall saguaro. Both squealed as they went down.

Other punchers were gaining ground too. Clay had to discourage them, so to that end he snapped off a swift volley that forced the cowboys to seek cover. Fiero joined in, but Delgadito and Cuchillo Negro held their fire.

For minutes the frenzied chase continued. The renegades held their own, riding flawlessly, at one with their mounts. All was going as well as could be expected until Delgadito's animal stepped into a hole.

Clay witnessed the spill out of the corner of an eye. He saw Delgadito leap clear as the animal went into a roll and heard the mount's tortured whinny as its foreleg shattered, the broken bone jutting through its skin. Since he was nearest, he skirted a wide saguaro to reach Delgadito before the cowboys did. He saw Delgadito rising unsteadily, saw a lean cowhand bearing down on the Apache and taking deliberate aim with a Winchester. Without giving a thought to the fact he was shooting a white man to save a redskin, he fired.

The cowhand sailed from the saddle with limbs outspread.

"Grab hold!" Clay shouted in Apache as he galloped up to Delgadito and lowered his left arm. Oddly, the warrior hesitated. And meanwhile, cowboys were converging from several directions at once.

Delgadito knew the *Americanos* were closing in on him. Yet he couldn't quite bring himself to reach for Lickoyee-shis-inday's hand knowing he would again owe his life to the white-eye. It was bad enough Taggart had saved him when the scalp hunters slaughtered his band; it was bad enough he had to live with the shame of having led his followers to their deaths. To be beholden once more to Taggart was like rubbing salt on a fresh wound. But a bullet clipping a cactus almost at his elbow reminded him he had to live in order to carry out his larger scheme to wreak vengeance on the *Americanos;* so, taking a short step, he leaped onto the chestnut behind White Apache.

Clay wheeled his mount and fled. He shoved his .44-40 at Delgadito, then palmed one of his ivory-handled Colts and banged two swift shots at the cowboys. With each shot a man fell. He faced front to devote his attention to riding and felt Delgadito lurch against him.

Fiero and Cuchillo Negro had slowed to allow them to catch up and were directing a withering hail of lead at the cowpokes, most of whom sought cover.

The chestnut struggled to maintain a full gallop bearing the weight of two men. Clay had to rein the horse in a little while keeping his eyes skinned for cowboys. He noticed several of the punchers were no longer pursuing and snapped off three more shots to discourage the remainder.

Gradually, one by one, the cowboys gave up, all except for a lanky pair who appeared determined to follow the Apaches to the gates of Hell, if need be. On the one hand Clay was annoyed by their persistence, but on the other he admired punchers who were so loyal to the brand they'd rather die than admit they'd been beaten.

A minute later even the last pair were forced to turn back when Fiero and Cuchillo Negro, their rifles reloaded, halted to steady their aim and cut loose with shots that clipped saguaros within inches of the cowboys. Reluctantly, the punchers turned around to rejoin their pards.

Clay was glad to see them go. He'd been riding with the Apaches for a while now but he still couldn't gun down men who were only doing their duty without feeling a pang of guilt. It wasn't like killing those who had tried to hang him, or those who wronged the Apaches.

Presently, the sea of saguaros ended. Chaparral provided cover, and Clay found a clearing among manzanitas where he reined up for the sake of their horses. He glanced over his shoulder and smiled at Delgadito. "That was a close one," he said in Apache before he realized Delgadito had his head bowed and saw that blood caked the warrior's shoulder and chest.

Sliding off, Clay turned just as the Apache pitched off toward him. He managed to get his arms out in time. Cuchillo Negro helped lower Delgadito to the ground.

The wound was high on the right side and still bleeding profusely. Clay had seen similar wounds before and knew they sometimes proved fatal. "We must help him," he said.

"I know a root that would do some good," Cuchillo Negro said, "but I do not know if I can find one quickly enough."

"Try," Clay said, and the warrior ran off. Clay looked up at Fiero. "We will need a small fire in case there are no roots. And I would like you to break open a cartridge so we can use the powder."

"Am I a woman that I should jump when another man tells me what to do?"

"No. You are Delgadito's friend and you want him to live."

Fiero sat there a full minute mulling what to do. He had agreed to let the *Americano* lead them, and he had on occasion helped the white man, such as the time he instructed Lickoyee-shis-inday in how to meet a formal challenge by another Chiricahua, but he wasn't one to take direct orders from anyone, not even another Apache.

Fiero gazed into Lickoyee-shis-inday's eyes and was surprised to see silent, sincere appeal. The thought struck him that this strange white-eye would probably do the same for him were he to be gravely wounded, a startling revelation. As Fiero saw it, whites and Apaches were inveterate enemies. Granted, Lickoyee-shis-inday had proven different from most of his kind, but the concept of a white man actually caring whether an Apache lived or died was virtually unthinkable. "Would you do the same for me?" he bluntly asked.

"Of course. We must always be ready to help one another. If we do not stick together, we will not last long."

The proposition needed a lot of thought. Fiero climbed down and walked into the trees, saying over a shoulder, "I will fetch wood for the fire."

"I am grateful," Clay said. With that problem taken care of, he studied the wound, gingerly probing around the bullet hole. The blood just wouldn't stop. He wondered if Delgadito would die, and what he should do in that case. The Apache stirred weakly. Clay shifted, his head lifting, and found the Apache's dark eyes regarding him with odd intensity.

"I will die soon, Lickoyee-shis-inday."

"You do not know that for certain," Clay responded. "It is not fitting for a man to talk of death when there is every chance he will live to be wrinkled with old age."

Delgadito gazed skyward. "An Apache knows when his time has come. This wound is worse than any other I have ever had. I can feel my insides growing wet with blood. They say when that happens there is no hope."

Alarmed by the news there was internal bleeding, Clay said brusquely, "Let me be the judge of whether you will pull through or not."

"Some things are beyond the control of men, and this is one of them," Delgadito said so softly the words were barely audible. "It is not for us to say if I will live." Sighing, he closed his eyes. "I do not mind telling you that I welcome death with a warm heart."

Exasperated, Clay switched to English. "How the dickens can you say such nonsense, pard? Life is too damned precious for us to chuck it aside without putting up a fight."

"I tired, White Apache," Delgadito said, and moved an arm enough to touch a finger to his chest. "In here."

"You're talking craziness."

Delgadito was fast losing consciousness. He spoke once more in his own tongue. "When the white-eyes took our freedom, they took our life. Those on the reservation are already dead but do not yet realize it." He coughed and his voice dropped even more. "It is better that I die now, before the *Shis-Inday* are no more."

"Don't give up the ghost yet," Clay said in English. He remembered hearing somewhere that it was best to keep people in Delgadito's condition awake and talking, so he went on, "If there's anyone who knows about taking the big jump, it's me. I was guest of honor at a string party, after all. But I didn't go meekly, and that's one of the reasons I'm still kicking. You've got to do the same. Like me, you have something to live for." Clay's features hardened. "I've got a no-account snake in the grass to settle with, and you have a whole passel of white-eyes to deal with."

Clay stopped on seeing that the warrior was unconscious again. Since there was nothing else he could do until the others returned, he slipped a rifle bullet from his bandoleer and drew his butcher knife. Prying the cartridge open took a while, but at length he poured the small amount of gunpowder it contained onto a flat rock.

Fiero showed up with an armful of wood and soon had a fire going. Not long after Cuchillo Negro returned to report no luck in finding the type of root he needed in order to make a poultice.

"Then we do this the hard way," Clay said.

The flow of blood had reduced to a trickle. Clay slowly sprinkled grains of gunpowder around the edges of the wound, then lightly pried the wound further apart and fed grains into the hole. He had to be careful not to use too much or the cure would prove instantly fatal.

Fiero and Cuchillo Negro watched without commenting. It was Apache custom for warriors to hold their own counsel when they had nothing worthwhile to say. Both wanted their former leader to live, but both also knew his fate was in the hands of *Yusn*.

Clay wished there was water nearby so he could wash the wound beforehand. As a substitute, he ripped off a small piece of his shirt, moistened it with spittle, and wiped off as much excess blood as the material would absorb. Then, tossing the cloth aside, he selected a slender firebrand and lifted it from the fire. Tiny flames licked at the air as he lowered the lit end close to the bullet hole.

Delagdito stirred but did not awaken.

"Here goes nothing," Clay said to himself, and dipped the burning tip. Immediately the gunpowder caught. There was a blinding flash and flames shot from the hole. The acrid scent of smoke and charred flesh filled the air.

Delgadito's dark eyes snapped wide, reflecting acute torment. He tried to sit up but couldn't. Raising his head, he stared at the smoke pouring from the wound, then at Clay. His mouth parted as if he were going to speak.

"I did the only thing I could," Clay said in his defense.

Eyelids fluttering, the tall warrior collapsed and lay insensate, his chest rising and falling.

Blood had stopped flowing from the hole. Clay eased a fingertip into it to ascertain whether the internal bleeding had likewise ceased. The flesh was a sickly black for over an inch deep. Underneath it was brown except at the bottom where it was a healthy pink. He found no trace of fresh blood.

"Do we go now, White Apache?" Fiero asked.

Clay could not quite believe his ears. "Go?"

"Yes. To kill the white-eye who is your enemy."

"And what about Delgadito?"

"We have done all we can for him."

"But he is too weak to move. We must stay the night to watch over him. In the morning we will head back to Sweet Grass."

"We will not go through with the raid?"

"No. We dare not leave Delgadito here alone. He cannot fend for himself. We will take him back to Sweet Grass where he can heal in peace."

Never in Fiero's experience had he heard of an attack being called off simply because a lone warrior had been hurt. Once, he would have objected strenuously to being denied his share of possible plunder because of the misfortunes of another. Apaches looked out for themselves. That was the essential creed by which they all lived, the acknowledged law under which they had existed since time immemorial. Yet here was this White Apache telling them that they must regard the welfare of other warriors as they would their own. It was an idea that would take considerable time to accept, if ever.

Cuchillo Negro had risen. "We will do as you say, White Apache. I will see to the horses."

"And I will hunt game for our supper," Fiero declared.

Watching them walk off, Clay smiled. Something told him he had won another round in his campaign to win them over to his way of thinking. Provided all went well, before long they'd be his to command as he pleased, and then Arizona would run red with the blood of those who had wronged him!

Chapter Eight

The young Chiricahua called Ponce arrived at Sweet Grass as twilight descended on the remote retreat. After setting the horses free to graze, he rode to the gurgling stream and squatted to drink. As his hand dipped into the cool water, his eyes drifted to a fresh set of tracks in the soft soil nearby. He immediately stiffened and glanced suspiciously around.

Apaches were masterful trackers. From an early age they were instructed in the art, taught by the very best warriors. So skillful were they, their ability was considered by many to border on the supernatural, an illusion the Apaches did all they could to foster.

Warriors learned, for instance, that when the toes of tracks pointed inward, then the prints had been made by Indians, and when the toes pointed outward, then white-eyes or the *Nakai-hey* were responsible. From the depth of tracks and the strides taken, Apaches could tell the approximate weight and height of those who made them. They were also versed in the many styles of footwear, from moccasins to boots to sandals.

So it was that the instant Ponce set eyes on the fresh prints he knew they had been made by someone wearing Apache moccasins. Since the other renegades were off on the raid, he knew it couldn't have been one of them. And since it was rare for reservation warriors who had accepted the white yoke to come to Sweet Grass, he immediately assumed the footprints had been made by another Army scout sent to ferret out the band.

Rising, Ponce scoured the stream and was confounded to see another set of fresh tracks, this time a trail left by a woman. His blood quickened as he hunkered down to examine them, for they were of a size and shape he knew as well as he knew his own. Yet they could have been made by any woman the same age, he reasoned, and stilled the alarm blaring in his breast.

The tracks led northward toward the rugged heights dominating Sweet Grass. Ponce levered a round into the chamber of his rifle and set off on the trail at a dog trot. Because he was following fellow Apaches, he took more precautions than he would have had he been following whites. Like a flitting specter he covered the rough ground, never still in one spot for more than a second at a time, never exposing himself for even the briefest of moments. Totally silent, he pressed upward until he came to a stand of ponderosa, and here he paused behind a wide trunk to adjust his mind to the rhythm of the woodland.

Somewhere to the east a squirrel chattered, to the west sparrows chirped gaily.

Ponce gazed up the mountain slope, a slope he was very familiar with from the many times he had explored it in search of game for their meals. Above the timber reared clusters of jumbled boulders, a maze few could negotiate. He couldn't imagine the couple going there.

Ponce was perplexed by the couple's presence. It made no sense for a scout to have brought a woman to Sweet Grass. Nor did it make sense for a reservation warrior to have done so. Apache women were every bit as hardy as their men and equally capable of living off the land, but women weren't permitted to take part in warfare. There were exceptions, of course, but they were rare.

Believing his quarry to be among the tall pines, Ponce advanced slowly. He was quite surprised when the tracks led straight through the trees to the rocky elevation beyond. From the base of the lowest boulder he swept the cluttered boulder field without spying anyone.

Ponce was about to go on when one of the woman's tracks arrested his attention. Marking the bare earth beside it were dozens of dark drops. Ponce touched one with a fingertip and sniffed his finger. It was blood, as he knew it would be. He took another step, saw where the woman had stumbled to one knee, and then spotted a severed finger lying close by.

Ponce stared at it, at the trickle of blood still oozing from the pink flesh, and felt an icy, invisible finger scrape the length of his spine. Quickening his pace, he went another fifty yards and came on the second finger. Like the other, it had been cut off mere minutes ago.

They were markers, Ponce realized, deliberately left for him to find. He ran now, recklessly, winding

110

among the boulders until he came on a small cleared space and there in the center, wedged upright in the soil, was a third finger.

Halting, Ponce raised the finger to his nose and inhaled. His jaw muscles twitched and he flushed scarlet. He darted behind a rock monolith and gently set the finger down. Then he sprinted onward, sheer rage filling him with blood lust so intense he could hardly think straight.

Two more fingers were found before Ponce reached the crest of a ridge. The twilight had deepened to near complete darkness and it was difficult for him to see the tracks. Often he had to feel the ground for the telltale impressions.

Once past the ridge, the slope steepened sharply. Ponce climbed in an awkward crouch, his pace reduced to a virtual crawl. A flat shelf afforded a place to ease the cramps in his calves. He saw a large flat rock in front of him, and on top of it the vague outline of something foreign. Only when he bent down did he make out the outline of a human foot, a woman's foot, sheared off at the ankle by a razor-sharp tomahawk.

The blood trail was a black ribbon leading ever upward. Ponce climbed on, the scent so strong he no longer had to bother finding footprints. He seemed to remember there being a clearing on top of the next slope, and there was. But the figure spread-eagled in the middle was a new addition.

Ponce ran to her, blood thundering in his ears. He'd done more than his share of torturing Mexicans and *Americanos* in his time, and had seen the gruesome handiwork of those who hunted his people, but those experiences did little to prepare him for the shock of seeing the woman he cared for butchered and dying.

Ko-do's eyes, ears, and nose were gone. Her left hand was a stump, her right leg ended at the ankle. Strips of skin were missing from her neck and arms. She breathed in feeble gasps, her body trembling. Looped around her neck was a length of rope.

Ponce knelt and touched her forehead. Ko-do flinched, shuddered more violently, then whined. "It is I," he said softly.

Somehow she found the strength to speak in a strangled whisper. "I am sorry. I told him where to find you."

"Who?"

"Tats-ah-das-ay-go."

"I will cut out his heart," Ponce vowed, running his finger across her brow.

"For my sake, do not fight him."

"You know better."

Ko-do's breathing slowed. For the longest while she made no comment. Then, "What are you waiting for?"

"It is a hard thing for a man to do."

"Please."

"He will hear."

"He already knows."

"I will miss you, Firefly."

"And I you." Ko-do convulsed briefly. "Please. Do it now. For me."

Without hesitation, Ponce placed the muzzle of his Winchester against her temple and stroked the trigger. As the blast echoed off across the valley he wheeled and darted into the boulders. He expected an answering shot, but there was none.

Anyone other than an Apache might have broken down at that point, might have succumbed to shock or tears or sorrow so profound it numbed body and soul. Ponce did not. He had been bred since infancy to control his feelings, to bend his emotions to the iron rod of his will, to achieve a state of complete self-mastery. So although inwardly profound sadness mixed with a raging thirst for revenge dominated him, he neither showed it in his expression nor allowed the upheaval to cloud his mind. He knew his judgment must be unimpaired if he was to stand any chance at all of beating the notorious Quick Killer.

Ponce listened, but heard nothing. He looked, but saw no one. Yet as sure as the moon was rising in the east, Tats-ah-das-ay-go was out there somewhere, waiting to slay him at an opportune moment.

Every Apache had heard of Quick Killer, the Army scout who rubbed out renegades for the price of a good horse. Yet Quick Killer's chosen line of work wasn't held against him. Many warriors would have liked to do the same but weren't as skilled at tracking or killing.

Several times Ponce had heard Delgadito mention that one day the white-eyes would send Quick Killer against them, most recently after Nah-kah-yen tried to wipe out their band. According to Delgadito, Tats-ah-das-ay-go was twice as good as Nah-kah-yen. Clever, tough, and as swift as lightning, Quick Killer was more to be dreaded than the whole *Americano* Army.

Knowing this, Ponce didn't hesitate. He was going to avenge Ko-do's death, come what may. In that respect, he was no different from all men everywhere. No man would ever sit idly by when their loved ones were threatened or slain. They will do what has to be done regardless of the consequences.

Ponce moved among the boulders with catlike speed and silence, senses alert for his enemy. He suspected that Quick Killer was aware of his movements and mystified because the scout didn't attack, especially after all the trouble Quick Killer had gone to in order to lure him to the spot.

The breeze picked up, as it often did at that time of the night, the fluttering whisper of its passage loud enough to drown out faint noises. Ponce turned this way and that as he sought his quarry, never rising higher than a low crouch, his cocked rifle clenched firmly.

Presently Ponce came to a cleared space and went to dart across it. He took a single step when a rifle boomed to his left and his right leg was jarred out from under him by a jolting blow. On elbows and knees he scrambled for cover, then took stock. He didn't return fire even though he knew the scout had moved after pulling the trigger and he had a fair idea where Quick Killer was now concealed. Any Apache would have done the same.

The bullet had caught Ponce in the fleshy part of the thigh and bored a neat hole clean through. There was scant blood and the bone hadn't been broken, so Ponce considered himself extremely lucky.

Crawling, Ponce bore to the right. He tried putting himself in Quick Killer's moccasins and decided the scout's next move would be to circle around and come at him from the opposite direction. Only he would be waiting. Once Delgadito and the rest saw Quick Killer's body, they would regard him with greater respect than had been their custom to date. Ponce could hardly wait.

The second rifle shot sounded much closer. Ponce jerked his head back as dirt spewed into his face, then he rolled against the base of a boulder where the deep shadow screened him. He touched his cheek and felt blood. By the width of a finger had his life been spared.

Quick Killer

Ponce didn't move for the longest while. He wanted Quick Killer to believe he was on the go, so every so often he picked up tiny pebbles and hurled them as far as he could. It was an old trick but one that often worked.

At last Ponce ventured out among the boulders. Here they were much larger, jagged monoliths squatting somber and black in the darkness. He made no noise on the hard ground, and he was confident he would soon have Quick Killer in his sights.

A sudden shout surprised Ponce and he turned toward its source, scraping a forearm on the soil as he did.

"Make this easy on yourself, young one. Give up and I will grant you a painless death."

Ponce thought he saw a vague form. He snapped off two shots and heard a mocking laugh that wavered eerily on the wind. Clearly he had missed, and he was ashamed for having fired without a definite target. It had been the wrong thing to do. Now Quick Killer had him pinpointed precisely.

Rolling to the left, Ponce pushed up and limped rapidly southward. He had a troublesome thought. It appeared that the scout was toying with him, treating him as if he were a mere boy and not a man. For Quick Killer to call out that way had been an insult. No warrior would dare do such a thing when fighting a foe worthy of the name.

Ponce didn't like being rated as of little regard. He had slain dozens since taking the renegade trail, and on forays into Mexico had held his own with the likes of Fiero and Cuchillo Negro. He deserved to be treated with caution, not contempt.

Briefly, the wind died, and Ponce paused so as not to give himself away. He scanned the vicinity without result, then moved on when the wind resumed. Due to his single-minded devotion to the matter at hand, he didn't realize he was near the spot where the maiden lay until he saw the outline of her body. The sight brought an odd constriction to his throat and he swallowed hard.

Ponce should have gone around. He should have stayed among the boulders to avoid detection. But he wanted one last glimpse of Firefly before going down the slope, so he dashed into the open past her. Too late, it registered that her body was much larger than it should be. Too late, he saw that the figure on the ground wore a buckskin shirt and leggings and not a beaded dress. And too late, Ponce tried to level his Winchester.

Quick Killer was a blur as he shifted and swung a sturdy leg, striking the younger warrior across the back of both feet to bring Ponce crashing down. Desperately, Ponce tried to brace a hand and rise to his knees but something smashed him in the temple and the next thing he knew he was flat on his side tasting dirt in his mouth as the barrel of a rifle was jammed against his ear.

"Do not move, young one, or you will die much sooner than you have to."

The tone was that of steel grinding on steel, of ice made into sound. Ponce did as he was told, but not out of fear. Every moment he was spared was another moment he might turn the tables and avenge Ko-do.

"You have talent, young one," Quick Killer said. "Were you to live another five winters, you would be one of the best."

"You did not need to involve the girl," Ponce said as a rough hand roamed his body searching for concealed weapons.

Quick Killer

"A wise hunter always uses the right bait to lure his prey into his snare."

"When hunting animals, yes."

"And since when is hunting men any different?" Quick Killer said. "Can it be that you have rode with Delgadito for so long and learned so little? Trickery is the Apache way, and has always been so. What we lack in numbers, we make up for with our wits. How else have we survived so long?"

Ponce was flipped onto his back. He couldn't very well refute the truth, so he made no comment.

"Where are the others?"

"I do not know," Ponce lied, and had to bite his lower lip to keep from crying out when the scout rammed a foot into his thigh wound.

"If you want the same treatment as your woman, I will not hesitate to cut you up. But I should think you would be smarter than she was."

"I am not afraid to die!"

"Then you are a worthy Chiricahua," Quick Killer said, the corners of his mouth twitching upward.

"Do you mock me, breed?" Ponce snapped. He never saw the blow that rendered him unconscious. When next he opened his eyes, he was flat on his back beside a small fire, his arms and legs bound. His head ached abominably. Twisting his neck, he discovered the scout had toted him to the valley floor and they were now camped a few yards from the stream. Tats-ah-das-ay-go was skinning a bloody rabbit.

"You have much to learn, cub," the scout said without looking up.

"How did you know I had revived?" Ponce asked, forcing his sluggish brain and mouth to work despite the terrible agony pounding in his temples.

"The rhythm of your breathing changed," Quick Killer disclosed. "It will give a man away every time."

"You must think you are crafty, like a fox," Ponce said scornfully.

"No, I know I am smarter than most," the other countered. "Otherwise my enemies would have killed me long ago." He cut off chunks of dripping meat and began impaling them on a slender stick he had whittled to a sharp point. "You, however, must be a weak thinker or you would not have let yourself be taken so easily."

"Save your insults, breed."

This time Quick Killer spun, the makeshift spit pointed at the young warrior's face. "Are you so stupid that you failed to learn your lesson the last time?" He sighed. "Respect, stripling. It is all that really matters in this life. When a man has earned it, he can hold his head high. Without it, he is as a lowly worm." Quick Killer resumed placing meat on the stick. "Surely I have earned yours."

"You dream with your eyes open."

"Delgadito would not be so childish," Quick Killer said. "He would be man enough to admit he had met his match."

"You?" Ponce said. "You flatter yourself, Tats-ah-das-ay-go. Delgadito is a better warrior than you will ever be. He has proven his ability time and again. None are his equal." Ponce coiled his legs and sat up, the effort aggravating the torment in his head. "Certainly not a man like you, who makes much of respect but who has earned only contempt by working for the white dogs who want to exterminate our kind."

"We do what we have to."

Ponce secretly tested the rope binding his wrists while saying, "No one made you a scout against your will. You went to the whites of your own accord and asked if you could work for them. And why? To kill for money." He adopted a haughty sneer. "When a man runs with dogs, what does that make him?"

Quick Killer jabbed the bottom of the stick into the ground so that the meat hung at an angle over the low flames. "You have a talent for insulting others," he remarked. "If I did not need you alive, I would slit your throat right now."

"Why have you spared me?"

"For the same reason I kept your woman alive after taking her from her village. To use as bait."

Ponce didn't like the sound of that. "To catch Delgadito? Do you really think he will fall into your clutches as easily as I did?"

"I have no intention of going to all the trouble of taking him alive," Quick Killer said. "All I need to do is lure him within rifle range, and for that you will serve most admirably."

"You are wrong if you think Delgadito would risk his life for mine," Ponce said, but he was not as sure as he tried to sound. "And besides, he will not be alone. There are twelve warriors in our band, more than you can fight alone."

"Twelve?" Quick Killer chuckled. "You speak with two tongues, young one. I read the sign in this valley most carefully when I arrived. There are five of you counting the one called White Apache."

"You are guessing," Ponce bluffed.

"Tracks do not lie. And they tell me that five different men have lived in this valley for some time. Four walk like Apaches, with light treads and short steps. One clomps about like a white-eye even though he wears Apache moccasins. He also drinks like a white-eye, by kneeling beside the stream instead of squatting as a true warrior would do."

"So you know, then," Ponce conceded. "But you are still outnumbered. Even if you should slay Delgadito, the others will stop you from collecting your blood money."

"Only if I fail to kill them first."

The insight startled the youth. "Delgadito is not the only one you are after?"

"No. I want him and the White Apache most of all," Quick Killer said. "But since long ago I learned not to leave a job half finished, I will kill the rest to prevent them from coming after me later."

Ponce offered one last argument. "Nah-kah-yen tried and lost his life. You would do well to learn from his mistakes."

"The only mistake he made was in thinking he was good enough to handle Delgadito." Quick Killer adjusted the stick to roast the meat more evenly. "A man who oversteps himself often falls flat on his face."

"As you will," Ponce predicted. He had given up on the ropes. They were tied too tight, the knots too secure. Yet somehow he must break loose or else find a way of alerting his friends when they arrived at the sanctuary.

The scout eased his hunting knife from its sheath and held the blade so that it reflected the firelight. "You might like to know that your woman was very brave. I had to remove both of her eyes before she told me where to find you."

The reminder provoked Ponce into attempting an awkward lunge. He wanted to knock Quick Killer into the fire but was swatted down instead.

"Behave, cub. Your time will come soon enough."

"So will yours. I just wish I could be there to see it." Ponce lay on his side, reflecting. He had one thing in his favor. Delgadito and the others wouldn't return for days, perhaps a week or more if they stole a lot of horses and had to go out of their way to evade cavalry patrols on their way back. In that event, the scout might lose interest and wander elsewhere. Or so he hoped until the next statement Quick Killer uttered.

"You have no idea how much killing Delgadito and the White Apache means to me. No matter how long it takes, no matter what I have to do, I will bring them back. And then everyone, whites and Indians alike, will look on Tats-ah-das-ah-go with the respect he deserves."

Chapter Nine

Delgadito appeared to be dying. His breaths were irregular and labored. His body quivered in convulsive bursts that made his breathing worse. The wound had discolored to an ugly black and blue, the flesh festering in a pus-filled sore.

Clay Taggart looked down on the pale warrior and made a critical decision. "There is a ranch over those hills to the south. I will go there and see if they have what we need to help him."

"Is that wise?" Fiero asked, remembering the last time Lickoyee-shis-inday had visited his own kind. "They will kill you on sight."

"I must do something," Clay said, partly out of concern for the warrior who had saved his neck from being stretched and partly because he suspected the others wouldn't help him in his vendetta against Miles Gillett without Delgadito there to goad them along. Hitching at his gunbelt, he stepped to the chestnut and swung up.

Cuchillo Negro came over. "We will wait until sunrise. No longer. The patrol we saw this morning might double back and find our trail."

"I understand," Clay said.

It had been two days since they tangled with the cowboys, yet they had gone less than twenty miles. In addition to Delgadito's condition slowing them down, they had to contend with a column of troopers that had arrived in the area with remarkable dispatch. Clay guessed they were the same bunch he'd run into at the road. They were conducting a thorough sweep that would eventually uncover the hiding place he'd picked deep in the chaparral if the band didn't move on soon. Say, by first light.

Clay rode with the cocked .44-40 in his right hand. He made a point of sticking to ground covered by grass and brush so as not to raise any dust. To his best recollection, the ranch he intended to visit was owned by a man named Welch, a devout transplanted Kentucky miner who had come West for his health and been able to build a thriving cattle herd. Clay had only met the man twice and visited the house but once, briefly. At that time, Welch had four hired hands.

On the lookout for punchers, Clay was puzzled when he spotted shimmering pinpoints of bright light along the bottom of the foremost hill. As he drew near the pinpoints resolved into shiny strands supported by regularly spaced posts.

"I'll be damned," Clay muttered. "Thorny fence." Or barbed wire, as some called it. A few ranchers had imported rolls of the stuff and drawn the wrath of their own neighbors for their audacity. Several had come to blows. And there were some who claimed worse trouble loomed on the horizon, that one day violence would erupt between those who reckoned they had the right to hem in their own property if they so desired and those who equated rangeland with wide open spaces.

The immediate problem Clay faced was getting onto the ranch. A fine jumper could clear the fence in a single hurdle, but he had no idea whether the chestnut was capable of doing so and he wasn't about to lose the horse on a gamble. Dismounting, he applied his Bowie to the top strand, in reality, a pair of thick wires wound together with keen spikes at intervals. He cut and scraped and dug slowly into the metal. In the process he was also dulling the edge on his knife, which he couldn't abide.

Clay rode westward, seeking a gap or break. He came to a draw where the wire had been strung about two feet off the bottom, not high enough for a cow to pass under but more than enough space for him to slide through. Tying the chestnut to a post, he proceeded on foot.

The afternoon sun beat down mercilessly. Twice Clay spooked lizards that darted off at astounding speed. To the east grazed cattle. To the west the grassland was replaced by mesquite.

It struck Clay as downright strange that here he was, a man who had once hated Apaches, risking his life to save one. And not just any old redskin. He was helping the most feared renegade in all of Arizona. Which proved that random circumstance had more sway in a fellow's life than all the good intentions in the world.

The hills were few. Beyond lay more grass, more cattle. A mile off stood the ranch house, stable, bunkhouse and corral. Clay saw no riders but left nothing to chance. He approached the ranch as he would a military post, with the utmost care. His training in Apache ways served him in good stead and presently he was secreted in shrubbery adjacent to the stable.

From the house wafted the merry tinkle of a piano and voices raised in harmonious song. Five buckboards were parked close to the hitching post. In the corral a pair of punchers were breaking a horse.

The peaceful scene tugged at Clay's heartstrings. Once again he was reminded of the rough but rewarding life he had forsaken for the sake of vengeance. Once again he longed to return to the old days, and his resolve faltered. But not for long because a striking, massive figure in an expensive suit appeared at the front window on the ground floor, a man endowed with a powerful frame so distinctive it could only belong to the man Clay longed to repay for the vile injustice done him: It was none other than Miles Gillett.

Clay was so amazed he forgot to use his rifle, and then Gillett strode back into the room. Clay flattened and wormed closer to the window. Apparently, Welch was having a get-together of some sort and had invited a number of friends and acquaintances. Where Gillett fit in, Clay had no idea. So far as he knew, Miles and Welch had never been very close. They'd always moved in different social circles.

Once abreast of the window, Clay saw many people moving about within. Blinding glare kept him from distinguishing features. He tucked the Winchester to his shoulder but held his fire, waiting for Gillett to reappear. He would only get one chance so he must make his shots count.

The singing went on and on, punctuated by loud conversations and much laughter. The guests were having a grand old time. Clay saw two people approach the window and tensed, thinking his time had come. They were women, however, and the sight of one sent a shiver down his spine.

Lilly Gillett was as ravishing as ever. Vivid images and sensations swamped over Clay; of the softness and scent of her luxuriant hair, the swell of her full breasts under his palms, the exquisite sweetness of her rosy lips on his. Lilly was the love of his life, the woman he'd yearned to marry, the radiant angel he'd set on a pedestal only to learn the hard way that her halo hid a set of devilish horns. For Lilly was the woman who had betrayed his love, who had played him for a fool so that Miles could steal his land. Next to her husband, she was the most treacherous, conniving creature in all of creation.

Automatically, Clay sighted on her chest. He'd never shot a woman before but at that particular instant he was ready and willing. Only a red haze shrouded his vision and his hands began shaking uncontrollably. He willed himself to relax, steeled his nerves, and smiled as the haze slowly faded.

Lilly and the other woman were gone.

Clay bided his time, hardly noticing the downward arc of the sun and the lengthening shadows cast by the oak trees in the front yard. The barking of a dog somewhere out back didn't disturb him either. Revenge was within his grasp and he wouldn't be denied.

The day was nearly done when the door opened and out bustled the guests. There were more women than men, and each and every one had to share a fond farewell with Welch's wife, who held the reason for the festivities bundled in swaddling in her arms. The women made quite a fuss over the infant, touching and kissing and hugging it as if it were their very own.

Clay had eyes only for Miles and Lilly Gillett. The wealthy couple were at the center of the crowd, talking to another husband and wife. Try as he might, Clay was unable to get a clear shot. When everyone moved in a body toward the buggies, he lowered his rifle and crawled to the left for a better shot. The new angle permitted him to see more of Miles and Lilly, but not enough to guarantee a kill.

Momentarily, the advancing ranks parted. Clay elevated the .44-40 and fixed a bead on the chest of his nemesis, but no sooner had he done so than the ranks closed again and he was denied the opportunity. He saw Lilly doting over the baby and thought of their own once cherished plan to have children some day, a plan ruined when Miles Gillett came between them. As a result, Clay would never know what it was like to take a stroll with a waddling little son at his side. He'd never know the joy of teaching his offspring to fish and hunt and ride and do the thousand and one things a man had to know to be worthy of the brand.

Clay aimed at the middle of the guests, his sinews as tightly strung as the barbed wire he'd seen before. His trigger finger was rock steady. All he needed was an unobstructed view for a mere second or two.

A heavyset woman with gray hair walked in front of Gillett, her bulk blocking him from eyebrows to toes. Clay saw her begin to turn, to lumber toward a nearby buckboard, and he lightly curved his finger on the trigger. He was on the verge of firing when harsh snarling broke out very close at hand and he twisted to see a large black cur bearing down on him with its lips curled up over its gleaming teeth.

Clay spun, leveling the Winchester just as the mongrel sprang. The boom of the retort rocked

127

his eardrums as the heavy caliber slug ripped into the dog's forehead, then exploded out the rear of its cranium. The mongrel slammed to the grass, sliding to within inches of Clay's moccasins. At the buckboards women were calling out, demanding to know what was going on, while some of the men stared suspiciously at the shrubbery. From the stable ran several punchers, unlimbering hardware.

As yet no one had spotted Clay. He dived and snaked toward the corral, keeping one eye on the guests and another on the cowhands. Welch was moving toward them, asking if they knew who had fired the shot.

Suddenly a short incline appeared. Clasping the rifle to his side, Clay rolled down to the corral and crouched beside a post. Rather than try to flee across open pasture, he dashed to the corner of the stable, checked to verify no one was by the open doors, and scooted within. A ladder brought him to a loft. He cracked the hay door so he could keep track of events and saw Welch and the three punchers moving toward the shrubbery, the hired hands with their six-shooters cocked.

"What is it, Arthur?" called out Mrs. Welch, her babe clutched protectively to her breast.

"We don't know yet, Ethel," answered Welch. He was about to squeeze through the row of bushes but a lanky puncher tugged at his jacket sleeve.

"Let me, boss," the man said, and went first, squeezing through to the other side. On spotting the dog, he dropped into a squat and pivoted right and left. "It's Buck!" he said. "He's been shot."

Welch and the other two men joined the lanky hand. They examined the mongrel, then straightened and scoured the area. From where Clay perched, he could just hear their voices.

"What do you think happened?" Welch asked no one in particular. "Who would shoot a good dog and run off?"

"Injuns," said the lanky one.

"Apaches, most likely," chimed in another.

"But why?" Welch replied. "It makes no sense, not even for those heathens."

"Apaches don't need an excuse to kill," declared the last cowpoke. "They do it for the thrill. I'd wager a month's pay that some wanderin' buck snuck in close for a look-see at the spread and had to gun down old Buck when the dog caught his damned scent."

"If so, where is the buck now?" Welch wondered.

The lanky cowboy wagged his shooting iron. "Me and the boys will poke around some, Mr. Welch."

"Thank you, Larry." Welch glanced at his visitors. "Under the circumstances it might be wise for me to have everyone go back into the house until the coast is clear. Let me know if you find anything."

"Sure thing, boss."

Clay watched Welch shoo the women indoors. The husbands, however, were eager to help in the hunt, and presently there were upwards of a dozen armed men prowling around the yard and the corral and moving out across the fields. Miles Gillett was one of them.

At long last Clay had the clear shot he wanted, yet now that he'd had a while to ponder on the situation, he refrained. Four men were in front of the stable, more on the sides. He knew he wouldn't live five minutes once he gave his position away. And as much as he craved vengeance, he craved life more. He had to live in order to mete out justice to the members of the posse that had done Gillett's dirty work.

Larry and another cowpoke were directly below the hay doors. The lanky puncher gestured at the stable and said, "I reckon it won't hurt to look in there."

"No Injun in his right mind would trap himself inside a building," said his companion.

"You never know," was Larry's argument. Together they entered, their spurs jingling lightly.

Clay lost sight of them as they moved below him. Outside, two more men came toward the corral, and he debated whether to fight or flee if he were discovered.

"No one in the stalls," said the companion.

"Same with the tack room," Larry stated.

"What about the loft?"

Clay slid to the right and furiously scooped with both hands. There were no bales to hide behind but there was plenty of loose hay, and in moments he had covered himself completely. He glimpsed the ladder, saw it jiggle as someone climbed. Larry's white Stetson materialized and the cowhand gave the loft a once-over. Clay could see the puncher's dark eyes narrow as they roved over the spot where he lay.

"Anything?" asked the man below.

"I don't rightly know yet," Larry said, coming higher. He set a boot on the hay and was lifting his hog-leg when a gunshot thundered to the west.

Clay was glad when the lanky puncher went lickety-split down from the loft and rushed from the stable to investigate. Shoving off the hay, he descended and ran to the back door. He spied several men running westward. Everyone was converging in that direction, so without delay he sprinted to the front, slipped along the corral to the shrubbery, and crouch-walked to the edge of the grass to the south.

In the distance was the mouth of the draw. So near, yet too far. He decided to wait for dark before moving from cover.

Folding his forearms under his chin, Clay made himself comfortable, pulled his hat low, and let his mind drift. The searchers had already been through the shrubbery from end to end so he felt safe staying there. He didn't count on having to deal with another dog.

Loud sniffing alerted him. Clay raised his head and peered through the bushes at four slim white legs moving along the next row over. It was smaller than the mongrel, a house-bred canine, he guessed. Mrs. Welch's pet, out relieving itself.

The dog came to Buck and circled the body three times, becoming more and more excited by the scent of blood. Moving in ever widening circles, the dog abruptly scampered toward the stable but drew up short less than six feet from Clay. He identified it as a Highland Terrier, a Scottish breed fancied by the well-to-do and noted for their courage and fighting ability. The last thing he needed was for the terrier to find him, yet it did.

Clay rose to his knees as the dog's strident yipping carried on the breeze. Everyone would hear. The animal danced this way and that, staying well beyond his reach, glaring and barking and snapping. Since someone was bound to come, Clay bent at the waist and sped off toward the draw.

The Highland Terrier advanced to the grass but would go no further. A bundle of energy, it bounced like a shaggy ball and continued to yowl madly.

Shouts signified people were hastening to the scene. Clay spotted a trio jogging past the stable but fortunately none were looking his way. He covered fifteen yards, then twenty. At thirty he straightened and raced like the wind.

"Lookee there! An Injun!"

Rifles cracked. Bullets thudded into the ground or whizzed past. Clay weaved to make it harder for them. Five or six men were in swift pursuit while others were hurrying to the corral for mounts.

Clay flew as if his ankles were endowed with wings. The grueling months spent among the Chiricahuas, hardening his body as it had never been hardened before, paid dividends now, enabling him to pull ahead of those on foot. Several slacked off, realizing they could never catch him.

The horsemen were a whole different problem. Two riders shot from the corral, a third from the stable, and opened fired as soon as they cleared the shrubbery. One was Larry.

Clay had to discourage them. Wheeling, he snapped off a shot that missed but caused them to swerve wide and bought him another twenty-five yards. In the meantime, women poured from the house and commenced cheering the riders on.

A full-blooded Apache would have proven a challenge for the horsemen to overtake. Apaches were incredibly fast over short distances, able to hold their own against ordinary mounts. Small wonder, since it wasn't uncommon for warriors to travel seventy miles in a single day and never stop to rest.

Clay wished he could do the same. A few more months, perhaps, and he would be that capable, but he wouldn't live a few more minutes if he didn't think of a means of escaping. The pounding of hooves told him that one of the riders was much too close. He stopped, whirled, sank to one knee, and put a slug through the man's chest. That gained him another thirty yards.

Quick Killer

More riders joined the chase, six of them streaming from the stable in a determined pack, some riding bareback in their eagerness to catch their quarry.

Clay was surprised that he wasn't growing winded. He held to a pace that would have tired most whites and made for a solitary tree, the only haven available. Larry and the other cowboy were forty yards off but holding their fire, perhaps thinking they could wait for the rest and cut him down in a hail of lead.

Inspiration, such as it was, prompted Clay to again turn, kneel and fire. He aimed most carefully and hit Larry high on the right shoulder, the impact flipping the puncher from the saddle, limbs akimbo. The third cowboy cut loose with his rifle in retaliation, four rushed shots.

Clay suddenly grabbed at his chest, stiffened, and sprawled onto his left side, letting go of the Winchester so he could drop his hand to one of his Colts. He had to resist the temptation to take a peek as the cowpoke's horse trotted nearer and nearer.

"Did you blow out the bastard's lamp, Wade?" someone yelled from the yard.

"Sure enough did," the cowboy answered. "Ventilated the vermin right proper."

Dust tingled Clay's nose. Through slitted lids he saw hooves halt in front of him, then heard the creak of leather as Wade dismounted.

"I reckon I'll take your scalp, Injun, and show it to my folks the next time I visit home. Won't pa be plumb proud! He's never much cared for you rotten redskins."

A hand fell on Clay's shoulder and he was flipped onto his back. In a flash he drew his Colt, pressed the barrel into the cowhand's abdomen, and thumbed

133

off two shots. Wade recoiled, staggering, red spittle rimming his mouth.

Clay batted the man's rifle aside and was on the sorrel before anyone else had awakened to his ploy. Hauling on the reins, he galloped past the tree, contriving to put the trunk between him and the majority of his pursuers so their outraged volley did no harm.

Or so Clay believed until the sorrel acted up. The horse flagged and kicked with a rear leg as if trying to stomp a pesky sidewinder. Bending, Clay found a crimson trickle seeping from a hole above its knee. Any notion he had of slowing to spare the animal misery was dispelled by another series of shots from the pack on his heels.

Clay hugged the pommel and used his Winchester as an oversized quirt, repeatedly smacking the sorrel's flank to goad it on. He got to within fifty yards of the draw before the leg buckled and the horse went down. He felt it start to fall and threw himself clear. Rolling to his feet, he sprinted onward.

"Stop him!" a gruff voice bellowed. "Can't somebody stop the son of a bitch?"

Lord knows, they tried. The ground was peppered by shots, some so close they nicked Clay's buckskins and hat. He darted into the draw, all the way to the barbed wire, and slid under as the sound of pursuit rumbled off the walls and loose dirt rattled from the rims. His enemies fired as he vaulted astride the chestnut, fired as he cut and ran. A stinging sensation in his leg was a reminder he wasn't bullet-proof.

Cursing and shouting, the riders drew rein at the barbed barrier, a few shaking their fists in impotent wrath.

Quick Killer

Clay never slowed. He'd saved his hide, but he experienced no joy. The way he saw it, he'd done poorly; he'd failed to kill the man he hated most and failed to obtain medicine that could help Delgadito. His days as the White Apache might be numbered, and without the renegades to back him up, he'd be that much easier to hunt down and kill. With every bounty hunter and soldier from Denver to Mexico City on the lookout for him, the thought was enough to almost make him wish he'd slain Gillett and gone out in a blaze of glory.

Almost, but not quite.

Chapter Ten

Delgadito, the Apache, did not expect to live much longer. His body burned with fever yet his skin felt icy cold. He had lost so much blood he was too weak to lift a finger. And overriding all was the worst pain he had ever experienced, agony so extreme it tore at the fabric of his innermost self. He expected to die and wanted to die so he would be spared further torment. And humiliation.

During his lucid moments, Delgadito felt an awful shame over having failed so many people. There had been his wife and relatives, massacred by scalp hunters because he hadn't exercised enough caution. There had been his loyal followers, warriors who had looked to him for guidance and shared his family's fate. As if that was not enough, he'd managed to turn the few survivors into outcasts shunned by their own people. And finally, he had failed himself by being unable to regain the leadership that should rightfully be his but which he had foolishly bestowed upon Lickoyee-shis-inday and apparently lost for good.

It was as if someone or something with powerful bad medicine was out to get him and had succeeded only to well, Delgadito mused.

In the Apache scheme of things, the supreme giver of life was known as *Yusn*. It was believed *Yusn* had created a number of lesser spirit beings who worked for the good of the tribe. But there were also evil spirits who took perverse delight in causing no end of misery. Apache medicine men and women were devoted to protecting their people from these harmful supernatural forces, but they weren't always successful.

Delgadito was convinced an evil *Gans*, or Mountain Spirit, intended to destroy him. Had it been possible, he would have gone to a medicine man for help. But it was too late now. He doubted he would live to see the new day dawn.

Suddenly Delgadito became aware of pressure on his brow. A hand touched lightly. Through a pale haze he saw the White Apache bending over him. Lickoyee-shis-inday spoke. In Delgadito's befuddled state the words sounded slurred, as if his ears were plugged tight with wax. He concentrated, trying to understand, a task made harder because Lickoyee-shis-inday was using English.

"—did my best, pard, but I've let you down. Don't worry none, though. Cuchillo Negro says we're bound to find some roots that will help, sooner or later."

Delgadito wanted to tell them not to bother but he couldn't move his lips. In his frustration, he groaned.

Clay thought he read confusion on the warrior's face so he switched to the Chiricahua tongue. "We are doing all we can for you, my brother. I would like to stay at this spot overnight but the *Americano soldados* are only five miles behind us and growing closer the longer we delay. Fiero is keeping watch on them in case they get too near."

Somehow Delgadito found the strength to say, "Leave me, White Apache. Take the others and go. I would like to die alone."

"A man should never give up while he can still take a breath," Clay responded, hiding his shock at the request. He'd long admired Delgadito's courage and toughness, and would never have pegged the Apache as being a quitter. "I will not desert you. I doubt the others will, either."

"Then you will waste your lives for my sake. And I am not worth it."

"You're talking nonsense," Clay said reverting to English. "Besides, it's our decision to make, not yours."

Delgadito would have liked to argue the point but a bout of paralyzing weakness silenced him. He couldn't understand why the white-eye was going to so much trouble on his behalf. But then, it had been next to impossible to understand anything Taggart did. No self-respecting Apache would allow himself to be used as Delgadito had used Lickoyee-shisinday. Chiricahuas were intelligent enough to look beyond a person's actions at the underlying motives, and only then act accordingly. Not Clay Taggart. The white-eye accepted everything at face value, as a child would do, and from what Delgadito had seen on the reservation, Taggart was typical of his kind. Sometimes Delgadito wondered if all white-eye infants were deliberately bashed over the head shortly after birth to addle their brains.

Clay Taggart saw the deep lines of pain etching the warrior's features and gave Delgadito a friendly pat on the arm. He glanced at Cuchillo Negro, who watched their back trail, and said, "Help me with him." Then, climbing onto the chestnut, he allowed Cuchillo Negro to place Delgadito behind him and lent a hand lashing Delgadito's body to his so the warrior wouldn't fall off.

"What of Fiero?" Cuchillo Negro asked.

"He will catch up later."

"That is not what I meant. You know how he is."

"I know he can take care of himself. Right now I am more worried about Delgadito." Clay galloped eastward, reaching behind him to keep the wounded warrior from flopping about. He put Fiero from his mind entirely, confident the firebrand wouldn't do anything rash under the current circumstances.

But had Clay only known, at that very moment Fiero was pressing his rifle to his shoulder and aiming at the white-eye in buckskins who served as tracker for the cavalry patrol. His reason was simple. He figured if he killed the tracker, the troopers would be unable to find White Apache and the others.

Fiero lay under mesquite on a knoll seventy yards from the soldiers. He had already picked out not only the scout but the *Americano* in charge and the bearded bellower who always relayed the officer's orders to the men.

During Fiero's short stay on the reservation, he had made it his business to study the various Army patrols he'd seen and to learn all he could about how they were organized. He'd learned that men who wore large patches on their shoulders were called officers and were the ones in charge, while those who wore colorful stripes on their sleeves were known as sergeants and although these sergeants served under the officers they had as much, if not more, influence with the troopers.

So Fiero easily identified the officer leading the patrol, and he knew the bellower was the sergeant. He observed them conferring with the tracker, who then forked a saddle and rode slowly forward. The man was skilled, but not as skilled as an Apache. Were the situation reversed, Fiero would practically fly along the trail.

The firebrand settled the front sight on the scout's sternum and aligned the rear sight with the front. Fiero allowed the scout to ride another twenty yards before he squeezed the trigger. The officer gaped in surprise when the scout hit the ground but recovered to shout commands and set the whole patrol into motion, bearing down on the knoll.

Scrambling backwards, Fiero dashed to his bay and leaped on its back. Legs flapping, he galloped southward, not eastward as his friends had gone. He intended to lead the patrol on a merry chase and slake his thirst for battle in the bargain.

Holding formation, four abreast, the soldiers swept over the rise and spotted Fiero. He looked back and grinned, mocking them. To fool the troopers into thinking they were gaining he held the bay in, and when they began to narrow the gap he let the bay have its head and pulled ahead.

Fiero had been pursued by soldiers before. Each time there had been a pattern to the chase. Invariably, the *Americanos* rode fast and hard initially, but when they saw they couldn't prevail, they gave up. Always it was the same, a fact Fiero could exploit to his advantage.

For over a mile the soldiers doggedly ate Fiero's dust, until at a barked order from the officer they slowed to a walk. Fiero kept on riding at full gallop until he was out of their sight, then he swung to the west in a wide loop that brought him up on the patrol without them knowing. Tying the bay, he stalked through the brush and shortly located the troopers taking their leisure while their winded mounts rested.

Fiero wormed his way within rifle range. He studied the uniforms and located both the young officer and the sergeant. Propping both elbows, he aimed at the bellower, going for a head shot. The sergeant was yelling at a pair of soldiers, who took the outbrust without complaint. Yet another white trait Fiero sneered at. For any man to tolerate such abuse was unthinkable.

Once more the sergeant consulted the officer. Then the bearded man removed his hat to wipe his brow and gaze at the sun as if gauging the amount of daylight left.

Fiero was ready. He fired, and instantly backpedaled, annoyed that at the very moment he'd shot, the sergeant had stooped to tug at a boot. Every last soldier scurried for cover, including the lucky sergeant and the officer.

Speeding to the bay, Fiero rode northward, his expert eye choosing the thickest growth, the most difficult terrain. He had little doubt the soldiers would be hopelessly inept in tracking him without the scout, and an hour later when he had circled again he saw them strung out in a ragged line seeking sign.

Fiero laid on his belly in high weeds and pinpointed the officer, but not the sergeant. He counted the patrol, learned there were four men missing, and guessed the sergeant was out looking for him.

Fiero settled for the officer, who squatted beside a flat rock on which a big piece of paper had been spread out. The officer and another man were running their fingers over the paper, then pointing in different directions. Maps, such papers were called. Fiero couldn't understand why the white-eyes relied on them. Apaches were taught to memorize the countryside through which they passed and to make note of prominent landmarks for future reference. If someone were to blindfold him and take him anywhere within a hundred and fifty mile radius, he would find his way back again with unerring accuracy.

The officer stood and stretched. Fiero sighted on the man's face and fired. Sent reeling by the impact, the officer fell among his men. Panic seized the troopers as they scooped up their carbines, went prone, and started firing at anything and everything.

Fiero stayed put to see if they would charge him. Amazingly, none had any idea where he was. They wasted scores of bullets before a skinny man with two stripes on his sleeves restored order. It wasn't long afterward that the sergeant and the other missing men arrived.

Slaying a few more would have been child's play, but Fiero did not. He studied them, learning how they reacted, learning their weaknesses for future encounters. Knowing an enemy was essential. Had the Chiricahuas known more about the white-eyes, they might have held out much longer than they did.

The soldiers were mounting. Fiero saw them form into four groups, one facing east, another west, the others north and south. He wondered what they were up to, and the answer came when the sergeant bellowed and they exploded across the plain, spreading out as they did, forming into a giant ring that kept expanding the farther they rode.

Startled by the brilliant strategy, Fiero ran to the bay. He had wasted so much time that several of the white-eyes were almost on him. They shouted excitedly as he bore to the northeast. Sporadic carbine fire sped him along. He wasn't worried in the least because he counted on the soldiers giving up after a while, as they always did. But these troopers proved to be the exception to the rule.

Those with poor horses fell out of the chase first. Others lasted a few miles more. Approximately eight or nine were on superior animals, and they stuck to Fiero like sap to a tree. He plunged into thorny brush but they were undeterred. He wound along a narrow gully for over two miles, thinking their poor horsemanship would be their undoing, but they showed they were as good as he was and actually gained ground.

The bay was slick with sweat when Fiero broke into open country and flew due north. The horse would last another ten miles, he judged, but by then he hoped to be in chaparral where he could elude the *Americanos* on foot.

A grim smile lit Fiero's countenance. He lived for warfare, as had his father, and his father's father. That his life was in danger added zest to his existence, not detracted from it. Killing without being killed was the Apache creed, and it was a way of life in which Fiero passionately believed. He would never accept boring reservation life as had the tame Chiricahuas; he would rather be flayed alive.

Although not given to introspection, Fiero had often pondered on the fate of his people. He had been hurt beyond measure when so many succumbed to the white invaders after offering token resistance. Fiero had argued with the leaders who advocated surrender until he was hoarse, without result. They had wanted peace at any cost, even at the price of their freedom, their integrity.

Fiero had seen the terrible toll the war took on his people, but he had been adamant. No one had the right to steal their ancestral land. No one had the right to tell them how they should live, how they should dress and act. The whites had gone so far as to require warriors to cut their long hair short as a symbol of their peaceful intentions, a symbol Fiero regarded as a mark of cowardice, as the final degrading act in a long line of requirements that had stripped the Chiricahua warriors of their manhood and reduced them to little better than well dressed dogs fit only to grovel at the feet of their white masters.

To Fiero it was unimportant that many of the white soldiers held no personal enmity toward his people. It was unimportant that many serving in Arizona would rather be elsewhere. They had taken his land, enslaved his people, and they would pay dearly for their audacity.

Presently Fiero reached the chaparral. He slanted to the right, then to the left. When the soldiers were temporarily blocked from view, he prodded the bay to go faster, then coiled his legs up under him, looked for a break in the brush, and leaped. He hit the ground running and was on his stomach before the dust of the bay's passage had settled.

His animal continued on at breakneck speed. The troopers poured around a bush, saw it, and never slowed, streaking past Fiero in a thundering string. Rising, he stared at their backs until they were gone. Tricking white-eyes was no challenge, he reflected.

"Tu no vale nada," Fiero said aloud to himself, and turned to head southward.

Twenty yards away stood a trooper with a leveled carbine, the reins of his horse held loosely in one hand. The animal was fidgeting and limped badly.

Quick Killer

Fiero had his own Winchester in the crook of his left arm. He made no move to use it since to do so invited certain death. The soldier addressed him but Fiero had no idea what the white-eye said. When the trooper motioned, he gathered that he was to put down his rifle, and slowly. The *Americano* seemed to relax a bit after he did.

Fiero had to do something. Soon the others would catch the bay and promptly swing around to search for him. He had a knife on the back of his right hip but drawing it would be too obvious.

The trooper motioned again, signaling for Fiero to step closer. Fiero did, and was made to understand he should kneel. Evidently pleased, the soldier tipped his carbine skyward and banged off two rapid shots.

Fiero's fingers were inches from his knife. He pretended to be cowed and bowed his head while secretly easing his hand to the hilt. The *Americano* let go of his mount's reins and edged to the left, the carbine trained on Fiero's head.

Fiero froze to deceive the white-eye into thinking he was going to submit without a fight, but he watched closely out of the corner of his eye. When the trooper twisted to scan the brush for his companions, Fiero whipped out the hunting knife and threw it in an underhand toss he had perfected through long practice.

The cavalryman had sensed something was amiss and turned as the warrior sprang into action, with the result that the long steel blade bit into the base of his throat before he could snap off a shot. Horrified, he clutched at the knife but couldn't get a grip on the slippery weapon.

Fiero grabbed the man's fallen carbine by the barrel and swung it in a vicious arc that caught the·

trooper flush on the face and felled him where he stood. Tossing the carbine aside, Fiero reclaimed his Winchester and his knife, then climbed on the soldier's mount. He didn't care if it had gone lame or not. He had to get out of there before more white-eyes arrived.

Wheeling eastward, Fiero goaded the reluctant horse into the chaparral, pausing once to break off a limb. The animal limped badly and grew worse as time went on. Whenever it slowed, Fiero lashed it with the limb so fiercely the blows drew blood and left nasty welts. The horse would then pick up the pace.

While Fiero's actions would have appalled a typical Easterner, he was unfazed. To Apaches, horses were just so much brute flesh, to be used as the Apaches saw fit. And since most animals wound up in cooking pots, seldom did a warrior allow himself to become attached to one.

In this instance, Fiero fully intended to ride the cavalry mount into the ground in order to put as much distance behind him as he could. He lashed and kicked and slapped, going well over five miles before the horse reached the end of its rope. On the slope of a small hill it finally faltered and would not go on no matter what he did. Leaping down, Fiero slit its throat and left it thrashing in a spreading pool of blood to die a slow but relatively painless death.

Legs pumping, Fiero scaled the hill, stopping at the top to check on the *Americanos*. They were still after him, all right, about two miles back. He jogged on, his pantherish muscles rippling, his stocky form flowing over the ground with exceptional, surprising grace.

Fiero ran for several miles, showing no signs of fatigue when he eventually halted at the edge of a narrow gully. It was so narrow that he could leap to the other side, yet it was thirty feet deep. On seeing it, he grinned, and when Fiero grinned, someone was bound to suffer.

Chopping off enough vegetation to cover the top took a quarter of an hour. Next Fiero pulled out entire bushes by their roots and arranged them so that they formed a seemingly natural aisle leading to the brink of the gully. Retracing his steps to a point fifty yards away, he snapped off a branch in so obvious a spot that even the white-eyes couldn't miss it. Then he crossed to the other side and hid.

The *soldados* were not long in coming. Seven of them, riding warily, the sergeant in the lead. He was the one who spotted the broken branch and called out to his fellows. In a compact group they thundered along the fake aisle, and because of Fiero's cleverly arranged bushes they were ignorant of the gully's existence until the sergeant's horse pitched into it with a panicked whinny. Two others suffered the same fate before the rest collected their wits and reined up.

Fiero thought their antics laughable. The three mounts that had fallen into the gully were neighing in an anguished chorus. The soldiers themselves were cursing and shouting to one another. He saw a grizzled one take a rope and lower it down. In turn, each of those who had taken a spill were hoisted out. None appeared the worse for wear except the sergeant, who held his left arm much like a bird would hold a crippled wing.

The troopers talked in low tones while staring down into the gully. Four of them formed a line, aimed their carbines, and blasted away until the last strangled whinny died to a gurgling wheeze. Riding double, the crestfallen *Americanos* headed back.

Fiero stood when they were gone. He walked to the gully, surveyed the carnage he had wrought, and quickly clambered over the edge. He picked a fine black and cut off a sizeable piece of its haunch.

Climbing out was simple. The warrior gathered enough kindling and wood and soon had a small fire crackling in a concealed nook. He trimmed the hide from his steak, impaled the dripping meat on a stick, and hunkered down to await his meal.

It gave Fiero pleasure to review his clash with the white-eyes and to think of the wailing women who would lament the loss of their loved ones. Countless Apache women had done the same in recent times, as one by one the proud Apache men were wiped out by the locusts from the north.

Fiero remembered how, many winters ago, he had heard white trappers boast that there were more of their kind than there were blades of grass on the prairie. Naturally, Fiero had believed the trappers to be rank braggarts who couldn't hold their whiskey. But the men had been right, after all, and the Chiricahuas had paid dearly for resisting the white invasion.

Numbers and firepower. Those were the keys to the white victory. Fiero was convinced that the war would have ended differently if the two sides had been evenly matched. Pueblos, Spaniards, Mexicans—the Apaches had beaten them all. It had taken a well-armed, limitless horde to do that which no one else had been able to do—subjugate the Apaches.

A soft rustling drew Fiero's gaze to a slithering rattler. He had the horse meat, but he darted over anyway and sank his blade into the snake's head as it curled to strike. A single, powerful stroke severed the tail, which he stuck in his breechcloth as he returned to the fire. He would save it, and later, when he had occasion to steal horses, the rattles would come in handy.

Fiero stared at the eastern horizon. By now, he mused, the others were halfway to their sanctuary. Being afoot, he'd take days to catch up. Not that it upset him. He preferred to raid alone, to kill alone, to exalt in the prowess that made him what he was; namely, one of the last true Apaches. Like Delgadito, Cuchillo Negro, and Ponce. And, yes, to a lesser degree, much like the White Apache.

Chapter Eleven

They were high in the mountains, less than a mile from Sweet Grass, when Cuchillo Negro reined up and announced, "I must go look for him."

Clay Taggart halted. "Do what you have to," he said. "I can manage by myself from here."

"I know he is a grown man and can look out for himself," Cuchillo Negro justified his decision, "but there are so few of us left, and he has a talent for getting into trouble. His hot head makes him commit acts that wiser warriors would know not to do."

"There is no need to explain."

The warrior lifted his reins, then said, "I would be grateful if you did not tell him I was concerned. He would think me weak."

"My ears never heard your words," Clay said, touching the upcurled brim of his hat. He rode on, anxious to reach their hideout so Delgadito would at last enjoy a long spell of rest and recuperation. It amazed him that the warrior still lived. Several times Delgadito had teetered on the edge of eternity, and in each instance the Apache had rallied, tapping an inner reservoir of endurance for which his tribe was widely noted.

A hawk circling high in the azure sky vented a shrill shriek as it winged lower after prey. Clay watched the streaking predator swoop onto a rocky slope and heard the death squeal of the animal it slew. Not until he came to live among the renegades had he fully realized how harsh a mistress Nature could be. In the wild, the only law was the survival of the fittest, a law that applied to beasts and man alike.

The Apaches had lived by this law for ages. In the unforgiving crucible of tooth and claw they had learned to meet Nature on its own terms, and endure. It had forged them into the fearless fighters they were. Or rather, the fighters they had been before their spirit was broken by the U.S. Army. By the whites. By his kind.

The thought bothered Clay. Of late he'd developed the habit of regarding himself as more Apache than white. Like a boiling kettle about to bubble over, he simmered with conflicting loyalties. On the one hand, part of him couldn't abide the cruel conduct of renegades who wiped out innocent families. On the other, he now saw the state of affairs through Apache eyes and had to admit their outrage was understandable. Who should he side with, he wondered? His own kind? When they had stolen his ranch out from under him and tried to make him do a cottonwood jig? He owed them nothing. Not a solitary mother's son of them. Let them all rot in hell.

The Apaches he owed a great deal. They'd saved his life, doctored him, fed and clothed him, accepted him as one of their own. They'd pulled his fat out of the fire when he was taken prisoner by an army patrol. And they'd stood by him when some of their own kind wanted to kill him. In short, the members of Delgadito's small band had done the sort of things true pards did for one another. So maybe, he mused, it was time for him to stop thinking of ever going back to his old life. Maybe he should throw his lot in with the Chiricahuas for keeps, come what may.

To enter Sweet Grass, a rider had to negotiate a long, winding ravine so high sunlight seldom bathed the bottom. Clay became absorbed in the many twists and turns, his left hand behind his back to hold Delgadito in place. He studied the ground to see if anyone had been through since they left and saw only the tracks made recently by the string Ponce had brought back.

Presently the ravine widened and the hidden valley unfolded before him. Clay sought evidence of a fire but saw none. Angling toward the cliff, he stayed vigilant, remembering the attack by Nah-kah-yen. He didn't think the Army would be loco enough to send in another scout so soon after losing one of their best, but he'd learned the hard way never to take anything for granted.

Oddly, there was no trace of Ponce at the camp. Figuring the youth was off hunting, Clay made Delgadito comfortable, then let the chestnut loose to graze. He took a water bag to the stream to fill it, and as he neared the pool where he had bathed last, he drew up short on beholding a tall pole imbedded in the soft soil at the water's edge. It wasn't the pole that startled him; it was the grisly head someone had impaled on top. Stunned, Clay advanced slowly, noting the long dark hair and butchered features of an Indian woman. An Apache, he deduced, a young maiden, going by the smoothness of her skin and her tresses, which although matted with blood and dirt had not yet lost all of their former luxuriant sheen.

The implications hit Clay like a bolt of lightning and he promptly squatted and brought the Winchester to bear. Ponce's absence took on a whole new meaning. He almost called out the warrior's name but caught himself in time.

Setting the water skin down, Clay sidled to the pole. There were tracks, a single set, so faint they gave the illusion the man lacked corporal substance. Clay knew better. Some Apaches were so light on their feet their prints were hard to read, just like these.

The killer had gone toward the stream, so Clay did likewise. He estimated the pole had been put in place ten to twelve hours earlier, so it was likely the man responsible was long gone.

The significance of the ghastly trophy eluded Clay. Was it meant as a threat of some sort? Or was it an Apache hex, tied in somehow with their belief in bad medicine and evil powers?

The tracks led into the water. Clay walked a few dozen feet in both directions, seeking the point where the killer emerged. On the opposite bank on the right were crushed blades of grass. He forded to examine them but was disappointed to learn a deer had been responsible.

Clay didn't know what to do next. It wouldn't do much good to aimlessly traipse around the valley looking for sign. He should make the killer come to him, provided the man was still in Sweet Grass.

First he must find a safe spot to secret Delgadito.

The thought electrified Clay into plunging across the stream and racing to the cliff. He had to skirt some pines before he saw the site clearly, and his pulse quickened when he discovered Delgadito gone. The killer had snuck in and toted the warrior off! He scoured the terrain in rising alarm but saw nothing other than the horses.

Kneeling, Clay found the same set of prints as those at the stream, only deeper because the killer had thrown Delgadito over one shoulder. Swiftly, Clay went in pursuit. The trail led along the base of the cliff for a hundred yards, then moved to the left, to the bottom of a slope covered with timber.

From behind a tree trunk Clay did as Delgadito had taught him and scrutinized every pine, every weed clump, every blade of grass. The trick lay in detecting where the pattern had been broken. Living things weren't ghosts. They couldn't pass through the wilderness without leaving some evidence of their passage. But this one had.

Clay continued his search, realizing his enemy was highly skilled. Rising, he ran to the left to use a thicket as cover as he ascended, but he had no more than gone three strides when a huge mallet seemed to slam into his torso and he was catapulted through the air. He glimpsed the earth rushing up to meet him, then the breath was jarred from his lungs.

Dazed, certain he had been shot, Clay rolled onto his stomach and crawled to a log. Gradually he recovered. His life had been spared by the merest fluke, the bullet having hit his rifle, striking the side plate and ricocheting into the stock. Both had been shattered, but better them than his rib cage.

Placing the useless Winchester down, Clay drew a Colt, then crept to the end of the downed tree and peeked around the twisted roots. Whoever shot at him must know where he was hiding. He needed to get out of there before the bushwhacker changed position and picked him off. Cocking the pistol, he dug his toes into the soil and bunched his legs.

"Maybe you make this easy on both of us, eh, Lickoyee-shis-inday?"

The unexpected hail rooted Clay in place.

"I know you still live, white man. I shot at your rifle on purpose. Throw out your other guns and I give you my word I not kill you."

"Who are you?" Clay wanted to know.

"Tats-ah-das-ay-go."

"Quick Killer?" Clay translated.

"You have heard of me," the man said, pride and arrogance equally thick in his tone.

"Can't say as I have."

A pause ensued. Clay stared at the nearest trees, ten feet off, and debated whether to make a try for them. He didn't care to squat there like a sitting duck when his foe was probably on the move.

Unknown to him, he was right. Quick Killer was thirty yards to the northwest, running to a boulder. Ducking down, he cupped a hand to his mouth and shouted, "But I have heard of you, White Apache. The Army wants you very bad. There is much money on your head, dead or alive."

"And you aim to collect," Clay responded, inching forward. He wanted to keep the man talking, to distract him long enough to reach the timber.

"I do," Quick Killer admitted. He was feeling quite sure of himself. Very shortly, all his careful planning, all his diligent effort, would pay off handsomely and he would not let anything go wrong.

"It won't be easy," Clay vowed. He was ready to make his dash, but he'd rather know where the killer was hiding first. To that end, he had to keep the man talking. "Others have tried and wound up worm food."

"I am better than them, Taggart," Quick Killer boasted. "I am the best."

"Why bother taking me alive?" Clay asked, probing the vegetation.

Quick Killer didn't answer right away. Initially, he'd intended to take White Apache in dead, but after thinking about it some more, he'd realized that practically anyone lucky enough to be in the right place at the right time could put a bullet through Taggart's brain. Taking White Apache back in one piece would be a greater challenge and would add more luster to Quick Killer's reputation.

"Did you hear me?" Clay goaded, deciding not to wait any longer.

"I hear," Quick Killer said.

And Clay was off like a jackrabbit, bounding into the pines and diving flat. He chose a wide trunk to lie behind and surveyed the slope above, wondering if the one who called himself Quick Killer had seen his move.

Indeed, the scout had. Quick Killer grinned and slid to the left a dozen feet. Propping his rifle on an earthen hump, he scanned the trees below and spied the lower half of a leg in plain sight. Snuggling his cheek to the Winchester, he sighted on White Apache's ankle. His finger caressed the cool trigger in anticipation. Then he heard footsteps.

Twisting, the scout surveyed the woods above. He listened to a rustling noise and a loud snap, as of a twig breaking underfoot. For a moment he thought someone was sneaking up on him but the sounds faded away as the person did the same. Since there was only one man it could be, Quick Killer leaped to his feet and sprinted higher.

Clay Taggart raised his Colt. He only had a glimpse of buckskins and a red headband but he banged off two rapid shots anyway, neither of which appeared to have any effect. He couldn't understand why Quick Killer was running off. Not one to look a gift horse in the mouth, he pushed upright and dashed madly toward the cliff.

Once there, Clay went into thick brush bordering the bottom and ran for over sixty yards. Here the cliff ended and a steep incline brought him slowly but surely to the summit. He had to stop often to seek solid purchase, and at one point he leaned out to see if the killer had followed him. He leaned much too far, losing his balance and nearly plummeting to the bottom.

At the summit Clay moved well back from the edge so he couldn't be seen from below and hastened to a vantage point directly above the camp. A Colt in both hands, he scoured the ponderosas but couldn't find Tats-ah-das-ay-go.

Quick Killer was in dense growth, close to a clearing where he had left Delgadito. Too cautious to blunder into the open, he circled the clearing, annoyed to see it empty. Delgadito's tracks were on the far side, leading higher, the footprints revealing Delgadito had moved with a short, shuffling stride, as befitted a man on his last legs. It would be no time at all before Quick Killer recaptured him.

The scout climbed to a ridge and hurried down the other side. He knew how weak Delgadito had been and counted on soon finding the unconscious warrior. Yet he went as far as an arrow could fly and did not come on the renegade. He would have gone farther but the tracks abruptly ended.

Mystified, Quick Killer searched in an ever widening circle, his movements growing more urgent as it became clear Delgadito had apparently vanished without leaving a clue to how it had been done. Quick Killer had never lost a trail before, and to do so now, at the worst of times, was doubly vexing.

Going to the last set of tracks, Quick Killer studied the partial impressions and the grass around them. He reasoned that Delgadito had tricked him and all he had to do was ascertain how. But it proved more difficult than he would have imagined.

Quick Killer chafed at the delay. He imagined White Apache catching a horse at that very moment, and foresaw the white-eye bringing the rest of the band back. Now that he'd lost the element of surprise, he'd either have to flee Sweet Grass before the renegades got there or resort to the special ploy he had in mind. And running from a fight wasn't in his nature. Giving the area one last survey, Quick Killer jogged off.

If the scout had looked back, he would have seen a low limb on one of the trees move and a face seared by affliction and anger appear. But Quick Killer was in a rush, and he didn't slow until he reached the top of the ridge and was starting down the other side. A glint of sunlight off metal caught his eye, sparkling briefly on top of a cliff to the southeast.

Quick Killer ducked into a cluster of aspens. The interplay of sunlight and shadows from passing clouds that dappled the cliff kept him from seeing the prone figure until it moved. "White Apache," Quick Killer said aloud softly, admiring his foe's mettle. Few adversaries were so resourceful.

Cutting deeper into the aspens, Quick Killer headed for the slope flanking the cliff. He no longer needed to rely on his special ploy. White Apache had unwittingly played right into his hands.

Over on the cliff, Clay fidgeted with impatience. He knew he shouldn't but couldn't help himself. The longer it took him to take care of Quick Killer, the less likely Delgadito would be alive when it was over. He snaked to his right a few yards, then crawled to the left. Neither in the valley proper or on any of the slopes was there any movement.

Clay glanced toward the entrance to Sweet Grass, wishing Cuchillo Negro and Fiero would show. The three of them would make short shrift of the man in buckskins. But he had no idea when they would arrive. It might be minutes, hours, or days. Something told him whenever it was, they would be too late.

As Clay fretted, Tats-ah-das-ay-go stalked steadily closer up the sparsely treed slope on the back side of the cliff. There were enough boulders and shallow depressions to serve his purpose, but he had to climb much too slowly to suit him. Near the top he had to adopt a virtual turtle's pace, resorting to all the stealth of which he was capable. Once he captured the White Apache, he would hunt down Delgadito and be on his way. The other renegades were unimportant, no more than mad dogs who would amount to nothing without Delgadito's leadership.

Up on the craggy heights, Clay Taggart concluded he had wasted his time. Quick Killer wasn't coming after him. Sliding back from the rim, he pushed to his knees and shoved the Colts into their holsters. He'd go down the back slope and swing around to outflank the killer. With a little luck, it would

all be over by sunset. Standing, Clay backed away
from the cliff, watching to be sure Tats-ah-das-ay-go
didn't appear below.

Quick Killer couldn't believe his eyes. The white
fool was backing straight toward him. He rose and
raised his rifle on high, the stock poised to bash
White Apache on the head. Three more steps and
he would have his prisoner.

Clay took the first step, his palms resting on the
butts of his pistols. He'd like to get his hands on
another rifle, and he knew where the renegades had
a cache of plunder that included several Winchesters, a couple of Henrys, and a few old Sharps.
Before tangling with Quick Killer, he'd fetch one.

The scout saw White Apache start to turn.
Smirking wickedly, Tats-ah-das-ay-go brought the
heavy stock sweeping down.

Chapter Twelve

During the many weeks Delgadito had spent teaching Clay Taggart Apache ways, the renegade had complained several times that Clay was as ungainly as a drunken mule. "You must have eyes in feet, Lickoyee-shis-inday," the warrior cautioned over and over in his imperfect English. "Many rocks, many holes. You trip over every one."

"I ain't doing that poorly, pard," Clay had countered, knowing full well his friend was right.

With practice, Clay had improved. But not enough to keep him from occasionally making mistakes that caused the warriors to look at him as if he were a blundering five year old.

This would have been one of those times. For as Clay turned without looking, his left foot came down on a rock. It wasn't big or jagged but it was smooth and his foot slipped out from under him just as a solid object flashed past his face. He fell to one knee and looked up into the feral features of Quick Killer.

The scout swung again, driving the stock low, but Clay was able to throw himself to the side. In a lightning draw Clay's Colt cleared leather, yet as fast as he was, Quick Killer was faster. A moccasin flicked out, connecting with Clay's wrist, and the nickel-plated Colt went flying.

Quick Killer tried to brain Clay a third time. Clay jerked backward, grabbed the rifle and pulled, jerking Quick Killer off his feet.

Clay tried to flip out from under, but Tats-ah-das-ay-go fell on top of him. Each had a hold on the Winchester. Grappling mightily, they surged this way and that, neither gaining the upper hand. Quick Killer broke the deadlock by ramming his foot into Clay's gut while simultaneously letting go.

Clay was sent rolling. He cast the Winchester from him and dropped his left hand to his second Colt, thinking he could draw and shoot much quicker than he could level the rifle and work the lever. And he was right, to a point. The Colt was arcing up when Quick Killer pounced.

Iron fingers clamped on Clay's windpipe, choking off his air. He saw a glittering knife spear at his shoulder and narrowly evaded it. To save himself he had to drop the Colt and seize Quick Killer's wrist so he could hold the knife at bay.

Tats-ah-das-ay-go had changed his mind. He no longer cared to take White Apache alive, not when his life was at stake. A dead body would be better than no body at all. So he strove his utmost to sink his blade into the white-eye's heart while choking the life from the American.

Clay exerted all his strength, yet couldn't pry the fingers from his throat. Meanwhile, Quick Killer's blade dipped closer and closer to his shirt. In another few moments either the knife would drink deep of his blood or his lungs would burst from lack of air. Desperation drove him to employ a weapon he rarely did; his teeth.

By suddenly shifting his weight, Clay was able to yank Quick Killer's wrist close to his mouth. He bit hard, his teeth sheering through skin and flesh. The salty tang of warm blood filled his mouth.

Quick Killer's eyes widened and his mouth parted in a soundless cry. Frantic, he tried to tear his wrist free and only succeeded in making the wound worse as Taggart's teeth ripped off a big chunk of flesh. To save his wrist he released the white-eye's neck and planted a fist in his foe's stomach.

Clay Taggart relaxed his jaws and heaved. Gagging for breath, he got to his feet and looked about for his six-shooters. He saw one and tried to snatch it but Quick Killer darted in front of him and made a vicious swipe with that big knife. Clay retreated, barely staying one step ahead of his enraged enemy.

Blood poured from Tats-ah-das-ay-go's wrist and a tingling sensation was creeping up his arm. He executed a wide slash, then adroitly tossed his knife from one hand to the other so his good arm was employed. Continuing to swing, he nicked Taggart's shoulder.

Clay saw the Winchester out of the corner of an eye. He tried darting over to it but Quick Killer guessed his intent and dashed in front of him. Defenseless, Clay was forced to back up as Tats-ah-das-ay-go rained blow after blow at him.

Neither of them paid any attention to their surroundings. The first intimation Clay had of a new danger came when he ducked under a cut and skipped to the rear, only to have his left foot cleave thin air. Shifting, he saw the precipice inches from his other foot and realized how close he had come to meeting his Maker. He faced front, expecting Quick Killer to press him harder. Strangely, the man just stood there.

"You have nowhere left to go," Tats-ah-das-ay-go said, pleased at the accidental outcome. Now he had a chance to take White Apache back alive, provided the white-eye listened to reason. "Give up and I let you live."

"Go to hell!" Clay responded, tensed to move either way depending on how Quick Killer attacked.

"Most men not so eager to die," Tats-ah-das-ay-go noted. While he would never admit as much, secretly he admired Taggart's fighting spirit. Not one of the many renegades he had tracked down over the years had proven half so difficult to subdue.

"Most men don't have bounty on their heads," Clay snapped, surprised Quick Killer was content to talk instead of finishing him off. "You'll have to earn your money the hard way, bounty hunter."

"I no bounty hunter. I am scout."

"Scouts wear uniforms," Clay pointed out, suspecting the man had lied.

"All but Tats-ah-das-ay-go. I do as I please."

"Were you sent after Delgadito or me, or both?" Clay asked, his future hinging on the answer. He'd about had his fill of his own kind. They'd cheated him, stolen from him, tried to rub him out. The marshal of Tombstone had the long arm of civilian authority arrayed against him. And now the government itself must be intent on doing him wrong. It was the last straw, if true. "Which?" he prompted.

Quick Killer

Quick Killer wasn't about to confess that he'd decided to hunt the band on his own, without official approval. He thought that if he lied, it would anger White Apache, perhaps even make Taggart mad enough to want to go back and confront those responsible, thereby rendering his job a lot easier. "They send me after you," he said. "Tell me to bring you. Say take as many moons as I want."

"I figured as much," Clay growled.

"So you come back, eh?" Quick Killer prodded. "You have your say. Tell army what you think."

"Never."

"You fool, white man."

Clay bristled, clenching his fists so tight his knuckles paled. "Don't call me that! No one is ever to call me that again. From here on out, for better or for worse, I'm the White Apache."

"You think you are Indian?" Quick Killer scoffed. "Take lifetime of living to be Apache."

"Just for the trimmings, I reckon."

"I do not understand."

"The trimmings," Clay repeated, moving a few inches to the right. He wanted to keep the scout jawing a little while longer, long enough for him to reach a small mound of loose earth a yard away. "Speaking the tongue fluently and knowing all the customs and such are what I call the trimmings of being an Apache. But there's a hell of a lot more to it than that."

"Oh?" Quick Killer grinned, amused by the notion of a white man claiming kinship with his father's people.

"Being an Apache has to do with what's in here," Clay said, thumping his chest over his heart and taking another short sideways step. "It has to do with craving freedom more than anything else, and not letting other folks tell you how you should live."

"You are wrong, white-eye," Quick Killer said. "Being Apache is in blood, not in heart. And you have wrong kind of blood."

"Which one of us is the renegade and which one is working for the white sons of bitches who make a habit out of stealing other folks' land?"

"You dare say you are more Indian than me?" Quick Killer rejoined in disbelief. "My father and all his fathers were Indians. Yours were white."

"Maybe so, but I don't want anything to do with the white part of me from now on. Like I told you, I'm Lickoyee-shis-inday."

"You are loco."

Clay had edged close enough to make his play, but there was one thing he needed to know beforehand. "Delgadito didn't think so." He paused. "Speaking of which, what did you do with him, you murdering bastard?"

The fiery insult scorched Quick Killer's pride but he controlled his temper. "Delgadito is alive," he said, "until I am done with you. Then he dies."

"You're counting your chickens before they're hatched, *hombre*," Clay taunted.

"We will see," Tats-ah-das-ay-go said, and lunged, extending his arm to its fullest in order to pierce the white man's torso.

Clay was in motion before the thrust commenced. He dipped, scooped up a handful of the dirt, and flung it squarely into the half-breed's eyes.

Quick Killer was a shade too slow in reacting. He saw the *Americano* bend but didn't divine Taggart's intent until the dirt was in flight. He shut his eyes, too late to keep some of the dirt from getting in and setting them to watering fiercely. Back-pedaling, he blinked over and over and wiped at them with his free hand, all the time swinging his knife in a random pattern to keep his quarry at bay.

There had been a time when the tactic would have worked, a time before Clay Taggart came to live among the Chiricahua renegades, before he learned to wield a knife as expertly as he already did a six-shooter. He'd learned well, this White Apache, and he resorted to his knowledge now as he glided to the right, crouched low to the ground and sprang, tackling Quick Killer around the ankles.

Quick Killer felt himself falling and stabbed at where he thought Taggart would be. But White Apache had let go and moved beyond reach. As the knife arm descended, White Apache pounced, gripping Quick Killer's wrist even as he drove his shoulder up and under Quick Killer's arm. Bending, White Apache heaved, throwing all his weight into the act.

Quick Killer felt air brush his cheeks and braced for the impact sure to follow. A second went by. Two. Three. And still he had not hit the ground. Furiously brushing at his eyes, he wondered how high the white-eye had thrown him. Abruptly, his vision cleared, and he realized it wasn't how high that mattered, it was how far.

Stark fear such as Quick Killer had never known seized him as he gaped up at the receding rim of the cliff and the grim avenger staring down at him. "Noooooo!" he howled. "It cannot end like this!"

White Apache's lips formed a mocking smile.

Thrashing and kicking, Quick Killer went into a frenzied panic. He twisted, saw the cliff face sweeping past him just feet away. Thoughtlessly, he reached out and tried grabbing hold to arrest his fall. His fingertips scraped solid rock, the rough surface shearing the skin from his fingers like a hot knife searing butter. He cried out, glanced down, and his stomach seemed to leap into his throat. He couldn't breathe, couldn't think. This wasn't supposed to happen, he told himself. He was Tats-ah-das-ay-go, the most feared of Army scouts, the man who had brought in more renegades than anyone else. His medicine was powerful, the most powerful of all. He couldn't be beaten by a deluded white-eye who wasn't half as skillful.

The ground loomed steadily closer, steadily larger, becoming Quick Killer's whole universe. The wind plucked at his buckskins, at his hair. He wanted to scream his defiance, to die as he had lived, but his insides had turned to water and were trickling down his leg.

The White Apache stood gazing down at the crimson smear of pulped flesh and busted bones for some time. Then he reclaimed his Colts and the scout's rifle and hastened to the base of the cliff. He was en route to the slope where Quick Killer had shot at him when a weaving figure stumbled into the open and called his name.

White Apache reached Delgadito as the warrior's legs buckled. He picked up the Chiricahua, carried him to the camp, and covered him with blankets. After building a fire, he went for water and permitted Delgadito to drink his fill. "How do you feel?" he asked in Apache.

"Much better. The fever has left me."

A hand to the brow confirmed it. White Apache nodded and said in English, "I always knew you were a tough son of a gun, pard."

For the first time since Delgadito met Clay Taggart, he didn't mind being called that. "I owe you my life. Again."

"I cannot claim all the credit. Cuchillo Negro and Fiero helped."

"What of Ponce?"

White Apache started, then blurted, "I plumb forgot about him. You lie still while I have a look-see." Since he hadn't seen Quick Killer's mount from the cliff, he figured it must be hidden among the trees. Twenty minutes of thorough searching brought him to a clearing in which two horses were ground hitched. On one, gagged and tied hand and foot with his legs lashed together under the animal's belly, sat Ponce.

"I thought you would be dead," White Apache said as he tugged the gag out.

"The breed was going to use me as a decoy," Ponce said. "He bragged how he would slap my horse and send it running past all of you and counted on you shooting me by mistake." The young warrior smoldered with wrath. "Where is the dog that I might kill him?"

"Dead."

"Who? You?"

"He tried to fly and forgot to coat himself with feathers first."

"You speak in riddles. Men are not birds."

"So he found out."

Two days later Cuchillo Negro and Fiero arrived at Sweet Grass. They were delighted to find Delgadito recovering, indignant to hear of Tats-ah-das-ay-go's attempt to destroy their band, and upset to learn that Lickoyee-shis-inday had left the day before on a special errand. To all their questions, Delgadito would only say that, "He took a gift to the *Americanos*."

At Fort Bowie, life went on as usual. Captain Vincent Parmalee, Chief of Scouts, stood in front of his commanding officer's desk. "You sent for me, sir?"

Colonel Reynolds looked up from the report he was filling out. Sometimes it seemed to him that he spent half his military career doing forms and the other half riding roughshod over incompetents like the captain. "Yes, I did. At ease."

Parmalee relaxed, but not much.

"If you'll recall, I sent word to you yesterday that I wanted your best scout, that fellow Quick Killer, sent out with Captain Derrick's next patrol. Derrick is going after Delgadito and will need all the help he can get." Reynolds leaned back. "Did you receive the message?"

"Yes, sir. The orderly delivered it promptly."

"Then why the hell isn't Quick Killer here? Derrick is out there with all his men, saddled and waiting."

Captain Parmalee shriveled inside. "I know, sir. But there's a slight problem."

"How can that be? Not two weeks ago Quick Killer was standing in the very spot you are, practically demanding that I send him after Delgadito. Has he changed his mind?"

"No, sir. It's not that."

"Damn it. Then what is the problem?"

"I don't know where Quick Killer is," Parmalee admitted, trying to shrink within his uniform. "He disappeared from the fort shortly after his little talk with you and no one has seen him since."

Colonel Reynolds began drumming his fingers on the desk. "Why wasn't I informed?"

"I was hoping I would find him before this, sir," Parmalee whined. "I didn't want to bother you over a trifle."

"A trifle!" the colonel exploded, coming out of his chair. "Our best scout up and vanishes and you don't rate it news worthy of my attention?" Reynolds swept around the desk and reared over the junior officer. "I've tolerated about as much of your bungling as I'm going to. I know you have a drinking problem. Hell, half the men stationed here do. But that's no excuse for gross misconduct. Didn't it occur to you that he might have gone off on his own after Delgadito?"

"Yes it did, sir," Parmalee answered, flushing with anger at the aggravation the damned breed had caused him. If and when Quick Killer did return, Parmalee was going to find a way to repay the scout in spades.

Reynolds lifted a hand as if to poke his subordinate in the chest, but then simply sighed and sat back down. "Captain, I want him found. Take as many men as you need. Scour the reservation from one end to the other if need be. But find him and bring him here before the end of the week, or so help me God I'll have you sent to a post that will make this one seem like the Ritz in New York City. Do you understand, mister?"

"Yes, sir."

"Good. Get the hell out of my sight."

Grateful for the reprieve, Parmalee scurried outdoors and hurried across the compound to his small, dingy office. He paused to glance back, and when assured no one was looking, he pulled out his flask. His hands shook as he shoved the door wide, stepped inside, and tipped the bottle to his lips. The whiskey seared his mouth, his throat, warming them and his belly as he gulped greedily. It used to be that he couldn't get through the day without a glass or two. Now he couldn't get through an hour without draining half the flask. But how dare the colonel accuse him of not being able to hold his liquor! he fumed. He did as good a job as—

Suddenly an awful stench assailed Captain Parmalee's nose. He jerked the flask down, almost gagging when he inhaled. Bewildered, he looked around, then felt his whiskey making the return trip.

A ghastly object rested on top of the captain's desk, positioned in the center where it leaked ooze and pus and gore. The flesh was discolored, the tongue protruded, the jaw split wide, but there was no mistaking those cruel facial features.

It was Quick Killer's head.

Jake McMasters

**Follow the action-packed adventures of
Clay Taggart, as he fights for revenge against
settlers, soldiers, and savages.**

#7: Blood Bounty. The settlers believe Clay Taggart is a
ruthless desperado with neither conscience nor soul. But
Taggart is just an innocent man who has a price on his head.
With a motley band of Apaches, he roams the vast Southwest,
waiting for the day he can clear his name—or his luck runs
out and his scalp is traded for gold.
__3790-4 $3.99 US/$4.99 CAN

#8: The Trackers. In the blazing Arizona desert, a wanted
man can end up as food for the buzzards. But since Clay
Taggart doesn't live like a coward, he and his band of
renegade Indians spend many a day feeding ruthless
bushwhackers to the wolves. Then a bloodthirsty trio comes
after the White Apache and his gang. But try as they might
to run Taggart to the ground, he will never let anyone kill
him like a dog.
__3830-7 $3.99 US/$4.99 CAN

Dorchester Publishing Co., Inc.
65 Commerce Road
Stamford, CT 06902

Please add $1.75 for shipping and handling for the first book and
$.50 for each book thereafter. NY, NYC, PA and CT residents,
please add appropriate sales tax. No cash, stamps, or C.O.D.s. All
orders shipped within 6 weeks via postal service book rate.
Canadian orders require $2.00 extra postage and must be paid in
U.S. dollars through a U.S. banking facility.

Name_____
Address_____
City _____ State _____ Zip_____
I have enclosed $_____in payment for the checked book(s).
Payment <u>must</u> accompany all orders.□ Please send a free catalog.

 **Jake McMasters**

Follow the action-packed adventures of Clay Taggart, as he fights for revenge against soldiers, settlers, and savages.

#9: Desert Fury. From the canyons of the Arizona Territory to the deserts of Mexico, Clay Taggart and a motley crew of Apaches blaze a trail of death and vengeance. But for every bounty hunter they shoot down, another is riding hell for leather to collect the prize on their heads. And when the territorial governor offers Taggart a chance to clear his name, the deadliest tracker in the West sets his sights on the White Apache—and prepares to blast him to hell.
_3871-4 $3.99 US/$4.99 CAN

#10: Hanged! Although Clay Taggart has been strung up and left to rot under the burning desert sun, he isn't about to play dead. After a desperate band of Indians rescues Taggart, he heads into the Arizona wilderness and plots his revenge. One by one, Taggart hunts down his enemies, and with the help of renegade Apaches, he acts as judge, jury, and executioner. But when Taggart sets his sights on a corrupt marshal, he finds that the long arm of the law might just have more muscle than he expects.
_3899-4 $3.99 US/$4.99 CAN

Dorchester Publishing Co., Inc.
65 Commerce Road
Stamford, CT 06902

Please add $1.75 for shipping and handling for the first book and $.50 for each book thereafter. NY, NYC, PA and CT residents, please add appropriate sales tax. No cash, stamps, or C.O.D.s. All orders shipped within 6 weeks via postal service book rate. Canadian orders require $2.00 extra postage and must be paid in U.S. dollars through a U.S. banking facility.

Name _____

Address _____

City _____ State _____ Zip _____

I have enclosed $_____ in payment for the checked book(s).
Payment <u>must</u> accompany all orders. ☐ Please send a free catalog.

DAN'L BOONE ❖ THE LOST WILDERNESS TALES ❖ DODGE TYLER

A mighty hunter, intrepid guide, and loyal soldier, Dan'l Boone faces savage beasts, vicious foes, and deadly elements—and conquers them all. These are his stories—adventures that made Boone a man and a foundering young country a great nation.

#1: A River Run Red. The colonists call the stalwart settler Boone. The Shawnees call him Sheltowee. Then the French lead a raid that ends in the death of Boone's young cousin, and they learn to call Dan'l their enemy. Stalking his kinsman's killers through the untouched wilderness, Boone lives only for revenge. And even though the frontiersman is only one man against an entire army, he will not rest until he defeats his murderous foes—or he himself goes to meet his Maker.

___3947-8 $4.99 US/$6.99 CAN

#2: Algonquin Massacre. Even as the shot heard round the world starts the War For American Independence, a Redcoat massacre of peaceful Algonquins draws Boone into a battle of his own. Determined to bring the renegade British troops to justice, Dan'l joins forces with a warrior bent on righting the wrong done to his people. But Boone and his new comrade soon learn that revenge never comes without a price—and sometimes even a man's life isn't valuable enough to buy justice.

___4020-4 $4.99 US/$6.99 CAN

CHEYENNE

JUDD COLE

Don't miss the adventures of Touch the Sky, as he searches for a world he can call his own.

Cheyenne #14: Death Camp. When his tribe is threatened by an outbreak of deadly disease, Touch the Sky must race against time and murderous foes. But soon, he realizes he must either forsake his heritage and trust white man's medicine—or prove his loyalty even as he watches his people die.

_3800-5 $3.99 US/$4.99 CAN

Cheyenne #15: Renegade Nation. When Touch the Sky's enemies join forces against all his people—both Indian and white—they test his warrior and shaman skills to the limit. If the fearless brave isn't strong enough, he will be powerless to stop the utter annihilation of the two worlds he loves.

_3891-9 $3.99 US/$4.99 CAN

Dorchester Publishing Co., Inc.
65 Commerce Road
Stamford, CT 06902

Please add $1.75 for shipping and handling for the first book and $.50 for each book thereafter. NY, NYC, PA and CT residents, please add appropriate sales tax. No cash, stamps, or C.O.D.s. All orders shipped within 6 weeks via postal service book rate. Canadian orders require $2.00 extra postage and must be paid in U.S. dollars through a U.S. banking facility.

Name _____

Address _____

City _____ State _____ Zip _____

I have enclosed $_____ in payment for the checked book(s).
Payment <u>must</u> accompany all orders. ☐ Please send a free catalog.

CHEYENNE

JUDD COLE

Follow the adventures of Touch the Sky as he searches for a world he can call his own!

#3: Renegade Justice. When his adopted white parents fall victim to a gang of ruthless outlaws, Touch the Sky swears to save them—even if it means losing the trust he has risked his life to win from the Cheyenne.
__3385-2 $3.50 US/$4.50 CAN

#4: Vision Quest. While seeking a mystical sign from the Great Spirit, Touch the Sky is relentlessly pursued by his enemies. But the young brave will battle any peril that stands between him and the vision of his destiny.
__3411-5 $3.50 US/$4.50 CAN